The Passing Bells

By the same author
FLICKERS
THE DEAD IN GUANAJUATO
THE EXTRAORDINARY SEAMAN

PHILLIP ROCK

The Passing Bells

HODDER AND STOUGHTON

LONDON SYDNEY AUCKLAND TORONTO

For Bettye Cooper Rock
from Kingston-upon-Thames –
with all my love.

British Library Cataloguing in Publication Data
   The passing bells.
   I. Title
   823'.9'IF   PS3568.033P/

   ISBN 0 340 24193 4

Acknowledgments

Grateful acknowledgment is made to the publishers of the following for permission to quote from material in copyright:

Excerpt from "I Have a Rendezvous With Death" by Alan Seeger, reprinted from "I Have a Rendezvous With Death" by Alan Seeger with the permission of Charles Scribner's Sons, © 1916, Charles Scribner's Sons.

Five lines from "Sons of the Widow" by Rudyard Kipling from "Barrack Room Ballads" with the permission of Eyre Methuen Ltd., London, and the National Trust.

From the last stanza of "The Send-Off" from *The Collected Poems of Wilfred Owen*: Edited by C. Day Lewis, © 1946, 1963 by Chatto & Windus Ltd. Reprinted by permission of the Wilfred Owen Estate and Chatto & Windus Ltd.

Excerpts from "The Dead" and "Peace" by Rupert Brooke from *The Collected Poems of Rupert Brooke*, © 1915.

Let there be rung the passing bells,
to call the living, to mourn the dead.

Author's Note

All the characters in this book, with the obvious exception of historical personages, are imaginary. The Royal Windsor Fusiliers will not appear on any list of regiments of the British army, past or present, but all other regiments are real and fought in the actions where mentioned.

I have tried to be faithful in the description of events, but this is not a work of history and if I have erred in places or taken licence may the historians forgive me.

No novel set against the background of the Great War could be accomplished without help from the works of other writers. I am especially grateful to the following: *Gallipoli* by John Masefield (the Macmillan Company, 1918), for details of the landings from the *River Clyde* and the battalions involved; *The Age of Illusion* by Ronald Blythe (Hamish Hamilton, 1963), for his chapter on the Unknown Warrior; *The Great War and Modern Memory* by Paul Fussell (Oxford University Press, 1975), for countless details; Siegfried Sassoon's *Memoirs of a Fox-hunting Man* and *Memoirs of an Infantry Officer*, both from Faber and Faber, 1928, 1930, and *Goodbye to All That* by Robert Graves (Cassell, 1957), a tattered paperback bought so long ago which inspired the writing of this book in the first place; and to Martin Middlebrook of Boston, Lincolnshire, for the superlative historical craftsmanship of his *First Day on the Somme* (Allen Lane, 1971).

And a special debt from the heart to all the poets who died too soon.

Book One

Blow, bugles, blow! They brought us, for our dearth,
  Holiness, lacked so long, and Love, and Pain.
Honour has come back, as a king, to earth,
  And paid his subjects with a royal wage;
And Nobleness walks in our ways again;
  And we have come into our heritage.

RUPERT BROOKE, 1914

I

THE DAWN CAME EARLY, TINTING A CLOUDLESS SKY THE PALEST shade of green. Cocks had been crowing before first light, heralding the June day the length and breadth of the shire. On Burgate Hill woodcutters paused to rest after the steep climb to the top, lit their pipes and watched the sun rise. It was another clear, dry day and the men could see Sussex and the South Downs far off across The Weald. The Vale of Abington lay below them still dark with shadows, but by the time they had finished their smokes – tapping the ashes carefully on to bare ground – the sun had reached the spire of Abington church and the brick chimneys of the great house, Abington Pryory three miles to the west, the house itself shrouded from view by the dense foliage of oak and birch woods. Beyond the vale the men could see a thin plume of smoke rise from the gentle hollows of the heath: the five ten from Tipley's Green bearing the rich harvests of Surrey to the London markets.

Anthony Greville, ninth Earl of Stanmore, heard the distant hoot of the train as it approached the crossing at Leith Common. He lay drowsily in bed, following in his mind's eye the passage of the goods train as it meandered across the county before joining the main line at Godalming. It was the same train, larger and more sophisticated, of course, that he had known as a boy, although in those days it had not crossed the heath but had come from Tipley's Green by way of Bigham through five miles of his father's land. When would that have been exactly? he wondered: Eighteen-seventy? Seventy-two? About then, he imagined. The early Seventies because the land had been sold off later in the decade and parcelled into farms. A new railway line had been built to skirt Abington proper, a much more efficient line he remembered the farmers saying, but he had missed the ancient train with its tall, bulbous smoke-stack and gleaming brass.

He turned his head on the pillow and glanced at the bedside clock, a ship's chronometer set in a rosewood case. Five twenty-three. The great house was coming alive, and he stretched his long, leanly-muscled body under the quilt and listened to the muted sounds: the murmur of pipes as the scullery maids drew water for the cooks, the far-away ring of shovels as coal buckets were filled, the faint whistling of a stableboy washing at the courtyard pump. Soon there would be scurrying footsteps in the halls as the upstairs maids brought hot water for shaving and pots of tea for the early risers. There were forty servants in the house, counting stableboys and grooms, and they could make a fair amount of noise as they began the day. It was a sound that the Earl of Stanmore found as comforting as memory.

He shaved himself, standing before the mirror in his stockinged feet, while his valet stood near him holding towels and a bottle of bay rum. His valet's name was Fisher, and he had been the earl's man for over ten years.

"And what does your lordship have in mind for today?"

He studied his face in the glass. "What do you think, Fisher? Is the moustache getting a bit too military?"

"It is rather fierce, if you'll permit me to say so."

"And ageing?"

"I'd hardly go that far, m'lord. Martial, yes."

"We shall trim it later, Fisher. Blunt the ends."

"Very good, m'lord. And as for your needs?"

The earl made one final stroke along the chin line and then dropped his razor into the shaving bowl.

"Morning clothes after my ride . . . and there will be guests for dinner. Black tie."

"Very good, m'lord."

The morning ride was the earl's unfailing ritual, the heat of summer or the dark, frosty mornings of winter. He dressed for it in old whipcord breeches and a Norfolk jacket, with a cardigan beneath it if the air were chill. There were thirty pairs of riding boots in the dressing room wardrobe, but his choice was habit set for the morning ride, a pair of Irish hunting boots, the tan leather cracked into fine lines like the face of an ancient, weatherbeaten man. The boots were as supple as gloves and fitted his long legs like a second skin. He was getting into them with Fisher's help when there came a discreet tap at the door and Coatsworth entered the room followed by one of the maids bearing a large, silver tray on which stood a teapot, a jug of hot water, milk, sugar, a basket of scones, a pot of marmalade and a dish of butter. The elderly butler walked slowly, his dark trousers almost obscuring his slippered feet.

"Good morning, m'lord."

"'Morning to you, Coatsworth. How's the gout this morning?"

"Better, I do believe. Soaked my feet in hot vinegar last night at Mr. Banks' suggestion."

"Hot vinegar indeed."

"Works wonders, Mr. Banks says."

"Been damned effective on the hunters, I'll say that."

Mr. Coatsworth cleared a table next to the chair in which his master was seated and motioned the maid to set the tray down. She was a young girl, slender and dark haired, with high cheekbones and a thin, uptilted nose. A very pretty girl, the earl thought as he smiled at her.

"Thank you, Mary."

"Ivy, m'lord," the girl whispered.

"Of course, Ivy." One of the new ones. Mary was the plump, ginger-haired girl with buck teeth.

"Shall I pour, m'lord?" the butler asked.

"Yes, please."

"You may go, lass," Coatsworth murmured. She was lingering, looking about the room. It took a while to train them properly. This one seemed more intelligent than most. She gave a proper curtsy before leaving. He poured tea into a cup and added a teaspoonful of sugar and a dash of milk. He then split a hot scone and buttered it. "I think you will find the scones to be quite delicious this morning, m'lord. Cook changed the recipe. A higher proportion of rye flour than usual."

"You don't say so."

"Ross says they remind him of the scones his mother used to bake when he was a lad in Aberdeen."

"Gets about a bit, doesn't he? Told me he came from Perth."

The butler chuckled as he spread marmalade on the scone. "I'd say Glasgow or the East End was nearer the truth."

"Perhaps. Still, a good man with a motor car."

"As you say, m'lord," Coatsworth said through pursed lips before turning to leave.

A bit of resentment there, and the earl knew it. Jamie Ross was a brash young man of indeterminate geographic origin, but a first-rate chauffeur and mechanic. He was badly needed now that the number of motor cars in the family had increased from one to four. The previous chauffeur had been a man of Coatsworth's age, an ex-coachman, who had known little about cars other than how to put one in gear and steer it in a reasonably straight line. He and the butler had been close friends and had spent their free hours together at the Crown and Anchor in Abington where dart-playing was an almost holy rite. Young Ross, on the other hand, preferred female company to darts and spent his half days off dashing about the countryside on his motorbike, impressing maids and shopgirls from Guildford to Crawley.

He did not linger over his first breakfast of the day, but drank his tea and munched his scones, a man in a hurry to be somewhere else. He could feel the tug of field and wood, hedgerow and thicket. There wasn't a part of the Vale that wasn't a challenge to a horseman, not a yard of the land that didn't provide a sense of exhilaration and triumph. There was no better way on earth to start the day than by riding full tilt across that blessed landscape. His only regret at the moment was that he would be riding alone on this bright and glorious morning. William wouldn't be down from Eton for another day or two and Charles had lost his zest for riding. The thought of his eldest son cast a momentary pall over his mood. He couldn't fathom the lad. All Charles had done since coming down from Cambridge had been to moon about, listless and apathetic. His scholastic record at King's had been most gratifying, but when the earl had tried to discuss his son's future with him he had drawn a total blank. The lad's direction seemed clear enough to Greville. He was, after all, the eldest, which would mean the eventual inheritance of the title. He should apply himself diligently to understanding the complex structure of the family holdings, not merely Abington Pryory with its score of tenant farms, but the land in Wiltshire, Kent, Northumberland and the West Riding, as well as the various parcels of London commercial properties. A job enough for any man. Of course, if Charles had expressed a desire to remain a scholar and wished to return to Cambridge he wouldn't stand in his way, but *any* discussion of the future had been met with what was fast becoming unendurable, aggravating, exasperating, bloody *ennui*! He drained his cup as though it contained a dram of whisky.

"I'm off," he said, getting abruptly to his feet. The valet hurried from the dressing room, carrying a jacket, tweed cap and a riding crop with a polished bamboo handle. Properly attired, the earl strode across the room to the door that connected his rooms with those of his wife. It was a source of inner satisfaction to him that never in the course of twenty-five years of married life had that door ever been locked, a symbol of love that effectively quelled the dark predictions of his friends, who had said that the marriage could not possibly last, *American women being what they are*. He had not understood the meaning of that remark then or now.

The contrast between the two sets of rooms symbolised the difference between men and women as the earl saw it. His rooms were panelled with dark oak, spartanly furnished and devoid of frivolous ornaments. A large, untidy bookcase contained works on country life and hunting, a novel or two by Hardy, Shakespeare's plays in five volumes, and a Bible given to him by the local vicar on the day he had left home for the first time to go to school at Winchester. Between the slim stacks of books stood hunting cups and other trophies of horsemanship. The sword that his grandfather had carried, but never used, at Waterloo rested in its scabbard above the brick fireplace and a large telescope, the gift of an admiral uncle, was fixed to a tripod in front of one of the mullioned windows. Study, bedroom and dressing room had survived intact the transition from young manhood to middle age.

The rooms of Hanna Rilke Greville, Countess of Stanmore, had been decorated by a man who had been under the spell of the *Belle Epoque*, rooms of deep pile carpets, embossed wall-

14

papers in shades of lemon and milky green, gilt-framed paintings, mirrors and rococo furniture. Silk curtains diffused the
light, bathing the rooms with a softly feminine glow. The
rooms of a warm and sensuous woman. In all the years of their
lovemaking she had never come to his rooms, only he to hers.

She was still asleep, her long, blonde hair tied into two thick
coils that lay across the pillow like strands of spun gold. The
earl did not intrude on his wife's slumber. It was his ritual to
simply stand for a moment at one end of the large bedroom and
look at her. He then closed the door quietly and retreated into
his own room, slapped his boot top with the crop and strode
briskly towards the hall.

"Good morning, m'lord." Four of the upstairs maids stood
on the landing and whispered their greeting in unison. They
curtsied as they did so, their heavily-starched uniforms making
a pleasant, rustling sound.

"Good morning, good morning," Lord Stanmore said,
barely glancing at them as he descended the broad staircase.

He left the house through the glass-domed conservatory with
its riot of potted palms and hanging baskets of ferns, and then
strode out across the shadowed west terrace, where two
gardeners' helpers were sweeping the flagstones with brooms
made of twigs. The men paused in their work long enough to
touch their caps in respect and he acknowledged their gesture
by a slight nod of his head. Steps of weathered granite curved
down to the Italian garden, where four men were busily at
work trimming the topiary work. An ornamental iron gate,
purchased long ago from the estate of the Duke of Fiori in
Urbino, led into the rose garden with its central fountain of
Carrara marble tumbling green water over carvings of
Neptune and Europa. Beyond the brick wall that enclosed the
rose garden, several long, low greenhouses marked the edge of
the vast kitchen gardens with their neat rows of vegetables and
well-spaded earth. A tree-shaded gravel path wound past the
gardeners' cottages, the compost pits and the storage sheds to
the stable area, separated from the domain of the gardeners by
a high stone wall. There was a scattering of musket and pistol
balls embedded in the chinks between the stone blocks,
mementoes of a brisk fight between Prince Rupert's Horse and

a company of Roundhead infantry in 1642. The earl had dug for them with a pocket knife when a child, but had recovered nothing but rusty flakes of iron and thin curlings of lead. A solid wooden gate painted a dark green pierced the wall and gave access to the paddock and stables beyond.

This was his world and he was intensely proud of it. The new wooden buildings with their slate roofs were painted in his colours, buff with accents of dull orange. They were the finest stables in England and the twenty-five hunters and jumpers housed in them were the best horses that could be bought, bartered or begged. His favourite of them all, a seven-year-old chestnut gelding, was being walked in the paddock by a groom while a stocky, bandy-legged man, wearing tweeds and brown leather gaiters, eyed the horse with a critical and practised eye.

"Good morning, Banks," Lord Stanmore called out cheerily. "Have a saddle on him, I see."

George Banks, trainer and vet, jocularly referred to as Master of the Earl's Horse, removed a knobby briar pipe from between his teeth and tapped out the ash against his palm.

"Fit as a fiddle, m'lord, and strainin' at the bit, as you can see. I'd venture to say that old Jupiter's as good as new."

The earl peered intently at the horse's left front leg as the groom walked it towards him.

"Not favouring the leg at all."

"No, m'lord," said Banks. "It's the hot packs what done the job good and proper."

"Let's just hope he won't be jump shy after this."

"Well, m'lord, we'll never know that till the old boy takes a fence, but he's had his knocks before this."

"Quite so, Banks, though not as severely." He patted the horse fondly on the neck and then ran his hand along its smoothly-curried withers. "Good Jupiter. Good old boy."

"Full of mustard."

"Quite so."

"He watched Tinker go and they're proper stablemates. I reckon he's eager to be catching up with him."

"Tinker? Who on earth . . . ?"

"Why, the captain, m'lord," Banks said, refilling his pipe from a yellow oilskin pouch. 'Captain Wood-Lacy. Came down from London last night, m'lord. Got in a bit late and didn't want to disturb the household so he bunked in with me. He was up with the lark and eager for a ride."

The earl swung up into Jupiter's saddle.

"Damn. Wish I'd known. Which direction did he take?"

"Towards Burgate and Swan Copse," the groom said. "But he weren't spurrin', m'lord. Just ridin' easy."

"Thank you, Smithy. Perhaps I can catch up with him."

He tapped the big gelding with his heels and the horse responded eagerly, breaking into a canter down the hard-packed, sandy path. He had to hold him from bursting into a flat-out gallop as they swept past the stables and the feed barns. The path curved to the right towards the Abington road and was bordered on the left by a five-foot fence.

"Take it, Jupiter." He tugged the left rein and the horse veered sharply off the path and soared over the fence with feet to spare. He could hear Banks and the groom give a cheer, but he did not glance back.

Captain Fenton Wood-Lacy, Coldstream Guards, rode slowly and morosely through the dappled shadows of a beech wood. He was a tall, square-shouldered man of twenty-five, with dark, deep-set eyes, a prominent, high-bridged nose and thin lips. It was a face with a look of studied arrogance about it and a hint of cruelty, like the face of a falcon. It was a face which, when angered, could reduce incompetent subalterns to twitching terror. But that was his parade-ground face, acquired with his commission. With friends, women, small children, and the meek and humble of the earth, the face underwent an almost magical transformation. The hard line of the mouth softened and the eyes lost their beady coldness and became warm with humour and compassion. At the moment, the eyes were leaden and the face troubled. A passing stranger seeing this man seated on a magnificent bay, dressed in fine, London-cut riding clothes and wearing a bowler of impeccable fit and style, would have taken him for a rich squire. In actuality, he carried in his pocket a letter from Cox's Bank, informing him in a respectful but terse manner that his account was seriously overdrawn. The matter of his unpaid bills at the Marlborough Club had been brought to his attention the day before by the club secretary.

"I should not enjoy mentioning this matter to your colonel, but you are so deeply in arrears that unless . . . ."

"Oh, go to the devil," he muttered without passion.

A ring-necked pheasant broke cover and whirled away towards the open fields beyond the wood. Fenton raised his riding crop and traced the bird's erratic flight with the tip, leading it just the proper distance to have assured a clean kill with a shotgun.

"Pity," he murmured. The pheasant went to ground and he lowered the crop and slapped it in a desultory fashion against his leg. The beauty of the morning, with the sun filtering through the leafy beech trees and the golden haze lying over the hedgerowed fields, mocked his mood. Something had to be done, but he couldn't for the life of him figure out what it could be. A hundred pounds would clear his present debts – and he could probably borrow that amount easily enough from Lord Stanmore as he had done in the past, but a hundred quid wouldn't solve his problems, merely delay the inevitable for a few months. His share of his late father's estate came to an inflexible six hundred pounds a year. That and his captain's pay were not enough to maintain himself in the Coldstreams, a regiment – like others in the foot Guards – that prided itself on the tone of its officers. All Guards officers must join the Guards Club, but as a captain it was almost mandatory that he should join the Marlborough as well. An unmarried officer in a less socially eminent regiment might live in quarters at the barracks, but an officer in the Guards was expected to maintain, at his own expense naturally, suitable lodgings in Knightsbridge or Belgravia – the higher the rank the better the address. His promotion to captain had merely hastened his ruin. And on top of all the other expenditure, there was the matter of clothing. Only mufti could be worn when off duty, except for certain social functions, and mufti of the most stylish and expensive cut. His tailor's bill had been outrageous and only a lucky spell at cards had permitted him to pay it. That luck had not continued long enough for him to settle matters with Cox's Bank and the Marlborough Club.

"Dash it to hell," he whispered to the trees. He gave his mount a gentle tap and the graceful animal trotted briskly on, threading its way through the wood and out into a meadow thick with cornflowers and buttercups. There Fenton reined in and sat stolidly in the saddle gazing ahead. Far off across the rolling meadows, partially obscured by the willows of Swan Copse, rose the Gothic façade of Burgate House. There was a permanent solution to his monetary problems in that place, but at a cost that he had so far been reluctant to accept. He was still reluctant, but he couldn't see that he had much choice. Archie Foxe lived in Burgate House with his daughter, Lydia. Archie Foxe of the bluff and hearty East-End manner and the dropped aitches. The Foxe of Foxe's Fancy Tinned Goods and the ubiquitous White Manor Tea Shops. Archie's offer of a place in the firm was genuine and of longstanding. One thousand pounds a year to start. Not a trifling sum that. He slipped a silver cigarette case from his jacket and removed a cork-tipped Abdullah. It would mean chucking in his commission, but there wasn't much of a future in the army anyway. His promotion to a captaincy at twenty-five had been the blindest of luck, one of those once-in-every-century reorganisations of a battalion. It would be ten to fifteen years before they raised him to major.

He blew a thin stream of smoke to the wind and watched the distant house through narrowed eyes, like a scout surveying the movements of the enemy. It was a hideous building, built by a duke in Queen Anne's time. The duke's only son had been killed, and the man had instructed his architects to alter the design of the place so as to create a monument to the boy's memory. They had outdone themselves by erecting a structure that looked more like a cathedral than a house. No one had ever been happy living there, except Archie. Archie Foxe loved the place. "Like livin' in Westminster Abbey," Archie said.

"Oh, damn," the captain sighed. His personal Rubicon lay in front of him. A thousand quid a year. And Lydia? That little question eluded an answer the way a will-o'-the-wisp eluded a man's grasp. Lydia Foxe would make up her own mind about that. She was beautiful, twenty-one years of age and the daughter of the world's most indulgent father. There were no restrictions placed upon her. She could flit over to Paris for a month or dash up to London for a weekend without fear of censure from Archie. It had been her suggestion in the first place that he turn in his commission and join "Daddy's shop", as she so quaintly understated the firm of Foxe Ltd. That idea had been given to him when she had helped to choose the proper furnishings for his flat on Lower Belgrave Street, her taste far exceeding his budget. "You're a man who should live among beautiful things," she had said. "You're quite wasted in the army." Well, he could have told her the same thing, but then didn't Archie see his rôle in the firm as a sort of military one? The stalwart ex-Guardsman, Archie's adjutant, reviewing battalions of apple-cheeked, nubile White Manor Tea Shop girls in their sky-blue dresses, starched white aprons and perky white caps? Of course he did. "Fenton," he had said, "Fenton, lad, Lydia tells me you might be chuckin' the army. Blimey, I could use your sort. 'Ow does a thousand quid per annum strike you?"

"Very well indeed, thank you very much. And yet . . . and yet . . ."

"Oh, damn," he whispered fervently, tossing his cigarette into a weed-choked drainage ditch. It just wasn't as simple as that. Six years with the colours. D Company's captain, First Battalion. A man's regiment became something a little sacred, whether one wanted to be seduced by the tradition or not. It was like a marriage . . . for better or worse . . . till death do us part. There were times when he despised the uselessness of his profession in an age where war was a virtual impossibility. And yet, when the regimental band struck up the march from *Figaro* and the long scarlet-and-blue clad column swung up Birdcage Walk from Wellington Barracks with the wind whipping the King's colours and the fifes shrilling, he felt an almost indescribable sense of pride. That was merely being boyish and he knew it. Echoes from childhood, when he had sat spellbound in front of Uncle Julian, back home after fighting the Pathans on the North-West Frontier or the cruel dervishes in the Sudan, Uncle Julian of the 24th Foot, the Warwickshires, with his V.C. pinned to his tunic, spinning his stories of bravery and battle and stalwart men.

Fife and drum and the colours streaming. The Guards marching shoulder to shoulder over the icy mountains of Corunna, Sir John Moore watching them with tears in his eyes and knowing by the very sight of those ordered, unbroken ranks that Napoleon was doomed. Boyhood dreamings. Uncle Julian's tales, Fortescue's *History of the British Army*, entwined inextricably with the social aspects of the game, for game it was, this playing at soldiering in London town. St. James's, Buckingham Palace, the Tower . . . an officer in the Coldstream Guards, the King's thin red line . . . a *Guards officer* and thus set apart in one's own exclusive and distinctive class. To give that up, to be merely *Mr.* Fenton Wood-Lacy of Foxe, Ltd., purveyors of meat pies and sixpenny teas, cheap food in tins, tea shops strategically placed on busy corners in major towns and cities – Brighton, Plymouth, Margate, Manchester, Leeds, Birmingham, Liverpool and the Greater London area – was to reduce himself to the level of the general herd. And if that be snobbery, make the most of it!

He leaned sideways in the saddle and sabre-cut a milkweed with his riding crop, a vicious, backhanded slash which reduced the tall and slender plant to stubble. On straightening up he heard a distant hallooing and glanced idly over his left shoulder to see Lord Stanmore, several fields back, coming on at the gallop, the chestnut gliding over hedges and blackberry thickets with the grace of a swallow.

The Earl of Stanmore in his proper element, Fenton mused. Coming on like the wind, horse and rider as smoothly integrated as a fine watch. It had been his initial view of the man when first visiting Abington Pryory at the age of nine. The sight had impressed him then as it impressed him now. He rode just as smoothly, he supposed. And so he should, for it had been Lord Stanmore who had taught him the proper way to sit a horse, and how to take a jump without flinching. The summer of 1898, he reflected, the year his father had submitted his plans for the restoration of the great old house. Abington Pryory had become a second home for the Wood-Lacy family during the years of restoration and his education as a horseman and huntsman had begun. A bond had been created between himself and the earl in that long-ago summer, a bond of friendship and respect that had grown stronger with time. He watched the man galloping towards him and his spirits lifted, the gloom that had been so crushingly pervasive beginning to fade.

"Dash it all, Fenton," the earl cried out as he drew alongside, the two horses whinnying, rubbing necks. "You could have waited for me."

"Sorry, sir. Didn't think you'd be up that early."

"Not up? What the deuce do you mean, *not up*? You know my habits as well as anybody."

The captain smiled and proffered the open cigarette case. The earl took a cigarette.

"My apologies."

"Accepted." He leaned towards Fenton for a light. "Well, now, caught up with you at least. Did you see how we took that last hedge?"

"Yes, sir, I did. Like a champion."

"You wouldn't think the old boy'd been laid up for two weeks, would you? I'll be taking him to Colchester next month for the point-to-point. By the way, did Hargreaves speak to you about the Tetbury Hunt?"

"We discussed it over lunch at the Savoy. His treat."

"You said yes, of course."

"I did."

"Fine. You shan't regret it. You can have your pick of mounts . . . except for Jupiter, of course."

"That's very kind of you, sir."

"Nonsense, my dear chap, nonsense." He patted his horse on the neck the way another man might pat a well-loved dog. "Let me rest him for a bit and then I'll race you to Hadwell Green. We'll knock up the publican at the Swan and have a pint and a wedge of cheese." He puffed on the cigarette, not inhaling. "Damn, but it's a fine morning. That crowd at the house don't know what they're missing, lying abed to all hours. Anyway, at least you're here. How long can you stay?"

"A lengthy weekend. I have palace guard on Wednesday."

"I suppose you know your brother's here."

"I assumed he would be. Roger wrote to me that he and Charles had plans for the summer – to celebrate graduating."

"Dashed if I can understand the lads. In my day chaps came down from Cambridge with a sense of purpose and a damned clear idea of where they were going in life. Neither Roger nor my dear son have the foggiest."

"It's just a phase," Fenton said abstractedly.

"Damned if I can see why your blessed mother had to sacrifice so much to keep Roger up there. Now, you take what occurred during snooker last night. Roger and Charles were in some sort of conversation about prosody and Roger said that in his opinion the Georgians were on the proper track. So I put in my oar after sinking the blue with a perfect bank shot, and agreed that *Childe Harold* was still a damn fine bit of poetry even if its author *was* a self-confessed bugger. Oh, Roger said, not those Georgians, sir, the *new* Georgians, Rupert Brooke *et al*. Rupert Brooke! Have you ever heard such nonsense in your life? The chap walks around with his hair down to his shoulders and no shoes on his feet. Well, later, after a glass or two of vintage, I asked Roger what he intended doing and he said, oh, edit a poetry magazine in London, starting in September. Editor, I say, good for you. How much they paying you? And *he* says, pay? Oh, there's no pay, one can't expect to make money out of poetry. Now, I ask you . . . !" His voice ended on a note of heartfelt exasperation. Four jackdaws rose from the top branches of a solitary oak and flew, cawing lustily, towards the granite towers of Burgate House. "Well, enough of that. Let's spur off."

"Can you lend me another hundred pounds?" Fenton said, gazing stolidly ahead.

Lord Stanmore tugged at his mustache. "Can I what?"

"Lend me a hundred pounds. I know that I still owe you . . ."

"Nonsense! No talk of that, my dear fellow. Of course I'll lend it to you, if you need it badly enough."

Fenton's smile was faint. "I suppose I shall always need it badly enough. I'm in a rather awkward position."

"I quite understand. You're in the worst possible regiment for a man of your means. I would like to make a suggestion, Fenton, and I hope you won't take offence."

"I'm sure that I won't."

23

"Well, then . . ." He took a final puff on his cigarette and then crushed it out against the handle of his crop. "It's quite simple, really. So simple that I'm rather surprised you haven't done it before this. The season is upon us again. London is simply overflowing with the marriageable daughters of substantial men, as well you know."

"Marry money," Fenton said flatly.

"Yes, and where's the harm in it? By God, you're a fine-looking fellow, positively gorgeous, I might add, when you're wearing your scarlet jacket at one of those Mayfair balls. Be honest, lad, is it such a crime to rescue a Manchester mill-owner's daughter from marrying some pasty-faced solicitor?"

The captain laughed for the first time in weeks. "I suppose it isn't, not when you put it that way."

"Only way to look at it, old boy. As Archie Foxe might put it, you're a marketable commodity."

"Like tinned beef."

"Precisely. Look, we'll be opening the Park Lane house next week and Hanna has half a dozen parties and balls in the works to get Alexandra launched. We could kill two birds with one stone. Find my daughter the right husband and you the proper wife. Will you co-operate to the fullest?"

"I have little choice."

"Why, dammit, man, you might enjoy it. Lord knows what pretty butterflies we may entangle in our net." He pointed his crop towards Burgate House where the jackdaws wheeled and cawed above the spires. "By Harry, there's a pretty one in that place I'd like to see taken off the market . . . for reasons I shan't go into, but I'm sure you understand."

"I believe so, yes," Fenton said quietly.

The ninth Earl of Stanmore frowned and looked away from the great monstrosity of a house that, to his way of thinking, only a millionaire Cockney with no sense of taste would consider grand.

"Dash it, Fenton, I've been more than accommodating over the years, permitted Charles his puppy love attraction to the girl when he was sixteen, but, by God, he's twenty-three now, time he got over it and faced reality. Then again, she may see

24

the futility herself and give him the . . . what's that slang word?"

"Gate?"

"Right, the gate – and opt for a more suitable mate, the quicker the better." He dug his heels into his horse's flanks. "Let's ride!"

More suitable to *him*, Fenton was thinking as he kicked his own mount into a gallop and trailed the chestnut across the field, meaning, of course, that the eldest son of an Earl of Stanmore didn't marry the daughter of a Shadwell greengrocer even if that greengrocer were richer than most of the peers of England. Archie Foxe's daughter, despite her Paris clothes and Benz runabout motor car, was still Archie Foxe's daughter. A friend of the family since her childhood, to be sure, but, to Lord Stanmore's way of thinking, no more than that – ever. The earl's canon of beliefs included a rigid view on the distinction between classes. He considered Lydia Foxe to be fated by her class to wed in her class. Not to the son of a greengrocer, Archie's millions obviated that, but certainly to someone less noble than a Greville. The soldier son of an architect perhaps? Fenton wondered. A knighted architect, the late lamented Sir Harold Wood-Lacy, refurbisher of old buildings, a master of his craft to the delight of such clients as Queen Victoria, for his work at Balmoral and Sandringham House, and the Earl of Stanmore for his painstaking restoration of Abington Pryory, work which the earl had paid for with part of his wife's dowry, the million dollars or more, which Adolph Sebastian Rilke had gladly handed over to see his daughter wed to a nobleman; dollars that had been earned in Chicago and Milwaukee, U.S.A., by the brewing of beer. No loss of social status in *that* union. Money was the American peerage: beer barons, steel barons, coal barons, robber barons of Wall Street, an occasional prince of industry tossed in for good measure. An American heiress ranked with a Hapsburg. And even if someone *had* sneered at the idea of a Greville, an Earl of Stanmore, marrying the daughter of a brewer, it could be pointed out that the Rilkes of Milwaukee, Chicago and St. Louis were simply a branch of the von Rilkes of Mecklenburg-Schwerin, and that Hanna Rilke had met the bachelor earl at a London garden party tossed in her honour by her fourth cousin, Princess Mary of Teck. Yes, one could so easily understand the difference between the Rilkes and the Foxes, even if one found the hypocrisy of it all slightly amusing.

"Come on! Come on!" the earl shouted over his shoulder. "Catch me if you can!"

"I'll give it a try, sir," Fenton yelled, spurring his horse, but keeping a politic half length behind.

2

"MR. COATSWORTH INFORMED ME HOW SATISFIED HE WAS WITH the way you conducted yourself this morning, Ivy. But you must remember what I told you about dawdling and staring."

"Yes, Mrs. Broome," Ivy Thaxton whispered.

"You may go and have your breakfast now and then give Mrs. Dalrymple a hand with the linen."

"Yes, Mrs. Broome. Thank you, Mrs. Broome."

Mrs. Broome, for all her formidable size and regal bearing, was not unkind or overly demanding. She prided herself on her ability to so train the household servants that reprimands were rare. There were some housekeepers who were veritable ogres and martinets, constantly bullying and punishing the staff. She had only contempt for such creatures. She looked approvingly at the slender, dark-haired girl and then reached out and touched her gently on the mouth.

"Let's see a little smile now and then, Ivy. You'll soon get used to it here."

"I'm sure I will, Mrs. Broome."

"That's the spirit, child. Now run off with you and have your breakfast."

"Thank you, Mrs. Broome," Ivy said, curtsying respectfully, before hurrying down the passage towards the servants' hall. Ivy Thaxton was seventeen years of age and this was her first week away from home, her first week of service, and she found it all very bewildering but not unpleasant. She was not unhappy as the housekeeper thought, not like that Mary Grogan from Belfast who cried all the time. It was just that there was so much to remember and so much to see. The huge, rambling house fascinated her. There were so many corridors and passageways, so many stairs and rooms that sometimes she got lost when instructed to go to the "Blenheim room in the east wing", or the "blue suite in the south passage". She had

27

grown up in a comfortable but crowded house near Norwich, the eldest of two boys and two girls with another child on the way. It had been the baby in her mother's womb that had necessitated her departure from the house. The older birds must make room for the fledglings, her father had said.

There were a dozen or more servants seated at the long table having their breakfast, but Ivy couldn't see anyone she knew. Valets, footmen and the kitchen maids mostly. The kitchens were just beyond the servants' hall and she went in there to get served, a plate heaped with bacon rashers, eggs, and a thick piece of bread, fried golden crisp in bacon grease. Urns of tea and pots of marmalade and jam were on the table in the hall. The amount and quality of the food that they were given still astonished her. There had always been enough food on the table at home, Mum had seen to that only God knew how, but it had been plain fare, heavy on boiled greens, carrots and thick barley soup with a few bits of meat in it. She found a place at the end of the table and ate her breakfast with a single-minded purpose that verged on gluttony. When she had finished, mopping up the last trace of egg yolk with a piece of fried bread, she became conscious of someone staring at her across the table. She glanced up into the amused face of a freckled young man with sandy hair, who was nursing a mug of tea and smoking a cigarette. He was dressed in livery of some sort, a tight black jacket with pearl grey buttons, the jacket unbuttoned, revealing a starched dickey.

"God," the young man said, "but you don't 'alf put your grub away. Where does it go? You can't weigh more'n a half starved cat."

"It's rude to stare," she said, looking down at her empty plate. Her face was burning.

"Sorry, lass, but I couldn't help it. I mean, I *am* sittin' here and you *are* sittin' there, you see. It was either look at you or look at one of them ugly mugs up the table. I'd rather glim a comely lass any old day in the week. Jamie Ross is my name, what's yours?"

"Ivy," she said, almost inaudibly. "Ivy Thaxton." She stood up, but the young man reached across the table and took hold of her wrist.

28

"Don't go for a minute. You didn't finish your tea. If I gave you a start, I'm sorry. I'm the sort of chap who says what he's thinkin'. It don't half get me into trouble sometimes, I can tell you."

She sat down again and he let go of her wrist and smiled warmly at her. It was an infectious smile and she smiled back.

"That's more like it," he said. "You've only been here a week, haven't you?"

"Yes, that's right. A week since Thursday."

"You from London?"

"Norwich. Are you from London?"

He tilted his head and blew a perfect smoke ring towards the high, vaulted ceiling.

"I'm from everywhere if you want to know the truth. Glasgow, Liverpool, Bradford, Leeds, London too. I get about a bit in my tea half hour, an' that's a fact. Like to keep on the go. That's why I took up chauffeuring."

"Is that what you do?"

He stared at her in disbelief. "Can't you tell? Can't you see the uniform I'm wearing? Of course I'm a chauffeur. I'm his lordship's and her ladyship's driver. The poor dears couldn't go anywhere without me."

One of the valets, a large, portly man, glanced down the table.

"Oh, put a cork in it, Ross."

The chauffeur dropped his cigarette in the dregs of his tea, leaned across the table and spoke in a harsh stage whisper.

"They're all jealous of me, see. 'Cause I've a proper trade and they don't know nothin' but how to polish a bloody pair of boots."

"I find you quite impossible," the valet said huffily. "I shall have to change my meal-times."

Ross ignored him. "I can do anything with a motor. I can pull it apart and scatter the pieces and then blindfold myself and put it back together again."

"I should like to see *that*," the valet said with scorn.

"Put up a quid and I'll give you the pleasure," he snapped.

"Can you really do it?" Ivy asked.

"Of course I can; an' make it run better than it did before.

I'm somewhat of an inventor, see. I think up all sorts of things."

"Think up a muzzle for your mouth," the valet said. There was a wave of laughter from others at the table and the man looked pleased with himself.

"Haw, haw," Ross said. "Very funny, Johnson, but it happens to be the truth. I bet I have a hundred inventions right up here in the old noggin." He tapped his forehead with a finger.

"I really must go," Ivy said. "I've got to help with the linen."

"Take 'im with you, lass," one of the footmen called out. "He has nought to do but drive to the village and back, like a ruddy omnibus!"

"Oh, is that so?" Ross said as he stood up and began to button his jacket. "I've got to drive Master Charles and his friend clear down to Southampton tomorrow morning. A relation of her ladyship is comin' in from America on the *Laconia*. You think *you* could drive a car to Southampton? Not bloody likely."

There was a sudden silence in the hall and everyone looked at him curiously.

"A relative? That's the first I've heard of it," one of the assistant housekeepers said. "I'm sure that Mrs. Broome would have told *me*."

Ross smiled smugly. "All in good time, dearie. They'll get around to telling you."

"Well, really!" the woman expostulated. "You do have a cheek."

"What sort of relative?" the valet asked. "Male or female?"

"A nephew, worse luck for you. Another pair of boots to shine."

No one appeared sorry to see the chauffeur leave. He strutted when he walked and Ivy thought he looked very grand in his black breeches and highly polished black leather gaiters. Rather like an Hussar. He walked her down the passage that led to the linen room.

"That bunch are nought but a gaggle of lackeys," he said. "They don't like me because I'm independent, see. I can go

30

anywhere I feel like goin'. A man who knows cars can write his own bloomin' ticket."

"Do you like it here?"

"Oh, it's not so bad. His lordship's a proper sort and the cars are right beauties, the Lanchester and the Rolls-Royce especially. I've been tinkerin' with the Rolls and found ten different things that could be done to make it run better. I might just write the factory and tell 'em about it. Yes, I might just do that one of these days."

They reached the linen-room door and Ivy held out her hand. "It's been awfully nice talking with you, Mr. Ross."

"Jamie," he said, taking her hand and giving it a slight squeeze. "When's your afternoon?"

"Next Wednesday."

"Well, if I'm off duty I'll take you into Guildford on me motorbike, treat you to the pictures. Do you like William S. Hart? He's one of my favourites."

"I've never been to the pictures."

"What? Never? Lor', you don't know what you've been missin'. Well, take care of yourself."

He gave her hand a final squeeze and then walked jauntily off, whistling as he went.

"Was that you whistling in the hall?" the linen keeper asked when Ivy came into the large, sunny room.

"No, Mrs. Dalrymple. It was Mr. Ross, the chauffeur."

Mrs. Dalrymple made a wry face. "I know who *Mr.* Ross is. You stay away from him if you've got any sense, and don't go fallin' for his blether, neither. He's ruined more than one poor girl's reputation, I can tell you." She took a pile of sheets and pillowslips from one of the shelves that lined the room and placed them on the long table used for folding the linen. "Take these up to the corner bedroom in the west wing. And make up the bed proper, mind. No sloppy edges."

"Yes, Mrs. Dalrymple."

"And try not to get lost this time. It's the spare room down the passage to the left of Lady Alexandra's rooms. And be as quick as you can. I'm short-handed this morning. Doris took to her bed with the cramps."

*

Roger Wood-Lacy walked slowly along the corridor towards the breakfast room with a look of hazy abstraction on his face. He had been awake since dawn, seated on the windowseat in his bedroom, watching the sun rise. The few moments between darkness and dawn had always been precious to him, a perfect time for creativity. The fifth stanza of the poem that he was writing on the legend of Pyramus and Thisbe was beginning to take shape in his head.

"Now hold the brittle garment of the night in jest . . ." he intoned softly, ignoring the portraits of seventeenth and eighteenth-century Grevilles who gazed stonily at him from their gilded frames, ". . . and scoff the wearing of day's bright mantle rare."

Not bad, he mused, not bad at all. He could hear a low rumble of voices beyond the breakfast-room door and he paused in front of an ornately-framed mirror to look at himself. The image pleased him: tall, imperially slender, the paleness of his face accentuated by his dark, unruly hair. He was wearing a well-worn pair of grey flannel trousers and his college blazer. A blue- striped shirt open at the neck and scruffy tennis shoes with no socks. The image of a poet if he ever saw one. A Georgian poet . . . *new* Georgian, if you please. The recollection of Lord Stanmore's *faux pas* made him smile.

"Good morning, all," he said, making an entrance, expecting Alexandra to be there as well as the Marchioness of Dexford and Lady Winifred Sutton, but only Lord Stanmore and, God forbid, Fenton were seated at the table.

"Hello, Roger," Fenton said.

The earl, Roger noticed with a flash of shame, was tucking a cheque book into his coat pocket and Fenton was slipping a folded cheque into his.

"Good morning, Fenton," he said tightly. "Good morning, sir."

"Ah, good morning, Roger," Lord Stanmore said. He took a final swig of coffee and stood up. "Got to be off. Must have a chat with that damned fool Horley before he strings any more of that bloody barbed wire across his field. The farmers know the rule, but they continue to ignore it. I suppose they want to see a good horse and rider cut up before they stop. Enjoy your breakfast, Roger. Is Charles up, do you know?"

"I tapped on his door, sir. He said he didn't feel too well and would breakfast in his room."

The earl only grunted and left the room scowling.

"Well, Roger," Fenton said, taking out his cigarette case. "How are you?"

"Fine. When did you get here?"

"Last night."

"Staying long?"

"A few days." He lit a cigarette and eyed his younger brother critically. "Your hair wants cutting."

Roger turned his back and walked stiffly to the sideboard on which stood half a dozen silver serving dishes, their contents kept warm by tiny alcohol lamps burning bluely beneath them.

"As long as you're creating an atmosphere of criticism, Fenton, let me say that what you just did is frightfully embarrassing to me."

"Oh? And what's that?"

"Cadging more money from the old boy."

"It was a loan, not that it's any of your business. I've never said a word about your cadging from Charles, now have I?"

Roger flushed. "That's a beastly thing to say."

"Maybe it is, but it's true. Not that Charles minds, I'm sure. It's just the principle of the thing, the pot calling the kettle and all that rot. Speaking of pots, try the kidneys. They're damned good."

Roger's anger began to dissipate, blunted by his hunger. He helped himself to a plate of kidneys, scrambled eggs and a slice of gammon.

"Changing to more pleasant subjects," Fenton said, "my little brother has covered himself with glory at King's. First class honours. I'm damned proud of you."

"Thanks," Roger murmured as he sat down to eat. It was impossible to maintain a grudge against Fenton. Like fighting feathers.

"How's mother?"

"Very well last time I saw her. You really should try and go up there once in a while."

"The regiment's kept me busy, but I have some leave

coming in September and I'll wangle a few days with her. Anyone staying here that I know?"

"House is rather empty for a change. Just that biddy Dexford and her daughter. You know, Winifred."

"Still as plump as ever?"

"Well endowed is the polite way to put it. And, let's see, one of Charles's cousins is due in tomorrow from Chicago, or some outlandish place. We're going to meet him at Southampton."

"And that's it?"

"Yes. Social activities will pick up, no doubt, when they move to London next week. Charles and I hope to miss that though, thank God. We're planning a walking trip through Greece."

Fenton's smile was sardonic. "Young Winifred had better work fast."

Roger nodded as he chewed. "Bit of a scene brewing, if you ask me. His nibs and Hanna are as keen as paint about joining the Grevilles to the Suttons. They keep pushing poor Charles and Winifred into the rose gardens every night to walk under the moon. Rather like pushing a couple of puppies out of the house. Not a thing's come of it. Charles can't think of a word to say to her. Anyway, he's . . . well . . . he has other matters on his mind. It's all rather hopeless. *Omnia amor vincit* . . . unless you're the son of an earl. Going to Greece might be just what he needs. One's troubles seem terribly puny in the shadow of the Parthenon."

The door opened and two servants came into the room carrying more food on covered salvers. The Marchioness of Dexford, and her daughter, Lady Winifred Sutton, followed them, Lady Dexford talking rapidly in staccato sentences, hands waving to the rhythm of her words, a tall, bony woman with a sharp, bird-like head. Her daughter trailed after her in silent resignation.

"Ah!" Lady Dexford shouted. "Both brothers Wood-Lacy! How nice! Fenton, you handsome rogue! I hear such naughty stories! My nephew Albert Fitzroy is in the Guards, you know. Grenadiers! Can't possibly be true, can they? Oh, dear, no! Well, here you are and I shall get at the truth, never fear. Say hello to Fenton, Winifred."

"Hello, Fenton," Winifred said, almost in a whisper. "It's very nice seeing you again." Her soft, unhappy eyes met Fenton's and then she dropped her gaze quickly, a blush appearing on her plump cheeks.

Pretty, Fenton was thinking. A bit too buxom and padded at the hips, but she would slim down when the baby fat left her. She would be Alexandra's age, just turned eighteen. Ripe for the marriage block.

He smiled pleasantly at her. "I'm happy that you remember me, Winifred."

"How could she ever forget!" her mother cried in a birdlike squawk. "Gave the child her first kiss! Sweet sixteen! Most gallant of you, Fenton. Most gallant!"

He could barely recall the incident. An avuncular peck on the cheek at her birthday party. He had been invited by her eldest brother, Andrew, a good friend from Sandhurst. Now she was a woman and a mate must be found. He felt sorry for her. The walks in the moon-drenched rose garden with Charles must be agony for her. A young woman longing to be loved. Charles, silent and moody, wishing with all his heart that he were in the rose gardens of Burgate House, walking beside Lydia Foxe.

"That's a charming frock, Winifred," he said. "It's very becoming."

"Th . . . thank you," Winifred stammered.

Roger choked on a piece of grilled kidney and coughed it up into his napkin. "Excuse me," he blurted.

Lady Dexford dismissed the apology with a wave of her taloned hand. "Nonsense, dear boy! Better to cough than to strangle, I always say."

It would be a good match for Charles, Fenton mused, and he could understand Lord Stanmore's desire for it. The Marquess of Dexford was not only a rich man with an ancient title, but also a possible prime minister, should the Conservatives ever regain power. As for Winifred, she was his youngest child and only daughter. He had four sons. No problem of handing down the title when he died. He would probably be content to see Winifred married to any man of good family and honourable profession. Andrew was a captain in the Horse Guards and the marquess himself had served briefly with the colours during the Zulu War, an act in which he took inordinate pride. There was food for thought there. He smiled warmly at Winifred and she smiled shyly back. An easy bit of fruit to pluck from the tree, but of course he could do nothing positive about it unless, or, rather, until Charles informed his parents that he would never become engaged to the girl, no matter what pressures they put on him.

Fenton stood up and gave a slight bow. "I leave you to breakfast. Perhaps we can form teams later for croquet."

"How marvellous! We will enjoy that, won't we, Winifred?"

"Yes, Mamma," Winifred said.

"All right with you, Roger? You could team up with Lady Dexford and show off your considerable skills."

Roger looked quizzical. "Fine. Although I must say, Fenton, I find your own skills to be downright humbling."

Ivy hurried up the back stairs cradling a pile of linen in her arms. The stairs were narrow and steep and the sheets and pillowslips felt like a ton weight by the time she reached the second-floor passage in the west wing. She opened the door slowly and peered hesitantly around it. The long corridor was empty. The housekeeping rules were emphatic: maids must never draw attention to themselves if at all possible. Should family or guests be seen standing in the halls, the maids should draw discreetly out of sight until the hall was empty. There were so many rules that Ivy's head spun trying to keep track of them all.

She looked to left and to right. The hallway that she was facing was known as the west wing gallery, an outer passage with tall, mullioned windows on one side. She remembered those windows from the day before, when she had come this way to help Doris make up Lady Alexandra's bed. The room that she was looking for was to her left, past Lady Alexandra's rooms and then down a short hallway which ran at right-angles to the gallery. She stepped resolutely out of the stairwell, closed the narrow door behind her and hurried towards her destination. As she passed Lady Alexandra's bedroom, the door flew open and the earl's daughter poked her head out.

"Velda?"

"No, m'lady."

"I can see *that*," the girl said petulantly. "I heard footsteps. Where's Velda?"

"I don't know, m'lady." She had never heard of anyone named Velda.

Lady Alexandra Greville took a step into the corridor and glanced up and down. "Oh, bother!"

Ivy stared at her in awe. She had only seen her from a distance before this. So pretty, like the portrait on a box of chocolates. A slim, oval face, blue eyes, thick, blonde hair curled into ringlets. And she smelt lovely, too. An odour of lavender soap and eau-de-Cologne. Her dress was open down the back, revealing silk lingerie fringed with frothy lace.

"You must help me," Alexandra said quickly. "Hurry up, or I shall be late."

"What?" Ivy said dully, gawking at this girl who was prettier than any princess in a storybook.

"Don't just stand there! Help fasten me up. I shall be . . ." The sound of a car horn cut off her words and she rushed across the corridor to the windows and looked out. "Oh, she's here! Drat that Velda!" She whirled in a fury of motion back towards the open door. "Quickly! Quickly!"

Ivy had no idea what she wanted her to do. She stood rooted, the linen in her arms. Alexandra disappeared from view for a second and then reappeared in the doorway, hands on her hips.

"I shan't ask you again. Now *please* do me up. Drop what you're carrying and come *here*."

"Yes, m'lady," Ivy blurted. Her arms parted as though they had a will of their own and the clean sheets and pillowcases fell to the floor with a dull thump. She hurried into the room to find Alexandra standing impatiently in front of a mirror.

"The buttons. Do up the buttons quickly, but don't miss any."

"No, m'lady." There seemed to be dozens of them, tiny ivory ones, running from the waist of the dress to the neck. She began to button them, her fingers trembling. "There's ever so many," she whispered.

37

Alexandra tried to look down over her shoulder. "Don't start off wrong or you'll have to do them all over again."

"I . . . won't . . . m'lady." The fabric was a beige wool challis, of such fine quality that it felt like silk to the touch. "Oh, m'lady, it's ever such a lovely dress."

"Do you think so?" she asked anxiously.

"Oh, yes. So pretty."

Alexandra scowled and ran her hands over the dress, smoothing the fabric across the hips.

"I was rather worried about it. I'm going up to London and I do so want to look nice. You're sure that you like it?"

"Oh my, yes, m'lady."

"I wasn't certain about the shade."

"It's so nice against your skin, m'lady. Like . . . like a pale brown mist."

The young woman turned around and smiled. "Why, what a lovely thing to say. Quite poetic of you. A pale brown mist. Oh, I do feel better about it now!" She turned back so that Ivy could continue with the buttons. "I have a lovely hat that goes with it, a beige sailor with dark brown velvet ribbons. You're new, aren't you?"

"Yes, m'lady."

"What's your name?"

"Ivy, m'lady. Ivy Thaxton."

"Well, Ivy," Alexandra began, then stopped as she noticed a middle-aged maid hurry into the room. "Well, Velda, it's about time. Wherever did you run off to?"

"I am sorry, m'lady. I . . ." The woman hesitated when she saw Ivy and her gaunt features clouded with anger.

"It doesn't matter," Alexandra said with a shrug. "I'm buttoned now. But do hurry and get my hat. I'm in a most awful rush."

"Yes, m'lady." Velda gave Ivy one final, withering look and then hurried into an adjoining room.

Alexandra bent quickly towards the mirror and gave her cheeks a firm pinch to redden them. "I shall ask one final favour of you, Ivy. I must kiss mamma good morning. Please hurry downstairs as fast as you can and tell the lady who just arrived, Miss Foxe, that I shall be down in a few minutes and

38

that we must drive like the wind or we shall miss our train."
She spun away, pirouetting in front of the glass.

Ivy backed towards the door, her brain in a whirl. "A . . .
Miss Foxe?"

"Yes, yes. Quickly, quickly."

Ivy flew out of the room and down the hall. She gave no
thought to taking the back stairs. There couldn't possibly be
time for that. She was on a mission, the importance of which
escaped her understanding, but a mission none the less. She
ran full tilt, clutching her little cap to keep it from flying off her
head, down the L-shaped hall of the west wing to the central
corridor of the main house. It was exhilarating to run along
such a broad, carpeted surface. She felt like laughing out loud.
It was like running down the High Street early in the morning
when all the shops were closed, racing Cissy and Ned and Tom
to school. She nearly collided with a footman on the upper
landing above the great hall.

"Sorry!" she called out, descending the stairs two steps at a
time. The startled man stared after her in mute astonishment.

The astonishment was shared by Mr. Coatsworth and two
other footmen standing in the entrance hall. They could merely
gape at the young maid coming so rapidly towards them and
could not have been more shocked if she had come sliding
down the banisters.

"What on earth . . . ?" Mr. Coatsworth blurted. "What on
earth . . . ?"

Ivy almost slipped on the highly-polished parquet floor and
came to a skidding, momentary halt in front of the butler.

"I . . . I must find a Miss Foxe. Have you seen her?"

Mr. Coatsworth could merely point in the general direction
of outdoors. The front doors were open and Ivy could see a
shiny blue motor car parked on the drive. A young woman with
red hair sat behind the wheel, a tall, dark-haired man in riding
clothes standing casually beside the car talking to her.

"Thanks," Ivy said, making a dash for the door.

"Now, see here . . ." the butler stammered. "See here . . ."

Ivy slowed her frantic pace when she stepped out of the
house and on to the hard-packed gravel drive. Her cap was
askew and she straightened it, then tugged at her apron which

had begun to droop off one shoulder. She walked demurely towards the car, revealing the kind of deportment that the housekeeper had stressed.

"Are you Miss Foxe?" she asked respectfully.

Lydia Foxe looked past the tall, angular form of Fenton Wood-Lacy. "Why, yes, I am."

"I have a message for you, miss . . . from Lady Alexandra, miss . . . she says for me to tell you that she shan't be but a minute as she has to kiss her mother and that . . . and that you will have to drive . . . like the wind to keep from missing the train."

"Oh, did she?" Lydia Foxe said with a husky laugh. "Dear Alex," she said, looking up at Fenton, the presence of the maid ignored. "Honestly, that girl would forget her head if it weren't firmly rooted to her neck. I told her that we were driving up to London. I hate that smelly train."

"Driving, eh?" Fenton said. "Bit of a rough trip for you, isn't it?"

"Oh, Lord, no. The road's quite decent once you're past Dorking."

"Going shopping?"

"Alex has some dress fittings and I have to see Daddy and then have the car looked at. There's a squeak of some sort in the differential."

"His nibs has a good man. Wizard with cars."

"I talked with Ross the other day in the village. He only knows English makes. And there's the question of tools. The Germans use different size bolts or something. There's a Benz and Opel garage on the Edgware Road."

"Won't break down on the way, will it?"

"No. It's just a noise. More annoying than anything else."

Ivy was at a loss over what to do. Stand listening to the conversation until dismissed, or just turn and walk away? Not that she was in any hurry to leave. The woman in the shiny blue car fascinated her. She had never seen anyone so attractive, not pretty and soft like Lady Alexandra, a different kind of loveliness altogether. This woman had a hypnotising, sensual beauty that caused Ivy to wonder if she might be on the stage. She certainly looked like an actress, not that Ivy had ever seen one except in the rotogravure section of the *Mirror*. Her hair was a deep chestnut red, coiled on top of her head and secured by a green velvet band. Her face was rather long, with high cheekbones and a slightly uptilted nose, the skin so fine as to be almost translucent. The mouth was large and full lipped, with a hint of wantonness in its moistness. Lip rouge? Ivy wondered. The woman's eyes were a luminous green that seemed to sparkle as she moved her head. Ivy gawked, spellbound, then pulled herself out of her momentary trance.

"Is . . . is there any message for Lady Alexandra, miss?"

A throaty laugh. "Oh, good heavens, no."

"Yes, miss . . . very good, miss."

"What an odd little creature," Lydia said as she watched the maid walk slowly back towards the house. "Did you notice her staring at me?"

"No, but then I was staring at you myself so I can't blame the girl. You're a damned attractive woman, Lydia."

She looked away from him, fingers toying with the heavy wooden steering wheel, eyes narrowed against the reflection of the sun off the shiny bonnet of the car.

"Please, Fenton, we promised to talk only in generalities."

He touched her shoulder, sensing the warm flesh beneath the cotton motoring coat and the silk dress. "I find that nearly impossible to do."

She could see the reflection of the house in the car's paint, mellow brick and smooth stone, the faultless façade of Abington Pryory, home of the Grevilles and the Earls of Stanmore for ten generations.

"I'm sorry, Fenton. Please don't make it difficult. You know how fond I am of you. You've been like a brother to me since I was nine years old and . . ."

His fingers tightened. "You can't look at me and say that, Lydia. But I shan't press you. I know what you're hoping to accomplish and I wish you luck. You shall need it."

Ivy made her slow way to the second floor of the west wing, taking the back stairs. The tableau on the drive lingered in her thoughts – the beautiful woman, the gleaming motor car, the tall, dark-haired man. What wondrous, exciting events lay in store for these people on this sunny June morning? Drive up to London, the woman had said. Ivy could not even imagine what that entailed or what Miss Foxe and Lady Alexandra would find when they got there. She had never been to London, although she had seen pictures of certain places in London, Buckingham Palace, St. Paul's, the Houses of Parliament and the Tower. A grand place, London, filled with pageantry: the Guards in their bearskin hats, the Beefeaters, the Lord Mayor with a great gold chain around his neck. Still, there must be more to it than that. A workaday sort of place, surely. Rather like Norwich or Great Yarmouth, only larger, more crowded. People doing ordinary things. Even some chaps repairing motor cars. It was all so curious. So far away. What fun it would be to be going with them, seated in the motor car as it raced like the wind through the countryside, whizzing through the little villages that she had seen from the train on the way down from Norfolk. Would they pause for luncheon on the way? Cold meat pies and cider in a little inn? Or would they eat when they got to London, dining in one of those posh hotels, with waiters in livery hovering around them? That would be the most fun. Would madam care to sample the cutlets? Would madam like a glass of bubbly champagne? The thought made her smile, and she was still smiling when she left the service stairs and walked down the hall. She was being served bubbly wine from a silver bucket when she suddenly became aware of a small crowd standing in the hall outside of Lady Alexandra's room. Mr. Coatsworth was there, and one of the footmen, and the maid, Velda – and Mrs. Broome. They were, all of them, staring at her and they were not smiling. Not at all at all.

"There she is, the little baggage," Velda said, sniffing back tears. "Oh, I'd give her such a thrashing if it was up to me."

Mr. Coatsworth and the footman nodded in agreement, their expressions like stone, but Mrs. Broome only sighed wearily.

"That will do, Velda. Kindly go about your duties."

"Yes, Mrs. Broome." Velda glared hatefully at Ivy before turning away and going into the room.

"If you need any assistance, Mrs. Broome," the butler said gravely, "I would be most happy to lend a hand."

"Thank you, no, Mr. Coatsworth."

"As you wish, Mrs. Broome. Come along, Peterson."

The butler and the footman walked stiffly away and Ivy was alone with the housekeeper who was now pointing down at the floor where the pile of linen was lying.

"Pick them up, Ivy."

"Yes, Mrs. Broome," Ivy whispered. She had forgotten all about them. She bent quickly and gathered them into her arms.

"We do not toss clean sheets and pillowcases on the floor in this house, Ivy."

"I . . . I'm sorry, Mrs. Broome . . . it's just that . . . that . . . ." Events had taken place so quickly that she could hardly sort them out in her mind. Dropping the sheets had been the only feasible thing to do at the time, but how could she make that clear to Mrs. Broome?

"Mrs. Dalrymple sent you to make a bed. Is that correct, Ivy?"

"Yes, Mrs. Broome."

"Very well, child, go and make it."

"Yes, Mrs. Broome . . . right away, Mrs. Broome."

"And I wish to see you do it. I wish to make sure that you have not forgotten *everything* that you have been taught."

"Yes, Mrs. Broome." Her face burned and there was an awful sinking feeling in the pit of her stomach. She walked down the hall with the housekeeper keeping a slow, measured pace behind her, like a turnkey in a prison.

The bed that needed making was a large four poster and Ivy made it with painstaking care, while Mrs. Broome stood silently watching. When the sheets had been stretched and smoothed and tucked in neatly, Ivy found blankets and a counterpane in a wooden chest at the foot of the bed. She spread them on, tucking in the blankets and straightening the corners of the counterpane and fussing with the folds so that it hung evenly, then she stepped back and waited for whatever comments the housekeeper might have.

"Very well done, Ivy."

"Thank you, Mrs. Broome."

"You were hired as an upstairs maid. I thought that I had made that clear. You were not hired as a lady's maid, nor were you hired as a messenger." Ivy opened her mouth as though to speak and Mrs. Broome raised a hand in admonishment. "It would pain me greatly to give you notice. Your vicar has recommended many girls to us over the years, both at Abington Pryory and Number Fifty-seven, Park Lane. The Reverend Mr. Clunes has always been a fine judge of character and I have never been disappointed with any girl he has sent us. Girls from Norfolk have always been level headed, intelligent, scrupulously clean and honest to the bone. I have never had a bit of trouble from one of them, but your shortcomings in the past half hour have more than made up for so many years of perfection."

"I'm sorry, Mrs. Broome, but you see – "

"Please do not interrupt me," Mrs. Broome said sharply. "There is, apparently, something that you are not aware of yet, and that is *place*. Everyone has his or her place in life, Ivy. Your place, at least for the time being, is that of an upstairs maid at Abington Pryory. Velda Jessup's place is that of a lady's maid. Mr. Coatsworth's place is that of a butler, mine is managing the household staff. What do you think would happen if none of us knew our place? Chaos, Ivy. An upside-down, queer sort of world. Can you imagine Mr. Coatsworth making beds or shining boots? Can you imagine me being told to empty chamber pots, and *complying* with such a request? Can you imagine cook and her helpers mucking out the stables? The mind rebels at such thoughts, but that is what you did, Ivy. You neglected . . . no, *ignored* your place and assumed the place of Velda. You then assumed the place of heaven knows what and went racing through the house like a Wild Indian. Mr. Coatsworth nearly had a stroke when he saw you leaping down the main stairs. He thought you must have had a fit and lost your mind."

"But, Lady Alexandra . . ." Ivy stammered.

Mrs. Broome stiffened. "Lady Alexandra is very young and inclined to dramatics. It is up to the staff to take her current, and I trust transitory, spirits into consideration and to keep them from demolishing the orderly procedures of the household. Lady Alexandra should not, of course, have asked you to dress her in the first place. And she should not have asked you to run downstairs with a message for Miss Foxe. She should

44

have waited for Velda to return, or rung down to me and I would have sent someone up to her and dispatched a footman who would have delivered her message in a proper manner. I cannot admonish Lady Alexandra, but I can, and must, admonish you or you may do something similar again. In the future, when asked to do *anything* that is not a regular part of your duties you shall decline – in a polite and respectful manner, needless to say – and will immediately convey the request to one of your superiors, to a valet, a lady's maid, a footman, a parlour maid or, in the unlikely circumstance that no one of such status is available, to either Mr. Coatsworth or myself. Do you understand, Ivy?"

Ivy could only nod her head numbly. Mrs. Broome then reached out and patted the trembling girl on the cheek.

"I shall not give you notice, Ivy, never fear. You have a sparkle and a brightness that I find most engaging. If there are no more unfortunate lapses of mind I shall start to train you as a parlour maid within the next six months. That will mean more pleasant duties and a bit more money to send home, which I'm sure will be appreciated."

"Yes, Mrs. Broome." The words were barely audible.

"Now, finish tidying up here. Check the towels in the drawer, open the windows and air the room. Her ladyship's nephew is arriving from America tomorrow and will occupy this room. We wish it to be nice and pleasant. When you have finished you will go downstairs and Mrs. Dalrymple will instruct you further."

And then she was gone, moving majestically out of the room, a tall, black-clad, white-haired woman who held the power of life or death over everyone at the house with the exception of Mr. Coatsworth and the outside staff. Ivy held her breath until the woman was safely out of sight and hearing, then she sank down on the windowseat and buried her face in her hands. She had come so close to losing her position, and then what would have become of her? She couldn't go home, not with the baby due any minute and Dad having enough trouble putting food on the table and paying the rent and seeing to it that her brothers and sisters had decent clothes and sturdy shoes to wear to school. Oh, sweet Jesus, don't let me get the sack, she prayed, *ever*. She felt like blubbering, but the tears wouldn't come and so she rested her suddenly feverish face against the cool window glass. She could see the side garden, an old brick wall smothered by clematis and part of the driveway. The shiny blue car came suddenly into view, going very fast, Miss Foxe clutching the steering wheel, her red hair gleaming in the sun. Lady Alexandra was looking backwards and waving, one hand clamped on top of her straw sailor, the long, brown velvet ribbons fluttering in the wind. "Goodbye," she was shouting happily to someone. "Goodbye . . . goodbye."

And that was *their* place, Ivy thought with a sharp pang of regret. It *was* a queer sort of world, come to think of it.

3

HANNA GREVILLE, COUNTESS OF STANMORE, SAT AT HER
writing desk fronting a deeply-set bay window in her sitting
room. The window overlooked a small, formal garden where
ordered ranks of boxwood shrubs and roses formed precise geometric patterns when viewed from above. The countess was
wearing a green silk peignoir with a downy fringe of marabou
feathers around the collar, cuffs and hem. Her long, blonde
hair was now unbraided and brushed into smooth, shiny
waves that cascaded over her shoulders and down her back.
She was forty-five, seven years younger than her husband, and,
except for a slight thickening around the hips and the begin-
nings of a double chin, had retained the golden good looks of
her youth. That she was Alexandra's mother there was no
doubt. She was the mirror of her daughter's middle age.

Hanna listened to the stuttering roar of a car engine as the
machine receded down the drive towards the Abington road a
mile away. That would be Lydia and Alexandra leaving for
London, she reasoned correctly as she refilled her coffee cup
from a silver pot. She did not entirely approve of women
driving cars, although more and more of them were doing so
these days. There were advertisements in all the better
magazines showing stylishly dressed young women seated
happily behind the wheels of Vauxhall, Benz and other sporty
makes. Alexandra had begged that she be given driving
lessons, but the countess had refused to allow it. She was
frightened enough by Charles having his own motor. There
were so many accidents. One read about them almost daily.

She finished her coffee and set to work, pushing her sleeves
back over plump, white forearms. The top of the oval desk was
nearly obscured by piles of papers filled with her neat and
almost microscopic handwriting. She had a formidable task
almost completed – the schedule and guest lists for the many

balls, fêtes, entertainments and extravaganzas planned for the balance of the summer, the "season" in London. The last two weeks in June and all of July would be spent at Stanmore House, the Greville mansion at Number Fifty-seven, Park Lane. The earl was not happy about it, of course, preferring to stay in the country. In previous years he had managed to avoid going up to London for the social whirl of those six weeks, but Alexandra had not been coming in then and it hadn't mattered to Hanna whether he came up for the full time or not. This year was different. She had insisted firmly that he should attend every function, meet every guest, for his daughter's future lay somewhere among the papers before her.

Somewhere. She sorted through the papers slowly, reading each name that she had written down, the guest list for each and every gathering. The list of names was long. Two hundred for the ball on Friday, June 19th, three hundred and fifty for the gala on July 4th – Independence Day – red, white and blue bunting everywhere, the American ambassador as the honoured guest. List after list: thirty for dinner on July 12th, twenty-five for a picnic at Henley, forty seats reserved at the Drury Lane Theatre to see Chaliapin in *Ivan the Terrible*. On and on. Everyone who was anyone had found their way on to Hanna's lists and were grateful to be there. Stanmore House had always been the glittering focal point of the entire London season. It was a clever trap, for sprinkled liberally among the names of Lord and Lady this, and the Viscount and Viscountess that, were the names of a score of young men, highly eligible bachelors all, and one of those names – and, oh, how she wished she could point to it – would soon be Alexandra's betrothed.

"Who?" she wondered, whispering the word, her finger moving slowly down list after list as though reading Braille. "Albert Dawson Giles, Esquire; The Honourable Percy Holmes; Mr. Paget Lockwood; Thomas Duff-Wilson." She paused at that name. A barrister, Inner Temple. Twenty-five years of age. Wealthy from inherited money, a fine sportsman – Anthony would be pleased at that – a nephew of Lady Adelaide Cooper, one of the queen's ladies-in-waiting, and certain to be knighted in a year or two. The man's name fairly

48

leaped at her. Yes, it stood out above all others and she sorted through the lists to make doubly certain that he had been included on all of them.

"Terribly busy, my darling?"

She gave a little jump of surprise and turned on her chair to see the earl standing behind her.

"Oh, you startled me. I didn't hear you come in, Tony."

He bent his head and kissed her softly on the nape of the neck.

"Of course not. I'm quite skilled at sneaking into boudoirs."

"That isn't a skill a *gentleman* brags about."

He kissed her once more through the river of hair. "I am not always a gentleman, Hanna."

"No," she laughed, reaching up for his hand. "You're quite a rogue sometimes." She gave his hand a quick squeeze and then turned back to her work. "Pull that armchair over, Tony, and let me go over these guest lists with you."

"Heaven forbid. That's your province, Hanna. Invite whom you like. You've never made a wrong choice yet."

"It's a little more important this year and you know it. Do you realise that these papers probably contain the name of our future son-in-law? That's a sobering thought, Tony, and I'd like to talk to you about some of these young men."

The earl frowned and walked slowly to the window and gazed down at the garden, his hands folded behind his back.

"I'm not concerned about Alexandra. I know that you will pluck just the right fellow out of the pack and that she will be happy over the choice. I have all the faith in the world in your ability to do that. No, I have no worries about Alex. It's Charles who disturbs me."

Hanna picked up a gold pencil and tapped it lightly against the edge of the desk.

"He's just going through a phase, Tony."

Lord Stanmore smiled wryly. "That's what Fenton said about Roger . . . going through a phase."

"Fenton? Is he here?"

"Yes. Got in last night. He'll be staying a few days. Damned glad to see him. Why is it that I can talk to Fenton and I can't talk to my own son? There's such a wall between us, Hanna."

49

"You were both chatting away at dinner last night."

"Oh, we *talk*. That is, we open our mouths and words come out, but that wall is there and we both know it, and we both know what that wall is. Or rather I should say *who* that wall is."

Hanna pressed the pencil against her pursed lips and then stood up and walked over to stand next to her husband.

"How pretty the garden is," she said quietly. "So wonderfully ordered and neat. It's a pity that lives can't be arranged in the same manner, but they can't and you know that they can't. We can merely guide people, train them, and I believe that we've trained Charles very well. He will never do anything that isn't the right and proper thing to do. He's infatuated by Lydia and always has been, but I know in my heart that when it comes to a decision he will make the right one, the one that pleases you and me."

"Perhaps," he grunted, eyes fixed on the geometric plantings below.

"But we mustn't press him . . . at least, *you* mustn't press him into building this wall you refer to any higher. It was a mistake inviting Mary and Winifred. I told you that."

"Winifred's father is – "

"A fine and honourable man," she cut in. "Yes, I know all that, and it would be wonderful if Charles fell in love with the girl and married her. But let me put in a little Yankee common sense, if you don't mind. You can lead a horse to water but you can't make it drink. Charles feels nothing for Winifred. Nothing at all. In fact, he probably hates the poor girl by now and if he does we're to blame. I made up my mind last night when I saw the expression on Charles's face when you *suggested* that he take Winifred down to see the new gazebo. I shall have a quiet, heart-to-heart talk with Mary and stop this nonsense before it goes any further."

"You can't tell the woman to leave and take her daughter with her. That wouldn't be right."

"I won't tell her to leave, just explain the blunt facts. She may be flighty, but she does have four sons who have minds of their own. She'll understand Charles's feelings and she won't resent it one bit. Mary's an old and dear friend and we've always been candid with each other."

50

"Well, all right," he said in a pained manner. "Perhaps you're doing the right thing."

"I will be doing the *only* thing." She touched him gently on the shoulder. "I'm a mother *and* a woman. I understand Charles far better than you do at this period of his life. And what's even more important, I understand Lydia."

"Oh, I feel so glorious!" Alexandra shouted, bouncing up and down on the car seat.

"Sit still," Lydia shouted back, "or you'll fall out."

Alexandra settled down firmly in the leather seat, keeping one hand pressed on the crown of her hat. Lydia, frowning slightly, concentrated on adjusting the controls until the engine stopped its stuttering roar and settled into a smooth, powerful howl. They were past the village of Abington, racing along a narrow road which curved in a succession of lazy S's through dense, old woods and sunlit patches of hedgerowed fields.

"Gloriously happy!" Alexandra cried into the slipstream of wind buffeting her face. "Oh, Lydia, do you realise that by this time next year I might be having a baby! That is, if we have a short period of engagement. I don't believe in long engagements, do you? Don't you think they're horribly old fashioned?"

"Oh, do be quiet, Alex," Lydia said in vexation. "You're enough to make a saint swear. Honestly you are."

The younger woman leaned closer to Lydia to keep from shouting over the noise of the engine.

"I went into mamma's sitting room last night after dinner and stole a long peek at her lists. Oh, Lydia, she's inviting every devastatingly handsome bachelor in London."

"How do you know they're *devastatingly* handsome?"

"I just know, that's all. Not a one under six feet, all destined for greatness – and one of them will sweep me off my feet and into his strong, ravishing arms."

Lydia rolled her eyes towards Heaven. "What trashy novel did you steal *that* line from?"

"Jane Bakehurst – you don't know her, she was my *very* best friend at school this year – well, she bought this book by Elinor Glynn, frightfully racy."

51

"Alex, you're impossible. The sooner you get married the better."

"I couldn't agree with you more. I can't wait to have babies, dozens of them – well, five at least – all fat, pink, gurgling things, and I shall stroll into the nursery every night with my devastatingly handsome young husband beside me and nanny shall parade them in front of us."

"Are you planning on having all five at one swoop?"

"No, silly, one at a time, a decent interval between each. But seriously, I believe marriage and babies to be a holiness. I truly do."

The countryside gave way to the suburbs. Epsom, Cheam, Merton and South Wimbledon, rows and rows of little brick houses, and semi-detached villas of mock Tudor design. The traffic became heavier when they reached Fulham and Putney; cars, lorries, buses and ponderous horse-drawn wagons. They crossed the river via Putney Bridge and so on into Mayfair. The House of Ferris, couturier, occupied an elegant Georgian edifice in Hanover Square. Lydia stopped in front and a doorman dressed in the livery of a Victorian coachman hurried from the entrance to open the car doors.

"Good day, m'lady . . . Miss Foxe," he said, touching the brim of his hat. "Shall I have a boy park your motor car, Miss Foxe?"

"Not today, thank you. I'm not staying."

Alexandra sprang from the car like a fluffy Persian cat. "Don't you dare pick me up before three. I don't want you to see my gowns until they're free of basting stitches. Promise?"

"Promise," Lydia said flatly. When the doorman closed the car door she put the Benz into gear and roared off in the direction of Oxford Street.

Foxe House was one of the largest and most modern office buildings in England. It had been designed by an American architect and completed in the spring of 1912 to a flurry of controversy. Letters had poured into *The Times*, the bulk of them decrying the erection of such a building within viewing distance of Nash's pristine Regent Street façades. But after a few months Londoners began to grow used to, and then fond of, the oblong multi-storey limestone-faced building near

Oxford Circus. It had long been Archie Foxe's dream to have all the varied departments of his vast enterprise under one roof, instead of being scattered hither and yon about the city. The efficiency of what Archie Foxe called "the Yank method" had been more than proved during the two years of the building's occupancy, and several of the larger British corporations were constructing massive office buildings of their own. The skyline of London was beginning to change and that was just what Archie Foxe liked to see.

Lydia turned into the entrance of the subterranean garage, where a boy in a smart blue uniform took the car from her. She removed her linen motoring coat and left it on the seat, then walked to a lift which whisked her upwards. The lift stopped at several floors and people got in and out, secretaries, office boys, mail clerks, men and women from Foxe's Fancy division, legal and real property departments. Lydia was instantly recognised by most of them and politely wished a good day, but she knew only one of her fellow passengers, a tall, ruddy-faced man named Swinton, who was chief of the advertising department. He got on at the first floor, a pipe jutting from his mouth and a large portfolio of drawings under his arm.

"Hallo, Lydia," Swinton said cheerily. "Come to take the guv'nor to lunch?"

It was a little joke they shared. Archie Foxe had never been known to have lunch. Once, long ago, Lydia had insisted that he should join her at lunch at the Savoy Grill and Archie had sent Swinton in his stead.

"No," she said with a smile. "Just come to pay my respects."

"He's as busy as a beaver. We're opening the new place at Charing Cross next week. Like to take a look-see at these?" He opened the portfolio to reveal half a dozen watercolours, rough sketches for advertising posters.

"They're very good."

"Thank you," Swinton said. "We're attracting some first-rate artists these days. The Slade School have finally stopped turning their nose up at us and we're getting some damned brilliant chaps from there, women, too. Any particular one strike you?"

"That night scene is very eye-catching."

Swinton slipped it from the portfolio and held it up. It was an impression of a London street on a rainy night, great blobs of brilliant colour shimmering in reflection on the wet pavement. People, heads bent against the wind-driven downpour, were scurrying shadows. Amid the gloom rose a brightly lit two-storey building with the words "White Manor" illuminated across the front of it. At the bottom of the sketch – which would be even more effective when done in oils – was a slogan in black ink, "GET OUT OF THE WET AND INTO A WHITE MANOR".

"Yes," Lydia said, "I like it very much."

"So do I. It's for the winter campaign. Well, ta-ta." He stepped out of the lift on the fourth floor and Lydia continued upwards to her father's office.

Archie Foxe had an office of his own, complete with a desk that had once belonged to the Duke of Wellington when he had been prime minister, but he rarely spent time there. He was a roamer, a compulsive walker, going from office to office and desk to desk, from the ground floor to the top, overseeing, supervising, suggesting, demanding, criticising and praising, as the case might be, every one of his employees from clerks to members of the board. Trailing after him would be one of his harassed, stout-legged male secretaries, a shorthand notebook and a pencil constantly at the ready. One filled notebook represented a very slow day indeed.

Archie Foxe had been destined to make money and had never felt the slightest surprise that he had done so. He had never thanked God for his good fortune and was quick to point out that neither luck nor the Almighty had had anything to do with it.

"Hard work and a bloody good idea," was Archie Foxe's sole business philosophy. He was sixty years old and had been born in the slums of Shadwell in London's East End on New Year's Day, 1854. He would not talk about his childhood to anyone, not even to his own daughter, nor to the woman he had married late in life and who had died when Lydia was a child, an upper-class woman from Cumberland who, had he told her, would not have comprehended his stories, or would have thought them mere Dickensian fiction. It had been a childhood of stinking hovels and workhouses, of a father drifting away in despair to gin-caused madness and a mother dying of consumption in a freezing attic. He could see the place of his childhood from the top-floor windows of Foxe House, the great serpentined stretches of the Thames below Blackfriars Bridge. It was not a distance that could be measured in miles.

Archie Foxe had been sent from a children's house of detention in Bethnal Green at the age of nine to be an apprentice in a butcher's shop in Smithfield Market. The butcher's brother owned a pie shop and Archie's job was to chop up scraps of near-putrid beef and veal which the owner turned into gelatinous meat pies. The vileness of those pies inspired Archie to make better ones, which he did after finishing his apprenticeship at the age of seventeen. He entered into partnership with a middle-aged widow who owned a tiny bakery near Covent Garden. The two of them made the pies at night and Archie took them round to various eating establishments and public houses and sold them during the day. They couldn't make enough of them and within a year they had rented a building and had ten meat-cutters and pastry men working for them.

"It was just a question of pilin' one thing on another," Archie would tell a magazine writer many years later. The bakery growing, the acquisition of horses and delivery wagons, the expansion of production, beef and veal pies, steak and kidney pies, veal and ham pies, pork pies with currants and apple chunks . . .

"And then the puttin' of the pies in tins, shippin' 'em to India, Australia; all round the bloody world."

The widow sold her share of the partnership to Archie in 1880 to spend the balance of her days in a comfortable house in the country with four servants.

"'Avin' it all to meself was really what did it. I could feel free like, just do what I ruddy well wanted."

What he wanted were a few shops in strategic places on a corner of major thoroughfares, clean, well-lighted places, where ordinary blokes could have a cup of tea or coffee and something good and filling to eat and be waited on by a pretty young woman dressed in a blue uniform with a starched white apron and a white cap and all for very little money. He wanted all these shops to look exactly alike so that people would recognise them instantly. He thought up the idea of painting the exteriors a glossy white and the first of all the subsequent hundreds of White Manor Tea Shops opened its door on the north-west corner of Ludgate Circus on June 3rd, 1883, the shops at Holborn and Gray's Inn Road opening two weeks later.

"Men must eat, you see, that's only nature. A man can go years on the same pair o' boots, a woman can wear the same coat from one year's end to the other or 'ave the same 'ousehold furnishin' for a lifetime, but they must eat, three squares a day and a cuppa char every few hours or so. That's the natural thing about it, that's why you can't 'elp but make a bit o' money at it, caterin' to that natural fact, you see. Can't 'elp it. And the only trick to it is in givin' just ordinary people decent grub at a fair price because those are the people you want to sell to, the people who've got to watch their pennies, see, because there's a lot more of them kind of people than there are rich people who don't give a damn 'ow much they spend for a meal. I don't care if they come into a White Manor or not. That is of no concern to me at all . . . not one bit . . . no. I built the White Manors with some bloke who clerks in an office in mind, with a shopgirl in mind. Yes. Only, of course, it grew a bit from that, you see. Got a bit more posh, you might say. Yes. There are White Manors where a navvy can hop in for his tea and two slices and there's the White Manors that got a ruddy six-piece orchestra and a duke couldn't find fault with the Dover sole. But the price stays fair, you see . . . that's the whole bleedin' trick . . . the price stays fair."

"Is my father about," Lydia asked the pretty, young receptionist.

"He went below, Miss Foxe," the woman said. "But I can ring down and I'm sure we can find him for you."

"Oh, that's all right. I'll just wait in his office. But if you hear from him, tell him I'm in there or I'll be waiting for ever!"

"Of course, Miss Foxe. And may I compliment you on your frock? It's very lovely."

"Thank you."

"Most becoming. Not English, surely."

"No. It's from Paris."

"Oh, yes. It does show, doesn't it?"

Lydia could see the envy in the woman's eyes. She was pretty but her clothing was drab. A girl who worked in an office and lived with other girls who worked in offices in some crowded lodgings in Holborn. It was quite pathetic.

She liked her father's office. It was what she imagined a judge's chambers would be like, or the study of a dean at Oxford. The walls lined with oak, the flooring oak as well, polished to a satin lustre with a fine old Oriental carpet to add the proper touch of colour and warmth to the room. Comfortable leather chairs. The grand old Wellington desk. A few pictures on the walls. A landscape by Constable. Two modern paintings of London by Walter Sickert. And there were photographs in silver frames, on the walls and on the desk, photographs of herself, her mother, George Robey, a music-hall comedian of whom her father was very fond, Herbert Asquith and David Lloyd George. (The nearly bottomless bankbook of Archie Foxe had been of great help to the Liberal Party in the General Election of 1906 and the prime minister and his chancellor of the exchequer would never forget it.)

The framed, enthusiastically inscribed photographs of the prime minister and Lloyd George made Lydia smile. She wondered what Lord Stanmore would do if he were in her shoes, standing alone with the images of *those* men confronting him. Toss them out of the window, probably, or smash them with his riding crop in righteous Tory rage.

There were some magazines on a table and she sat in a chair next to the window and leafed through a copy of the *Illustrated London News*. There were pictures of the King and Queen at Cowes, the King looking trim and fit in an admiral's uniform, the Queen beautiful and terribly austere in an ostrich-plumed hat. There were three pages of photographs of the rebuilding of a cottage in Derbyshire, an article by Mr. Hilaire Belloc on the French Revolution – the first of five articles – lavishly illustrated with old engravings of the period, and several pages on German army manoeuvres in East Prussia: ranks of drably-uniformed men, with *Picklehaube* helmets, marching across fields, squadrons of gorgeously uniformed Uhlans and Hussars passing the Kaiser and the Crown Prince in review. How operatic and *costumed* they all looked. She wondered which of the Kaiser's arms was withered. It was impossible to tell. She turned the page. An advertisement in half-tone showing the newly completed White Manor in Charing Cross: three distinctly different restaurants for your dining pleasure, two orchestras, tango teas, saloon bar . . .

"Well, this is a welcome surprise."

She looked up and there was her father coming into the room, full tilt as usual, nearly running, a gaunt eyed, pink-complexioned young man at his heels.

"Hello, Daddy," she said.

"You can go, Thomas," Archie Foxe commanded over his shoulder. "Get the Manchester directive in the post by five, that's all that's important. Give the rest to the typists."

The young man visibly brightened. "Yes, sir, I'll do that."

"Well, well." Archie Foxe rocked back and forth on his heels and gazed at his daughter with obvious pleasure. He was a stocky man who looked younger than his years, with reddish hair parted and combed carefully to help conceal a round bald spot, like a monk's tonsure. The East End was engraved on his puckish features, the face of a street imp grown old – and much wiser. "Well, well. What brings you up from the country? Money, I suppose."

She was looking at him through narrowed eyes, a critical stare.

"You promised not to wear checked suits. They make you look like a bookmaker."

He touched the loudly patterned jacket with his heavy, blunt hands. "I like checks . . . an' bookmakers. Smartest bloke I ever met in me life was a bookie at Newmarket."

"Oh, Daddy," she sighed. "You're quite impossible." She stood up and walked over to him, kissing him on the cheek. "I've missed you. Can't you come down for a few days?"

"There's been too much to do, but I'll try and manage. You keepin' busy?"

"Oh, yes, with one thing or another. I drove Alexandra up for a dress fitting."

"How is the girl?"

"Excited. Hopes to be married any minute."

"Oh? Who's the lucky gent?"

"She hasn't met him yet, but I gather any man will do as long as he's tall, handsome and can walk on water."

"Seems to me that walkin' on water is your ruddy standard." He took a leather case from an inner pocket and extracted a long, Cuban cigar. "That and curin' lepers and raisin' the dead."

She turned away from him and walked stiffly to the windows. London had never looked so beautiful, almost like a picture postcard rendition, a too blue sky, a perfectly formed nimbus of white, fleecy cloud framing the dome of St. Paul's. How wonderful it would be to fly above the city – not in an aeroplane, she had done that and it was far too noisy for enjoyment – but as a bird flew, on silent wings.

"I find your impatience with me depressing, Daddy."

"Oh, do you?" he snorted, biting the tip off his cigar and propelling the fragment towards a shiny brass spittoon. "Well, my girl, it's normal for a man to want kids, his own kids or grandkids. Natural fact that, ask anybody."

"I wish I'd been born a boy," she sighed. "It would have made everything so much simpler."

He came up behind her and rubbed the side of his hand against her neck. "Yes, Foxe and Son right from the start. Only thing, see. He would 'ave looked like me instead of his mother. I would 'ave 'ad a short, ugly, red-headed nipper instead of a bloomin' ravin' beauty of a girl."

She turned with a smile and put her arms around him, hugging him, inhaling his scent of fine wool and good tobacco.

"You're a dear. I'll give you scads of little nippers one day, Daddy. I promise."

"I've never doubted it, but I wish you'd hurry up and get started."

"I have plans," she said quietly. "Really quite wonderful plans."

Hanna gave some thought to her nephew as a maid brushed and combed her hair for her.

59

"Would her ladyship like it swept up this morning?" the maid asked. "With a few curls on the sides?"

"I think so, Rose, yes, the way you did it the other day."

"Very well, your ladyship. I'll just heat up the tongs."

The telegram was in the centre of her desk, sent from New York: "Will arrive Cunard S.S. *Laconia* . . . docking Southampton Friday June 12 . . . Eagerly awaiting seeing you again . . . Give my regards to all . . . Martin Rilke."

Just thinking of the telegram made her smile. It was so American. So filled with uninhibited eagerness and friendliness, a pat on the back and the big hallo, the Chicago manner. *Give my regards to all*. Only a Mid-Westerner would cherish such presumptions towards people he had never met, nor even corresponded with, simply because they were *family*. She could understand his attitude because although she had left Chicago at the age of nineteen, to return there only once for the briefest stay, she had never lost her awareness of American attitudes. It would have seemed perfectly natural and right for him to send such a telegram – *give my regards to all* – to Uncle Tony, Cousins Charles, Alexandra and William. Indeed, it would have seemed wrong, in his mind, not to do so. The unfortunate fact was that her husband and her children would have been bewildered had she passed on such sentiments to them. She had merely said after receiving the telegram, "My nephew will be arriving on the twelfth. He is looking forward to meeting all of you." That, of course, was understandable. They were, in a mild fashion, looking forward to meeting him. (William, not having been home and knowing nothing about it, was excluded.) She had told them two months before that Martin would be coming to England, to stay for a week or two before travelling on to France, Germany, Austria and Italy, so that the announcement of a specific time and place of arrival had come as no surprise.

"Is he, now?" her husband had said. "So soon. Well, we shall have to send Ross down to the docks to fetch him . . . and one of the footmen to help with the luggage."

"I think it would be nicer if Charles went also."

"Yes, quite so, my dear, by all means."

Charles had shown a certain reluctance. "It's not as though

I knew the chap, mother . . ." but her will had prevailed. "I just hope to heaven he's not like that other Rilke who descended on us last year."

"No, dear," she had said. "I'm sure that he isn't. He's my brother William's son. You remember my telling you about him."

Charles had nodded in the affirmative, but she doubted whether he had remembered very much of what she had told him, in bits and pieces over the years, of her brothers William and Paul and of the polar distance between them – Paul successful and rich, William a failure, poor . . . and now dead. It had been Paul's son, Karl, who had come over the previous summer for a brief visit before going on to Paris and Berlin, a contentious, brash young man who had prefaced almost every sentence that he had uttered with the words, "Well, at Yale we . . ." They had all grown rather irked at the Yale standard for everything by the time he had left. Now another young Rilke was coming from across the sea and she could not guarantee that he would be any different from the last one, although she had sensed from the letter he had written to her in March, telling her of his plans for travel in Europe, that he was very different indeed. Willie's son. They had met for the first time in Chicago when she had gone back for Aunt Ermgard's funeral in the summer of 1903. He had been twelve years old then, a month younger than Charles. A quiet, polite boy who had rather startled her by quoting a passage from Goethe in a German untainted by New World idiom or accent. But why should that have been a surprise? Willie's son, after all. It was impossible to think of her dead brother without feeling a tug at the heart.

"Keep steady, m'lady," the maid cautioned. "The tongs are quite hot."

After her hair was arranged to her satisfaction, the maid helped her into a morning dress of white lawn and she left her room and started down for her breakfast, passing her son's room on the way. The door was closed and she hesitated in front of it for a moment and then rapped gently. She distinctly heard him call out – "Go away" – but she ignored the directive and opened the door.

61

"Good morning, Charles," she said cheerfully.

He was fully dressed on the bed, his back against the head-board. A breakfast tray, the food barely touched, was on the bedside table. He put down the book he had been reading and smiled in apology.

"Sorry, Mother, I didn't know it was you."

"I'm going down for breakfast. Have you eaten?"

"I was brought something, but I'm not hungry."

"Don't you feel well? You look a bit pale."

"I'm fine."

"Are you sure?"

"Yes, Mother, quite sure."

How gaunt he has become, she was thinking, the face of a troubled man. She could see the unhappiness in his eyes and that hurt her deeply. He was her firstborn and they had always had a special relationship, a closeness.

"Can we have a little talk, Charles?"

He looked away from her and tossed the book on to the bed.

"What about?"

"Winifred Sutton, among other things."

"Ah," he said with a thin smile. "Winifred."

"I convinced your father this morning that there is no possible chance of your becoming attracted to the girl and that any dreams he may have had about the two of you are simply that . . . his dreams, not yours. I intend to be quite candid about the situation with Winifred's mother."

"Well, that's a step in the right direction, I must say." He sat on the edge of the bed and placed his hands on his knees, a pose that always reminded her of her husband. They were so alike in looks and mannerisms, the same long legs and slender body, the same clean features, and yet so opposite in character. The room reflected his tastes, just as her husband's rooms reflected his. Books were everywhere, stacked, piled, some open, some closed with scraps of paper jutting from the leaves. She had no idea of his purpose in all that reading. He had mentioned in an off-hand manner his interest in the Seven Years War and the expansion of the British Empire. Did he intend writing a book? It seemed to her an odd subject to devote one's time to.

"You look instantly better," she said.

"Yes, as a matter of fact I am." He grinned at her. "And I'm quite sure that Winnie will feel better as well. I frighten her. Do you know that? It's true. She told me last night down at the gazebo. She called me moody and intense. There's quite a simple, passionate soul beneath all that *embonpoint*. I'm not the man to bring it out and she knows it."

"That's a pity, in some ways."

He nodded emphatically. "The dynastic blending of two fine old names. A gilding of coronets. I feel a bit of a rotter disappointing everyone, except Winnie, of course. I wouldn't say a word to her mother, though. I'll take Winnie for a drive into Guildford, treat her to a cup of chocolate and an éclair at the tea shop and break the terrible news to her. That's the gentlemanly thing to do, isn't it?"

"Yes, I suppose it is."

"Then she'll tell her mother whatever she feels like telling her, that she's fallen in love with the Prince of Wales or discovered in the nick of time that there is galloping insanity in the Greville blood, and in a day or two they will both depart seeking more receptive game. I'm sure that Lady Dexford has a list that beggars the one you've compiled for Alex."

"Charles! What an awful thing to say!" Her indignation was so patently artificial that they both laughed. "Very well, you deal with the entire matter, but don't put it off."

"First thing this afternoon."

She walked further into the room and stood looking about with a wistful expression.

"You used to keep this room so neat at one time. Everything in its place. It must be the despair of the maids now."

"I won't let a maid in it. They have a compulsion for tidiness."

"I think the room reflects your state of mind, Charles. A topsy-turvy confusion."

Their eyes met and he looked away. "I sense the preamble to a motherly lecture. I think I can guess the subject matter and I'd rather you didn't get started. Not now."

"If not now, then when?"

He turned to the book he had tossed aside and flicked through the pages idly.

"Soon. When . . . when I get it all clear in my mind as to just what I want to say."

Hanna's face seemed suddenly drawn and tired as she looked pityingly at her son.

"I know what you're going to say, Charles. I can hear every word of it, and I can hear your father's reply. He's a proud and inflexible man. No need to tell you that. Yes, Charles, I can hear his reply, anticipate his actions. I should like to leave you with just one thought and I want you to face that thought and dwell upon it honestly. Will you promise me that?"

"Of course," he said, frowning at the pages.

"I hope you won't think me cruel."

"No."

"I've known Lydia since she was a child and I'm fond of her. Her mother was a dear woman and it was a great tragedy that she died when Lydia was so young. I think she would have grown up to be a more – well, a more *traditionally* minded woman had her mother lived." The branch of an elm moved gently in the wind outside one of the windows. Charles used to climb out of that window when he was a little boy and clamber down the tree into the garden below. "The question I raise is this. Should you marry Lydia without your father's blessing he might publicly disavow her as his daughter-in-law. The social implications of such an action would be devastating. I ask you in all honesty, Charles – if Lydia knew for certain that your father would ignore her in such a drastic fashion, would she have quite the same affection for you as she does now?"

Twilight lingered until past nine o'clock, a soft blue glow in the sky with cobalt shadows lying across the fields. On Burgate Hill, the top branch of the tallest tree caught the last ray of sun from the west. A golden bough turning slowly to black.

Lord Stanmore leaned back in his chair and waited for Coatsworth to pass the cigars around the table. The ladies had left for the drawing room, the younger women to the music room off the conservatory, where recitals were sometimes held and where Alexandra kept her Victrola. He could hear the steady, far-off beat of music. He felt satisfied, with just a small tinge of regret. Satisfied by the dinner, an exceptionally fine baron of beef, the company – old and dear friends – but regretful over the way things had turned out between Charles and Winifred Sutton. He had allowed Hanna her way and the situation had no doubt been resolved. Charles had been a little less moody, although that could have been because Lydia had been at the table, and Winifred had acted as though a great weight had been lifted from her shoulders, chattering away to Alexandra and Roger Wood-Lacy like a plump magpie. The young knew what they wanted and didn't want, he supposed. Still, it was a pity. It would have been a damned fine match for both of them.

Coatsworth had decanted a fresh cask of port, the first of the shipment from Messrs. Lockwood and Grier, Lisbon, and he stood expectantly beside the earl's chair waiting for him to taste the first glass poured.

"Nice colour, Coatsworth," he said, holding the glass up to the light.

"Yes, m'lord, it is."

He sniffed the rim. "Aroma, too." He tasted, holding the wine in his mouth for a moment before swallowing. "Ah!"

Coatsworth took the sigh as a signal of approval and placed the crystal decanter on the table on the earl's left, where Mr. Cavendish, a local squire and one of the earl's oldest friends, was seated. Cavendish filled his glass and passed the decanter on to Fenton, who filled his glass and handed it down to a florid-faced man who was the Conservative M.P. for Caterham. And so the port went the rounds of the ten men at the table, only Roger Wood-Lacy, who could not physically tolerate alcohol in any form, declining.

"Well, Fenton," a retired brigadier, and one of the leading horse-breeders in the county, called out from the far end of the long oak table. "Well, sir, what do you hear from Ireland? You chaps still standing pat at the Curragh?"

Fenton dipped the end of his cigar in his port. "One never knows from one day to the next, sir. But I believe it's all rather more sound than fury, like Irish politics in general."

There was a muted chorus of "Hear, hear."

"It's all the newspapers, if you ask me," a tall, bald-headed man said. "You can always rely on Northcliffe or Lord Trewe to toss oil on a fire. I'm certainly against this damned Home Rule Bill as you all know, but I do believe that it's irresponsible journalism to intimate that the British army is on the verge of mutiny over it."

"Only the Irish garrison," someone remarked in clarification.

"Quite so. Still, you get my drift."

Fenton lit his cigar and blew a contented puff towards the high, beamed ceiling. "Oh, a few officers might resign rather than lead a force against the Ulster volunteers, but I'd say that would be the size of the so-called mutiny. And if push comes to shove, you'll see the Orangemen back down. They'll have to settle this Home Rule business around a table, not by taking pot shots from the bogs."

Lord Stanmore shook his head. "That's giving the Irish too much credit for common sense, Fenton. I'm sure they could work out a solution if they tried, or if they wanted a solution badly enough, but they have dug themselves into fixed positions."

"Oil and water, Tony," the brigadier said. "Two things that simply will not mix. The whole concept of Home Rule for Ireland is as foolish as trying to tamper with God's design."

"That's the Liberals for you," Mr. Cavendish said. "They feel above the laws of God or physics. Take Lloyd George and his Home Rule for Ireland . . . Home Rule for Wales . . . Home rule for Scotland. He'll be wanting Home Rule for India next."

"I met Parkhurst at the Carlton Club last week," the brigadier said with a chuckle. "He quipped that one sure way to get that randy Welshman out of office was to offer him an earldom in Glamorganshire and half interest in a coal mine. He'd be off like a shot!"

"There might be something to that, sir," Charles said solemnly, "I have no doubt that the man's ambitious, but I rather think he fancies himself above material gains or honours at the moment."

"A leader of the people," Roger said. "A sort of Celtic Napoleon or benevolent tyrant in the Greek manner."

"Friend of the common man," someone scoffed. "Quite an

easy matter to make friends if one is in the position of sending five bob a week to every old duffer in the country. But the people who thank Lloyd George and Asquith for their pension money should really thank me, and the rest of us at this table. The money comes from *our* pockets."

"No politician ever lost support by taxing the rich," Mr. Cavendish remarked drily.

Fenton let his attention wander. The gramophone was playing a fast two-step, the ragtime music barely heard. He was a good dancer, an attribute that was an outright necessity for any officer garrisoned in London. The regimental adjutant insisted that all new subalterns attend dancing classes, conducted three evenings a week by Corporal Booth of C Company, who had been a professional dancer in the music halls before enlisting. An inept dancer would have socially disgraced the regiment. It was Corporal Booth who had taught Fenton to dance the Castle Walk, Turkey Trot and the Texas Tommy and to keep abreast of all the latest steps coming out of America. His right foot began a soundless tap-tap-tap on the carpet.

"I'd gladly have them double my taxes," the brigadier declared stoutly, "if it meant another Dreadnought or two."

"Nonsense," the M.P. for Caterham said. "Let Germany pour millions into sabre-rattling. War is being fought now, today, and we're winning it hands down. The British merchant navy is the most powerful on earth and getting more powerful minute by minute. By Jove, it seems only yesterday that the *Lusitania* and the *Mauretania* were being touted by Cunard as the grandest ships afloat and now they come up with the *Aquitania* which simply beggars them. North German Lloyd and the Hamburg-American line will never be capable of building or operating anything like it."

An elderly surgeon from Guildford, a well-known hunting man, cleared his throat.

"Still, it isn't simply a question of merchant bottoms, is it? It's a question of production. Fritz may be trying to imitate his betters by venturing out into the sea lanes, but they out-produce us in steel and chemicals. One simply can't argue about that."

"The *manufacture* of chemical products," the M.P. said firmly, as though making a point in the House. "They must import every ounce of nitrate and other raw materials. You know a bit about that, don't you, Tony?"

"Yes, quite so," the earl said. "My wife's relations in Mecklenburg and Waldeck, the von Rilkes. Very heavily involved in the chemical industry. Import a great deal of nitrate from South America, I believe. Still, rather amazing how many things they can make in Germany out of coal tar. A cousin of my wife's, Baron Heinrich von Rilke, you met him last year, Percy, the scientific chap."

"Yes, of course," the Guildford surgeon replied.

"Well, he told me of some truly remarkable things that they were doing at his laboratory in Koblenz. Quite astonishing. One mustn't sell the Germans short."

The Caterham M.P. blew a stream of cigar smoke past the candelabra, the smoke curling above the steady candle flames.

"My point exactly! We must rise to their challenge, not with more battleships, but with increased productivity and better technology . . . bicycles, motor cars, farm tools. Fight them to a standstill in the market place with better and *cheaper* goods."

Fenton stifled a yawn. How many hundreds of hours had he suffered through listening to after-dinner conversations? It wasn't so bad at the Guards' Club where they could talk shop or sport – but not sex – or at the battalion mess where they could talk sex or sport – but not shop. He couldn't think of one brother officer who cared a tinker's damn about Germany, or England's social, political, or economic affairs. Cheaper goods indeed! That was the province of America, wasn't it? Ford cars and buying one's clothes through the post from an illustration in a catalogue.

"I say, sir," he said, hoping to sidetrack any further discussion of English industrialisation, or lack of it. "Roger tells me that one of Lady Stanmore's relations is arriving from America tomorrow."

"Quite so," Lord Stanmore said without enthusiasm. "From Chicago. Newspaper wallah of some kind. Never met him." He stood up, an august figure in his evening clothes. "Gentlemen, let's join the ladies."

Roger, Fenton and Charles lingered in the dining room until the older men had left, trailing cigar smoke down the corridor towards the drawing room. Charles drew a silver watch from his waistcoat.

"Not bad, a damned sight shorter than usual. A master stroke, Fenton, or we'd have been stuck in here for another quarter hour at least."

Fenton looked puzzled. "What are you talking about?"

"My cousin from Chicago. Father wished to avoid any probing questions about the fellow from his cronies."

"What on earth for? Is he some kind of desperado, like Jesse James?"

Charles laughed. "I hope so, but in all seriousness, no, he's just a chap who works on a newspaper. But there's some kind of skeleton in mother's cupboard, the chap's father, her brother William. I forget the story. All I know for sure is that he died years ago . . . of drink . . . or suicide. Something rather nasty. She named our William after him."

Fenton grimaced and flicked cigar ash into a plate. "I'm sure young Will appreciates *that*."

"Well, they couldn't change his name, could they? It happened after he was born. Poor chap is stuck with it. Are they gone, Roger?"

Roger had been peering down the corridor. "Yes, safely turned the corner. Let's hop it before someone comes back and insists we form bridge fours."

They left the dining room by way of the french doors that led on to the terrace. The gramophone grew louder as they passed the domed glass structure of the conservatory, designed by Sir Harold Wood-Lacy as a scaled-down replica of the Crystal Palace. Beyond the carved stone balustrade of the terrace lay the Italian gardens, bright under the rising moon, the topiary elephants and giraffes bobbing their cypress heads in the warm wind.

Alexandra and Lydia were dancing together to the trombone, cornet and snare drum beat of a Texas Tommy. Winifred stood beside the Victrola, one hand on the crank, her hips moving slightly to the syncopated sound.

"Charming!" Fenton said loudly, watching the girls prance

about the room, their images reflected from the mirrors on the walls, mirrors installed when Alexandra had been twelve and avid to study ballet. "Most inspiring!"

Roger stepped fully into the room, arms spread wide.

"All hail the antic Bacchae, chaste and fair!"

"Oh, don't be an ass, Roger," Alexandra called out over her shoulder. "Dance with Winnie."

Winifred looked startled. "Oh, no, I don't know how."

"Of *course* you do," Alexandra said breathlessly. "Don't be a frump."

The frantic music came to an end and the two girls broke apart, flushed and laughing.

"Oh, I did enjoy that," Alexandra said. "I could do the Texas Tommy all night."

"I prefer a waltz myself," Roger said.

"That's because you're staid and dull."

Roger stiffened with indignation. "I am not."

"Yes, you are."

"All right, play a tango then. I'll show you how staid and dull I am *not*. I dance the tango with a great deal of *sensuality*."

Fenton helped Winifred find a tango record among the pile in the Victrola cabinet. The girl's hands, he noticed, were trembling slightly.

"Don't you really know how to dance?"

"No," she whispered. "I never learned, at least, not properly. I have no ear for music, that's the trouble. I can't keep time."

"I'm sure I could teach you in a few minutes. It's really quite simple. No trick to it at all."

"Which tango are you playing?" Alexandra asked.

Fenton glanced at the label. "The Sans Souci."

"Fine. I like that one." She held out her arms. "Come on, Roger, and try not to step on my toes."

Charles bowed to Lydia with exaggerated formality. "Miss Foxe, may I have the pleasure?"

She curtsied. "You may indeed, Lord Amberley."

He put an arm about her waist and she moved closer to him. Their hips touched and his body became tense. When he took her right hand in his left she could feel the dampness of his palm.

"Relax," she said softly.

"We must talk, Lydia."

She smiled coquettishly into his taut, pallid face. "Why, Lord Amberley, whatever about?"

The music began, the pulsating Latin rhythm that had all Europe in thrall. Charles stumbled slightly, as though his knees had become locked from tenseness, and she had to lead for a moment until he was able to co-ordinate his body to the throbbing sound.

Fenton took Winifred by the hand. "Shall we try it?"

Her smile was wan. "I . . . I don't think I can."

"Nonsense. I saw you swaying to the Texas Tommy when I came into the room. You were keeping perfect time."

"Oh, I can dance by myself. It's just that . . . when I . . ."

"I quite understand." He held her firmly, one hand in the small of her back. "It's simply a question of practice, and confidence in oneself. I know I could teach you to tango in a very short time."

"You don't mind?"

"Why, of course not, Winifred. It would be a pleasure."

She was really quite pretty, he was thinking, smiling down at her. She smiled back, shyly, a pink glow spreading across her cheeks and throat. She had been casting glances at him all day. A young girl's sudden infatuation, a crush. He had done nothing to encourage her. Always the correctly formal officer and gentleman. Her brother Andrew's friend. He guided her expertly through the steps, the sensual movements of the dance.

"You're doing very well," he said. "Just follow me, don't look at your feet."

She had little grace, but that was probably nervousness. Her hand clenched his tightly and the hand on his shoulder kept straying down as though she were not sure where it belonged. Her eyes were hazel, he noted, and her hair the palest shade of brown. Yes, a very pretty girl, and if she lost a stone or so in weight she would have a quite fetching figure. Lady Winifred Sutton, only daughter of the Marquess and Marchioness of Dexford. A substantial yearly income when she reached the age of twenty-one. A dowry of . . . ten thousand pounds?

71

"Are you going up to London for the season, Winifred?"

"Oh, yes," she blurted, staring down at her feet. "Mamma will open the house next week. Number Twenty-four, Cadogan Square." She looked up at him and there was a wistful look in her eyes. "That isn't very far from the Guards' barracks, is it?"

"No. And it's just a short walk from my flat on Lower Belgrave Street."

He detected a sudden change in her breathing. The exertion of the dance? Hardly, she was barely shuffling her feet across the floor. A faint line of perspiration had formed on her upper lip.

"Perhaps . . ." she said hesitantly, "perhaps you could attend one of our . . . entertainments. That is . . . if . . . if your diary isn't completely filled."

"Why, no, it isn't. I'm quite flexible this season. Quite flexible indeed."

Her hand tightened on his arm. "My coming-out ball is on the twenty-second of next month. Alexandra will be there, of course, and Charles . . . and I know that Mamma would be pleased if you could come, also. Do you think that you could?" she added anxiously.

He appeared to think about it. "I believe so, yes. You can tell your mother that I'd be honoured to receive an invitation."

She smiled brightly and her dancing improved to a remarkable degree.

He's toying with her. The Fenton charm. Was it just for her benefit, Lydia wondered, or did he have a serious motive in mind? Winifred Sutton was rich, as Fenton well knew. Rich and dowdy. A good deal of poundage and not an ounce of chic. No one knew that more than her mother and father. A dashing, handsome man like Captain Fenton Wood-Lacy, son of the late Sir Harold, nephew of Major-General Sir Julian Wood-Lacy, would hardly be ignored if he asked permission to call on their daughter. Would he do that? He was smiling at her and Winifred was smiling back. She looked away.

Charles bent closer to her. "Let's dance out on to the terrace."

"Oh," she said, forcing her attention back to him, "if you wish."

They stopped dancing as soon as they had tangoed out of the music room. Taking Lydia by the arm, Charles led her across the terrace and down the stone steps into the Italian garden.

"You've been practically ignoring me all evening," he said, his hand pressing into her bare arm. He stopped at a stone bench and pulled her down on the seat beside him. "You look so beautiful tonight, Lydia. That dress, your hair – everything about you is like music . . . poetry. You knew I wanted to talk to you alone before dinner, but you deliberately stayed in . . . in *groups!*"

"It would have been rude not to mingle."

"So much has happened today," he said excitedly, running a hand through his hair. "I told Winnie, in a very nice way, that I could . . . well, that I could never become *emotionally* involved with her. She took it quite well."

"So I noticed," she said stonily.

"But that doesn't really solve anything, darling. I'm afraid that Father is going to be as intractable as ever as far as we're concerned."

She smoothed her dress over her knees. It was a long evening dress of pale green silk embroidered with seed pearls, the bodice cut with a discreet plunge.

"Charles, I think that the time has come to be honest with each other. I love you and I *think* you love me."

He stared at her with his mouth open. "You *think*? Good God! You dominate my thoughts day and night. I wake up in cold sweats a dozen times a night because I have nightmares of losing you. There's not another woman on this earth that I would care to even *look* at, and you *think* I love you!" He put his arms around her and pressed her close to him. Her perfume made his head reel. "Oh, Lydia, how can you question my feelings?"

She pulled back from him slightly and placed a slim, cool hand on the side of his face. He was gravely handsome, a noble, intelligent face that reminded her somehow of the portrait of Shakespeare, the engraving in most editions. Much younger,

73

but the same high domed brow, the soft eyes. An Elizabethan man, courtly and gallantly romantic.

"You had a talk with Winifred and I'm sure that you were very tactful and considerate."

"And direct," he cut in.

"Yes, direct. But tell me, Charles, are you ever that direct with your father, regarding us?"

He looked away from her, towards the house. It reared up against the moon-streaked sky; most of the rooms were lighted, and yellow squares of light fell across the dark lawns.

"I . . . I intend to have a long talk with him."

"You might begin by reminding him that we're living in the twentieth century."

He smiled sardonically. "The twentieth century? Father doesn't recognise it socially."

"Perhaps he doesn't, but most people are beginning to. I don't think he would be ostracised in the House of Lords if I married into the family. After all, it would be apparent to everyone that I hadn't *bought* my way into the peerage. Now, if I should marry Lord Peter Manderson, or the Earl of Darnil, that would be quite a different story, wouldn't it? There are a number of impoverished peers in this country, Charles. You'd be utterly amazed at how easy it would be for me to marry one of them if that was all I wanted, as your father seems to think."

He was staring at her with a look of dread. "Lydia, you . . . you'd never marry a rotter like Darnil. My God, I . . ."

"Of course I wouldn't." She draped her slender white arms about his neck and pulled him gently down to her. Her lips roamed teasingly across his face. "You're my own, sweet darling and I love you very much. I want to stop being *Miss* Foxe and start being *Lady* Amberley. I want to experience all the joys of marriage, and I want to experience them with you, no one else."

He held her tightly, kissing her lips, her neck, the soft hollow of her throat. He could feel her firm breasts against his chest.

"Lydia . . . Lydia . . ." he murmured.

She stroked the side of his head and traced a fingertip across his earlobe. He was really such a boy, she was thinking, so torn between duty and desire, so deferential to the Victorian codes of his father Charles Greville, Lord Amberley, the future Earl of Stanmore pressing trembling kisses on her skin.

"I've thought of a way to approach your father, Charles," she said quietly, stroking his soft hair. "It will require a positive attitude on your part, darling. You'll have to beard the lion in its den, but I've given quite a bit of thought to this."

"Whatever you say, Lydia," he mouthed against the narrow opening of her dress, the deep cleft between her breasts.

"But we must talk it over thoroughly first. Spend the day with me tomorrow. Daddy's still up in London. We can be alone, have the day to ourselves, perhaps take a luncheon basket to Leith Wood and talk, talk, talk."

"Lovely," he murmured, "lovely . . ." He suddenly stiffened and pulled away from her, his face even more pallid than it had been before. "Oh, God! I can't . . . I . . . I have to go to Southampton tomorrow and greet some bloody cousin from America. Oh, damn. I'm sorry, darling, but . . ."

Her smile was cryptic. "I understand, Charles. There's no need to explain. I quite understand."

4

MARTIN RILKE DOUBLE CHECKED HIS TINY CABIN TO MAKE SURE
that he had left nothing behind. He had packed in a hurry,
having spent the entire morning on deck gawking at the coast
of England as the S.S. *Laconia* moved up the Channel towards
Southampton.

"You won't see a better day than this in a long while," one of
the ship's stewards had told him. "We 'ave quite a bit of mist
most days, sir."

Not a speck of mist that morning. Martin had gulped down
his breakfast and had gone on deck to share a pair of binoculars
with a fellow passenger, a Dr. Horner from Cincinnati, who
was on his way to London for a month's seminar on neuro-
surgery. Both men had been fascinated by the vivid greens and
whites of the land, the sparkling blue of the sea. The passage
had been marred by a summer storm on the second day out of
New York, grey seas and a clammy rain staying with them as
far as the coast of Ireland. Of the Emerald Isle they had seen
nothing but great banks of cloud, but the clouds had parted
when they entered the English Channel and there was not so
much as a scrap of vapour to mar the scenery.

"'This royal throne of kings, this sceptred isle . . .'" Dr.
Horner had recited grandly as he leaned against the rail, the
binoculars cradled in his hands. "Shakespeare, *Richard the
Third*."

"Second," Martin had corrected. "*Richard the Second*. 'This
precious stone set in a silver sea.' It does look like a precious
stone, doesn't it?"

"Fire opal, Martin. Gosh, I wish my Agnes had been able to
make this trip. And she thought *New* England was beautiful
when we went up to the Berkshires last summer. Can't hold a
candle to the Old." He had handed over the glasses. "Take a
squint at that little village beneath those cliffs. If that doesn't

76

put the icing on the cake I don't know what will."

The landscape had at last given way to less pastoral views, reminding them both that England was not all quaint villages and rolling hills. By noon they were steaming up the Solent into the crowded roadstead of Southampton, the shoreline cluttered with iron cranes, docks, wharves and warehouses.

"It's been a pleasure travelling with you, Martin," Dr. Horner had said before going below. "Perhaps we can have lunch one day in London. I'll be at Guy's Hospital, the Sir William Osler seminar group."

Martin hoped that the good doctor had been better organised than he himself had been. A sailor with a trolley waited impatiently outside the cabin door.

"Okay," Martin said. "You can take the steamer trunk and the suitcase, but leave the leather attaché case."

"Yes, sir," the sailor grunted as he pushed his trolley into the cabin.

Martin took one last look around, under the bunk, in the dresser drawers, the cupboard. He suffered from a vague absent-mindedness at times and it wouldn't have surprised him to have come across a drawer filled with socks and underwear. But everything had been packed. Though rushed, he had been thorough. There was nothing of his left in the cabin except the attaché case, a brown woollen jacket and a Kodak folding camera in a leather carrying case. He put on the jacket and checked his appearance in the mirror. He wasn't all that happy about the fit of the jacket. It had been bought off the peg at Marshall Field and was a bit too tight across the chest. He solved that problem by leaving it unbuttoned.

Well, he thought as he slung the Kodak over one shoulder, you look every inch the world traveller. He was, finally and irrevocably, a long way from Chicago.

Jamie Ross soon managed to find a suitable space for the big Lanchester touring car, but they were a good distance from the Cunard dock.

"Can't you get a bit closer, Ross?" Charles asked.

"Afraid not, m'lord. Take us an hour to crawl through that mess."

The mess he referred to was a nearly solid line of lorries, taxicabs and lumbering horsedrawn wagons jamming the narrow approaches to the Cunard and White Star Line piers.

"Looks like three big ships came in at once this afternoon, m'lord," Ross said as he slipped his driving goggles from his face.

"So it seems," Charles said, suppressing an urge to swear. He picked up his straw boater from the seat and placed it squarely on his head.

Roger Wood-Lacy did the same. The hats of both men bore the Cambridge colours on a silk band around the crown. "Nothing for it, old boy, but to plod resolutely ahead."

"I hope we can snare a porter, Ross."

"I'm sure we can, m'lord," the chauffeur replied as he got out of the car and hurried to open the passenger doors.

"A thought just struck me," Roger said as they walked away from the car, the nattily uniformed Ross keeping a respectful six paces behind them. "How do we go about finding the chap? Do you have any idea what he looks like?"

"Haven't a clue. My age, a bit Germanic, I expect. I suppose we shall have to have him paged."

Charles glared balefully ahead. The street was narrow, dingy, lined with small shops and eating places. The fumes from the backed-up vehicles poisoned the air. He was in a bitter mood, the thought of what he would have been doing at this moment galled him. But for Martin Rilke's inopportune arrival, he would have been resting his back against an oak tree in the cool glades of Leith Wood while Lydia, her body uncorseted beneath a light summer dress, served him watercress and ham sandwiches from a wicker basket. Damn!

Both young men found the jumble of large wooden structures along the wharf bewildering. Beyond the roofs of the buildings they could see the tall funnels of the *Laconia*, wisps of smoke still trailing after them. Ross stepped forward and suggested that they head for an enormous, open-sided structure which bore a sign marked "BAGGAGE DISPERSAL – CUNARD LINE". Hundreds of people could be seen inside, milling about under twenty-six large metal signboards that dangled from the roof beams and had the letters of the alphabet painted on them. A regiment of dockers in blue overalls trundled carts filled with luggage into the building from the ship.

"Good thinking, Ross," Charles said. "The chap's bound to be under the 'R' sign sooner or later."

There were a great many people under the "R" sign, roaming through canyons of steamer trunks and stacked suitcases. Several officious looking men representing various tour organisations walked about calling for their groups to stay together.

"Raymond Whitcomb people over here, please!"

"Will all passengers on Cook Tour Number Seven please wait at the Customs shed? Will all passengers . . . ?"

"Is that him, do you suppose?" Roger asked, pointing discreetly down one of the aisles of luggage.

Charles contemplated the man Roger had pointed out, seeking a family resemblance. He saw a man in his early twenties, of medium height and stocky build, blond haired and square jawed. His nose was long and high bridged, the eyes blue and merry. Very much a masculine version of his mother's face. And he certainly had the Rilke mouth, wide, full lipped and quick to smile – as it was smiling now in his direction, a warm, faintly lopsided grin.

"Say," the man called out, "you wouldn't happen to be Lord Charles Amberley, would you?"

"Yes, I am," Charles said, taken slightly aback. He hadn't expected to find him so quickly.

Martin came towards him with his right hand thrust forward. "Don't ask me how I knew," he said, grinning more broadly. "I guess you just look like I thought you'd look." He took hold of his cousin's hand and pumped it vigorously. "Gosh, it's nice of you to meet me. Is Aunt Hanna with you?"

"No," Charles said, managing a weak smile—his hand felt as though it had been gripped in a vice. "I came down with my friend." He gestured towards Roger. "Martin . . . Roger Wood-Lacy. Roger . . . my cousin from America, Martin Rilke."

Roger took a step forward. "How do you do?"

"Very well, thanks," Martin said. "Had a swell trip, a bit rough for a few days, but all the passengers were good eggs. Had a really great time."

"Glad to hear it," Roger said. A pleasant-looking fellow, he was thinking, although a bit on the boisterous side – like most Americans. Not one of the millionaire Rilkes, he remembered Charles remarking. Some kind of poor relation. The jacket he was wearing certainly confirmed that fact. "Welcome to Merrie England."

"Thanks." He let go of Charles's hand and stood facing them, arms folded, grinning like a fool. "I just can't believe I'm *here*, that I'm actually on the other side of the Atlantic. Travel is really fantastic when you think about it. Just a week ago I was in Chicago and now I'm in the Old World."

"The *old* world?" Roger repeated dully.

"Take some getting used to," he went on blithely. "But here I am, Martin Rilke in the flesh, or on the hoof, as they say on the South Side. Maybe you guys wouldn't mind helping me find my trunk. It's dark brown leather, a bit scuffed, and it has my name painted on the side."

The two inhabitants of the Old World exchanged bleak glances and then helped Martin in his search. The trunk and suitcase were soon located and Charles asked Ross to collar a porter, tipped the man half a crown and the luggage was soon safely strapped to the rack on the back of the Lanchester.

Martin sat between Roger and Charles in the back seat, his attaché case on the floor between his feet, his camera case on his lap.

"Beautiful scenery," Martin said as they left the outskirts of Southampton and drove into the open countryside. "I hope you won't mind if I ask your driver to stop now and then. I'd sure like to take some pictures of this."

Oh, God, Charles groaned silently. He couldn't look at Roger. "Well, it's rather a long drive and we'd like to get there before dark. But we shall stop soon at Taverhurst for lunch. A quite ancient inn, the Three Talbards, and you can take all the pictures you want."

"That'd be fine. Thanks a lot. Where are we now? The county, I mean."

"Hampshire," Roger said.

"Hampshire? Near Thomas Hardy country . . . well, I'll be darned."

"The edge of it, yes," Charles said. "Dorset more than Hampshire, of course."

Roger arched one eyebrow. "I suppose Hardy's novels are required reading everywhere. *Tess of the D'Urbervilles* and *Jude the Obscure*."

Martin nodded. "That's right, but to be honest, I never could get into the novels. I prefer Hardy the poet."

"Oh, I say," Roger said with exuberance. "Jolly good for you. I feel the same way about him. Have you read 'Channel Firing' yet?"

"Yes, just before I left home. I especially liked the last stanza where he talks about Camelot and Stonehenge." He glanced wistfully at the green hills of the South Downs. "I'd sure like to see those places."

"But you shall, old boy," Roger cried. "We'll see to that, won't we, Charles? Oh, I say, this is absolutely marvellous. Think of old Hardy's poems being read in *Chicago*!"

Their accents and mannerisms began to grate on Martin's nerves a little. They seemed so affected, like certain theatrical people he had known. But, unlike actors, Charles and Roger were not trying to be something they were not. They were, in the slang of the city room, "genuine articles". He knew enough about England to recognise that and so he did not inwardly sneer at their way of speaking, their attitudes or their posturings. They did everything and said everything in a manner designed, consciously or unconsciously, to set them apart. It was something they had been born to practise, a manner carefully nurtured by their parents, steadily built upon at Winchester and then honed to a silver perfection at Cambridge. They were by every gesture, every nuance of speech, English gentlemen. They could have been set down in rags in the middle of the Arabian desert and that fact would have been apparent to the lowliest Bedouin, just as it was apparent to the chauffeur, the porter at the docks and the young women who waited upon them at the Three Talbards Inn in the village of Taverhurst. Driver, porter and barmaid treated these two young men without the slightest sign of servility, but with a natural deference. This he knew was what the English called *class*, the lower class recognising and accepting without resentment the superiority of the upper class. It was not an exportable commodity, like English woollens, although a great many rich Americans had tried to import it. He thought of his Uncle Paul and Aunt Jessica Rilke in Chicago, their huge palace of a house – referred to as the North Side Horror by many of Chicago's younger architects – staffed by footmen in knee breeches, butlers and grooms. A façade of upper-class splendour, no more than that. The servants needed the money they were paid, but they had no ingrained respect for their master and mistress. None at all. They felt degraded by their costumes and saw the difference between themselves and the Rilkes not in terms of *class*, but in terms of *money*. Paul Rilke owned breweries, a brokerage house, real estate in the Loop, iron foundries in Gary, Indiana, Toledo and Cleveland and a half share in a baseball team of the American League. That made him rich, even powerful, but did not ensure by right of heritage or custom that a porter would tip his cap to him and say *"sir"*.

"Here you are, sirs," the barmaid said as she approached their table with a loaded tray. "All piping hot."

"And very good it looks, too," Roger said, rubbing his hands. "I tell you, Rilke, it's steak and kidney, in pudding or pie, that is the true secret of British fortitude."

"Has my man been taken care of?" Charles asked.

"Oh, yes, sir," the barmaid said. "He's out at the back, sir."

She placed the steaming steak and kidney pie on the table along with mugs of dark brown ale, curtsied and departed.

"I understand you work on a newspaper, Rilke," Roger said after a few minutes of silent eating.

"That's right, the Chicago *Express*. I joined the paper when I left college last June."

"Where'd you go?" Charles asked. "Yale, I suppose."

"No. University of Chicago."

"Thank heaven for that. We had our fill of Yale men when Cousin Karl was over here."

Martin laughed. "Yeah, I know what you mean. We have a saying in the States, 'You can always tell a Yale man, but you can't tell him much'."

"Oh, I say," Roger chuckled, "that's rather good. I must remember that."

"Anyway," Martin said, "I joined the paper hoping to become a reporter, on the police beat. You see, I'd like to become a novelist and I thought a year or two of seeing the seamier side of life would be a big help. That's how Theodore Dreiser started, and Frank Norris and . . . oh, a lot of good writers. But they stuck me in a little office of my own and have me writing book reviews and theatre reviews. I'm getting sick of that and may quit when I get back unless they give me a more challenging job."

"Jolly good for you," Charles said. "There's nothing worse than being stuck in something you don't like."

"Well, I liked it okay at first, but I'm not going to learn very much about life reviewing the novels of Gene Stratton-Porter or Harold Bell Wright."

He wondered if he should mention that he had the first sixty pages of a novel in progress with him, a saga of Chicago, the struggle of men to break the power of the street railway barons? The manuscript was in his attaché case, but he decided against it. He was apprehensive about the direction the book was taking. It was – although he hated to admit it even to himself – too imitative of the "class struggle" novels of others. And besides, looking at the two faultlessly-dressed men, he doubted whether they would have the slightest empathy for the problems of poor Chicago streetcar motormen.

"What are your plans, Martin?" Charles asked.

"Well, let's see. Ten days here in England, then I go to Paris, Berlin, Zurich, Milan, Rome, then home on the White Star liner *Majestic*, from Naples. Six weeks in all. Not exactly the grand tour, but the limit I could afford."

"We may go to Greece in July," Roger said. "Pity you couldn't hop over for a week or two and join us. But you must at least make a point of seeing Perugia and the Abruzzi. That's the true Italy, Rilke, the true Italy."

They arrived at Abington Pryory in time for tea, which was being served on the terrace. It was a hectic moment for both

Martin and Hanna, he trying to remember the names of the people he was introduced to, and she trying to greet him in a proper "auntly" manner while not neglecting her guests. Two of the guests were leaving for London, a Lady Somebody-or-other and her daughter, a Winifred something, and their departure added to the confusion.

"We shall have a long talk later, Martin," Hanna whispered, giving his arm a little squeeze. "I'm sure you'd like some time to yourself before dinner. I'll have one of the servants show you to your room. And it *is* your room, Martin, to stay in as long as you wish."

He blurted his thanks to her and then excused himself to the dozen or so people whom his aunt had invited for tea. "My fellow members in the Abington Garden Club," Hanna had explained to her nephew before introducing him to them. They had seemed pleasant enough people, but they had studied him with unabashed curiosity as though he were some rare breed of plant that was entirely foreign to them. He was grateful when a footman arrived and ushered him into the house.

His trunk and suitcase were in his room, looking shabby against the pristine furnishings, but he only had eyes for the bed and flopped wearily on to it. He wondered what time they served dinner and whether he could take a nap for an hour or two. He had just closed his eyes when someone coughed to draw his attention. A middle-aged man, wearing a black linen jacket and grey striped trousers, stood just inside the room, one hand on the handle of the door.

"Yes?" Martin said, raising himself on his elbows.

"Beg pardon, sir," the man said. "I'm Eagles, your valet. If I may have the trunk keys, sir, I shall unpack and see to your clothes."

He wanted to tell the man not to bother, but his aunt had obviously ordered the valet to come and she might feel affronted if he told him to go away. He got off the bed and searched his pockets for the small, flat keys.

"Here you are," he said, handing them over.

"Thank you, sir. Shan't take but a moment. Travel is terribly hard on clothing, sir."

"Yes," he said lamely. "I guess it is."

"Oh, terribly hard, especially a sea voyage, sir. The salt air sets the creases."

It was embarrassing to Martin to watch the man go through his luggage, like standing by and watching a total stranger sort through his dirty laundry, piece by piece – and that was what most of his suitcases seemed to contain, soiled shirts, underwear, pyjamas and socks. The valet did not actually cluck his tongue, but his lips remained pursed as he sorted out the dirty clothes and removed wrinkled suits and jackets from the steamer trunk. It was obvious even to Martin that everything needed a good press, but the valet singled out one article of clothing for immediate attention as he held up a particularly wrinkled tuxedo.

"I shall give this a sponge and press immediately, sir. Dinner is always black tie, at least."

The *at least* had an ominous ring. He didn't own tails. The tuxedo was his only article of formal wear, and it was nearly two years old, bought for a fraternity dinner in his senior year and not worn since. It would be tight, but maybe a sponge and press would stretch it a little.

"Thank you . . . Eagles?"

"Eagles, yes, sir. I shall get right on to this, sir, and have the rest of your clothing back in the morning."

After the valet had gone, Martin sat on the edge of the bed and debated whether to flop back and go to sleep or take a hot shower. A shower sounded good, but it was obvious that the room didn't contain a bathroom. He was puzzling over that dilemma when there came a gentle knock on the door.

"Come in," he called out.

The door opened and a slender, dark-haired girl in a maid's uniform came into the room bearing a large bouquet of flowers in a glass vase. She seemed to shrink into the room like a scared doe.

"Hi," Martin said cheerfully. "Who sent the flowers?"

The girl mumbled something inaudibly and set the vase down on a table next to the windows. She barely glanced at Martin before turning to go.

Martin stood up and blocked her exit to the door. "Wait a minute, maybe you can help me."

85

"Help you, sir?" the girl whispered, almost shrinking away from him.

"Well, I'd like to take a shower. Where's the bathroom?"

"The bath, sir, or the W.C.?"

A water closet! He recalled all the tales he had heard about primitive British plumbing facilities. An English mansion might have thirty bedrooms but only two baths and a couple of water closets, almost as an afterthought. There would be, he felt certain without taking the trouble to look, because he'd be damned if he'd use it, a chamber pot under the bed.

"Well," he said, "both, I guess."

"Yes, sir," the girl said, looking past him towards the door. "The W.C. is the last door at the end of the corridor, sir, and the bath is the third door to your left . . . no . . . to your *right* as you leave the room, sir."

She was a daisy of a girl, Martin was thinking as he looked at her. Seventeen or eighteen, skin like the proverbial peaches and cream and eyes that were almost violet, with the thickest and longest lashes he had ever seen.

"My name's Martin," he said impulsively. "Martin Rilke. What's yours?"

"Ivy, sir."

"Ivy what?"

"Thaxton, sir."

"Thaxton." He repeated the name slowly, savouring it. "*Thaxton*. That's really a good *English* name, isn't it?"

She was looking squarely at him for the first time and a smile appeared to be lingering just below the surface of her face.

"Yes, sir, I suppose."

"I guess that's because it rhymes with *Saxon*."

"It does, yes." The smile came, faint, curious. "You're from America, aren't you?"

"That's right. Chicago."

She nodded. "Chicago, the state of Illinois, situated on Lake Michigan, railways, cattlemarkets . . ."

"Say, you've really done your homework, haven't you?"

"My what?"

"You know, study. You seem to know a lot about Chicago."

"I was very good at geography, sir, at school. It . . . it was

86

my favourite subject . . . that and arithmetic."

"Arithmetic? You're the first good-looking girl I've ever met who liked arithmetic."

A bright crimson glow appeared suddenly on her cheeks. Lowering her eyes she started past him towards the door.

"If you need anything, sir, just ring the bell. The pull's on the wall, sir."

"Hey, wait a second." But she was gone, and he could hear her footsteps going rapidly off down the hall.

The bathroom was large, its walls and floor covered with tiny white tiles. There was nothing in the room but a mammoth cast iron, porcelain-enamelled tub, and an oak cabinet containing fresh soap and extra towels. There was no shower. The hot water came in fits and starts, rattling the pipes and belching occasional puffs of steam, but eventually the water rose in the tub and Martin sank gratefully into its warmth. Odd, he thought as he soaped himself and lathered his hair. The room was totally out of proportion to its use. Ten bathtubs could have been placed in the room along with half a dozen stall showers. On the other hand, the W.C. had been no larger than a closet, a dark, evil little place to get out of as quickly as nature would permit. The bathroom had four wide windows along one wall with a view of trees and distant hills. The W.C. had only one tiny window, near the ceiling, which had emitted the palest shaft of light – the window in a dungeon far above the prisoner's reach. Odd. Well, the English were an odd race. No question about that. Everyone on the paper had warned him about what to expect, although only Comstock Harrington Briggs, the managing editor, had ever been to England and that had been during the Boer War. Primitive. That had been the most common word bandied about. A cultured but primitive race. Trying to pin people down as to their interpretation of the word *primitive* had led to little or no elucidation. To Briggs, primitive had meant warm beer and boiled food. To others it had meant King-worship, the class system, and the bull-headed preference for cricket when it was obvious to anyone with even a grain of sense that baseball was a better game. So far, the only area for criticism he could find was in their plumbing.

87

The tuxedo was back, hanging from a peg on the closet door. Its appearance had been bettered, but not by much. Martin eyed it dubiously and prayed that he could get into it without popping any buttons. He dressed gingerly, but, glory be, the suit fitted quite well. He was struggling with a black tie when there came a tap on the door. It was one of the liveried footmen informing him that whisky would be served in the library at six thirty.

Lord Stanmore set down his glass of whisky and soda and walked towards the door as Martin entered the room.

"My dear fellow," he said, advancing with hand outstretched in greeting. "I'm delighted to meet you. Pity we've never met before this, but your aunt talks of you often."

Martin could only assume that the tall, ruddy faced man with the iron-grey hair advancing on him was his uncle. He had never seen a photograph of him. How did he greet him? Uncle Tony sounded too familiar. Your lordship too formal.

"How do you do, sir?" he said, shaking the man's hand. The grip was strong, friendly.

"Come," he said, placing an arm about Martin's shoulders. "You know my son and his friend, Roger . . . let me introduce you to the others." He steered his nephew towards a small group of men standing at the far end of the room with glasses in their hands. Charles and Roger were among them. Their dinner jackets, Martin noted with a touch of envy, were faultless – as was the jacket of every other man in the room.

"Gentlemen, my nephew from America, Martin Rilke. Martin, may I introduce Mr. John Blakewell, Master of the Doncaster Hunt . . . Major Tim Lockwood, retired, I'm afraid, a great loss to King and country . . . Sir Percy Smythe, finest barrister and the best horseman in the county . . . and Captain Fenton Wood-Lacy."

Martin shook hands and greetings were exchanged. Then Charles put a drink in his hand and he was on his own, the earl rejoining an interrupted discussion about horses with Blakewell, Major Lockwood and the barrister.

"Well, Martin," Charles said, "did Eagles look after you all right?"

"Yes, thank you."

"By far the best valet I've ever had. Just take his word on all sartorial matters and you won't go wrong."

"I'll remember that," he said, thinking of his pile of laundry.

Roger sipped a ginger beer and pointed to the towering shelves of books that lined two walls of the room.

"As a budding writer, I'm sure you find this rather interesting." He bent closer. "Though I doubt if a tenth of them have been read. Charles is the only reader in the family and he keeps his books quite separate. You won't find much in this room written after 1880."

Charles laughed. Some sort of private joke, Martin supposed.

"So you're from America," Fenton said.

"That's right. Chicago."

"Ah, Chicago. And how do you like England so far?"

"Very much. Beautiful country."

"And by far the best time of year to see it. Planning on a fairly full itinerary?"

"Yes, I suppose so."

"Then you must see the Lake District, Stratford, of course, Bath, the Chilterns."

"I'm sure he knows where to go, Fenton," Roger said.

"Just thought I'd be helpful. If you care to see the Changing of the Guard, I'll get you a first-rate view."

"Are you a captain in the army?"

"Yes. Coldstream Guards."

"That must be exciting."

Fenton took a long pull on his Scotch before answering.

"Well, if you want to know the truth, it's deadly dull most of the time. The only excitement is when we're off duty. London is not without its perils."

"Women and cards," Roger said.

"Yes," Fenton said. "Quite so. They've cut more than one promising fellow down in his prime."

Martin caught the twinkle in the tall, hawk-faced man's eyes and they both grinned.

"We have those kinds of perils in Chicago, too. But getting back to the army, don't you serve a good deal of time in India?"

"No such luck. The Guards don't leave the country without the King's permission. We're his household troops and he does not want to squander us on the North-West Frontier keeping the wild and wily Afghan in line."

"Saving you lads for something really big," Roger said.

Fenton nodded. "Right you are. The next Hundred Years War."

After dinner, Martin played one game of snooker with Fenton and then excused himself and went up to his room. The cover had been removed from the bed and the sheets neatly turned down. His last clean pair of pyjamas had been laid across a chair along with his robe and carpet slippers. The quiet efficiency of the house impressed him. All of the servants moved about without anyone, at least apparently, telling them what to do. He had seen quite a few maids during the course of the evening, but the pretty Ivy Thaxton had not been one of them. Had she turned down his bed? he wondered. He hoped that she had, not knowing why he hoped so.

There was a good bedside lamp, and he sat in bed and placed his leather attaché case beside him, opening it and rummaging through it for one of the new notebooks he had brought along. The first section of the novel-in-progress lay at the bottom of the case, like a flat corpse in a flat coffin, he thought ruefully. "*City of the Big Shoulders*." He didn't even like the title any more.

"Write out of your own personal experiences of life."

Theodore Dreiser had told him that . . . and all the other members of the Pen and Quill Club at the university. That had been during the Fall Term, 1912, and Dreiser had been the guest speaker. The big, slow-speaking, gloomy-faced man had told of the difficulties he had faced in the publication of *Sister Carrie* and *Jennie Gerhardt*, and had spoken to them about the need for truth in writing, honesty and realism. They had spoken afterwards in German – their common heritage as German-Americans creating an instant bond, although their childhoods and upbringing had been poles apart. It had been Dreiser who had advised him to work on a newspaper so as to see life as it truly was, the raw, hard, often ugly side of the human condition, and it had been Dreiser who had told him to write down his thoughts and observations every day and to keep them for reference later, a free-flowing sketch book written in Pitman shorthand.

He took a notebook and a fountain pen from the case and then placed the case across his legs to serve as a desk. Opening the shorthand notebook to the first page, he began to write:

Observations and reflections. Friday night, June 12th, 1914. Here I sit, feeling like everyone's country cousin come to stay with rich relatives . . . the country mouse and the city mouse fable. A paradox there as I come from Chicago – which is about as big a town as you can find – and the cousins come from Abington, Surrey, which is about as hick a place as you'll find anywhere. But, oh Lord, do they ooze sophistication! Debonair. What an overworked word that was during my last year in school. Any guy who smoked Murads was debonair . . . or wore a wristwatch, or took a girl up to the Loop in a taxicab. Well, we never really understood the meaning of that word. If the fellows in the frat house want to know what debonair means they should watch Captain Fenton Wood-Lacy for about ten minutes and then crawl off somewhere and write UNCOUTH across their foreheads.

I feel depressed – by my clothes. I caught my uncle . . . no, I shall clarify my thoughts on that subject first. The Earl of Stanmore is not my uncle. He is the man my aunt married. An uncle should have at least some common ground to share with his nephew. Uncle Paul and I have little in common, but we can at least get into a roaring argument on the subject of Cubs versus White Sox, Connie Mack vis-à-vis McGraw as the best manager, or any other comparison between the two leagues. It might have helped my financial status if I had grown up to be a lover of the American League, but Uncle Paul respects me, I think, for sticking to my guns on that score . . . which is probably why he has taken me to every World Series game since I was twelve years old and left Karl behind. His excuse to Aunt Jessie being that he didn't want Karl to miss any school. Why does Karl detest baseball, I wonder? Dr. Sigmund Freud would probably come up with a good answer. I can merely

guess at one. Returning to the matter of clothing . . . I could see
the earl glancing with definite disapproval at my dinner jacket
at least five times during the course of the evening. This was
true also of my cousin Charles and Captain Wood-Lacy. Roger
Wood-Lacy does not appear to share the others' fixation about
clothes. He looked a bit rumpled himself, but then he appears
to go out of his way to "play the poet". Have not read any of
his verses but, judging by the number of Greek and Latin
phrases he drops like pearls, I imagine he is not a budding Carl
Sandburg or Vachel Lindsay.

Brief impressions. House is magnificent, a mixture of
architectural types, Tudor, Queen Anne, Georgian and Victorian. But there is a unifying cohesion to the style, the entire
façade having been rebuilt, or reconstructed, by the Wood-
Lacys' father, a prominent architect, now dead. Charles told
me something about the house's history. The Normans built a
priory here in the twelfth century and it was written into the
Doomsday Book as pryory, with a "y" instead of an "i". The
structure was torn down in the fourteenth century and the
Duke of Abington built a manor house here and retained the
name, poor spelling and all. The dukes of Abington, a family
named de Lys, died out during the Wars of the Roses and the
property was bought by the first of the Grevilles during the
reign of Henry VII. The Grevilles had been firm backers of the
Tudor cause and were given knighthoods and land, but the first
earl was not created until 1660 at the restoration of the
monarchy – the Grevilles having weathered the political tur-
moils of the struggle between king and parliament. The first
earl had been a Greville who had hitched his star to the king
and had gone into exile with the future Charles II. They are a
land-owning family who have always been blessed with sons.
Country Gentry. One earl had fought with the Duke of Marlborough and lost an arm at the Battle of Blenheim, but, from
what I can gather, soldiering has never been a family tradition
as it is in some great English families.

Brief impressions. The earl is a political conservative, but
not rabidly so. He had some good things to say about the prime
minister, Mr. Asquith, but his *bête noire* is Lloyd George, a
Welshman who used to be a solicitor – lawyer. Lloyd George is

92

chancellor of the exchequer and the earl blames the man for the rise in taxes and for pressuring the prime minister into taking an inflexible stand on the question of Home Rule for Ireland. The Irish question did not come up at dinner – no politics are discussed until the ladies have left the room – but it was woven into the general conversation when port and cigars were passed around after the women had left. I say woven, because politics take a decided back seat to talk about the coming hunting season and horse riding in all of its phases, point-to-point, jumping, dressage. I was asked if I rode and I said yes . . . not a total lie because I have been on a horse a few times, not enjoying the experience any more than the poor animal beneath me.

Brief impressions. Hanna has three children. William – named after my father – is sixteen and will be home from Eton for the summer holidays any day now. Charles is my age. He seems like a nice enough sort of guy but vaguely indecisive about things. I have no idea what he wants to do in life, but I gather that that isn't terribly important to him or to his parents. Young men of his class – he will inherit the title one day – are not expected to do anything except ride a horse and look after the lands and the tenantry. A friend of Charles from Cambridge, the son of a lord somebody or other, had shocked his friends by "going into trade". He had taken a job with a company that makes automobile engines. I gathered by the way they talked about him that he had committed some kind of sin against the peerage. Peers, or the sons of peers, may serve on the board of directors of business concerns, but they don't get involved in the day-to-day grind of making or selling the product. This class structure is arcane, but I shall fathom it out in time. A million and one taboos. Alexandra is eighteen and just about the prettiest girl I've ever seen in my life. Honey blonde. Blue eyes. Angelic face. Not too much behind it, I'm afraid. The kind of girl who has no room in her head for anything but boys, clothes, parties and sugar-whipped dreams of perpetual happiness.

Brief impressions. Aunt Hanna. She took me aside after dinner and we walked for a quarter hour on the terrace. She talked about my father, her beloved Willie, and how much I reminded her of him. Perhaps we were alike when she last saw

93

him. He left home at twenty. She would have been seventeen. She never saw him after that time. In other words, her image of him is vastly different from my own. She referred to him in rather schoolgirlish French as *le beau Bohème*, as though his act of leaving home and finally being disinherited had been romantic. She should have come to Paris and seen him in his final days, drugged with absinthe, our apartment filled with mad paintings that would never sell. God forgive me, but his death was a blessing. Aunt Hanna feels a certain sense of guilt for not having come to Paris after father died. She was ill at the time, she says. Perhaps she was, or perhaps she couldn't face seeing her beloved Willie in the awful light of truth. Anyway, she had let Uncle Paul pick up the pieces, which is just as well in retrospect. I can't imagine the Earl of Stanmore being overjoyed at taking into his ancestral home the Catholic daughter of a Paris shopkeeper and her eight-year-old son. In all fairness, Aunt Jessie hadn't been that overjoyed either, nor Uncle Paul. But he had bought mother the house on Roscoe Street and paid all the bills and given her a generous allowance and . . . but why are my thoughts roaming so far afield tonight?

Brief impressions. Captain Fenton Wood-Lacy. British army officers walk around in civilian clothing except when on duty at their barracks. Captain Wood-Lacy in the Coldstream Guards. I gather by his air of superiority that that is one of the better regiments to be an officer in. They are quartered in London to guard the King. Against whom? Three or four regiments of infantry, two of cavalry, and yet, according to Fenton W.-L., the only real protection the King has from bomb-throwing anarchists are a few stolid London bobbies who walk flatfooted in the background, overshadowed by the scarlet-coated Guardsmen who are not issued bullets for their guns. All a grand show. Tradition at work. Fenton appears to be bored and dissatisfied. I asked him while we were playing snooker if he liked being in the army. He simply shrugged and muttered something about it not being a bad sort of life. He's been in for six years, but has taken several extended leaves. He spent three months in Somaliland and Abyssinia last year, hunting game, and plans to join some fellow officers for a major mountaineering expedition to Nepal in 1916. A restless man, and not a happy one. Not a particularly good snooker player either. Certainly not in my league, but then I was the best pool player in Chicago – bar none . . .

His eyes began to blur and he capped the pen and closed the notebook. He had a pair of glasses in the case, but he was tired of writing. His heart wasn't in it. Thinking about the house on Roscoe, only five blocks from the home of the ever glorious Cubs, the palace of Frank Chance, the domain of Frank Schulte, triggered too many memories. They flooded in upon him and he shut them out. The novel that Dreiser had advised him to write was in *that* Chicago, not the Chicago of stockyard workers and striking trolley motormen. If he was serious about becoming a novelist he must attempt to weave the tangled threads of his childhood into a cohesive pattern. The plight of Chicago's working poor was not his element. Neither, of course, was Europe.

He turned off the lamp and sat in the darkness watching the curtains float gently in the night wind. The silence was almost unnerving. He wasn't used to it. A big city boy, born in Paris, raised to manhood in Chicago. He missed the muted thunder of traffic, the distant rumble of trains. He felt a pang of home-sickness for Pastor's saloon on Clark Street, the sawdust and the shots of rye with beer chasers, the pool and the poker games, the lean, hardboiled talk of newspaper men.

He got off the bed and placed his attaché case on a table, then stood in front of the open windows. A long way from home, but maybe this was the perspective he needed. Europe was the past, changeless, drowsy and content with old glories, fiercely proud of its ancient traditions. Nothing stood still in Chicago. The city was bursting outward and upward. Even the old house on Roscoe was gone to make way for the new apartment houses being built on the North Side. Looking out on the ordered patterns of the garden, he could see the little house much clearer than he could have seen it in the windy city. He had debated with himself about coming to Europe, blowing the bulk of his savings, putting his job in jeopardy (for there was no guarantee that Comstock Harrington Briggs would take him back after being away for six weeks – the hard-nosed little editor's idea of a vacation for his staff was three days in Waukegan), but he was here and by God he'd make the most of it. He'd let himself drift to Europe's stately music and then go back to the New World's ragtime clear eyed and refreshed.

The garden and an old wall could be seen clearly in the moonlight. Gazing down he felt a strong sense of time. People had lived on this spot for seven hundred years, Normans, English, Roundhead and Cavalier . . .

"'. . . Every hyacinth the garden wears dropt in its lap from some once lovely head . . .'" he whispered. He had never thought too much of the *Rubaiyat*, too fervently romantic, too much quoted to get girls in the proper mood for spooning. But the words brought a shiver to his spine as he repeated them now. How many *once lovely heads* had passed below? he wondered. He could almost see women in Elizabethan costumes move serenely past the roses. Yes. This was the past and he could see his own future more clearly because of it. He would scrap *"City of the Big Shoulders"* and begin another, a novel rooted in his own heritage.

"I wrote *Jennie Gerhardt* out of love and pain . . . facing my ghosts," Dreiser had said. It was what he must do. He would take his time, plan the book carefully, write it with honesty, the saga of the Rilkes which was the saga of America over the past half century: money, power, success and failure. Uncle Paul would be fictionalised in the book, as well as his father, mother and even Aunt Hanna and the Grevilles. The awesome scope of it stunned him for a moment. Was he up to the challenge? Well, he thought turning away from the window and getting into bed, he had six weeks in the tranquillity of Europe to think about it, to make notes and plan the outline. He felt both awed and excited and wondered whether he would be able to fall asleep, but the moment he closed his eyes that question was no longer in doubt.

5

CAPTAIN FENTON WOOD-LACY WALKED ACROSS A STUBBLED field with a light fowling piece under his right arm, the gun uncocked, and, for that matter, unloaded. He had brought a game bag which dangled from his left shoulder, but no shells.

"I might try and bag some of those rooks," he had told Lord Stanmore after their early morning ride. It was the type of shooting that the earl felt was beneath his dignity as one of the premier grouse-shooters in the British Isles, but he did not discourage other men from killing the grain scavenging birds.

"Try and get a pigeon or two while you're at it."

"I'll try," he had said.

He was now within sight of the crows. They were in the same spot they had been the morning before, wheeling and cawing above the chimney stacks of Burgate House. He wondered if the raucous noise disturbed Lydia's sleep. He walked on slowly and it was nearly nine o'clock when he reached the edge of the formal gardens that were spread out on both sides of the house like pruned wings. A gate to the east gardens was open and he sauntered through, leaving the gun and the game bag on a carved stone seat. He followed a path that meandered through groves of yew and willow to the terrace that encircled the house in a broad stone ring. A maid washing an upstairs window waved at him and he waved back. The servants at Burgate House reflected their master. They were all Londoners, as cheery and cheeky as sparrows.

As he approached the tall, bow windows of the morning room he could see Lydia inside, just as he had hoped, seated at a table having her morning coffee. She was wearing a pale yellow peignoir and her hair hung loosely to her shoulders. He tapped gently on the glass and she looked up, first with a frown, then with a bemused smile. He waited patiently until she got up from the table and opened a side window.

"Good morning," he said.

"What on earth are you doing here? Don't they serve breakfast at the Grevilles'?"

"They do, but the company can't compare to this place. May I come in?"

"Through the front door or through the window?"

"Which would you prefer?"

She stepped back. "The window, by all means. But take care Harker doesn't mistake you for a burglar and put buckshot in your backside."

"I'll take the chance." The casement window was narrow but he managed to squeeze through after stepping up on a ledge. "*Voila!*" he cried, stumbling into the room. "Amazing the skills one learns in the Guards."

She returned to her coffee and he could tell that she was not overjoyed to see him. She would be polite, of course. Lydia was always polite even when she was on the verge of being her most shrewish.

"Well, now," he said, straddling a chair and folding his arms along the back of it. "I just happened to be passing by . . ."

"Please, Fenton, don't be any more ridiculous than you are already. Want some coffee?"

"Wouldn't mind."

Her foot sought the buzzer bell under the table. "Jenny baked a seed cake. You can have a slice." She sipped her coffee without looking at him. "The Rilke cousin get in all right?"

"Yes. Pleasant chap. Open faced and honest, hardly your type."

She finished her coffee and set the cup down with great delicacy, as though it might shatter if she did not.

"That was a crude remark, Fenton. Quite beneath you."

"I feel a bit crude this morning, to tell you the truth. Had a rotten sleep. By the way, Charles telephoned you at least five times last night that I know of. He kept ducking out to the hall while we were playing snooker. Were you out?"

"No. I didn't wish to be disturbed."

"Well, you certainly disturbed *him*. I think you'll be getting quite a few more calls today. Going to speak to him?"

98

"Does it matter to you?"

He shrugged. "Yes and no. Is Archie here?"

"You do jump around, don't you? What's Daddy got to do with it?"

"I wanted to tell him that I'm serious about joining the old firm. I sat up most of the night, if you want to know the truth, writing my resignation of commission letter." She was looking at him now and he smiled into her narrowed, questioning eyes. "It's a great deal easier getting out of the Guards than getting in. It took Uncle Julian at least six letters to get me posted from Sandhurst, and God alone knows how many lunches at his club for old comrades in arms. Must have cost the old boy a tidy sum, depending on his choice of wine, of course."

"Don't be facetious," she hissed. "What the hell are you up to?"

The door opened before he could answer and the Foxe butler stepped into the room.

"You rang, Miss Lydia?"

"I'm sorry, Spears; must have hit the button by mistake."

The butler was a huge, florid faced man who had once been a publican in Cheapside. He had known Lydia from the day of her birth, and Captain Wood-Lacy from the age of nine. His gaze at the moment went over both of them.

"Very good, miss," he intoned and then departed, closing the door silently behind him.

Fenton chuckled and took a tin of cigarettes from the breast pocket of his Norfolk jacket.

"Poor old Spears. He probably thinks I spent the night."

"Stop grinning," she said icily.

The telephone began to ring far down one of the halls, the sound muted by the walls. Fenton lit a cigarette and Lydia sat motionless, one hand toying with a silver spoon. The ringing stopped and after a few moments there was a tap on the door and the butler appeared again.

"Lord Charles Amberley on the line, Miss Lydia."

Fenton blew a passable smoke ring. Lydia played with the spoon.

"Thank you, Spears. Tell him . . . tell him that I'm still sleeping."

"Very good, miss."

They sat in silence until the butler's footsteps receded down the hall, then Fenton stood up and sought out an ashtray.

"When *are* you going to speak to him?"

"I'm going to invite him for dinner," she said. "Not that it's any of your bloody business."

"My, my, aren't we touchy this morning, and after I walked all the way over here to ask you to marry me."

He was standing very close to her, reaching across the table to snuff out his cigarette in a crystal plate. Her hand was on the spoon and he noticed that it was trembling slightly.

"Anything the matter with your hearing?"

"No," she said softly. "Please go away, Fenton."

He straightened up and stepped behind her, placing his hands gently on her shoulders.

"We could hop into your spiffy little motor and drive up to Scotland. Get married in Gretna Green. I know an inn overlooking Luce Bay with a magnificent view of the Solway and the deepest, softest feather beds one ever sank into." His fingers slipped through her hair and stroked the back of her neck. "Give up on Charles. Nothing can ever come of it. You know that, if you're honest."

"He'll marry me," she said, so quietly that he could barely hear the words.

"I'm sure he *wants* to, but his nibs has something to say about it and that's an obstacle you'll never get around. And Charles won't be much help. He'll never take any step that isn't *right* and *proper* according to the unwritten code of the Grevilles and the untainted Earls of Stanmore. Christ, is marrying into the peerage so damned important to you? Of course, you could always pick up a lord on the cheap, pay off his debts and add a title to your name. But you don't want that, do you? People would only make jokes about how one can buy anything at a White Manor Tea Shop these days."

She jerked her head away and turned quickly, lashing out at his face with her right hand. He grabbed her wrist in full swing and pulled her roughly to her feet, knocking the chair over.

"You bastard!" Her lips were taut, bloodless.

He held tightly to her wrist and pulled her against him, bent his head and kissed her mouth. She didn't struggle – he hadn't expected that she would – and he could feel her body relax, submit, bend into him.

"Marry me," he said, pulling gently away. She shook her head, eyes closed, lips parted. "You love me and you damn well know you do. But then love doesn't count, does it? Marriage is too important for that."

She stiffened as though slapped in the face and stepped back. Her eyes smouldered, passion and rage mingling.

"You're a fine one to talk. You and Winnie Sutton . . . what a fine exhibition that was. The Fenton Wood-Lacy prelude to seduction." She mimicked his voice. "*It's so easy to tango . . . let me teach you.* What else do you plan to teach her?"

"I felt sorry for her."

"Yes, that's easy to do. She's such a dowdy, awkward creature. Simply makes your heart bleed to look at her! Don't insult my intelligence. You weigh your charities very carefully. You looked at poor Winnie as just so many pounds sterling to the ounce. Is that how you look at me?"

He smiled sheepishly and rubbed the side of his nose. "*Touché.* Yes, I admit part of that. I feel a bit of a cad about my behaviour the other night. I'm a good sportsman. Never shoot ducks on the ground. You're quite right. I'm in a rather nasty spot at the moment and endearing myself to Winnie and her loving parents would pull me out of it, very nicely, too, I might add."

"I'm sure it would, but that would be nothing to how nicely you'd be *pulled out* if you married *me*. Daddy would be so happy he'd probably thrust a million pounds into your hot and greedy hand!"

"Hands," he said, holding them up to her, palms out. "Two hands. Drive a spike into each if I'm not speaking the truth. I'm not after Archie's money. If I thought you'd be content living on my twelve shillings and sixpence a day pay, less mess fees, of course, I'd never ask the old boy for a farthing. But you couldn't live on it and so I'd be willing to go to work on civvy street. It's as simple as that. I'd make you a damned good husband, in bed and out, and you bloody well know that, too."

She nodded solemnly. "Yes, I know it."

He placed his hands on her hips, feeling the softness of the flesh beneath the silk morning gown.

"We're very much alike. We both want things that are just a shade beyond our grasp. I'm in a regiment that I can't afford and you want a social standing that all the money in the world won't buy. I have a minor confession to make. I didn't sit up half the night drafting a letter to my colonel. I just couldn't sleep. My mind was a jumble of thoughts. I kept seeing the expression on poor Charles's face after trying to reach you on the telephone. Did you have a tiff with him?"

"No. Nothing like that."

His smile was knowing, a bitter twist of the lips. "Letting him dangle on the hook?"

"That's unkind," she said stiffly.

"Perhaps, but I know the game. He might just become desperate enough to take a positive stand with the lord of the manor, an ultimatum that he may or may not win; that *you* may or may not win. You're a reckless gambler, Lydia, and for what? There has to be more to life than living in Abington Pryory and becoming a countess one day. And more to life than my strutting around Buckingham Palace in a red coat. Do you remember when you were eight or nine years old and my father was working at the Pryory? You used to follow me up the scaffolding and do every dangerous thing I did. Charles and Roger were afraid, but you weren't. You used to say that you'd follow me anywhere. Well, I wish you'd follow me now."

He was very handsome in a dark, piratical way. A swash-buckling bounder with fine manners. His hands on her hips had a strong surety, as though they had a right to be there, or anywhere else they wanted to rest on her body. It would have been easy to succumb, to rush upstairs and pack a bag, to drive to Scotland and then to follow him anywhere. But it wasn't what she wanted. It wasn't enough.

"I'm sorry, Fenton. I'm not a little girl any more."

He let go of her hips. Not with any obvious reluctance. He simply allowed his hands to drop away from her body.

"No need to apologise. It was a forlorn hope anyway." He held out his hand. "Still friends?"

Her fingers brushed his. "Always."

"May I leave by the front door? I'm not too adept at going *out* of windows."

"Of course. What are you going to do? About Winnie, I mean."

"Oh," he said vaguely, "I haven't really given it much thought."

"Are you horribly in debt?"

"That's one way of putting it."

"I can give you a cheque, or would that be too painful to bear right now?"

He bent stiffly from the waist and kissed her on the forehead. "As a matter of fact it would be. No, I'll land catlike on my feet as usual. I have some plans afoot, prospects in mind."

She winced and looked away from him. Gardeners in dark green smocks could be seen through the windows, moving down one of the paths towards the rose trees. They carried spades and hoes over their shoulders and looked like medieval soldiers off to the wars. She had a vivid mental picture of Fenton and some featureless debutante walking beneath an arch of drawn swords, rose petals strewn at their feet. The image pained her. She looked past the gardens at the distant chimney-tops of Abington Pryory faintly visible above the green frieze of Leith Woods.

"Let's wish each other good fortune," she said tonelessly. "And much happiness."

Martin slept late and was the last one down for breakfast, but there was plenty of food left and he was amazed by the variety. He heaped his plate with scrambled eggs, grilled kidneys, two slices of a ham-like bacon, grilled tomatoes and thin, fried potatoes. He also had some hot scones and a fruit compote. There was a humidor filled with slim, mild "breakfast" cigars on the table and he lit one after finishing his meal and strolled contentedly out on to the terrace. He was walking slowly around the house, admiring its architecture and the view of the gardens, when a ground-floor window suddenly opened and Lord Stanmore leaned out.

"Good morning, Martin. Had your breakfast yet?"

"Yes, sir," he said, removing the cigar from his mouth.

"More breakfast than I should have eaten."

"Have some coffee with your aunt and me. See that door? Just follow that passage to your right."

The earl was waiting for him in a corridor and led him into a room which contained a roll-top desk, several filing cabinets, a leather sofa and some chairs. Hanna was seated at the desk, papers strewn in front of her.

"My office," the earl explained. "The heart of Abington Pryory."

Hanna glanced up from her work. "Good morning, dear. We were just discussing you." She tapped some papers with a pen. "We have so many functions planned for later this month and all through July. I don't believe you'd find all of them interesting, but I've written your name down on every list containing lots of pretty girls."

"That's swell of you, Aunt Hanna, but, you see, I'm only planning to be in England for two weeks or so and I . . . well . . . I was hoping to see as much of the place as possible, travel around, leave my steamer trunk here, if you don't mind, and just pack a suitcase." He felt embarrassed, hoping he wasn't insulting her. Then she smiled, almost with relief it seemed to him.

"That's a wonderful idea, Martin! Isn't that wonderful, Tony?"

"Yes, it is," the earl agreed, nodding his head vigorously. "When I was your age I went on a walking tour, all around the country, from the Channel to Thurso Bay in Caithness, then back along the West Coast of Scotland, through Wales, glorious time I had, too. An ash walking-stick in my hand, a rucksack on my back. Yes, my boy, a capital idea. The London season may be heaven for the ladies, but it's hell on us men."

"Now, Tony," Hanna chided.

"It's true. A non-stop round of parties and balls. I require two valets in London and I wear them both out before the season is half over. And I shan't even mention the effect of all that partying on one's liver."

"Oh, Tony!" Hanna laughed. "What a dark picture you paint. But in all seriousness, Martin, I think your plans are splendid. When do you want to get started?"

"The sooner the better. There are so many places I want to go, I thought I might take the train up to London today and make arrangements with Cook's . . . you know, join a tour group of some kind. Maybe I could take off Monday or Tuesday."

Lord Stanmore drew a silver watch from his waistcoat and flipped the lid open. "Jolly good way to go about it. Those chaps make all the arrangements in advance for accommodation in decent hotels and inns. Let's see, you could catch the eleven thirty from Godalming. I'll have Ross drive you to the station. Get a taxi at Waterloo to Thomas Cook's. They're in the Strand, I believe."

Hanna sorted her lists back into order with an air of finality.

"Of course, I am a bit disappointed. I was looking forward to showing off my handsome nephew. But I will have you meet some of my friends before you travel on to Germany."

"I would like that," Martin said politely. He understood her approval of his plans. Aunt Jessie had found him socially redundant on more than one occasion. It was probably his destiny, he thought ruefully, to go through life messing up people's seating arrangements.

Lord Stanmore clapped him on the back. "And we must get in a day's riding. The only way truly to enjoy the English countryside is from the back of a horse."

The earl walked with him to the main hall, talking ecstatically about the joys of riding, a subject that Martin was incapable of warming up to.

"I shall inform Ross and he'll bring the car around. Do you have any English money?"

"I have a pound or two, sir. I imagine I can cash some travellers' cheques at Cook's."

"Yes, they provide that service, but I'd better give you a fiver just to be on the safe side." He was reaching into his jacket for his wallet when he spotted Fenton entering the hall from the direction of the conservatory. "Ah, Fenton, have a good shoot?"

Fenton, walking slowly and apparently lost in thought, seemed startled by the question.

"What?"

"The bloody jackdaws. Get any?"

He had left shotgun and game bag on the seat in Lydia's garden. Well, someone would find them. "Bagged a couple."

"Jolly good for you. Young Rilke here is going up to London, book a Cook's tour of the British Isles. Sensible way to go if one doesn't know the country."

"Yes, I suppose it is. Are you going up this morning?"

"Yes," Martin said.

"I'll go with you, then." He smiled ruefully at Lord Stanmore. "I ran into the telegraph boy as I was crossing Fern Lane. The adjutant needs me back."

"Whatever for?"

"A battalion matter that could easily have waited until next week, but he's a nervous old aunty of a man."

"Damn. Well, at least we got in a couple of decent rides."

He sat in a moody silence halfway to London. Martin had made an attempt at conversation, but Fenton had responded with a few grunted monosyllables so he gave up trying. He sat opposite the tall officer in a first-class carriage and contented himself with watching the scenery. As the train entered the suburbs of South London, Fenton emitted a deep sigh and reached into his pocket for cigarettes.

"Do you smoke, Rilke?"

"Yes, thanks." He preferred cigars, but he took the offered cigarette, grateful for the breaking of the ice.

"Rather a blistered landscape, isn't it?" Fenton said, gesturing towards the window. "I suppose all England will be like that one day, every inch of turf paved, every hill crawling with brick villas. I really detest progress."

"So do I, sometimes. It's the same way in Chicago. New things going up all the time, the city growing like a weed."

"Yes, I dare say. Still, in America there is so much land to expand into. I mean all those prairies and deserts and things." He puffed on his cigarette and eyed Martin narrowly through the smoke. "I really hate to bring this up, Rilke, but that jacket doesn't fit you at all. Who the devil is your tailor?"

"Marshall Field," he blurted.

"The man should be shot. Look here, old chap, I hope you

won't take offence, but a gentleman is judged by his clothes and you're too nice a fellow to be snubbed. My tailor is a wizard. He could make you a couple of outfits in no time at all, a few days. He's in Burlington Street, just off Savile Row. What do you say we pop around there after you leave Cook's?"

"Well, I . . ." He felt like ripping the offending jacket from his body and tossing it out of the speeding train.

"And if ready cash is a problem," Fenton went on blithely, "don't give it a thought. Old Purdy wouldn't expect an earl's nephew to fork out vulgar coin. Just pay him when you get around to it. And you'll find him surprisingly reasonable." He sat back with the contented air of a man who had just settled a question once and for all. "Yes, we'll do that straight away."

Martin squirmed. He felt humiliated, but the man had only been speaking honestly. The jacket was terrible, there was no question of that.

"But don't you have to report to your unit?"

Fenton brushed a fleck of cigarette ash from the knife crease of his grey flannel trousers. "As a matter of fact, I pulled a slight deception on his lordship. There never was a telegram from the adjutant. It was an excuse to get out of staying for the weekend. I hope you won't say anything."

"Of course not."

"Thank you. I just felt like getting back to London for . . . personal reasons."

They took a taxicab from Waterloo Station to the Strand. The office of Thomas Cook & Sons was found and arrangements quickly made for Martin to join a tour group leaving Euston Station on Thursday morning for "Ten days of wending one's way slowly through the beauties of the British Isles . . . the pageantry of her great castles . . . the historical significance of Stratford-on-Avon . . . the Roman wall . . . Bath . . . the Lake District where the great poets roamed . . ."

The clerk had spoken with evangelical zeal and had congratulated Martin for his foresight in choosing Cook's. He had then cashed one hundred dollars in travellers' cheques for him and handed him a printed sheet detailing the schedule for his trip – British Isles Tour, Number Thirty-two.

"Rather painless," Fenton remarked as they left, "though

Lord knows what your fellow tourists will be like. One should at least be given a choice of travelling companions."

The two hours spent with Fenton's tailor, the firm of Purdy & Beame, were equally painless. Both Mr. Purdy and Mr. Beame looked on Martin as a challenge to their worth as makers of fine gentlemen's apparel. They exchanged knowing glances and raised eyebrows as they divested Martin of his clothes, clucking their tongues over the shoddiness of Yankee cloth and workmanship. Martin was so much clay in their capable hands. He ended up purchasing three outfits which, according to Fenton and the tailor, would see him through the day in impeccable style. They would be ready Wednesday afternoon.

"Two fittings on Tuesday, Mr. Rilke, in the morning and again in the afternoon. It is not customary for Purdy & Beame to work under such pressure of time, but we will be, I can assure you, equal to the task."

Martin was then helped back into his offending garments and that was that.

"A decent bowler and an umbrella with a silk cover and you'll look like the Duke of Norfolk," Fenton said as they stepped out of the shop. He pointed in the direction of Old Bond Street. "My hatter's a short walk away. Come along."

As they turned into Bond Street, Fenton suddenly stiffened and then faced about to peer intently into a window displaying pipes and tobacco.

"Christ," he said under his breath. "I hope he didn't see me."

"Who?" Martin asked, looking around.

"Don't look. Just stand beside me. Perhaps he'll pass on by."

Martin stared at the racks of pipes, the tins of tobacco and then he sensed someone approaching and looked to his left. A young man was coming towards them, somewhat hesitantly. Martin's first impression was that it might have been a girl in man's clothing. The body was slim, almost willowy, and he was more pretty than handsome. Black, curly hair framed a narrow, high cheekboned face, the skin a pale olive-ivory. The man's nose was thin but prominent, the eyes large, oval and a

soft brown like the eyes of a fawn. But the fawnlike character-
istics were negated by his mouth, a wide slash that seemed to
be fixed in a permanent sneer.

"Captain Wood-Lacy, I presume," the man said. "And
companion."

"Why, hallo, Golden," Fenton said, doing a poor job of
imitating surprise. "Fancy running into you."

The man's lips curled even tighter in derision. "Fancy! And
in Bond Street to boot. I never knew you to be taken by pipes."

"I'm not, as a matter of fact, but any port in a storm."

The man threw his head back and laughed, a rollicking peal
of such depth and timbre that it was difficult to associate it
with so delicate a throat.

"Oh, Fenton, I do admire you. You are positively the most
candid man I've ever known. But mind your manners, introduce me."

"Golden . . . Martin Rilke from Chicago. Rilke, Jacob
Golden the Fleet Street gadfly. Rilke is a fellow journalist, by
the way."

"Oh?" Golden said, peering at Martin intently. "What
paper?"

"Chicago *Express*."

Golden closed his eyes for a second. "*Express* . . . Republican
attitudes, hostile to President Wilson, distrustful of organised
labour . . ."

"Hey," Martin said with a nervous laugh. "Lay off. I only
write book reviews."

"That's what you should be doing, Golden," Fenton said
drily. "Might keep you out of mischief."

Golden sighed deeply and pulled a long face. "My father
feels the same way, I'm afraid. No more reporting on the Ulster
farrago or Balkan intrigues. It's nothing but murders and *crimes
passionnels* for the immediate future. I'm covering the Goodwin
case at the moment. You know, the Birchington dentist who
drilled his sister-in-law to death because God told him to do it.
Very nasty business, but I believe God knew what he was saying. The victim was an absolute horror. Everyone in the family
is overjoyed that the biddy is gone. The paper is paying for his
defence."

"And if it wasn't," Fenton drawled, "I'm sure you'd be just as enthusiastic over his hanging."

"Yes, I dare say I would." He spread his hands outwards in a gesture of helplessness. "But that's the old newspaper game, isn't it? One must cater to the public tastes, or even create tastes to cater to." He winked slyly at Martin. "But then I'm sure you know all the devious ramifications of our noble profession. It must be rather pleasant being a soldier. At least one is *told* who to shoot. No inspired judgments in the thin red line."

Fenton faked an exaggerated yawn. "Same old Golden. No wonder your friends duck into shop doorways." He pulled a watch from his waistcoat pocket and glanced at it. "Time for tea. Let's hail a cab and go to the Marlborough."

"My dear Fenton," Golden said, "they don't like Jews at the Marlborough."

"I know. An odious rule. It should merely be *certain* Jews." He scowled at his watch. "Bother, we're a bit late for tea there anyway. Where do you suggest?"

"A White Manor by all means. The two shilling de luxe. And speaking of White Manors, have you seen the beautiful Lydia Foxe lately?"

Fenton appeared preoccupied as he scanned the busy street for a vacant cab.

"No, not for some time."

"I saw her in Paris two months ago. At the opera, clinging to the arm of a major in the *cuirassiers*. She seems to have a penchant for military men."

The captain turned slowly and gazed down into the smaller man's blithely innocent face.

"Why in God's name did I ever befriend you in school, Golden? You are truly the most insufferable – "

The laugh came again, deeper and louder than before. "It was an act of pure Christian charity, old boy. And like any worthwhile Christian act, needs to be paid for with a modicum of suffering. Ah," he cried, dashing suddenly into the street, "there's one . . . Taxi! Taxi!"

Martin arrived back at Abington Pryory at ten thirty that

night, taking a rattletrap taxi from Godalming Station to the house. The butler informed him that his lordship and her ladyship had retired early, that Lord Amberley was not at home and that Mr. Wood-Lacy had also retired for the night . . .

"But if you care for supper, sir . . ."

"Perhaps a sandwich and a glass of beer, if it's no trouble."

"Not at all, sir."

"In my room, if you don't mind. I'm pretty tired."

"Indeed yes, sir," Mr. Coatsworth said with genuine understanding. "A trip up to London is always most fatiguing."

He wasn't sure if it had been the trip or the company that had been fatiguing. A bewildering day, he decided as he put on his pyjamas. A footman brought ham sandwiches and a tankard of pale ale which Martin wolfed down before getting into bed, placing his attaché case on his knees and taking from it a notebook, pen and his eyeglasses:

Observations and Reflections. Saturday night, June 13th, 1914. The upper-class Englishman's attitude towards "trade" is an interesting one. Fenton is probably not upper class, in the strictest meaning of the term, but as an officer in a socially prestigious regiment he is entitled to all the prejudices of that class. Trade is, loosely speaking, any purveyor of services or products – haberdashers, wine merchants, bootmakers, tailors, etc. Doctors are not in trade, nor are journalists, the military, professional sporting people and etcetera. Upper-class Englishmen rely on trade for their comfort and well-being, but consider it proper form to delay paying their bills for as long as possible. Cash, it seems, is vulgar. After tea, Fenton took me to his hatter where I was measured for a derby – the hat to be ready Wednesday afternoon. I insisted on paying cash in advance and both Fenton and the hatter appeared slightly nonplussed.

We had tea at a White Manor in Oxford Street near the Marble Arch. It was a huge, multi-storied place with several dining rooms, a string orchestra, bakery shop and continental delicatessen. The food – small tea sandwiches and a variety of cakes – was both good and inexpensive. The service is first-rate, hordes of young women in crisply-starched blue uniforms taking orders and carrying trays, all of them pretty and cheerful. Fenton told me that they are well paid and that they live in hostels owned by the company, are charged very little for their rooms, practically nothing for their meals, the bulk of their wages going into a savings plan. Golden added that this benevolence has resulted in a shortage of maids for the gentry. Girls prefer the short hours and fine working conditions at the White Manors to going into service – like Ivy Thaxton – where they must work long hours and receive practically nothing for their labours. Maids in big houses get one afternoon off a week and are on call twenty-four hours a day. I wonder if Ivy Thaxton has ever heard of the White Manors? Probably must have. Fenton said they are all over England, but not all of them as splendid as the one on Oxford Street. It seems to me that it would be a far better place for a young girl to work. Being a maid in a place like Abington Pryory must be gruelling. So many rooms to clean, beds to make, chamberpots to empty. I have a horror of that white ceramic bowl under the bed, but I can readily understand why one would use it, especially in the winter. That little room down the hall is as cold as death and it's only June! I imagine that if I were living here in December I'd think twice about getting out of a warm bed in the middle of the night and trotting down the hall to that icy cubicle.

Brief impressions. Jacob Golden is twenty-four, about a year younger than Fenton, a year older than me, but wise beyond his years, as the saying goes. From conversation at tea, and from what Fenton told me about him later, I can piece together a sketchy biography of the man. He's the only son of Harry Golden, the great Lord Trewe. Trewe is as well known in Chicago as William Randolph Hearst is in London. Publisher of the London *Daily Post*, largest daily circulation of any newspaper in the world. A rag. Yellow journalism at its most blatant, a paper slanted for the lowest common denominator of mass interest – lots of pictures, short texts, stories of murders and other crimes, falls of the mighty from grace, lives and loves of theatrical people and motion picture performers, scare stories of civil war in Ireland, damnation of the German Empire for having the temerity to compete with Britain in the building of a war fleet and the maintaining of colonies. Jingoism and sensationalism in a heady mixture.

Jacob Golden is amused by the paper his father built up from nothing, but I can detect an air of gravity beneath his cynical posturings. The paper, he says, wields a far greater influence on the masses than the Bible. The Gospel according to St. Trewe. Golden sees the world as being divided into two distinct classes, *yahoos* and *nabobs* – a few nabobs who rule, millions upon millions of yahoos who do what they're told and believe what they read. He can see nothing wrong in this division, provided all of the nabobs are intelligent, compassionate and enlightened men – which of course they are not. The nabobs, he says, are donkeys sprinkled with a few apes. He says all of these outrageous things with a smile; a perverse pixie gleefully watching humanity stream towards the edge of a cliff. Fenton referred to him as an ass several times and I'm half inclined to second the motion. And yet . . . I wonder?

Jacob and Fenton went to school together, a well-known preparatory school near London, which sends the vast majority of its pupils on to Eton or Harrow. There were only a couple of Jews in the school and Jacob had a miserable time until Fenton took him under his wing. From what I could gather, Fenton's father had designed the *Daily Post* building in Whitefriars Lane off Fleet Street and was a good friend of Jacob's father. Jacob went on to Eton and then to Balliol College, Oxford. Fenton went to Sandhurst and the army, but there has been a tenuous bond between them since their prep school days.

Jacob was expelled from Balliol and seems proud of the fact. He didn't say why he had been sent down, but I'm sure the powers at Oxford University didn't lack for reasons. His father gave him a job on the paper as a roving correspondent and he has been to a great many places. I felt a pang of envy as he talked about the Balkan Wars, tramping along with the Servian army during its thrust across Albania to the Adriatic in 1912. An interesting anecdote, one that illustrates Jacob's theory about the nabobs. It seems that Lord Trewe objected to reportage of the *Servian* army. He felt that the word sounded too much like servile and so he ordered his editors to substitute a "b" for a "v". So Servia became Serbia overnight, at least to the readers of the *Daily Post*. Nabob power! The changing of a nation's name by the mere stroke of a blue pencil.

Reflections. Jacob Golden is a newspaperman. I work on a newspaper. What a gulf separates our occupations! While I was toiling over a review of Frances Hodgson Burnett's latest novel, Jacob was sending dispatches from Ireland suggesting that Germany was supplying rifles to the Ulster volunteer army. He went a bit too far, I gather, and accused a British general of corresponding with the Germans in order to equip the Protestants with Maxim guns. Lord Trewe wouldn't print that story and Jacob was brought home to cover local events. Still, even the reporting of murder trials is far and away more exciting and meaningful than anything I have done on a newspaper. Jacob made a suggestion to me. He said that his paper might be interested in half a dozen articles about England as seen through the eyes of a visiting American – "A Yank's View of Britain", he suggested as a lead title. Advised me to make the pieces short and laudatory, although a gently chiding humour would be okay. The paper would pay three to five pounds per article. That won't pay for my trip, but it will make a slight dent in the tailor's bill. It will also be good training . . . the observation and reporting of life around me . . . people, places . . .

A gentle tapping at the door interrupted his train of thought. He assumed it was the footman coming back for the tray and called out for the man to enter. He was surprised when Charles opened the door and stepped into the room, dressed in evening clothes and carrying a bottle of champagne.

"I hope I'm not disturbing you," Charles said.

"No, not at all." He capped the pen and closed the notebook.

"I saw your light as I came up from the garage. Thought you might enjoy a nightcap." He held up the bottle. "Found this in the butler's pantry. Still reasonably chilled, and a truly decent year. My father has impeccable taste in wine."

Martin shoved notebook and pen into the attaché case, got out of bed and put on his robe. Charles found two glasses on the chest-of-drawers, one of which had a toothbrush resting in it.

114

"Just right for swizzing out the bubbles," Charles remarked as he undid the wire around the cork. There was a tiny, satisfying pop and then the pale amber wine flowed into the tumblers. "Enjoy your trip up to London?"

"Yes," Martin said, taking one of the glasses. "I'm going on a Cook's tour of England next week. Leave on Thursday morning."

"That should be pleasant. You'll probably see a good deal more of old England than I've ever seen. But that's always the way, isn't it? The traveller sees more than the native."

There was only one chair in the room and Charles sat in it. Martin leaned against the bedpost, feeling self-conscious in his bare feet.

"Well, here's how," he said, raising his glass.

"Yes, to your health." Charles sipped the wine, staring moodily into the glass. "Nice and dry, don't you think? One of the few things the French can do well."

It seemed to Martin that something was troubling his cousin and that he had come to the room for more than a friendly nightcap, but what it could be or why he had come was a mystery.

He endured five minutes of small talk and then Charles said, "Odd, come to think of it. Here we are cousins – blood relatives – and yet I know next to nothing about you. Oh, just a few things that mother has told me."

"I know very little about you," Martin said.

"There isn't that much to know. I went to Eton and Cambridge. Would like to be an historian, or teach history. I've been to France, Germany, Italy and Greece. Enjoy good music, books; used to enjoy hunting. Rather an ordinary, uneventful life."

There was a long pause and Martin struggled to think of something to say.

"Were you born here?"

"In this house, do you mean? Yes. You were born in Paris. Is that correct?"

"In the Montparnasse."

"Is your mother French?"

"Was. She died four years ago."

"I'm sorry. That's my point. I should have known that."

Martin drained his glass and Charles stood up quickly to refill it.

"I don't know why you should," Martin said, sitting on the edge of the bed, "your mother only met mine once. And besides, her death wasn't really a family matter."

"The disinheritance, you mean?"

So he knows about that, Martin thought without bitterness. The midnight conversation was becoming curiouser and curiouser.

"Yes, the disinheritance. That took place before I was born so I don't know too much about it. I never knew my grandfather, but I gather he was a tough old bird, very old-fashioned and puritanical." He paused to drink some more champagne. Charles was watching him, hanging on to every word with taut-faced concentration. "I guess my father was a rebel. He was the second son, five years younger than Uncle Paul and three years older than Aunt Hanna. Paul was in the family business – half a dozen breweries – but my father didn't want any part of it. He wanted to paint. I guess my grandfather gave him a choice. It was as simple as that. Anyway, when he died he'd cut my father out of his will. A dollar. I think he left him that much." He felt dispassionate about the whole thing. It was like telling the life story of a total stranger.

Charles wet his lips with champagne. "I wonder what my mother felt about it. She was very fond of your father. At least I've always had that impression that he was her favourite."

"I think he was, when they were kids. But my father alienated people. He had a talent for that at least."

"Not much of a painter?"

"I couldn't say," Martin shrugged. "He died when I was eight and I don't remember his work, except that it didn't sell. My mother was a *modiste*, and a good one. That's how we lived. I remember my mother telling me that Aunt Hanna and Uncle Paul used to send father money from time to time, but he always mailed the cheques back, torn into scraps. He cut himself off totally from them – getting back at them for being cut off himself, I guess. Although Uncle Paul and your mother had had nothing to do with it. I suppose they gave up trying to help

116

him after a time, as did everybody he knew in Paris. He had a terrible reputation and I don't think anyone was sorry when he died. I'm sure you know your Conrad. I can't read *Heart of Darkness* without thinking of my old man. Paris was his Congo. It found him out early, the way the jungle found out all there was to know about Kurtz. 'It whispered to him things about himself that he did not know', or hadn't known in Chicago. I often wondered if he died like Kurtz, whispering 'the horror . . . the horror'." His mouth was as dry as stone and he reached down for the bottle which was on the floor next to the chair. Charles picked it up and handed it to him. His face was pale and tiny beads of sweat clung to his wide, smooth brow.

"How did he die?"

Martin took his time answering. He filled his glass and drank half of it.

"He cut his wrists. He spared my mother and me the sight, thank God. It was his most noble act. He did it in the apartment of one of his models in Montmartre. My mother believed he was just trying to scare the woman, but he'd been drinking heavily and I guess he lost his sense of caution. Anyway," he continued in a flat monotone, "he died."

"That's horrible," Charles whispered.

"Yes. A wasted life."

"It seems so cruel to be disinherited for such a trivial thing, wanting to be an artist."

"I guess it wasn't a trivial thing to my grandfather. He expected obedience from his children. That was over twenty-five years ago, remember. A different age. And he was very Germanic. Never bothered to learn English properly or to assimilate American customs. I suppose he felt it was his duty as supreme head of the house to punish a prodigal son."

Charles stood up abruptly, as though shaken by what he had heard.

"I'm glad you told me all this. I've always had the feeling that my mother wanted to tell me how her brother died. She started to tell me once, but perhaps she found me unreceptive or the matter was too painful to discuss in any detail."

"Could be," Martin muttered into his glass.

"Anyway, I appreciate your frankness." He combed a stray

lock of hair from his forehead with stiff fingers and began a slow pace of the room. "One wonders what effect all that had on her. It must have been a shock to see her favourite brother destroyed by such a harsh, uncompromising directive and be unable to raise a voice in protest or, anyway, be unable to alter the outcome."

"Being disinherited was a lousy break, but that wasn't what destroyed my dad. If he had been a different sort of man . . ."

"Perhaps, perhaps," Charles cut in, speaking rapidly. "Still, that patriarchal edict was the first blow. If that blow could have been softened, if there had been someone in the family willing to take your father's side, to arbitrate, to conciliate . . ."

"But there wasn't. Uncle Paul told me quite a lot about my grandfather. His word was law. But that was a long time ago. There's not much point in talking about what could or could not have been done. Or is there? You won't mind if I'm blunt, will you? A little Chicago spade-calling. Is there anything bothering you?"

Charles stood very still, eyes fixed on the windows where the curtains fluttered in the night wind. Then he returned to the chair and slumped wearily into it.

"I asked a woman to marry me . . . a positive, irrevocable commitment."

"Congratulations. But you don't look very happy about it."

He stared down at his hands folded tightly in his lap. "It's something we both want. Something we've talked over many times. The final decision rested with me . . . not in asking her, but in facing my father squarely and resolutely."

"And did you?"

He looked up, his expression carved into a mask of firm resolution.

"I intend to tell him in a few weeks, on my birthday. It seems like the best moment. I'm terribly afraid that he might withhold his blessing. It's not the girl – father likes her – it's what her father does, and what his political views are, that my father finds totally unacceptable. Having him as an in-law would be a constant source of embarrassment." His resolution appeared to waver and Martin could detect a slight trembling of the lower lip. "I'm certain Father would resign from some of his clubs because of it. What else he might do I . . . I . . ." His voice trailed off into silence.

Martin bent down for the champagne. The bottle was half empty and he divided the contents between his glass and his cousin's.

"I think I understand what you've been driving at. Are you trying to say that your father might disinherit you? I mean, could something like that happen these days?"

"No, I can't be legally disinherited, but he could turn his back on me, disclaim me as his son. That might sound harsh, but it could happen. There's nothing to prevent him from doing that, except my mother. She's always had a great influence over him and would probably take a firm stand. I think she'd remember your father, how he was cut off from the family and what it did to him – or, what she believes it did to him. I'm banking on that."

"Jesus," Martin said softly. He took a swallow of champagne. "Maybe you'd better talk to her first."

"No. She'd just tell me to think it over, to wait. She's hoping my feelings for Lydia will undergo a change, or hers for me. That won't happen." He drained his glass and leaned forward. "God, but she's lovely. She's leaving for London tomorrow, but when you get back from your trip I want you to meet her. When you do, you'll understand my feelings about her. Lydia Foxe is the most beautiful, most captivating, most exquisite creature that God ever gave the breath of life."

Martin avoided looking Charles in the eye. He drank his champagne, the wine tasting musty all of a sudden. He was thinking of Jacob Golden and his remark to Fenton about seeing Lydia Foxe in Paris. Could there be two Lydia Foxes? It didn't seem likely.

"I sure hope it all works out for the best."

"I have a strong feeling that it will," Charles said a little too fervently. "Yes, I really believe it will."

He became euphoric and wanted to go downstairs and bring back another bottle of champagne, but Martin talked him out of it and persuaded him to go to bed. He wasn't in any mood for an all-night bull session. After Charles had gone he turned out the light and flopped wearily into bed, but it was impossible to get to sleep.

"God damn it," he whispered, staring at the ceiling. His father wasn't a ghost that he couldn't face, it was just that he preferred not to think about him. The image was blurred by time. A tall man who had slipped in and out of the apartment on the rue Dupin like shadow and smoke.

He tossed and turned under the light blanket for a long time and then got out of bed and stood in front of the open window. He gazed down at the gardens, so ordered and geometric, so faultlessly pruned. The serenity seemed a paradox as he thought of his cousin's problems. Perhaps that was symbolic of England. A carefully-nurtured façade of grace and tranquillity behind which emotions seethed as strongly as they did in New York or Chicago. He had been falling into an artful trap. England could do that to visiting Americans. The old stones and the imperial customs tended to overawe Yankee common sense and lull one into a misty shortsightedness. Even the perceptive Henry James had fallen into that trap at least once, writing a book that had been filled with rhapsodic descriptions of buildings and sylvan glades but devoid of people. England was more than Gothic spires and Roman ruins, Tudor castles and Georgian spas, it was a country of people, rich and poor, with all the vices and virtues that human flesh was heir to. He would keep that in mind when he wrote his articles for Jacob Golden's paper. He would be a true reporter and write what he saw and felt and heard and if the editors of the *Daily Post* didn't like it that was just too damned bad.

6

Jamie Ross was happy to be in London. Every day there helped to brighten his spirits. Strolling up and down the narrow, cobblestoned mews behind Stanmore house, he inhaled the aroma of burnt petrol wafted by the morning wind from the motor traffic on the Bayswater Road and nearby Oxford Street. That aroma was sweeter to him than any country wind. London was motor cars and the company of his true peers, the men who drove those motor cars and made them run. London was a pub near Paddington Station where chauffeurs, garagemen and mechanics met over a pint or two and talked seriously about magnetoes, carburettors, fuel pumps and horsepower. London was also pretty girls, droves of nursemaids and housemaids, typists and God knows what else in Hyde Park, Piccadilly and the Strand. It was heaven for a bloke like him, he was thinking as he walked up and down, the heels of his boots ringing sharply on the stones. He was wearing a new uniform of dove-grey serge, black boots and leggings, a grey cap with a black leather peak and tight-fitting black leather gloves. He strutted a little, feeling certain that a maid or two would be peeking through the curtains of the big house. Up and down he walked, past the old limestone buildings that had once been coach houses but were now garages with living quarters above them for the servants. The rear of Stanmore House rose four stories on the other side of the alley, a grim stone block of a building, its marble-columned front facing Park Lane.

One of the garages was open, its wooden doors folded back to reveal the Rolls-Royce parked there. Ross paused for a moment to look at it. A good car. Polished to a rich silver sheen. Fine bit of machinery beneath the bonnet, but it could be better. He had written a letter to the Rolls-Royce company suggesting a method for improving the carburation system and had posted it that morning in the letterbox on Brook Street. He wondered idly if anything would come of it.

"'Morning, Ross. Care for a fag?"

He looked away from the car to see one of the elderly footmen coming towards him. The man was in his braces and wore carpet slippers. He took the offered Woodbine and the footman lit it for him.

"Keepin' banker's hours, aren't you?"

The footman made a sour face. "Didn't get to me bed till after three this mornin'. They had thirty-five people for dinner last night. Nothin' on for tonight, thank the Lord. Goin' to the theatre."

"I know," Ross said.

The footman sat down on a stone step and unfolded a newspaper that he had been carrying under his arm. Ross leaned against the edge of the garage door and looked over the man's shoulder.

"What happened at Newmarket yesterday?"

The footman turned the large pages of the newpaper. "Let's see . . . Ah. Kennymore took the Princess of Wales Stakes, no surprise there."

"Who took the second race?"

"Sheba . . . went off at seven to one."

He whistled softly through his teeth. "Wish I'd had a bob or two on her." He leaned closer to see the paper better. "That Jack Johnson. No one's ever going to whip that lad."

"Well, it's for sure Frank Moran was never the one to try, but it says here the darkie was in poor form. He's not what he used to be, an' that's for certain."

Ross squinted down at the sporting page through a haze of cigarette smoke. There was nothing much there that interested him. Cricket scores mostly; Winchester versus Eton, Navy beating Army at Lord's. He hated cricket, a bloody soppy boring game. America's Cup trials at Torbay, *Shamrock IV* wins; doubles play at Wimbledon; polo at Ranelagh. There would be nothing to interest him until football started.

"Did you hear about the archduke?" the footman asked, turning the page.

"What archduke?"

"The Austrian one."

"What about him?"

"Got scuppered yesterday. Him and his missus."

Ross removed the cigarette from his mouth and tapped ash on the ground.

"Go on," he said, "who'd do a thing like that?"

"Anarchists. Tossed a bomb at him, than shot the poor blighter dead, and her, too."

"Get off it," he said with a tone of disbelief.

"It's in the paper." The footman turned the pages until he found the one with the archduke's photograph on it. "See. Archduke Franz Ferdinand, heir to the Austrian throne – and his consort – murdered in Sarajevo. A student's political crime, it says here."

"I can read." He leaned over the man's shoulder. "Where's Sarajevo?"

"Bosnia."

"Never heard of it. One of them queer penny farthing countries. Couldn't happen here. Too bloody civilised."

"The King's puttin' the Court into mourning for eight days."

"Our King? Why? The boogger wasn't a relative, was he?"

The footman closed the paper in disgust. "You don't know a bleedin' thing except motor cars, and care less. It's just common courtesy, that's all. Just plain common decency. One king to another."

Ross straightened up and walked slowly away. "Thanks for the fag, mate." He didn't much like the footman, or any of the male staff for that matter. Not a drop of spirit in any of them. Content. That was their problem. Content to walk around in knee breeches and powdered wigs like a packet of bleedin' Drury Lane fairies. He took a final drag and flipped the cigarette away. It was starting to get hot, the sun bouncing off the walls of the old stable houses, their slate roofs intensifying the rays. The high, tight collar of his jacket was beginning to feel uncomfortable and his hands felt sweaty in the gloves. Well, what the hell did he expect on the twenty-ninth of June, snow-flakes? The church in South Audley Street began to toll the hour of eight.

"Thank God," he muttered as he walked quickly to the open garage and got into the Rolls. Before the bell had finished ringing the hour he had driven out of the mews and had turned on to Park Lane. Lord Stanmore was just coming out of the front door, preceded by a footman.

"Bloody good timing." He drew the car up to the kerb, the footman opened the rear door and the earl got in.

"Good morning, Ross."

"Good morning, m'lord."

Lord Stanmore sank back against the seat with an audible sigh.

"Ah, a perfect morning, Ross."

"Indeed it is, m'lord," he said, watching the traffic streaming down from Marble Arch, waiting for his moment to slip the car into it without causing any other driver to brake or sound his klaxon.

"Too nice a day to waste in the city. Should all be back in Abington, eh, Ross? Breathing that fresh country air."

"Indeed we should, m'lord."

"I have to go to the House, Ross. Shan't be too long, though. Drafting a message of condolence . . . that beastly assassination of the Austrian archduke."

"I was just now reading about it, m'lord. Told Mr. Picker that it would never have happened in England, m'lord."

Lord Stanmore leaned forward to make conversation easier over the hum of the traffic. He was fond of young Ross. A bright, intelligent man. Bit of a rough diamond. A good example of what was admirable among the lower classes.

"Quite right, too. Jolly well put. We may have our anarchists in England, but they have a sense of fair play. And shooting the man on a Sunday, too. But the deed was done and that's the end of it. I shall tell you something, Ross, that you won't read in the newspapers. They won't be shedding many tears in Vienna."

"You don't say so, m'lord."

"The fellow was neither liked nor trusted." He was about to add that the archduke's morganatic wife had been *déclassé*, no better than a housekeeper, but thought better of it. "Well, *de mortuis nil nisi bonum*. One shouldn't speak ill of the dead."

Ross drove the earl to the Houses of Parliament and found a parking space in Parliament Square. He spent the next two hours in enjoyable conversation with the other drivers who had parked their motors there and he told them about the carburettor fuel mixture device he had thought of and of the letter he had written to the Rolls-Royce company. Lord Curzon's chauffeur, a tall, white-haired man, spoke up.

"I say, Ross. Did you take out a patent?"

"No. Why?"

"Why? To keep anyone from stealing your idea."

Ross winked broadly at the other men. "Well, if someone does, I'll know who to thank."

"Don't be daft," Lord Curzon's man said with some annoyance. "I hope you didn't send a set of drawings to Rolls-Royce."

"No . . . just wrote 'em." He was beginning to feel a bit uneasy. "Told 'em enough to wet their whistle like."

"Good." The man drew a piece of paper and pencil from his coat and leaned against a mudguard to write. "I'm going to give you the name of my brother-in-law and his establishment. He's chief clerk for a firm of solicitors in New Fetter Lane near Lincoln's Inn. Go and have a chat with him soon as you can. He'll tell you how to go about getting a patent."

"I've got dozens and dozens of ideas."

"Have you, Ross? Well, lad, put a patent on the best of them. It could turn out to be a good deal more rewarding than spending your money on skittles and beer."

He wondered for a moment if the elderly chauffeur was making fun of him in a sly way, but there was no hint of mockery in the man's eyes as he handed him the slip of paper.

"Thanks, mate," Ross murmured.

"Think nothing of it, lad. And good luck to you."

"Hop to it, lads," a driver warned, flipping away his cigarette. "Here they come."

Lord Stanmore and a dozen other peers could be seen crossing Palace Yard, all of them smoking cigars and chatting away in high spirits. Hardly the proper mood for men who had just drafted a message of condolence, Ross was thinking. He straightened his cap and walked towards his car.

"Mind what I said," Lord Curzon's chauffeur called out. "Go and see him straight away."

There was a faint aroma of sherry as Lord Stanmore got into the back of the Rolls.

"Pall Mall, Ross. Drop me at the club and then see to her ladyship's needs, or my daughter's." He chuckled wryly and contemplated with favour the ash on his cigar. "I can well imagine how they've been keeping you hopping the past ten days or so."

Ross doubted that as he turned the gleaming, silver car into Whitehall. The earl had only to attend the various parties that were almost a nightly feature at Stanmore House, he didn't have to prepare for them. Ross estimated that he had been on duty an average of fourteen hours a day since the family and most of the servants had moved up from Abington Pryory. For the maids, cooks and footmen the hours had been even longer and more taxing. As he drove sedately towards the hurly-burly of Charing Cross he wondered what her ladyship or Lady Alexandra would have in store for him the rest of the day. Her ladyship's passion was for hand-delivered invitations. That meant driving all over London with one of the footmen, in full livery, powdered wig and all, seated beside him, to the hooting delight of every passing lorry driver. Miss Alexandra was party mad, which meant long hours waiting outside the Café Royal or any number of houses in Belgravia and Chelsea, jawing with other chauffeurs while tango music drifted into the dark street. It was such a bloody waste of time. Somehow he had to find a spare hour to visit the solicitors' office in New Fetter Lane. A patent with his name on it. The thought awed him. Of course, it would take a bit of money, perhaps every penny he had saved up. He might be forced to sell his motorbike, but that was not a great sacrifice. And he'd have to give up his pleasures for a bit. No more walking out with girls and taking them to the pictures. A penny saved was a penny earned.

"I say, Ross," Lord Stanmore called out, "turn into the Strand."

He obeyed without question, although it meant cutting in front of other cars, ignoring the squeal of brakes and the irate blowing of horns. Lord Stanmore was leaning forward and pointing across the lowered glass partition that, when raised, isolated him from his chauffeur.

"There, Ross, in front of Cook's. Yes, by Jove, thought I'd spotted the fellow. Pull up in front."

There was a great press of traffic inching towards Charing Cross Station, but Ross sliced neatly through it to the kerb and parked behind a touring bus.

"Martin!" The earl rolled down the rear window and poked his head out. "Martin, dear boy!"

Martin Rilke was standing on the pavement talking to the tour director. His attaché case was under his arm, an old leather suitcase beside his feet. He turned at the sound of his name and walked over to the car.

"Hallo, sir." He still couldn't find the courage to call the man *Uncle Tony*. "This is a surprise."

Lord Stanmore extended his hand through the window and squeezed Martin's arm. "And a very pleasant one at that. All done with your tour?"

"There are two more days of it, the sights of London, but I'd rather see those on my own. I was just saying goodbye to the guide."

"Just got back in town?"

"Yes, drove in from Cambridge this morning in the bus. It's been a good trip, but tiring. They keep up a fast pace."

Lord Stanmore opened the door. "Hop in, lad, and we'll take you to the house. All your gear's up from the country as promised and there's a room waiting for you."

Martin hesitated. "Thank you, sir, but I wrote a few articles about the trip that I think I can sell to the *Daily Post*. I'll hail a cab."

"Busman's holiday, eh? Jolly good for you, but hop in anyway. I'm just going to my club and then the chauffeur will drive you to the *Post* building." He shifted over on the seat. "Won't hurt your chances of a sale if you arrive in style."

New Fetter Lane was practically around the corner from the *Daily Post* building. Ross was out of the car with alacrity, not giving Martin time to refuse the offer of a ride.

"I'll get your luggage, sir," he said, hurrying across the pavement. "And may I say that it's nice to see you back again, sir, very nice indeed."

The *Daily Post* building was an architectural fusion of Gothic cathedral and Victorian railway station. Slender Ionic columns of soot-blackened stone and dull green copper flutings bound myriad windows into an awesome monolith, designed to impress even the most casual observer with the power of the press.

"Do you want me to wait for you, sir?" Ross asked as he stopped at the main entrance.

"No, thanks," Martin said. "I'll get a cab. Fifty-seven, Park Lane. Is that right?"

"Yes, sir. Stanmore House."

And then the chauffeur was gone and Martin, clutching his attaché case under his right arm, mounted broad stone steps and entered the palatial lobby of the newspaper building. A uniformed page escorted him up to the second floor, to a vast room filled with oak desks and shirtsleeved men. Taut steel wires were suspended horizontally from the ceiling, crossing and criss-crossing the room. Small metal canisters rocketed back and forth on the wires like artillery shells whizzing from one target to another. Typewriters clattered, men shouted over telephones or cried out for the copy boys, the message containers hummed over the wires and a bank of teletypewriters added their own chatter to the din. It was a room that made the editorial offices of the Chicago *Express* seem like the interior of a funeral parlour.

"Mr. Golden's down there, sir," the page said in a Cockney accent so thick as to be barely intelligible to Martin. "Fourth desk in the centre past the glass cubicles."

Martin pondered what "glarssubles" were, but he could see Jacob Golden, bent over a desk, a green eyeshade pulled low on his forehead and so he thanked the boy and made his way through the aisles, walking ankle deep in scrap paper at times. A harried looking man at one of the desks glanced up as Martin came abreast of him.

"How in God's name do you spell Count Marish Szogyeny? My bloody mind's gone blank." A metal tube whizzed overhead and then plummeted down a curved track that jutted up from a corner of the man's desk, coming to rest in a little contraption that looked like the breach of a gun. The man flipped a lever and the canister plopped into his hand. "Oh, God! Not more memos! The chief's gone bloody bonkers!"

Martin left him to his troubles and walked on to Golden's desk.

"Hallo, Rilke," Golden called out cheerfully. "Pull up a wastepaper basket and sit down."

"I think I'm intruding. You guys seem pretty busy."

"Not me, *they*." He leaned back in the chair and locked his hands behind his head. "I'm polishing an item about a clerk who made off with five thousand pounds of his firm's money and is now living in splendour in Brazil. The other lads in this room are not so much busy as they are confused. Austro-Hungarian internal affairs have never been their forte and now the chief, meaning my dear old man of course, is demanding reams of articulate, incisive prose in order to explain Bosnian political aspirations to a multitude of unwashed, unlettered readers. I have my own views of that dark corner of the world, but no one around here is interested in hearing them expressed."

"That was a terrible thing. But there doesn't seem to be any major crisis over it."

Golden's slash of a mouth twisted in derision. "Precisely, my dear Watson. It's the case of the dog that didn't bark all over again."

Martin scratched the side of his jaw. "Sorry, Holmes, but that's a bit too cryptic for me."

Golden uncoiled his hands and reached to the desk for a tin of cigarettes.

"A bit backward in our knowledge of the European ant heap, are we?"

"A bit, yes."

"A common enough fault, I'm afraid, but don't despair, Professor Golden is at hand with pungent commentary and a full assortment of descriptive material." He tapped the cigarette tin after removing two cigarettes and handing one to Martin. "The Austro-Hungarian Empire, a simple tin of Abdullah smokes – only not so simple in real life. A hodge-podge of Germans, Magyars, Croats, Slavs, corrupt and monumentally stupid, exceeded in stupidity and corruption only by the Russians who border them to the east." He shifted an inkwell into position. "The mighty Russian inkwell, murky with serfs, Cossacks, mystics and dark plots, most of them hatched in Viennese coffee houses."

"I'm not totally ignorant of European politics," Martin drawled in his best laconic Chicago manner.

"No, I'm sure you're not, Rilke, but you've watched it all from a long distance, across a wide ocean. I've seen it from the gutters of every capital. Hate. That's the binding word on the Continent. Everyone hates everybody."

Martin picked a match off the desk and lit his cigarette and Golden's.

"I know that, too. My mother was French, from Lorraine. She mourned the lost province to the day of her death."

"And your father was German?"

"German-*American*. She never held the Franco-Prussian War against him. They had more personal wars to fight."

Golden's smile was arcane. "French hatred for Germany is a normal hate, almost quaint. To see true hatred one must go to Servia, to the little cafés in Belgrade, and, casually, over a glass of slivovitz, bring up the subject of Austria and whether or not she has a legitimate right to keep all those Slavic people in Bosnia and Herzegovina enfolded in the Hapsburg wing. *Then* you will see hate, my dear Rilke. A violent, hot-blooded people those Serbs. They cut one of their kings down nine years ago and most of his household. Sliced them up like dog meat and tossed the scraps from the palace windows. The king they have now is very imperial looking, tall and straight, a rather kindly face. Only one minor deficiency in the man – he's insane. It's a country ruled by a weak regent and strong-armed ministers. Plot and counterplot, Pan-Slav radicals, the Black Hand. Oh, quite a charming little country Servia, but we love them because they're so small and plucky and Austria is such a big bully."

A man darted over from an adjoining desk. "Do you have a pen I can borrow? I just broke my last nib."

Golden pulled out the centre drawer. "Help yourself. Care to hang about for a few minutes? I'm explaining the Balkan crisis."

The man grabbed two pens from the drawer and turned quickly away. "Good Lord, no."

"I have few listeners," Golden sighed, puffing smoke. "The reason being that no one can conceive of a world that isn't neatly divided into villains and heroes. Well, they're *all* villains across the Channel, every bloody one of them." He moved a box of paper clips into position below the flat tin of cigarettes. "Servia. On Austria's southern flank. That's why the Russians love them. They keep the Austrians off balance and tie up half their army. Austria could never go to war against Russia, not with all those Serbs facing their soft underbelly. Well now, what have we got right at this moment? One dead archduke. Not much of a loss. A typical Hapsburg who had a girdle on his belly and one around his brains. But his death will give the Austrians an excuse to crush Servia if they can prove it was a Serbian activist who committed the crime and there's no doubt in my mind that one did." He pushed the tin sharply against the box of clips. "Austria moves against Servia, but not in swift anger – a dog who doesn't bark can't be heard, can it? Oh no, they'd never cross the Danube unless they can be assured that Germany will keep the Russians in check, and they'll be given that assurance in due time. That will anger the Russians no end and so we can move the inkwell against the smokes. Hordes and hordes of bearded Russkies, more than enough to deal with Austria and the Germans, too. And what will France do if war flares from the Baltic to the Adriatic? She has a treaty with Russia, just the excuse *la belle France* needs to avenge 1870 – Alsace and Lorraine – the holy names. With the Russian bear scaring the wits out of the Germans in East Prussia, the French will attack across the Rhine and storm to Berlin with their magnificent élan, march in triumph down Unter den Linden the way the Germans marched on the Champs Elysées forty-four years ago."

He leaned forward with a gleeful smirk and pointed his cigarette at Martin's face. "But the Germans are such clever chaps. They know all this; they've worked it out on paper years ago. They prize and honour generals with brains while we despise ours and the French ignore theirs. Rather a sad omen that. Anyway, the Germans have a plan to deal with French moves. It's not a secret. Every *sous lieutenant* in the French army scoffs at the details. It calls for a massive flanking sweep through Belgium in order to fold the French armies into a net, to crush them in less than three weeks before the Russian bear can even stumble out of its cage. Not a plan without its flaws, dear Rilke, but it might well work and even work well. The French refuse to believe that Germany would violate Belgian neutrality. So do we. It wouldn't be sporting, would it? Not playing the game. Belgium is sacred and inviolate. There's a paper to prove it signed by us and all the great powers years and years ago. One more holy relic to toss on the scrap heap."

"Oh, shit," the man at the next desk cried out in exasperation. "Put a sock in it. I can't hear myself think."

"You can't hear what you can't do, old boy." He sighed wearily. "Oh, well, I suppose all prophets are without honour in their own countries."

The man leered at him. "That makes you rather unique, Jacob. You're without honour in every bloody country. Bar none. But thanks for the pens. You're a generous soul at heart."

Golden leaned back in his chair and stared into space, the cigarette drooping from his lips.

"Where was I?"

"Damned if I know," Martin laughed. "Bucketing along through Belgium."

"Yes. Crying havoc as usual. I don't really blame people for ducking under tables when I come into a room. Hope I didn't bore you."

"Not at all. I'm glad you brought me up to date."

Golden stubbed out his cigarette and tidied up the European scene by moving the inkwell to its proper place and dropping the box of paper clips into the top drawer. "Back to more pleasant subjects. So the Yankee tripper has returned safe and sound. How did you find little Britain? No revolutions in Manchester, I trust. Is the wild and hairy Scot still keeping to his side of the border?"

"I had a grand time," Martin laughed. He placed the

attaché case on the desk top. "Wrote half a dozen sketches. In shorthand, I'm afraid. If I could borrow a typewriter . . ."

"No need for that. I learned Pitman at my old dad's knee. It *is* Pitman, I hope, not that awful American stuff."

"It's Pitman."

"Good." He lit a cigarette and pushed the tin towards Martin. "Leave your copy and go and wander about for a bit. You'll find a canteen of sorts down that corridor to your right. Acidulous tea and stale buns, all profits to a home for venereal mill girls in Huddersfield. Ta-ta and leave me to it."

The tea was fresh, the buns were soft and the charity was a trade school for orphaned boys in Southwark. Martin sat at a small table next to a window with a view of the Temple gardens and the river. He was finishing his second mug of tea and his third bun when Golden came into the canteen with the travel copy papers rolled into a tight cylinder. He sat down and tapped the roll against the edge of the table.

"Spend much time on these, Rilke?"

"No, not much."

"Just off the top of your head?"

"Sort of, yes." He could feel his face beginning to burn.

"Well, they're bloody damned good. You have a sharp eye and a finely tuned ear. I laughed out loud over the Yorkshire cattle-show piece. The judges were right out of Dickens. Gentle satire. Just the ticket." He looked thoughtful. "When are you leaving for the Continent?"

"The day after tomorrow."

"Is it absolutely vital that you should go?"

"No, I guess not. Why?"

"Because perhaps you could postpone it for a bit. I think your style of writing would go over very well with our readers. A Yank's eye view of Britain, with the emphasis on the upper-middle-class types, mildly satirised, like the Yorkshire squires. It'd probably be good for eight weeks at least, and being a roving feature writer for the *Post* would be jolly good experience for you. Or do you have to be back in Chicago by any fixed date?"

"No. As a matter of fact I don't even know if I'll have a job when I get back."

"Does that mean you're interested?"

"Sure."

The sardonic mouth softened into a warm smile. "Jolly good. Let's hop upstairs and I'll introduce you to the chief: give the old boy the pitch, as they say in America."

The top floor of the building was in awesome contrast to the lower depths. No harried men there, no nerve-racking type-writers. Deep carpets and oak-panelled walls subdued all sound. Massive oak doors lined a broad, carpeted corridor, all of them closed, all of them bearing discreet brass plates with engraved names: MR. KEENE, MR. UPSHAW, MR. ROSENBERG . . .

"The real powers," Golden whispered as though in church, "reside here as the prophets reside in heaven. Policy-makers all." The hooked little smile returned. "A terribly difficult job. Does one advocate votes for women now, or wait and see how the wind's blowing? And what stand do we take on birth control? Ribald plays? The income tax? Should décolletage be more or less this season? If one stands very still and listens hard, one can hear the brains creak like rusting gears."

The corridor ended in a double set of oak doors. No brass nameplate. None was needed. The doors opened into a vesti-bule in which several men were seated in leather armchairs, all of them with the resigned expression of men who had waited a long time and knew they would wait a good deal longer. A male secretary sat behind a small desk adjacent to another set of double oak doors.

"Is he busy?" Golden asked.

"Naturally," the secretary drawled in Oxonian tones. "You know better than to ask, but he'll see you if it's important."

"It is," Golden said. He leaned towards the man and spoke in a stage whisper. "The chap I'm with fired the fatal shot yesterday and is willing to tell all for fifty quid."

A few nodding heads stirred. The secretary faked a stage yawn.

"Go in, Jacob, and take your assassin with you."

Beyond the doors was a cavernous room that seemed to be part office and part museum. Glass cases filled with Egyptian artefacts stood next to teletypewriters enclosed in soundproof glass domes. Paintings by Reynolds, Gainsborough and Turner competed for wall space with two-shilling maps of Europe, Russia, Africa and other sections of the world, which were pinned to the oak panels with drawing pins. Secretaries and typists, both male and female, abounded, scurrying in and out of glass-enclosed cubicles, all of them moving in a soundless frenzy. At the far end of the room was a broad oak dining table used as a desk, and behind it, in a Beidermeier chair, sat Harry Golden, Lord Trewe.

"Guv'nor," Jacob said, "meet Martin Rilke, from Chicago. An eminent journalist on the *Express*."

There wasn't even the remotest family resemblance, Martin was thinking as he extended his hand across the table. If Jacob was a willow, his father was an oak, and a substantial one at that; the king of all oaks, a dark brown trunk of a man with arms that could truly be called limbs. A sailor, Martin dimly recalled, a constant contender for the America's Cup races, and as constantly fated to lose in the trials to Sir Thomas Lipton. The hand that reached out and took hold of his own was as hard and horny as a sailor's foot.

"Rilke, did you say?" The voice fitted the man, deep and growling like a storm at sea. "Any relation to Paul Rilke of Chicago?"

"My uncle, sir," Martin said, tensing, expecting a vice-like squeeze. The big, brown hand was surprisingly gentle.

"One of my good friends. Saw him two years ago, come to think of it. Right in this room. How is he?"

"Fine, sir, just fine."

The brown hand slipped away and joined its mate in a lock fingered grip across a waistcoat broad as a sail. A hawser of gold chain dangled in a loop from the pockets.

"Then you'd be Hanna Stanmore's nephew as well. Yes. I can see the resemblance."

Martin could detect a likeness to Jacob now. It was in the mouth. The same slash of lips. Nothing else was the same, only that. Jacob's eyes were large and luminous, his father's tiny, like black beads almost lost in a great meaty, sunburnt face.

Jacob leaned across the table and placed the tightly-rolled sheaf of articles in front of the press lord.

135

"Young Rilke here took a Cook's tour of jolly old England and came back with some very amusing observations of about a thousand words each. I'd like you to read them."

Lord Trewe merely glanced at them. "If you say they're good, Jacob, give them to Blakely."

Jacob scooped up the articles and shoved the roll under his arm like a baton. "Right. My idea is to run a short column every day by Rilke, his unjaundiced view of the London social and sporting scene. Use a *nom de plume*; Yankee Cousin, or something on that order. He's staying with the Stanmores, which gives him an inside look at society high jinks – thus the *nom de plume*, Rilke – can't have you being accused of biting the hand that feeds you, can we?"

"He can feed himself," Lord Trewe rumbled. "We've never been accused of underpaying our correspondents."

A harassed-looking young man darted up to the table with handfuls of paper torn from the teletype machines.

"Berlin and St. Petersburg reports, sir."

Lord Trewe snatched them from the man's hand and read through them rapidly. His face was expressionless, the carved figurehead on a ship's prow. When he was through with them he tossed them casually aside.

"I'll have a few memorandums to shoot down. Ask Miss Fisher to come over."

"Yes, sir," the young man said, hurrying away.

Lord Trewe looked at his son with a faint smile. "All your fears are proving groundless. Serenity reigns. The world is used to Hapsburgs getting themselves murdered. The new heir apparent is well thought of. Not a ripple in the European pond."

"Still waters run deep," Jacob said, "I do believe."

Lord Trewe settled back in his chair. "Get on with your work, Jacob. And have the decency to telephone your mother once in a while."

More messages were rushed to the press lord who turned in his chair to scan them. The interview was clearly over and Jacob led Martin back towards the bedlam of the news room.

"Well, Rilke," Jacob said. "How does it feel to be writing for the most powerful newspaper in the world?"

"Pretty good, but I can't stay with the Stanmores. It wouldn't be right."

"You'll have a hard time finding suitable lodgings, old boy. This is the height of the season and London's bursting at the seams. Tell you what, I have more rooms than I know what to do with, a big old flat in Soho above the finest Hungarian restaurant this side of the Danube. And I know you'll like the digs, Rilke. Every chorus girl in London has a key to the place."

By leaning out of the garret window and craning her head to see around a chimney Ivy Thaxton had a fine view of Mayfair. A bit lopsided, more roofs than streets to be seen, but, still, it *was* London and she *was* there.

Dear Mum and Da and my own dearest sisters Mary and Cissy and brothers Ned and Tom and our own dear baby Albert Edward. I am penning this to you all in London town. Oh, it is the grandest place you ever did see.

Just below the window there was a flat, secluded spot near the base of the tall chimney that had probably been used during the building of the house to stack slates for the roofers. It was an easy matter to climb out of the window with notebook and pencil and to sit with her back against the chimney. The roof was a wonder that she would have loved to explore, a vast place of triangular slate hills running in all directions with narrow valleys in between to catch the rain. In the winter those valleys would be rushing torrents of black water tumbling to the drains. Rising amid the sharp ridges was a forest of chimneys and vents, some of them emitting clouds of steam or black smoke like thin volcanoes. Her happiest moments of the long day were the few minutes she could sneak in total aloneness by popping out of the window with the sureness and silence of a cat.

The sun was hot and she turned her face to it for a moment and closed her eyes. The sun was thought to be death to a woman's beauty; she had read that somewhere, but Norfolk girls loved the sun because there was so little of it to be seen in the watery, misty fens.

The letter had been started days before, but she had so little time to complete it. Velda Jessup had thrown a fit of some kind shortly after they arrived in London, falling to the floor and frothing at the mouth. She had been carried out of the house on a stretcher, her body as rigid as a broomstick. Her inopportune departure had created a crisis, as Lady Alexandra was left without a lady's maid at the hour of her greatest need for one. Mrs. Broome, who ran the Park Lane house with the same calm sureness as she ran Abington Pryory, had given the job to Ivy.

"It's a big step up the ladder, my girl."

It was also hard work. Alexandra was in a perpetual fever of activity, her days and nights spent at parties, balls, fêtes, luncheons, garden party teas, dinners, dances, riding in Rotten Row, attending fashion shows, concerts and plays. Each activity required a new costume from shoes to hat and she could never make up her mind about just which dress she wanted to wear. She would try on a dozen before settling for one that halfway pleased her. And talk! The girl never ceased. A constant stream of chatter about this boy and that boy, and should she marry a barrister or should she give her hand and heart to a dashing Hussar who was the youngest son of a duke? And gossip, gossip, gossip as Ivy struggled to turn up a hem or sew on a button . . . Lady Blake, it was rumoured, was seen at the Café Royal with a devastatingly handsome Russian ballet dancer while Lord Blake, surely the ugliest little man in London, was away in Dublin, and had Ivy heard the hilarious *bon mot* that George Bernard Shaw had uttered to Granville-Barker in the foyer of the Lyceum?

Ivy smiled in the blessed, sun-filled tranquillity of the rooftop, lulled by the muted rumble of traffic and the cooing of a pigeon preening itself on a chimneypot. George Bernard Shaw indeed! How could she have possibly heard what the man had said. And who was Granville-Barker? She truly liked Lady Alexandra, but she was a flibbertigibbet if there ever was one.

Dear Mum and Da and my own dearest sisters . . .

The words seemed to wriggle across the page in the heat. She licked the point of her pencil and placed it against the notebook, but she couldn't get her thoughts together.

I am penning this to you all in London town. Oh, it is the grandest place you ever did see.

That was true enough – what she had seen of it: a few shopping trips with Lady Alexandra and one afternoon off which she had spent sitting in Hyde Park watching the rowers on the Serpentine. Ross had offered to take her to the pictures, but she had overheard one of the parlourmaids telling another maid what Ross liked to do in the dark of the picture palace.

"Put his hand clear up me knickers," the girl had said, tittering. Tittering! Ivy glared up at the pigeon. If any man had done a thing like that to her she'd make *him* titter, right out the other side of his mouth. She began to write in a slow, precise hand . . . *I have been given a much more enjoyable and responsible job here, quite a rung up for your Ivy . . .*

Was it? She stared thoughtfully into space. What was she? A lady's maid. Ironing and sewing and smoothing, folding things into drawers and hanging things in cupboards all day and half the night, too. Lady Alexandra never put so much as a stocking in its proper place, but then one didn't keep a dog and expect to do the barking.

How cheeky the pigeon was, strutting back and forth as though it owned the house beneath its tiny feet. The true London spirit, all right. She had noticed that in the park, the London air, everyone strutting along the paths, rich and poor alike, cocky as lords. She had sat on a bench in her plain brown dress, one hand pressed to the crown of her straw sailor hat to keep it from spinning away across the pond in the wind. Three girls had come along the path sharing a bag of sweets between them, nice-looking girls, her age or perhaps a bit older. Well dressed. Nice linen skirts, white shirtwaists. They had sat for a moment on the bench, talking and laughing, and then one of them had drawn a silver watch on a silver chain from a small pocket in her shirt and had glanced at it and said, "Oh my, we'd best get back to the office or Mr. Parrot will be ever so upset."

The other two girls had laughed merrily and one of them had

replied, cheeky as can be, "Well, you know what Mr. Parrot can do!"

Then they had walked on, not hurrying one bit, down the path towards Stanhope Gate and on into the great city to work in an office somewhere, and surely no later than six in the evening. Typing, she supposed. They hadn't taught typing at school. Hadn't taught much of anything, if it came to that. How to do sums, read, spell. The library in Norwich had been her real school. She had begun with the "A's" – Jane Austen, the historical romances of William Harrison Ainsworth, the collected essays of Addison. "Don't you think they're a bit too deep for you, Ivy?" The librarian had held rigid views on what was proper reading for young girls. She had persisted doggedly, volume after volume in proper order: Dickens, Galsworthy, Shakespeare, atlases and almanacs, dictionaries and encyclopaedias. Well read, but nothing learned of any practical value.

. . . Quite a rung up for your Ivy and Mrs. Broome said that I'd be making an extra shilling a week from now on.

It was too much of an effort to write. Her heart wasn't in it and she couldn't keep her thoughts from wandering all over the landscape. It was almost with relief that she heard the sound of Mrs. Broome's voice calling for her.

"Ivy? Jane, where is Ivy Thaxton?"

The girl was sure to tell. She shared the garret room with four girls. Sneaks all.

"Out the window, Mrs. Broome. I told her. I said, Ivy, I said . . ."

Ivy sighed and closed the notebook, looking up to see Mrs. Broome's incredulous face in the garret window.

"Ivy Thaxton! You come up from there this instant before you fall to your death!"

"It's impossible to fall, Mrs. Broome."

"Perhaps. It is also impossible to permit one of his lordship's staff to scamper across the rooftops like a common chimney sweep! Come up! Come up *at once!*"

She returned to the small, stuffy garret, climbing in through the window with the same agility as she had climbed out of it. She brushed dust from her skirt while Mrs. Broome stared coldly at her and the other girl in the room pressed a hand to her mouth to keep from laughing.

"Honestly, Ivy," Mrs. Broome said, "you are incorrigible. Never let me see you out there again."

"No, Mrs. Broome, you won't."

The housekeeper appeared dubious. "Well, we shall see what we shall see. At least I won't have to concern myself with your extraordinary behaviour for the next few days. Miss Alexandra has been invited to Somerset. You will go with her, of course. So hurry along and begin packing. Your mistress will choose her dresses, but you can get started on the underwear and accessories."

"Yes, Mrs. Broome."

"Take an extra dress for yourself and plenty of clean aprons and caps."

"Yes, Mrs. Broome."

"And don't look so penitent, girl. You're not fooling me one bit. Sitting on a roof indeed!"

They would be leaving first thing in the morning, the eight thirty train from Paddington. Lady Alexandra was more bubbly and talkative than usual as she agonised over her selection of clothing. The occasion was a three-day house party at the Duke of Avon's ancient and beautiful – but restored, with all the modern conveniences – castle. She had gone to school with the duke's daughter and all the *most* eligible bachelors in England, perhaps in the *entire* Empire, had been invited.

"Oh, Lord, I can't possibly be seen in this rag!"

By eleven o'clock that night the clothes had been selected and carefully packed away. Supper had been brought up on a tray – sandwiches and tea. Ivy barely had two bites of a ham sandwich, being too busy smoothing dresses and skirts.

"Should I take the taffeta? Do you like the yellow silk from Worth's?"

A hem or two needed a few stitches, a button or so was gone and had to be replaced. At last all of the work was done, the cream-coloured leather trunks with the Greville coat of arms embossed upon them in gold leaf closed and ready for the foot-men to take downstairs in the morning. A three-day house-party! Ivy shuddered to think what work would be involved if her mistress had decided to take a world cruise.

"Good night, Ivy. Be up bright and early in the morning."

"Yes, m'lady."

She walked wearily down the corridor and then up the curved staircase to the third floor where a narrow stairway led to the garret rooms. As she passed one of the doors which faced the landing it opened and Martin Rilke stepped out. He was wearing a dressing-gown and was holding a toothbrush and a tube of Pepsodent.

"Ivy . . . Thaxton?" he asked, smiling.

"Yes, sir," she said, staring blankly at him.

"Don't you remember me?"

She nodded. "Yes, sir. Mr. Rilke from Chicago."

"Right! Cattlemarkets and railways." She was looking at him curiously and he suddenly felt lost for words. He wanted to say that he'd been hoping to run into her again, that she was just about the prettiest girl he'd ever seen, but he knew that would only confuse and embarrass her. In England gentlemen didn't speak to maids that way. Maybe they didn't do it in America, either. But then he'd never grown up around maids.

"Well," he said helplessly. "How do you like being up here in London? Do you miss the country?"

"No, sir."

"Do you come from here? I mean, are you a Londoner?"

"No, sir. I come from Illingsham, near Norwich."

He hadn't been to either place on the tour. He was starting to feel silly standing in the hall in his bathrobe, holding toothbrush and paste. He couldn't think of another thing to say to her.

"Are you going back to America soon?" she asked.

"No," he said quickly, glad that she had broken the impasse. "I've got a job on the *Daily Post*. I'll be in England for another couple of months, but I'll be leaving here tomorrow, moving in with a friend in Soho."

"That should be nice. I'm going down to Somerset tomorrow with Lady Alexandra."

"That should be nice, too."

"Yes, sir," she said, looking away from him and starting off down the hall towards the garret stairs. "Goodnight, sir."

*

Two of the girls in the room snored – loudly. Great fleshy lumps of girls, both Scots, strong as horses. They worked in the kitchen and their hands were beetroot red from being in water so much. They laboured like navvies and she didn't have the heart to wake them and tell them to turn over to their sides. The other two girls were Irish, parlourmaids, sisters from Belfast. God's wrath couldn't have wakened them.

Ivy sat up in her narrow bed and then got out of it to stand by the window. She could see the dark shapes of a dozen pigeons on the chimney, huddled against the tall pots. There was hardly any sound of traffic. The city was asleep, or holding its breath on the brink of July.

Dear Mum and Da and my own dearest sisters Mary and Cissy and brothers Ned and Tom and our own dear baby Albert Edward. I am penning this to you in my thoughts on a hot night in London town. Tomorrow I go to Somerset to stay at the castle of a duke. I have met a very nice young American who is from Chicago, in the state of Illinois, on Lake Michigan as Tom will understand because we both know the atlas better than we know the streets of Illingsham. He is quite taken by me, I think, but bashful and shy and he knows his place. He wouldn't dare say, Ivy, may I go walking with you tomorrow? Or, Ivy, may I take you to the pictures on Saturday? After all, he is really nothing but an American boy with shabby suitcases and pyjamas which are a bit thin in the knees. Tomorrow I go to Somerset to the castle of a duke. The plumbing, I believe, is sound. Every eligible bachelor in the world will be there and I will startle them with my inexhaustible supply of starched aprons and crisp caps.

"Damn," she said softly, staring out across the shadowed roof, the sleeping city. "Damn . . . damn . . . damn."

7

LORD CHARLES AMBERLEY EMERGED FROM THE COOL FOYER OF the Carlton Club and waited patiently in the afternoon heat for the doorman to signal a taxi. To anyone passing by he looked elegant, cool and detached – the attributes that one would expect of any man leaving the Carlton. Inside, he was seething, He had just left his father and absolutely nothing had been resolved. They had had lunch together, Scotch salmon and a superb bottle of hock followed by fruit, cheese and a hundred-year-old brandy, his father waiting for the brandy before toasting his birthday.

"To the twenty-third of July. The date of my son's birth. May it always be a day of sunshine."

"Thank you, Father."

"Drink up, my boy. A true Napoleon."

His father had been in a good mood. The season was beginning to wind down, more and more people were moving out of London, back to their country estates. He could decently do the same. Abington Pryory would be back in full swing by Bank Holiday.

"I tell you, Charles, I miss the horses, damned if I don't. Banks will have 'em in shape to suit Banks, but I like 'em a good deal leaner. I'll have to run the fat off them. And speaking of horses, my lad, why don't you come with me in September and ride in the Tetbury? Be like old times."

"Perhaps I'll do that, Father."

"Happy to hear it. By the way, thought you and Roger were intending to go to Greece this month."

"We decided against it. Roger is preparing a book of his poems for publication, a slim book."

"A fruitful summer, what? Did Alex tell you that she's finally made a choice?"

"No. How did she do it? Stick a pin into a list?"

"Something like that, I'd say. The chap's name is Saunders. Good-looking fellow. Went to Trinity. He's in the Foreign Office, Lord Esher's nephew and heir. Of course, that's her choice for *this* week, but I hope she stays with it."

"So do I. And Father, I've made up my mind to marry Lydia."

How soft those words sounded to his ears, a melody. They had rung a different tune for his father, but he had said little. Sipped his brandy, lit a cigarette.

"Oh? You know my feelings on that subject, Charles. The thought of your being Archie Foxe's son-in-law is most painful to me."

"Because Archie's in trade?"

The earl had cradled his glass of brandy between his hands, sniffing the aroma. "Archie Foxe is an extremely successful shopkeeper. More power to the man. I don't hold that against him to any great extent. What I simply cannot abide about him is his contempt for the British class structure. Damned if I don't believe the man's a socialist at heart. And his closeness to Lloyd George and all that scruffy bunch of icon smashing Liberals is repellent to me. I'm sorry. Lydia has been welcome in my house since she was a child. I would never by thought or deed snub her because I disapprove of her father's views. But marriage? That is out of the question."

"And if I marry her anyway, Father?" His voice had sour l tinny and ineffectual in the vastness of the dining room. He had studied his father's face but had discerned no drastic change of expression. He had looked, if anything, slightly bored.

"I do not wish to discuss the matter any further, Charles." He had set his glass on the table and reached for the bottle. "Have another drop of Napoleon. Do you good."

The luncheon had dragged on interminably for Charles, as several of his father's friends had come to the table and joined in the birthday toasts. But at last it had ended and he had taken his leave.

The taxi arrived and he slumped on to the back seat. Anger and frustration made him mute and it took several seconds to compose himself enough to give the driver directions. God, he agonised, what was he going to do? He felt like a man tied to two horses pulling in opposite directions. It was obvious that his father would not be pinned down as to what specific action he might take. He couldn't actually stop him from marrying Lydia, wouldn't create a scene and bar the church door, but he might let them both know in no uncertain terms that as far as he was concerned the marriage did not exist. A marriage between two strangers, a union that he would neither witness nor acknowledge. Would Mother forbid him from taking such baleful measures? And if she did, would Father be swayed by any of her arguments on his behalf? He squeezed his hands tightly until the knuckles ached. Everything was in doubt and it was impossible to get solid, concrete answers. Evade the issue, play for time; that was his parents' game. And what of Lydia? What in the name of all that was holy would be her reaction if he couldn't assure her that she was marrying into the family. No woman would wish to marry a man ostracised by his own father. He didn't quite believe her assurances that he was all she wanted. Acceptance by society was important to Lydia; she couldn't be blamed for that.

He stared gloomily out of the window as the taxi turned into the Mall. The park had never looked so beautiful, the trees a startling shade of green against the sky – a sky almost impossibly blue for England. An Italian sky, the kind one saw in Amalfi in August. The red brick towers of St. James's rose above the trees and the guardsmen stood in front of their sentry boxes at Buckingham Palace. The Scots Guard, he noticed as the taxi swung past the palace towards Lower Belgrave Street.

The Earl of Stanmore's daughter-in-law.

He could only speculate on the importance of that relationship to Lydia. What doors would it open for her socially that no amount of Archie's millions could ever have breached? Lydia *Amberley*. That name carried an almost indefinable aura of prestige and privilege. It meant garden parties and balls at homes where Lydia *Foxe* would not have been welcome, or, at best, merely tolerated. It meant a final and irrevocable acceptance in even the most rarefied levels of society – provided, of course, that the union had been publicly blessed.

"God," he whispered fiercely. What would she say if he had to tell her that it would not be blessed? That his father's presence at their wedding would be thunderously conspicuous by its absence? Would she smile, kiss him, tell him that it didn't matter in the slightest? He knew in his heart what her reaction would be and the thought turned his blood to ice. Lydia loved him, he had no doubt of that, but her love was based, at least in some measure, on his position in life. But what if he were wrong? What if she didn't give a tinker's damn about it and wanted a marriage, blessed or not? What then? Could he defy his father and run off with her? Toss away so casually every vestige of his sense of duty and obligation?

He felt that he was in the grip of a nightmare. His emotions were in such a whirl that when he arrived at his destination he handed the driver a five-pound note and told him to keep the change. The man drove off in a hurry before this madman regained his senses.

Fenton Wood-Lacy's batman opened the door of the captain's tastefully furnished flat which Roger was sharing while in London. Roger was in the drawing room, seated on the floor surrounded by printed proofs of his poems. Sprawled on the floor next to him was Rupert Brooke, shoes and socks off, a white tennis shirt open down the front revealing an expanse of brawny, tanned chest. Brooke's friend, Lascelles Abercrombie, sat in a chair, puffing on a pipe and reading the afternoon edition of the *Globe*.

"Hallo, Rupert," Charles said. It was good to see the man again. The poet had left King's College when he and Roger had gone up to Cambridge, but his influence had been strong, had set a stamp on all literary societies that had flourished there. And Brooke had lived for a time near the college, at the Old Vicarage in Grantchester, and he and Roger, and many others, had spent hours there talking endlessly about books and poetry, or swimming in the dam above Byron's Pool . . . *yet stands the church clock at ten to three? And is there honey still for tea?*

"Hallo, Charles," Brooke said with a lazy smile. "Happy birthday."

"Yes, Amberley," Abercrombie muttered. "Many happy returns of the day."

"I gather Roger's been advertising the fact," Charles said.

Brooke nodded. "In the hope we can all pressure you into

147

giving a party for the occasion, or at least a bang-up feed at some small, but epicurean restaurant."

"My pleasure," he said thickly.

Roger looked up for the first time and noticed the sickly pallor of his friend's face.

"I say, Charles, do you feel all right?"

"I'm fine, thanks."

"Well, you don't look fine. Webber!"

The batman darted into the room. "Yes, sir?"

"Fix Lord Amberley a large whisky. And Mr. Brooke and Mr. Abercrombie could go for a Guinness, if there's any left."

"There's one bottle, sir."

"Divvy it up, that's the good chap." He watched the soldier-servant scurry off. "My dear brother runs a niggardly house. No, Charles, you look as pale as a ghost."

Charles sat on the edge of a sofa. He really didn't feel well at all. "It's just the heat and the petrol fumes. God," he blurted, "I'd like to get away for a month or two. Can't you postpone that blasted book? Let's go to Greece. Train to Trieste and then Shanks's mare to Epirus."

Abercrombie lowered his newspaper. "I'd stay away from that section of the world for a few months. Austria just sent a perfectly shocking demand to Serbia, a veritable slap in the face with an iron glove. There's bound to be another war in the Balkans. We were just discussing it before you arrived. Care to read the dispatch from Belgrade?"

"Oh, bugger Belgrade!" His tone had a bitterness that surprised even him.

"Oh, I say," Roger said. "We like little Serbia, don't we?"

It was all perfectly proper, Fenton Wood-Lacy was thinking as he walked slowly towards Number Twenty-four, Cadogan Square. It was the day after Winifred Sutton's coming-out ball and it was socially correct to return, leave one's calling card or thank the hostess for a splendid time. He had come to do more than that. He had had only one dance with Winifred, but it had been the final one, a waltz, and after it was over he had overheard a woman mention to Lady Dexford that her daughter looked beautiful, ". . . and they make such a lovely

148

couple". Lady Dexford had beamed radiantly. He had then brought Winifred a final cup of punch and had asked her if he might call the next day and perhaps, if she wasn't too tired from the exertions of the ball, go for a walk.

"I am so glad you asked," she had said. "And I shall let you in on a secret. Mamma will be pleased as well."

And so now he stood on the front steps of the Dexfords' London house feeling, he thought ruefully, very *suitorish*, with a box of sweets from Fortnum and Mason under his left arm. A butler anticipated his ringing the bell and opened the door.

"Good afternoon, sir."

He was ushered, almost reverently, into the drawing room where Winifred and her parents were waiting. They all seemed immensely relieved when he walked in.

"Ah, Fenton," the Marquess of Dexford cried. He was a stout, balding man with the slightly bowed legs of a lifetime horseman. "Jolly nice of you to drop by, what? Care for a glass of sherry? Did I tell you I saw your uncle t'other day? At the Army and Navy. Looked fit. His division did damned well at Salisbury in the old manoeuvres, what?"

The one-sided conversation became increasingly more fatuous and then, blessedly, Lady Dexford gave her husband a discreet nudge. Excuses were uttered and they withdrew from the room.

Fenton smiled at the plump girl seated so demurely on the divan.

"Well, Winifred," he said with a forced cheerfulness, "your coming-out ball was a total success."

"Did you think so?" she asked shyly. "I do hope you had a pleasant time."

"I enjoyed myself thoroughly."

"Mother was so pleased that you came." She looked down at her hands twisted tightly in her lap. "And quite happy that you called on me today."

"Well," he said, clearing his throat, "it's my pleasure, Winifred. A chance for us to . . . talk."

"Could we go for a walk? It's so stuffy in the house."

Anything was preferable to Fenton than staying in the Dexfords' drawing room where the possibility existed of the

Marquess returning to tell yet another anecdote about his brief, but vivid career in the army. A few moments later they were going down the front steps into the golden sunshine.

"Shall we walk up to Kensington Gardens?" he asked.

She put a hand on his arm. "Let's walk slowly to the river. I love Chelsea, don't you?"

He admitted that he did. He also told her that she looked lovely.

She blushed fiercely and her hand tightened on his arm. "Thank you. Is it wrong for me to say that you look lovely, too? That's not the proper thing to say to a man, I know, but it happens to be true. I feel very proud walking beside you."

Her usual reticence vanished once they were away from the house. She was candid about herself, aware of her short-comings.

"But I *am* trying to better myself. Take this frock. I think it's very becoming, but Mother said no at first. She thought it was too daring in the bodice, but I don't think a woman should feel ashamed that she has a . . . well, a female chest, do you?"

"Certainly not."

"One of my problems has always been a sweet tooth. I'm mad for cream buns and confectionery of all sorts, but if one hopes to achieve slenderness, one must firmly resist such treats. I shall treasure your box of chocolates, but I shan't eat them."

"I'm sorry. My next present to you will not be edible."

She slipped her arm through his. Her intimacy was childlike. He felt like a favourite uncle. Lord, he thought, how terribly young she is.

The Thames was sluggish in the afternoon heat and their conversation about Chelsea began to wear thin. A public house in Cheyne Walk looked inviting, but he couldn't take her there. She seemed content just to be with him, walking decorously by his side, arm-in-arm, not caring whether they spoke or not. A tug ploughed up-river pulling a string of empty coal barges. Some grey birds rose from the mud flats in the shadow of Albert Bridge and flew off across the river towards Battersea. They walked on, leaving the Embankment and walking slowly up Kings Road in the direction of Sloane Square. A sentry standing by the iron gates of the Duke of York's barracks tapped the butt of his rifle twice against the pavement as they walked past him.

"Why did he do that?"

"Because he recognised me as an officer," Fenton said after acknowledging the salute with a slight nod of his head.

"Is he in your regiment?"

"He's in the Royal Sussex, but I've been to the barracks a few times. Perhaps he remembered my face."

"No. You just look like a captain in the Coldstream Guards. I think it's the way you wear your boater. It's the way I imagine Kitchener would wear his."

He leaned towards her and whispered loudly in her ear. "Don't tell anyone, but Lord Kitchener doesn't own a straw hat. Nothing but uniforms, even his pyjamas – scarlet with rows and rows of medals."

Her laugh was throaty and rich. "Oh, dear, poor Lady K., how she must suffer!"

He was enjoying her company. Was, in fact, beginning to like the girl. And that mildly bawdy allusion to old K. and his missus proved that she wasn't a prude. Yes, he liked her. She was on the dowdy side, no question about that. Even the new frock was of no great help. It showed her figure, to be sure, but it wasn't exactly a figure that would set a man's blood on fire. Her hair was pretty in the sun and her complexion clear and rosy. Good teeth. Lips that looked soft and kissable. He liked her. She was easy to be with and one could, in a sense, relax.

"Are you feeling a bit peckish?" he asked. "A cup of tea, some sandwiches?"

"I'm always peckish. It will be the death of me. On my tombstone they will write, 'Here lies Lady Winifred Sutton, fasting at last'."

His laugh was a gunshot that turned heads. He took hold of her hand and steered her across the busy street, dodging cars and lorries, and into an Italian restaurant that he remembered with favour. He had taken Lydia there once. She had enjoyed the Milanese food, but had been bored by the Chelsea types, the actors, writers and painters who haunted the place from morning to night. Winifred, on the other hand, was delighted by the revelation of a side of Chelsea she had never seen, nor even knew existed. The dimness of the shuttered room, the candles stuck into wine bottles on each table, the Bohemian crowd fascinated her. A burly man with a ragged red beard, a shabby velvet cloak draped across his shoulders, paused in front of their table and eyed Fenton up and down.

"You look like the Prince of Wales."

"Only when I'm sitting down," Fenton said, then rose to his full six feet two inches.

Red-beard nodded. "So I can see, mate. You and your lady want your portraits done? Half a crown each."

"And a bottle of chianti, of course."

"Of course."

The man sketched while they ate, using charcoal and pastels. The results were very good.

"May I have yours?" Winifred asked. "I shall treasure it always."

She felt slightly tipsy from a glass of wine and so he ordered a taxicab and asked the driver to take a long way back to Cadogan Square. Her head cleared as they drove around the park, but she remained euphoric.

"This has been the most wonderful afternoon of my life."

"I'm glad you enjoyed yourself, Winifred."

She clutched the two portraits and turned on the seat to look at him.

"Can we do it again sometime?"

She was his for the asking. Hooked, netted and placed in the creel. He felt a nagging sense of shame for being so cold-blooded about it, but, damn it all, he *did* like her.

"As often as you like. Although, I suppose you'll be leaving London soon."

"Yes," she said quietly. "We go back to Dorset on August 1st." Her eyes had an almost haunted appeal.

"May I ask your father for formal permission to call on you, Winifred? Here in London . . . and . . . as often as possible at Lulworth Manor?"

She seemed to stop breathing for a moment, then she let out a tiny cry and leaned against him, her lips brushing the side of his face.

"Oh, yes, yes. Oh, my dearest, *dearest* Fenton. May God bless you and keep you always ... *always* ..."

Martin Rilke tried to keep his mind on what he was typing, but the chatter of the teletype machines intruded on his thoughts. He had been given the courtesy of a glass-enclosed cubicle, sharing the space with the theatre reviewer, but the top of the cubicle was open and the sounds of the enormous room rolled over like great waves over a dyke. The banner of the morning edition had been made up and he could see it as a copy boy hurried the proofs to one of the editors.

SERBIAN CRISIS GROWS

That was a feather in Jacob's hat, he was thinking. They had pulled him off murder trials and sent him hurrying off to Belgrade. He envied him. The pages from his typewriter mocked the severity of the European situation ...

There is something about Lord's cricket ground that is humbling to even the most uninitiated of spectators. Standing in the Long Room, amid the almost holy relics of the game's past, looking up at the severe visage of W. G. Grace whose bust dominates the pavilion, even this Yankee was struck by ...

Struck by what? The absurdity of the game? Men in white clothing standing about in the sun? The lack of passion? The elderly men seated in the shade murmuring, "Good play ... Oh, well done, sir"? Where was the explosive snap of the ball from home to second to catch the runner? And where was the runner himself, sliding in with his spikes high, trailing dust?

But the piece must be laudatory with just the gentlest of digs at the more stuffy types of club men with their "haw, haw" fatuity, a few thorn pricks amid the roses.

"Are you finished, Mr. Rilke, sir?" a copy boy asked, poking his head around the doorway. The accent was strong East End, but no longer incomprehensible to Martin's ear. He was becoming Anglicised.

"Another fifteen minutes, Jimmy."

"Right you are, sir."

Twenty minutes to the midnight deadline. He'd make it with ease, even with the rambling of his thoughts. When he was done he raised his hand and the boy darted into the cubicle and raced away with the copy. Martin took off his glasses, wiped them with a handkerchief and placed them in his pocket. The theatre reviewer, a cadaverous man who had never been seen by anyone on the paper dressed in anything but evening clothes, white tie, rose stretching and yawning from behind his desk where he had been sound asleep for the past two hours.

"All done, Rilke?"

"Yes. Put to bed."

"That's where I should be."

"You could have been there for the past two hours."

The reviewer yawned and drew a cigarette from a silver case.

"I know, but I feel restless. I rather miss Jacob. He's the only one I know who might conceivably understand what's going on. The other chaps around here are no bloody use at all." He smiled thinly. "They know only what they read in the papers. I tell you, Rilke, I'm most apprehensive about the Balkan situation. I can't see how it can possibly ease off or where it will end. Oh, well, worrying about it won't make it change, will it? Can I buy you a drink at Romano's?"

"No, thanks, I think I'll go straight home."

"I'll share your taxi, if you don't mind. I have this absolute horror of being alone lately. Can't explain it. Damnedest feeling."

It seemed to be a feeling that many people shared. It appeared to Martin that the streets of the city never emptied. The cafés in Soho weren't open twenty-four hours a day, but if they had been, they would have done good business. Perhaps it was no more than the unusually hot weather that drove people, mainly young men, from their rooms and set them to wandering in restless bands through the West End. The groups were orderly, excessively polite as a matter of fact, and the police were not concerned. It was almost Bank Holiday time and a certain anticipatory excitement was normal. And yet, somehow, this behaviour could not be explained that easily. One of the *Post* editors had just returned from Berlin and had observed

154

the same thing occurring in Germany but on a vaster scale, masses of young men hiking across the country to the Black Forest or to the mountains of Bavaria, singing *Brüderschaft* songs, drawn by some deep urge that none could adequately express. It had struck the editor as being quite odd, but then the Germans had always been a mystical people. An atmosphere of impending climax seemed to hang in the air like heat haze. Lord Trewe, stalking through the City room on his daily tour of inspection, had remarked that what Europe needed right at this moment was a bloody good thunderstorm with plenty of rain to cool the blood. But there was no rain. The skies were a savage blue. Jacob wrote from Belgrade, "*One can see the Austrian gunboats prowling the Danube which has never looked more beautiful, more conducive to song.*"

The flat in Soho smelled of furniture polish and ammonia. The cleaning woman had been in during the day, not that she could have found much to do from her last visit. With Jacob away, the spacious rooms in Beak Street remained clean and orderly – and empty. The girls who used to taxi over to the place from their theatres on Shaftesbury Avenue between performances, many of them still in costume, for champagne and cold lobster stayed away when Jacob was gone. Martin wasn't sure whether Jacob had told everyone that he was leaving London or if they simply knew he was gone. Some sort of seventh sense. The theatrical grapevine, more likely. He missed the ribald gaiety, the perfume, feather boas and expansive flesh of the chorus girls. He also missed Jacob's untidy presence, the litter of papers and books on floors and furniture, the blue haze of his strong Turkish cigarettes, the torrent of his conversation which was mordant, exasperating, seditious and profane – but always worth listening to.

There was nothing much to eat in the kitchen except for tinned Strasbourg pâté, water biscuits, thick glass jars of Russian caviar and a cupboard stacked with champagne. More substantial meals were eaten out or brought up on trays from the Hungarian restaurant below, Jacob doing the ordering by shouting out of the back window into the alley where the cooks and waiters lounged during their breaks, playing cards on an upturned milk crate. The restaurant closed at eleven and so he was stuck with appetisers. He put a bottle of champagne in the ice chest to cool, then got into his pyjamas and carried his attaché case into Jacob's study, the only room in the flat that had decent lighting.

The notebooks had lain untouched since June. He hadn't had the time, not with five articles a week to turn out for the paper and the travelling involved in getting material for them. Also, he just hadn't felt like writing down his thoughts. He had hoped that his novel would take shape out of those random jottings; current observations drifting into thoughts of the past. That hadn't happened. His perspective of Chicago and the Rilkes had not been freshened in any way whatsoever. And Jacob had cast a pall of doubt over the project.

"Every first novelist feels that the story of *his* life and *his* family is a world-shaking event that simply screams for print. I went through that stage myself, Martin. I was twelve at the time and I suddenly noticed something that perhaps you have noticed yourself . . . that I simply do not look at all like my father. Well, I began to ponder on that and reached the febrile conclusion that I was the result of a liaison between my mother and the King of Spain. Then, filled with plans for an epic saga of my first twelve years on earth, the little English Jew who was in reality bastard claimant to a Catholic throne, I went browsing in the attic and found a trunk. In that trunk were tintypes of my father and his long dead sister, Rose. I was exactly like her, a carbon copy of the poor departed dear. Not a royal bastard at all, simply a throwback to certain Whitechapel physical types, the influx of Sephardim into London in the eighteenth century. Ah, well, the world lost a great popular novelist and gained an unpopular newspaperman. My dear fellow, the times spin on at a dizzy pace. Do your utmost to at least keep abreast of them. You have a talent for keen observation of the pathetic, sometimes endearing, sometimes mundane foibles of mankind. Put it to use. Bang out copy with the fury of the anchorites shrieking their predictions to the stones. Hone your pen to a knife. Cut . . . cut . . . cut! And save your memoirs for venerable old age."

The champagne cork made a satisfactory pop and flew over

the leather sofa. Jacob was as easy to live with as a mad wasp, but he made a certain amount of sense sometimes. The epic novel of the Rilkes would join his saga of the striking Chicago motormen in oblivion.

He poured a glass of champagne, spread a thick layer of pâté on a water biscuit and then leafed through the stack of mail which the cleaning woman had placed on the desk. Dunning letters for Jacob mostly. One envelope addressed to him. Marlborough Club stationery:

Dear Rilke,

I have the unfortunate honour to be assigned Captain of the Guard over Bank Holiday. Promised you a look at the inner workings of Buck duty. Might make an item for the penny press. If you are not otherwise engaged, I look forward to your joining me and a few friends for dinner in Guards quarters, St. James's, Tuesday evening, August 4th. 7 p.m. Black tie.

R.S.V.P. if possible.
Sincerely,
Fenton Wood-Lacy.

He made a mental note to reply in the morning. It should be interesting. He could probably squeeze two articles out of it.

The notebooks lay piled in the attaché case. The last entry had been at Abington Pryory before he had left on the tour. He had a hundred comments and reflections to write down, but he could do no more than enter the date and time on the top of a blank page: July 24th, 1914. Early morning. He toyed with the pen and sipped champagne. He felt too weary to write and too keyed-up to sleep. One singular event stuck in his mind, lingering with a peculiar poignancy. Why should that be so? It had only been a couple of weeks before, a picnic beside the Thames at Henley with the Stanmores and a party of their guests, and yet the scene seemed to belong to another age, suspended in time and misted by a golden light. The Royal Regatta held on the smooth green water of the river; gleaming, highly varnished rowboats gliding as noiselessly as the Royal swans; great bowers of willow trailing leafy tendrils in the stream; women in white dresses and large hats strolling along the banks; a band playing in a gingerbread pavilion.

Jacob's dispatch from Serbia had triggered the remembrance of that day. *One can see Austrian gunboats prowling the Danube* . . . The squat iron hulls became superimposed over the delicate pageant on the Thames. There had been no talk of crisis that day as they sat on the grass and ate strawberries and cream. The archduke two weeks in his grave. Long forgotten. Now Austria-Hungary prepared for war as Serbia held firm. What would Russia do? France? England? Treaties and alliances bound country to country like bands of steel. Now lights burned all night in the chancellories of Europe.

Strawberries and cream and a white wine, the wine served by the Stanmore butler – for of course there were servants even at a picnic in a meadow – from a silver bucket filled with ice. He had met Lydia Foxe on that day. What had they talked about? He couldn't remember. Nothing of any consequence. A stunningly beautiful woman. Easy to understand Charles's infatuation, but he had detected a shrewd toughness behind the lovely face and the gracious manners. Charles leaped at her every request, clung to her every word. She was bright, charming, and yet once he had happened to glance at her while she was watching the earl and Hanna eat their strawberries. The woman's eyes had been pure steel.

He put the pen down and closed the notebook. There was no point in even trying to write. He felt a sense of waiting, as though the entire world was holding its breath. Outside in the street he could hear the sound of footsteps ringing on the cobblestones, a group of young men heading up Carnaby Street towards Oxford Circus. He didn't even have to get up and look to know that there would be a dozen or more of them, arms linked, cloth caps perched on the back of their heads, cigarettes dangling from their mouths. Out on the town on a hot July night. Several of them were singing a popular music-hall song, their voices loud and beery, but the sound fading rapidly as they moved up the short, narrow street . . . *It's a long way 'ome, so don't wait up for me . . . I'll give you a kiss an' a thrup'ny bit, but don't wait up for me . . .*

*

They all seemed to be watching the clock, although Roger Wood-Lacy tried to keep the conversation going by telling a few jokes. Uniformed mess attendants removed the dinner plates. There was, Martin noted, a good deal of uneaten food. But not on his plate. The rack of lamb with Cumberland sauce had been delicious.

"You have good cooking in the army," he said.

Fenton sat at the head of the long table in his scarlet jacket, brass buttons reflecting the candlelight.

"The palace chefs actually, but our own chaps don't do too badly in the mess. Do you know who provides this dinner, Martin?"

Martin raised his wine glass. "You, I suppose, so I offer a toast to the host."

Roger clapped his hands, the sound echoing in the vast room with its black oak Tudor beams and dark brick walls.

"A toast to the host! I say, we're all rhymesters tonight."

"I suppose we'll be telling puns or reciting limericks next," Charles said gloomily.

A pink-faced lieutenant looked blank. "Rhyme? What rhyme?"

"Never mind, Ashcroft," Fenton said. "Getting back to what I was saying, the answer is no, I don't provide the dinner. The meal comes from the generosity of King George the Fourth, the great Prinny, better known to history as Beau Brummel's friend. Anyway, he was a lover of fine food and blowsy women. Unfortunately, he only willed the Captain of King's Guards provision for the former. The meal is his legacy for which generations of hungry captains and their guests have been truly thankful."

"Here, here," Lieutenant Ashcroft murmured.

Charles checked the time again. "Ten thirty."

"That makes it two minutes later than when you last looked," Fenton remarked drily.

One of Fenton's mountaineering friends, a ruddy-faced barrister named Galesby, frowned and shook his head slowly.

"You're taking all this very lightly, I must say. After all, what happens or does not happen in the next hour and a half

159

concerns you a good deal more than it concerns any of us, Lieutenant Ashcroft excepted, of course."

"Of course," Ashcroft said stiffly.

One of the messmen brought around a box of cigars. Fenton selected one and passed it slowly under his nose.

"We have a rule in the Guards quarters against talking shop. War, my dear Galesby, is shop."

"To you. I never took the king's shilling so I'm legally entitled to speak my mind. I ask you straight out, Fenton. Do you believe Germany will back down by midnight and refrain from marching into Belgium?"

Fenton lit his cigar. It was so silent in the room they could all hear the hissing of the match. The messmen walked as though treading on clouds.

"We are long past the moment when anyone can back down. The Germans are in front of Liège and God himself couldn't turn their troop trains around. The politicians, the statesmen, the kings and emperors have done their jobs and now the soldiers take over. It's simply come down to that. If we could whisk old Golden back from Serbia, he could probably explain it better than I can – although, on second thoughts, I doubt it. It's rather like explaining the colour blue to a blind man."

The barrister accepted the port decanter as it made the rounds of the table.

"Lord, what a bloody awful week this has turned out to be."

The clock was ancient, a triumph of rococo design, a small face nearly lost in a welter of ormolu. A Grenadier officer had found it in the baggage of a Russian general after a battle in the Crimea. The room was filled with the souvenirs of old glories. Silver candlesticks brought back from Portugal after the Peninsular campaign, silver salvers given to the Brigade of Guards by the Duchess of Richmond a year after Waterloo. What would they add this time, Martin wondered. He looked at the clock. The minute hand made a tiny jump. He could visualise trains . . . hundreds upon hundreds of them rolling west across Germany in the night, rolling east across France. Along the Danube there had been war for six days. By all rights it should have stayed there, toe to toe between Austria and Serbia. Jacob had written that Serbia was small but tough and the Austro-Hungarian empire rotten from the core out. The Serbs would maul the Austrian invasion and if no one rushed to the aid of either side, the war would be over in three weeks with a treaty of mutual compromise. A grudging, bitter peace perhaps, but still a peace. Jacob had added to his dispatch – but does the world want peace? One of the editors had scratched the question out.

"With your permission, sir, I would like to propose a toast," Lieutenant Ashcroft said, his face becoming pinker by the minute.

"By all means," Fenton said, scowling at the tip of his cigar. "It's a night for toasts."

The lieutenant shot to his feet. "To England!"

The minute hand jumped. In the silence after the toast had been echoed around the room they could hear the soft whirring of the clock's gears. The port was passed along. Glasses were refilled.

"Odd," Galesby said. "Incredible, really, if one stops to think about it. Just last week I was making plans to go to Lanersbach and stretch my legs with some good alpine rock climbing."

Fenton puffed a lazy plume of smoke. "Well, you can always go to Wales."

Fenton and Lieutenant Ashcroft had to inspect the guard at Buckingham Palace at midnight and so the guests left at eleven thirty, a gravely formal parting in the austere, treeless court-yard of St. James's.

"Shall we share a taxi?" Galesby asked as they walked into Cleveland Row.

Charles took a deep breath of the clean night air. "No, thanks. Can't speak for the others, but I could do with a walk."

The barrister hesitated. "Jolly good idea. I think I'll join you. Heading down to Whitehall, I suppose."

"We might as well be among the first to know," Charles said.

They walked in silence to the Mall. St. James's Park was shadowed and gloomy across the wide, tree-lined road. A night heron glided across the still surface on the lake.

"Yes," Galesby said, almost to himself. "Quite odd. One would have thought that intelligent men could have settled issues across a conference table."

"That would be contrary to fate," Roger said, his tone strangely fervid. "War is a form of rebirth. A rite as old as time. I was talking to Rupert this morning on the telephone and I've never heard him so enthusiastic, so revitalised. To go shining to war in defence of little Belgium has all the nobility and purity of Arthurian quests, Rupert said. I think it's more Grecian myself. A sailing for Ilium."

"I don't know about that," the barrister said, tossing his half-smoked cigar into the gutter. "All I bloody well know for sure is that nothing will be quite the same again."

"That might be a blessing," Charles said quietly.

They stopped at the end of the Mall, the Duke of York's statue looming up against the sky, the lights in Admiralty House twinkling through the trees at the edge of the park. Big Ben tolled the hour, twelve hollow iron peels. They could hear distant cheering and then the sound of a rushing crowd, hundreds of feet ringing on the pavements. Shadows raced past the pools of light cast by the windows of the Foreign Office. Other shadows streamed across the wide expanse of Horse Guards Parade. The streams converged, split apart, some moving rapidly along Birdcage Walk, others coming into the Mall. Men, mostly young, running with a wild exuberance.

"War!" they were yelling. "It's war!"

Martin and Galesby stepped back to keep from being bowled over by the frantic rush towards Buckingham Palace which was now blazing with lights. Roger grabbed Charles excitedly by the arm.

"Come on, Charles! Come on!"

And then the crowd swallowed them. They were one with it, borne along.

A middle-aged man, red-faced and puffing, ran out of the shadows of Waterloo Place.

"Is it war?" he shouted. "Is it war?"

"Yes, you damned fool," Galesby said. "It is."

Book Two

On, marching men, on
To the gates of death with song.
Sow your gladness for earth's reaping,
So you may be glad, though sleeping.
Strew your gladness on earth's bed.
So be merry, so be dead.

CHARLES HAMILTON SORLEY (1895-1915)

I

Major-General Sir Julian Wood-Lacy, v.c., c.v.o., stood beside his staff car on a low hill in the shadow of a derelict windmill. The road to Maubeuge lay below, the poplars lining it standing motionless in the heat, their leaves white with dust. The army had been moving up the road from Le Cateau since dawn and had ground the surface to a chalky powder. The general's division was coming along, the first battalion of the Lancashire regiment almost abreast of him now, the Royal West Kent behind them followed by three batteries of field artillery. The rest of the division was far down the road, a crawling line of khaki barely discernible through the dust. Two squadrons of the 19th Hussars, the troopers dismounted to spare the horses, moved across the skyline of a distant hill. By God, the general thought, rendered dumb from emotion that choked him, what a wonder!

The division had been on the move for three days, dawn to dusk across the rolling plains of Northern France. Three days of gruelling route march from the port of Boulogne under a pitiless August sun, and now here they were at last, a mere ten miles from the Belgian frontier. The general removed his cap from his balding head and waved it vigorously. The colonel of the Lancs, riding in front of his leading company on a sorrel horse, waved back, then turned to shout something at the men striding along behind him.

The infantry, by Harry! The general replaced his cap and stiffened as though about to salute his King. God, how he loved the infantry. And there they were, the battalions of his division, marching at ease, rifles slung, dust-streaked, uniforms black with sweat, whistling, some playing mouth organs or jew's harps, but every man Jack of them keeping in step and in unwavering columns of four. The general was sixty-one years of age and had been an infantryman since his seventeenth year, when he had joined the old 24th Foot as a subaltern. God! How many roads had he marched along in Zululand, Egypt, the Sudan, India? Uncountable miles. He could remember the hardships of those stony ways, the poor food and the stinking roadside water, the ranks dropping like flies that terrible September on the road from Jalalabad. All that was changed. Now, behind every company in each battalion came the horse-drawn transport wagons loaded with supplies, an ambulance wagon and the field cookers, comforting plumes of smoke drifting from the stovepipes.

The passing men looked towards the low hill and burst into a shout, "Are we downhearted? NO-O-O." The sound of the company's voices rocketed up to the general like a burst of cannon fire. And then the men broke into song, the music-hall ditty that the British Expeditionary Force had taken for its own: "*It's a long way to Tipperary . . . it's a long way to go . . .*"

Succeeding units kept the verses going, rank after rank, the Wiltshires and the Royal Irish, the Highland Light Infantry and the Middlesex Regiment, sweated, sunburnt faces turned towards the hill where "Old Woody" stood saluting them, yes, by God, until the last of his nineteen thousand men had passed by – or at least come into view.

"*Goodbye, Piccadilly, farewell, Leicester Square . . . it's a long, long way to Tipperary, but my heart's right there.*"

The château at Longueville shone silvery white under the moon, a fairyland castle with conical towers and pointed spires. It was the temporary headquarters of the Third Division, Second Corps, of the B.E.F. and the cobblestoned court-yard was crowded with staff cars, tethered horses and the motorcycles and bicycles of dispatch riders and battalion runners. Captain Fenton Wood-Lacy rode his tired horse under the graceful, wrought-iron arch that spanned the stone columns of the gateway, showing his identity papers to the sergeant of the guard and then dismounted and led his mount to the horselines where a cheerful farrier corporal offered to wipe the beast down and give him a good feed. Fenton handed him some cigarettes for his trouble and then walked stiffly towards the terraced stone steps of the château.

The entrance hall was a place of bedlam. Signallers were struggling to set up their telephone equipment in one corner and staff officers hurried up and down a baroque marble staircase, while clusters of company and battalion commanders stood about in glowering impatience. Fenton felt conspicuous among so many majors, colonels and brigadiers, even more so when Colonel Archibald Blythe, General Wood-Lacy's A.D.C., spotted him and cut through the crowd of expostulating brass with a deaf ear.

"Ah, Captain," the colonel said, pumping Fenton's hand, "glad you received the message. The general's most anxious to talk to you. Come along upstairs."

Fenton ignored the glares of his superiors as the elderly colonel, who looked more like a professor of Greek than a soldier, led him up the winding staircase to the second floor and ushered him into a large room.

"How about a whisky?"

Fenton made a futile dab at his dust-streaked khakis. "I'd like that *and* a clothes brush."

"Good Lord, no," the colonel said. "Dusty uniforms and dirty boots are strictly *de rigueur* in this division. I believe your uncle would court-martial any officer who showed up in clean kit." He gave Fenton a pat on the arm. "Dammed good to see you again, lad. Just stroll about and I'll send for a bottle and some Vichy. His nibs'll be along in time."

"How is the old boy?"

"Happy as a lark in spring. He was planning his retirement two months ago and now he's leading a full strength division against Fritz. Rather makes one ponder."

Fenton walked slowly around the room, a gallery filled with bucolic paintings and *objets d'art*. The château of a cultured man. A soldier brought whisky, Vichy water and glasses and Fenton made himself a stiff drink and sat down on an impossibly delicate Louis XIV chair to enjoy it. He was several degrees past weariness, having been in the saddle since dawn. The men of his company were even wearier, having been foot-slogging since dawn, but at least they were asleep by now in and around the haystacks of Neuf-Mesnils.

He had just finished the drink and was contemplating having

another when the general came striding into the room. His uniform, Fenton noted, was suitably dust-ridden. He jumped to his feet, shifted the empty glass from right to left hand and made a proper, if hasty, salute.

"At ease, boy, at ease." Sir Julian faced his nephew and smiled broadly. "By thunder, but you're a sight to behold. Dirty as a collier. Glad to see the Guards doing honest soldiering for a change."

"Well, sir, it's good to be out of a red coat, I'll say that."

"Yes, by God, I bet it is." He clapped Fenton on the shoulders with both hands. "Damn, but it's nice to see you, boy. How's young Roger?"

"Hurrying to enlist, last I saw of him."

The general tugged at his bristly, walrus mustache. "Jolly good for him, but this flap'll be over by the time he gets his uniforms tailored. Our Teutonic friends bit off a bit more than they can chew. They'll be scurrying back across the Rhine before the leaves fall."

"Do you think so, sir?"

He leaned forward and lowered his voice a notch. "I *know* so. They've been taking fearful losses at Liège and they'll be taking worse if they try to storm the forts at Namur. Those Belgians are fighting like terriers. By God, I hope we get a crack at 'em, but I'm afraid they'll pull in their horns and rush back to cover their centre. The Frogs have been on the attack since this morning, towards Morhange and Saarebourg. They should be deep into Lorraine by this time tomorrow and Fritz will be in bloody hot water. Never did think much of this tactic of theirs, thinning the centre and throwing all their power on their right wing. Bloody damned silly, if you ask me. The Frog first and second armies will cut through Fritz's belly like hot knives through wax. How about another whisky?"

"Only if you'll join me, sir."

"Sorry, lad. Can't take the time. Got a devil's amount of work to do." He folded his arms and rocked slowly back and forth on his heels. "I shall be brief, Fenton, and to the point. I've just arranged your transfer to my staff."

Fenton glanced away from his uncle's bright, piercing eyes.

"That smacks a bit of nepotism, wouldn't you say?"

167

"Smacks? Why, good Lord, it positively reeks of it. But let lesser tongues wag if they will. My senior staff are all for it. We move north into Belgium tomorrow, the entire army. I suppose you can visualise what that means: ninety thousand men on the move and hardly one decent map among all of 'em. Your brigade is supposed to stay in close contact with my right flank. That might be a bit tricky because of the roads and the terrain. I need a trustworthy liaison officer, someone who won't rub the Guard's brigadier the wrong way, if you get my drift."

"I do, yes, sir."

"You're just the chap for the job. Blythe will give you a map showing our intended position by the evening of the twenty-second and indicating where the Guards Brigade should be at that time. Your job is to make bloody sure they're in that position. If they're not, then I must know exactly where they are so I don't leave my flank dangling in the blue. The signallers aren't laying wire except along the line of march. I can pick up the telephone and ring through to Calais or even Paris, but I can't bloody well speak to anyone five miles to my right or left. I hope you don't resent my turning you into a messenger boy?"

"No, sir, not at all."

"Good. It's settled then. Fortify yourself with another whisky and then go over the details with Blythe." His hard, brown hand shot out and squeezed Fenton's arm. "By Gad, it's good to have you with me. I made you my second-in-command when you were eight years old. Do you remember?"

"Yes, sir," Fenton said, grinning. "And Roger was adjutant."

"Wooden sword, paper hat and all."

Colonel Blythe appeared in the doorway and coughed discreetly for attention.

"The battalion commanders are assembled, sir . . ."

"Right," the general said, snapping out of his sudden reverie. "Take our new young thruster in hand, there's a good chap." He turned abruptly and strode out of the room, his spurred boots pounding a brisk tattoo on the landing.

Colonel Blythe smiled faintly. "Comforting sound."

"He certainly exudes confidence."

"Yes, and we should be grateful for that. The troops are

cheery enough, and cocky as hell, but except for Old Woody
the high command is as nervous as a maiden aunt in a men's
smoking room." He poured himself a whisky and downed it
neat. "The French Fifth Army is off to our right somewhere, but
there's no communication between them and us, no co-
operation of any kind. They may be massed along the Sambre
and then again they may not. They may be about to attack
Fritz and then again they may be planning to fall back. No one
knows for sure. Nor do we have the foggiest idea what Fritz is
up to. There may be two German corps ahead of us or two field
armies, but I dare say we'll find out soon enough." He drew a
map from a leather case fastened to his belt and handed it to
Fenton. "We start north at dawn tomorrow. Our corps area
will go along the canal from Condé to Mons. Third Division
H.Q. will be a couple of miles south of Mons, at Frameries. We
want you up there with the advance party. When battalion
areas have been established and you can place them on the
map, you're to scurry over to First Corps and make certain the
Guards Brigade has reached Villers-St. Ghislain and that they
have at least two batteries of eighteen pounders covering the
road from Thieu – if there *is* a road. The maps are bloody useless when it comes to minor details like that." He ran a hand
through his thinning, grey hair. "Lord, what a way to go to
war."

D Company was in bivouac in a field, most of the men rolled
up in their blankets beside the haystack, but a few sprawled on
the ground, smoking and talking. The company had been
brought up to full strength with reserves, two hundred and
forty men in four platoons, and Fenton had hoped to lead it.
But strict adherence to custom had prevailed; only majors to
command companies. The majors would have preferred the
captains to have had the job. Most of them were well into their
thirties and some, like Major Horace Middlebanks who was
now in active command of D Company, had been on extended
leave for months, Middlebanks on his estate in Ireland where
he raised steeplechase horses and distilled whisky. Too much
sampling of the latter had played havoc with his liver and he

was far from joyous to see his second-in-command pack up to move out.

"Hells bells, Fenton," he grumbled, pacing the tiny farmhouse room they shared as a billet. "I really feel rotten."

Fenton shoved his gear into a canvas kit bag and tried to ignore the major stalking back and forth in his underwear.

"Go and see the M.O."

The major snorted in disgust. "All he'll do is give me one of those blue pills, or yellow pills – anyway, whatever the bloody colour they'll keep me chained to a latrine for a week. It just isn't fair for me to lose you now. What if I ruddy well collapse in the saddle tomorrow and have to be sent back to Boulogne to see a real doctor?"

"Then Ashcroft will take over. He's a good man."

"He dosesn't have the experience," the major said with a snort.

"None of us have the experience, do we? I mean, this isn't manoeuvres. Have you ever heard a gun fired in anger? No, neither have I . . . neither has Ashcroft. What difference does it make? Go back to sleep, Horace, and stop worrying about everything."

The major tossed and turned in restless slumber, grunting and groaning. It didn't matter to Fenton. He found it impossible to sleep anyway, his brain wouldn't allow it. Thoughts swirled around in a hodge-podge of vivid images. It seemed unbelievable that he had been in France for less than a week. Six days ago he had been in Southampton waiting to board the transport ship. The Marquess of Dexford had been permitted to come to the docks and had brought gifts for his son Andrew embarking with the 4th Cavalry Brigade and for "*my future son-in-law*".

He sat up in the hard, narrow bed and looked through a hazy mica window at a distorted image of the moon. Lord Dexford's gifts had been appreciated – a box of tinned delicacies from Harrods, Abdullah cigarettes, a bottle of whisky and a beautifully made, but totally impractical pocket pistol. He had traded it to a captain in A Company for some extra socks. Among the gifts had been a letter from Winifred.

*

My dearest Fenton,

God protect you in this hour of trial. I know you will be brave and daring and help achieve a quick and glorious victory. I am most vexed at Germany for starting this war, but they shall soon rue it. All of the newspapers predict that it will be over by Christmas. I pray they are correct in that assumption and that we will be tangoing at a victory ball on New Year's Eve.

Ever . . . Your Winifred

He groaned as loudly as the liverish major. *Your* Winifred! It was a struggle to recall her face.

He was dressed and out before dawn, walking across the stubble field towards the crossroads where a staff car was waiting. Private Webber, his batman, trailed along behind him carrying the bags and whistling softly to himself. Happy to be leaving, Fenton was thinking. The idea of his officer being attached to staff was pleasing to Webber. No more thirty-miles-a-day marches, no more sleeping on the hard ground. No wonder he was whistling. The tune was certainly appropriate to their change in station and Fenton mouthed the words: *"I'm Burlington Bertie, I rise at ten thirty . . . and go for a stroll like a toff . . ."*

"What's that, sir?" Webber stood still, head cocked to one side. There was nothing to be heard other than the thin, distant call of a nightingale from the dark woods that bordered the field, but something had moved against them, a pulse of air that was not wind, that could be sensed rather than felt. Then sound came, dull, persistent thuds far off to the north-east, a rumble of thunder bumping the horizon. Sheet lightning flickered against a sky that was beginning to pale.

"Blimey," Webber said, sniffing the air. "Don't smell like rain."

Fenton walked slowly on, watching the sky, the dim, shimmering orange and red glow that was, after six years of being a soldier, his first glimpse of war. Not his war . . . not yet. The heavy guns were miles east, at Charleroi or even Namur. It could be French or Belgian fire and the German army might be reeling back from those withering blasts, but doubt gnawed at

171

him. His palms became wet and he stuck his hands into his pockets and strolled to the car with studied nonchalance.

The boat train from Cherbourg was seven hours late arriving in Paris, having been shunted off the main track half a dozen times to allow troop trains to speed by. When it finally reached the Gare St. Lazare there were no porters available and the passengers were obliged to carry their own luggage into the station. Soldiers thronged the platforms while harried sergeants and corporals struggled to sort the men into their respective companies and battalions. Bugles blew. Regimental colours were unfurled to serve as rallying points and gradually the soldiers moved out of the station in orderly lines, before more troop trains arrived to add to the confusion. A band standing in the square in front of the church of St. Augustin played the "Marseillaise" and the "Sambre et Meuse" on bugle, drum and fife as the troops marched down the rue de la Pépinière into the Boulevard Haussmann. Thousands of Parisians thronged the pavements cheering the long columns of men in their blue coats, red trousers and red képis.

To Martin Rilke it was a vision of childhood. He was seven years old again, standing with his mother and her cousin Bette on the Champs Elysées. The fourteenth of July. Bands and marching soldiers, the giant horses of the *cuirassiers*, tall men riding them, steel breastplates and crested helmets gleaming in the sun. There were troops of *cuirassiers* now, turning out of the rue Pasquier to trail the infantry. They looked the same as they did then except for a covering of brown cloth over their horseplume helmets. A concession to *la guerre*.

Tom Ramsey, an artist for *Leslie's Weekly*, murmured in appreciation.

"Colourful . . . and old world. They look like they're ready to fight the battle of Sedan all over again."

"The *pantalon rouge* is sacred to the French Army," Martin said. "Although you'd think khaki would be more practical these days. Those red pants and hats are going to be easy to aim at."

Ramsey removed a curved briar pipe from his mouth and dug ash from the bowl with his finger.

172

"I was just thinking the same thing, but it's none of my business how they want to dress for war. Anyway, it's sure going to make my pictures a damned sight prettier." He stretched his arms in an expansive gesture, embracing the scene. "Paris! City of light and beauty. Red trousers and blue coats against chestnut trees. I'll do watercolours of regiments of *cuirassiers* and battalions of *pantalons rouge* in the gardens of the Tuileries."

Martin laughed. "What if they aren't there?"

The artist shrugged. "So what? Artistic licence. Anyway, if they're not there they should be." He breathed deeply. "Paris. Like coming home for me."

"Hey, you said you'd never been here."

"I haven't. Took my training in Philadelphia, but boy, have I ever dreamed of this town. I guess I've looked at a million pictures of the place. I know it by heart. I can't tell you how much I envy you, Rilke, *born* here. My God."

That fact had impressed all of the eleven American newspapermen who had been on the train. Most of them spoke French in varying degrees of ineptness, could ask for simple things – a cup of coffee, a glass of wine, the direction to the lavatory – but more complex thoughts had been beyond their abilities to express. Their papers had arranged for interpreters to meet them in Paris and Martin had been their spokesman during the interminable train journey as not one porter, conductor or waiter in the dining car could, or would, speak English.

"Why?" Jasper King of the *New York Herald* had wanted to know. "This is a boat train, for cryin' out loud. They must be used to English-speaking passengers."

"They all understand English," Martin had explained after conversing with a conductor in faultless French. "They're just irked at Americans. There was an editorial in one of the Paris papers about America's decision to maintain an impartial neutrality and to honour trade commitments with Germany. They're just giving us the needle."

Along with his linguistic ability Martin had been pumped for information about Paris: the best restaurants, the location of various hotels, the metro system. There was nothing he could tell them. Paris was an alien city to him. All he could remember with any clarity were a few streets near the Luxembourg and the small park off the rue Campagne where he used to fly kites with his friend Claude. Paris was not his home town. He would have traded the Champs Elysées for one block on State Street.

But here he was, seated in one of the taxis provided by the French minister of information, an army officer riding in the leading taxi, the little cavalcade wending its way through the twisting streets of Paris to the Quai d'Orsay, to the grim stone building housing the ministry. His reason for being there was in the form of a letter in his attaché case, a letter that he had been asked to present to the third deputy assistant to the minister of information along with his passport. The letter was from Comstock Harrington Briggs authorising Martin Rilke to serve as sole European correspondent for the Chicago *Express*. The deputy assistant solemnly checked a list before him on his desk, a list of those newspapers in the United States that had revealed pro-German attitudes. There were quite a few of them in Milwaukee, Chicago, St. Louis, Philadelphia and New York. The *Express* was not on the black list.

"You may go in and see the minister, Monsieur Rilke."

They were all acceptable to the deputy, as the deputy knew they would be since their credentials had been checked in London before visas had been issued. It was a formality and the deputy assistant was a stickler for formality.

"We are at war, monsieur," he had said icily to the war correspondent of the *New York Times* who had had the temerity to lose his patience when the deputy had taken ten minutes to study his papers.

"Damn it, sir," the *Times* man had blustered. "I know it. Why do you think I came to France?"

"You did not come at our request, monsieur. I can assure you of that."

The chill deepened when the minister of information himself, a man of great girth and regal bearing, entered his chambers nearly an hour after the last newspaperman had been ushered into the room and told to wait. He offered no apologies for the delay.

174

"Gentlemen," he said, speaking English with barely a trace of accent. "Let me welcome you to Paris. I hope your stay here will be pleasant. This ministry will do everything in its power to provide you with up-to-date information on the progress of the war. Let me caution you on the use of the telegraph service and the postal service. Censorship has been imposed. Nothing pertaining to the war may be sent out of the country unless it has been approved by this office and stamped accordingly. No foreign journalist may venture into the Zone of the Armies without the written permission of Marshal Joffre. Such permission is not likely to be granted in the foreseeable future."

The silence was total. Finally, the war correspondent of the *New York Times*, a man with an international reputation for his coverage of every war since 1890, cleared his throat and got to his feet.

"Your Excellency, do you mean to say that none of us can visit the front? That we are forbidden to view with our own eyes the current battles in Lorraine?"

The minister's tone was bland. "There is no necessity for it, sir. We shall provide you with that data. Captain de Lange who travelled with you from the station will keep you abreast of all developments. The official communiqués will be at your disposal every afternoon at four o'clock in the Military Information Centre on the second floor. Room Number 225. Captain de Lange will give you today's communiqué which you are free to transmit to your journals. If there is any way I can be of further service to you, do not hesitate to call upon me. Good day, gentlemen."

And then he was gone, striding as regally out of the room as he had entered it. A solid oak door closed noiselessly behind him. Captain de Lange, a tall, thin, grey-haired man, who wore a pince-nez on the very tip of his nose, walked stiffly from the back of the room and occupied the spot vacated by the minister. He removed a single sheet of paper from the breast pocket of his uniform jacket and unfolded it.

"The following communiqué has been received from General Castelnau in Nancy. The Second Army, in close coordination with the First Army under General Dubail, has everywhere been successful in its drive towards Morhange. Our

175

infantry has inflicted grievous losses on the enemy and has re-captured many towns on the sacred soil of the lost province . . . the flag of France flying above the town halls of the following places for the first time since 1870: Burthecourt, Moyenvic, Lezey, Donnelay, Marsal, Salival, St. Medard. Château Salins is expected to fall by dawn tomorrow. Our losses have been insignificant and reports from field commanders indicate that the German Sixth Army is in a disorderly retreat. On the Alsace front, General Pau is in firm possession of Mulhausen and expects to reach the Rhine within three days." He folded the paper and placed it back into his pocket. "That is the termination of today's communiqué. Copies will be available. Are there any questions?"

Baker of the *Journal-American* stood up. "We heard a rumour in Calais that the Germans are well past Liège in force. That they crushed the forts there with some exceptionally powerful, highly mobile siege guns and are approaching Namur in strength, bringing these guns with them. It seems to me that if the Belgian forts at Namur should fall –"

Captain de Lange interrupted with a tight little smile. "Let me advise you not to pay heed to defeatist rumours. There are a great many German spies on the loose. We are discovering them daily and putting a speedy end to their intrigues. The truth will be found in Room 225 every day at four p.m. Are there any more questions? No? Then let me bid you a good afternoon."

It was evening when they left the ministry and walked across the broad courtyard towards the waiting taxis. Martin shared a cab with Tom Ramsey and three other men, one of whom was struggling to unfold a large map of France which he had bought in Cherbourg. The taxi crossed the Seine on the Pont Alexandre III and plunged into the brilliantly lit boulevards beyond the Petit Palais. Pavement cafés were jammed with people. Soldiers and pretty girls strolled arm-in-arm under the street lamps and the traffic along the Boulevard des Capucines was at a standstill. The city was in fever of holiday.

"Got it!" the newspaper man said grimly. "Here they are, those towns he told us about. Burthecourt, Moyenvic, Salival; why, they aren't *towns*, just dots on the map. There may be a

176

pigpen or two but there sure as hell is no *town hall* in any of 'em."

"I think we made a mistake in coming to Paris," another man said. "We should have gone straight into Belgium by way of Holland. They're just going to feed us a daily dose of pap."

"That's all *Leslie's* is after," Ramsey said. "Pretty pictures of marching soldiers and cheering crowds. They think this war is going to be nothing but a lot of sabre rattling and martial posturing. What does your paper expect from you, Rilke?"

Martin shrugged. "General background stuff, as objective as possible. We have a lot of German-American readers."

The letter from Briggs had come as a surprise to Martin, but the editor had been candid:

. . . as long as you are already in England there doesn't seem to be any point in sending another man from here, although Jack Pierson expressed a desire for the job. You speak French and German which was another point in your favour. Martin, just keep your eyes open and write what you see. Don't slant your reports one way or the other. Most people I've talked to here believe this war is based on an economic struggle between Germany, France and England and there is a good deal of sympathy for Germany's position. I had a long talk with a brigadier-general in the Illinois National Guard and it is his opinion that the war will last only four to five weeks and that the French army, being in his view, seriously antiquated, will fold and that the token English force will go back across the channel without ever firing a shot at the Prussians. He does not believe Germany will occupy any part of France, but will withdraw their armies in a hurry. If they don't, they'll be overrun by the Russians in the east. The way he sees it – and you can take this for what it is worth – is that the Germans' only intent is to eliminate France as a military threat to them. To be frank, I don't think the general knows any more about this war than the guy on the street – who knows nothing. I sure as hell don't understand it.

You're a sensible young fellow with no axe to grind, so just remain objective and write down what you see. Don't fall prey to rumours which always abound in a war and take all official communiqués with a grain of salt. I discovered that when I was covering the Boer war for the old *Gazette*. I will arrange monetary matters, salary and expenses, through American Express. I would suggest that you spend no more than ten days in France and then go to Berlin via Switzerland and get the German viewpoint. I want your articles to be as balanced as possible.

P.S. I saw your uncle at the Union Club and he wishes you well. He picks Cleveland to win the pennant.

There seemed to be little point in staying in Paris. He spent the night, wandered about the city the next day with Ramsey, who was delighted with every stone and made innumerable sketches, then went to the ministry at four o'clock along with a score of other reporters and listened to Captain de Lange read a communiqué.

". . . Chateau Salins and the town of Dieuze were captured this morning by General Castelnau's Second Army. However, a strategic withdrawal was advised by Marshal Joffre in order to consolidate the efforts of the First Army's drive on Saarebourg . . ."

An English journalist was foolish enough to ask a question. "Was this withdrawal in the face of German counter-attacks?"

Captain de Lange looked piqued. "If there had been an enemy counter-attack it would have been mentioned in the communiqué."

The line to Basle passed through the French Zone of the Armies and only a few civilians had been issued travel permits. Even with papers properly stamped and signed Martin was given no guarantee that he would be allowed on any of the trains rumbling out of the Gare de l'Est, trains that left every fifteen minutes filled with troops, horses and supplies. It was five o'clock in the morning before he and twenty sombre Swiss nationals were given reluctant permission to board a small passenger car that had been attached to the rear of a freight train loaded with field guns and *caissons*. The train groaned slowly eastwards along the Marne, stopping every few miles on sidings to allow faster trains filled with soldiers to go by. Late that afternoon they had reached Epernay and the wagons of seventy-five millimetre guns were uncoupled and hitched to another train heading north for Reims. No one at the station seemed to care what happened to the detached passenger carriage, although a railway official made a vague reference to another train due in that night from Paris and bound for the Swiss frontier.

The carriage was hot, the Swiss were sullen, there was nothing to eat and only lukewarm water to drink and so Martin decided to leave. Judging by the heavy rail traffic going north, the war lay in that direction and he just might be able to see something of it. He was so deep inside the Zone of the Armies that no one he enountered in the crowded station questioned his right to be there, even though he looked like a commerical traveller, a lone civilian in a sea of uniforms. While having a meal of sausage, bread, cheese and wine in an *estaminet* near the depot, an artillery major pulled a chair up to his table and sat down.

"Are you in the chamber of deputies?" the man asked.

"No," Martin said, "the ministry of information."

The major toyed with his moustache which was heavily waxed.

"Information, eh? Well, I'll tell you something that you can pass on to your superiors. It is cannon and only cannon that the Boche will have any respect for. The minister of war has given us a good field gun, but we must have bigger and better ones."

"I'll make a note of that."

The major twirled the points of his moustache into firm needles.

"They say it is the infantry who will drive the Boche into the Rhine, but I say it is the cannon."

"I agree with you wholeheartedly. Have some wine."

"Thank you," the major said, reaching for the bottle. "You seem like a fine fellow. Civilians don't understand the first thing about war. You mention cannon to them and they stare at you blankly. I can tell that you are different."

"I understand the need for cannon. Absolutely."

The major drank carefully from the bottle and then wiped a drop of wine from his lower lip.

"I admire a civil servant who understands the needs of the military. However, I do not believe that you are a civil servant. A man from the ministry would not wear a brown jacket and checked trousers. He would wear a black suit and a shirt with a stiff collar. Also, you speak with a slight accent that is not familiar to me. Are you Swiss?"

"American – of a French mother."

"And you are . . . ?"

"A journalist."

"Ah." He took another drink of wine and then leaned forward across the table and lowered his voice. "Papa Joffre does not like journalists. No one in the high command likes them one bit. Are you trying to get up to the war?"

"That was my hope."

"Then I will take you. And in payment for my generosity, you will, please, inform the world that it is cannon that wins battles. I will give you an artilleryman's cloak to cover yourself with, and a képi. My battery is entrained and we leave for the Ardennes in an hour. We're the 27th Regiment of Artillery in the Third Colonial Corps. Veterans, I can tell you. We've used our beauties more than once in Morocco. Fifteen rounds of shrapnel a minute . . . bang . . . bang . . . bang."

Trains moved liked snails along the line north of Reims. On the second day after leaving Epernay they crossed the River Aisne and the major's battery was taken off the train, hooked up to the horse teams and put on the long, tree-lined road to Mazières. Martin rode in one of the transport wagons that creaked along behind the clattering gun teams, nestled down among the men's packs and jumble of other gear. He wished he had brought his camera to France, but the French consulate in London had advised him against it. His eyes must be the camera lens, the notebook on his knee the photographic film. He jotted down impressions to be fleshed out later:

*

Montigny-sur-Vence. August 22nd. A small village of white-washed stone houses, thatched roofs. Orchards beyond the village. Vineyards covering the low hills. Peasants in smocks working trees and vines and not turning their heads as the endless columns of troops pass through the village and ford the sluggish, weedy little river. Dragoons on black horses, *cuirassiers* on greys. Infantry in great, untidy masses, like a crowd pouring out of a baseball stadium. They wear blue wool greatcoats despite the heat, the tails of the coats pinned back. Their red trousers are chalky with dust. The officers carry swords and many of them wear white gloves . . . French officers, after all, *très chic*.

Fontaine-Gery is a few miles up the road. Rolling hills, heavily wooded. The Ardennes is a dark green cloud-mass along the horizon. A dispatch rider on a bicycle catches up with the battery and the major has ordered the guns pulled off the road next to an ancient church and a crumbling cemetery wall. A Zouave band stands in the sunpatches and shadows of an orchard. They wear yellow Turkish trousers, vivid blue jackets and red fezes. Like parrots among the trees. They play the "Sambre et Meuse" march on drums and fifes. Troops cheer and weep. We are not far from Sedan. Germany ground the face of France into this road in 1870 and now her sons are coming back to make them pay for it.

There is a sound like rolling thunder ahead of us. We have heard it since dawn, but intermittently, extremely far away. Now it is closer, a continuous bumping and thumping as though hundreds of empty freight cars are rolling back and forth inside a long tunnel.

Congestion on the road. Peasants from the north, driven from their farms by the fighting that must be raging ten or fifteen miles away, push against the on-coming troops. They pull carts and wagons loaded with their belongings. Children sit crying on top of bundles of goods. The refugees are oblivious of the soldiers who yell at them and try to make them leave the roads. Mixed in with the refugees are wounded soldiers. Some are in horse-drawn ambulance wagons. Others walk as though in a daze clutching bloody bandages. The troops seem embarrassed by the sight of them. A colonel lying in the back of a wagon with a blood-caked bandage wrapped clumsily around his chest mutters "*C'est catastrophe*", over and over.

Hannogne-St. Martin. The battery has been moved at the gallop along dirt lanes and across fields to this village, which is seven miles closer to the front. It is late afternoon and the beech trees and poplars are pale gold in the waning sun. The guns are drawn up on a low hill screened by thick clumps of grape vines. Seventy-five millimetre guns. An ammunition limber is beside each cannon. A seven-foot metal ladder has been bolted to one of the limbers and the major stands on the top rung behind a narrow metal shield, powerful binoculars in his hands. He scans the woods and fields ahead of the battery and then shouts, "*Fantastique! Magnifique! C'est incroyable!*"

Martin put aside his notebook and climbed out of the transport wagon. The major was coming down the ladder, shouting out directions to the gunners for range, elevation and type of shell. He tossed the binoculars to Martin.

"Have a look! Oh, my God, the poor bastards of infantry!"

Martin climbed up the ladder and focused the binoculars. He could see French infantry advancing out of a valley and up the grassy slope of a hill towards a dark line of woods. They were in long lines, shoulder to shoulder and walking slowly, rifles held at the hips, the long bayonets catching the sun. Officers with drawn swords walked in front of them. The red and blue of their uniforms, the white gloves of the officers created a living flag, the tricolour rippling across the green hills of France. On they moved, a thousand or more in three waves. A hundred yards from the trees the first wave began to falter, to stumble and fall, to wither away as some unseen, unheard force scythed through them. They fell over in heaps and the second wave moved on over their bodies.

"Guns ready!" a sergeant cried out.

"Fire for range on command," the major shouted. He clambered up on top of the limber and stood on the ladder, holding on to Martin's waist and grabbing the binoculars from him. "Fire!"

A gun barked and a few seconds later the shell burst above the treetops. Leaves and small branches disappeared in a froth of debris. The infantry were still advancing, tumbling forwards, sinking to their knees, turning and twisting in a slow, silent dance of death.

"Machine guns," the major yelled. "The damned Boche! Down a hundred . . . fourteen degrees . . . Fire! Fire! Fire!"

Every gun in the battery began to slam shrapnel shells towards the tree-line four miles away; black bursts of smoke blossomed violently in the shadowed wood. Breech blocks clanged, empty shell cases rattled against the iron tailpieces of the guns. The artillery fire was accurate and devastating, but it was too late to save the soldiers. The Napoleonic formations had disappeared. There was nothing on the slope but rows of corpses raked in heaps, like haystacks, wounded struggling to crawl back down the hill and a few men running for cover, the tall grass rippling around them as machine-gun bullets mowed through it.

The major tugged at Martin's clothes. "Get down before you lose your head. Those damned Boche have cannons too."

A Renault whined up from the village in low gear. A colonel of artillery stood in front beside the driver, clutching on to the windshield.

"Drag your battery out, Duchamp," he shouted over the cracking reports of the guns. "The whole front's caving in. Pull back to Omicourt and be quick about it." He spotted Martin climbing down from the observation ladder, the civilian clothes showing under the artilleryman's cloak. "Who in God's name is that?"

The major shrugged. "An American, from Chicago."

The colonel tugged at his Van Dyck beard. "I won't ask you how he got here, Duchamp. I'm in no mood to listen to your tall tales. Get him into the car before someone shoots the bastard as a spy. I tell you it is all falling apart. A débâcle!"

There was a roaring sound above their heads, a short, sharp whistle and then a shell exploded in a patch of woods behind the village. The shock wave sent Martin stumbling off his feet. The noise cracked against his skull. Trees and soil rocketed upward in a cascade of smoke and flame.

"Howitzer!" Major Duchamp yelled. "Two hundred and ten millimetre! Those damned Boche!" He grabbed Martin and propelled him towards the car. "Write about *that*. Tell them we can't fight against two hundred and ten millimetre howitzers with our seventy-fives. Tell them —"

But what else the major wished him to tell was lost in the shriek of heavy shells, one following the other, the explosions rocking the hill. Geysers of earth and shattered trees blew upwards in a whirlwind of blinding flashes. A field gun lurched brokenly into a yawning, steaming hole. An ammunition limber began to explode, the hot rounds whirling off across the vineyard like giant catherine-wheels. Martin half fell, half dived into the back of the Renault. He felt the car turn and twist crazily as the driver gave it full throttle and spun the steering wheel. Martin lay on the floorboards, his face pressed against the bottom of the seat. Clods of dirt and bits of wood showered down on his back. Oh, God, he thought wildly, I wish I were on Maxwell Street . . . I wish I were on Maxwell Street.

2

"I'M AFRAID I'M LOST, SIR," THE DRIVER SAID.

"It's not your fault," Fenton said, scowling at his map. "That *was* Givry we passed through, wasn't it?"

"Yes, sir."

"It's the map then. Bloody work of fiction. This road doesn't go to Villers-St. Ghislain or anywhere near it."

The driver tapped his gloved hand against the steering wheel and whistled softly between his teeth.

"Stop that bloody whistling," Fenton snapped irritably.

He was sorry that he had lost his temper and thought of offering an apology. That wouldn't do, of course. One didn't apologise to a man in the ranks under any circumstances. Poor chap was only whistling in the dark. It was an eerie feeling being alone in the middle of God knows where. The road they were on might lead them straight into the German army for all they knew. Ninety thousand British troops in France, the French Fifth army off to their right somewhere, and not a man to be seen. It was damned discomforting. He settled back in the seat and glared at the map. Why would a cartographer mark a road that didn't exist? Perhaps one had been planned and the map maker had simply jumped the gun in marking it down. That was a possibility. They weren't on a road, not a proper *pavé*, more in the nature of a cow path that wouldn't have warranted inclusion on a map. He tried to figure out its eventual destination. Bray? Spiennes? A score of place names were clustered east of Mons. The path could lead to any one of them – or to none of them. He removed his cap and wiped his forehead with a handkerchief. Lord, it was hot, the noonday sun beating down from a cloudless, brazen sky. His batman was groggy from the heat, slumped sideways in a listless, soggy bundle. Poor old Webber, far past his prime. The driver, Lance-Corporal Ackroyd, was a thin, wiry Londoner of the

Middlesex Regiment. He'd hold up all right. Fenton reached into his pocket and took out a tin of cigarettes.

"Care for a fag, corporal?

"Thank you, sir," the driver said, perking up noticeably. "Been 'alf dyin' for a smoke, sir."

"Take a handful of them."

The driver did as he was told. "Blimey. Abdullahs."

"Might just spoil your taste for Woodbines."

"Might at that, sir."

Fenton smiled and the man grinned back. A certain amount of familiarity was unavoidable. They were, in a manner of speaking, in the same boat. He lit the corporal's cigarette and then his own.

"Bloody dismal country."

"Yes, sir. Mucked up a bit."

It was an ominous landscape, chilling even in the brightness of an August day. Dank, overgrown patches of woodland, untilled fields, the sour smell of neglect. Weed-dotted slag heaps and conical structures of rotting timber marked the sites of abandoned coal shafts. This was the edge of the Borinage, coal, slate, and darkly polluted streams.

Fenton folded the map and slipped it into its case. "Drive on another couple of miles. We're bound to reach some sort of village that'll give us a fix."

Lance-Corporal Ackroyd put the car into gear and they rolled bumpingly along the narrow, deeply-rutted road, past eroded hills of slag, the edge of a gloomy wood and then into more open country, flat fields of unharvested oats stretching away on both sides of them. Ackroyd suddenly braked and pointed ahead.

"Look at that, sir! Comin' straight for us."

The aeroplane had side-slipped over a line of poplars and was flying towards them no more than thirty feet off the ground. It banked sharply and the pilot leaned far out of the cockpit and pointed towards the field.

"One of ours, sir?"

"Yes," Fenton said, studying the slow moving machine carefully. "An Avro, I think. What the hell keeps them in the air?"

186

"Thinkin' the same thing, sir. Looks like a Chinese laundry cart, don't it?"

The plane's tiny engine popped and fumed and the ungainly contraption of canvas, wood and wire made a sickening lurch, straightened up scant feet from the surface of the field and then glided to a perfect landing, no ng over slightly against the bamboo skids fastened in front o wheels.

Fenton and the corporal got out of the car and ran across the field. The pilot was climbing carefully out of the cockpit, threading his way through the maze of wires connecting the bottom wing with the top.

"Hallo, chaps," the pilot called out. "Any idea where I am exactly?"

"Only roughly," Fenton said. "You're somewhere between Givry and Villers-St. Ghislain. About eight miles east of Mons."

The pilot removed his leather helmet and scratched his head vigorously. He looked no more than eighteen years old to Fenton.

"Oh, I say. I thought I was *west* of Mons. No wonder I couldn't find the ruddy place. Been circlin' for hours, it seems. Can you spare some petrol? I'm down to my last few drops."

"There's a five-gallon tin in the boot," the corporal said.

"Thank the Lord. I can get to Le Cateau on that."

"Is it all right, sir?"

"Yes, of course," Fenton said. "Go and fetch it."

The corporal ran back towards the car and the pilot leaned wearily against the edge of the plane's lower wing.

"F. A. M. Weedlock here, Lieutenant Weedlock actually." He held out a grimy, oil-smeared hand. "And you are?"

"Fenton Wood-Lacy."

The pilot glanced at the pips on Fenton's sleeve. "Nice of you to help me, captain. I shall do you a good service. Turn your car around. There's absolutely nothing ahead of you but Huns. Bloody hordes of 'em."

"How far away?"

"Ten miles or so. I've been as far as Nivelles and Charleroi this morning. Germans on every road, crossing every field. Bloody bunch of locusts. Never seen anything like it. Flew very

187

low over 'em and the silly bastards waved at me. Thought it was quite a lark, they did."

Fenton drew out his map. "Where are they exactly?"

"Oh, Lord, *everywhere*." He drew his finger across the map, leaving a faint smear of oil. "From Charleroi all across to just north of Mons. There must be two hundred thousand of 'em. Looks like a grey river from the air. And artillery, miles and miles of horse-drawn gun transport. I've got to get my report to H.Q., if I can ruddy well find it."

"Yes," Fenton said drily. "I think they might be interested. See any French troops on our right?"

"Well, some of their cavalry – tossing plumes, breastplates shining in the sun – all that fancy dress rot. A few infantry, all going south. If our chaps are at Mons then their flank is in the air. I went up to ten thousand feet over Charleroi and I could see nothing but battle smoke from the Meuse. Poor old Frenchy must be catching hell. Looked as though their whole line of battle was caving in."

The pilot ate some cheese and bread from the hamper in the car while Ackroyd refuelled his plane. He then instructed the corporal on how to spin the propeller without decapitating himself and flew off, the plane rising as effortlessly as a swallow from the field. He made one stuttering turn around the car at a hundred feet and then headed south. They stood in the road and watched until the little plane was lost to view.

"Rather a pleasant way to travel," Fenton said quietly.

They reached the brick schoolhouse in the village of Frameries that was now Third Division H.Q. shortly after nightfall. The road to Mons was jammed with horse-drawn artillery and supply wagons, pipers of the Gordon Highlanders skirling away to help ease the tempers of the cursing drivers. Fenton dismissed Lance-Corporal Ackroyd and Webber for the night and then made his way through the building which was crowded with staff and line officers. There was an atmosphere of frenzied confusion, but Colonel Blythe assured Fenton that everything was firmly in hand.

"I suppose you know by now what's ahead of us," Fenton said.

The colonel nodded. "We've been getting reports in all day. It's the bulk of a German army . . . Von Kluck's, we believe. The field marshal rang up from Le Cateau to tell us there's no more than two corps facing us, but we know better. The cavalry wallahs have been out all day and doing damned well too. They even brought in some prisoners. We're horribly out-numbered, but the old boy convinced the corps commander that we can stop them along the canal. I hope to God he's right. How are the Guards settling in at Villers-St. Ghislain? Do they have enough artillery in support?"

"They may, wherever they are. We finally found that damned village after driving around in circles for bloody hours, but there are no troops there. Not one. Your flank is, if you'll pardon the expression, naked."

"Good God," the colonel muttered. "Old Woody won't be happy to hear that, although I imagine he won't be terribly surprised either. High Command is trying to run this show from thirty miles back, abysmal roads, faulty telephone wires, wretched maps. It's a bloody balls-up, that's what it is. Well, I'll go and tell him the good news. We have a mess of sorts down that hall. Get yourself a hot meal and a whisky. It may be your last of both for some time to come."

Cooks were opening five-pound tins of stew and heating the contents over an oil fire. Foxe's Fancy Old Irish Stew, Fenton noted wryly. He wondered what Archie would be dining on at his London club. Not stew like his own, surely, although it was certainly tasty enough. He ate two helpings and washed it down with a large whisky and soda. One of the other officers who sat squeezed at the long table which had been designed for children's legs eyed him sourly.

"Where the hell is the First Corps? Should be in position on our right flank by now, shouldn't it?"

"Should be. But it's not, and it won't. There's nothing on *their* right flank. The French are falling back all along the line."

The glum officer toyed with his stew. "Could have told 'em that. Knew it would happen. We should have landed at Antwerp and let the bloody Frogs fight their own war."

So much for allied co-operation and friendship, Fenton thought as he sipped his whisky. But why should officers of the

189

Second Corps of the British Expeditionary Force have a feeling of comradeship with the French army when they didn't have it with their own First Corps? A major in the Manchester Regiment was glaring at his Coldstream Guard badges with open hostility. Fenton downed his whisky and left the room without bothering to thank anyone for the hospitality of the mess.

The H.Q. was cleared by one a.m. as battalion commanders and their aides returned to their units. General Wood-Lacy, slurping away at a mug of steaming tea, continued to pace slowly back and forth in front of a wall map, a pathetically inadequate map but the best one available. Fenton sat behind a child's desk in the schoolroom and watched his uncle in silence. After ten minutes the general turned away from the map and sat on the edge of a desk, tapping a wooden pointer idly against his booted leg.

"Well, Fenton, tomorrow will be all battle and Second Corps will go it alone. No matter. We can cut it. We're blessed with Smith-Dorrien as corps commander. A good infantryman. Knew him well in Africa. Zulus almost scuppered him when he was a subaltern as they almost scuppered me. By God, this division won't let him down."

"What do I do, sir? Seems to me I'm a bit of a fifth wheel around here now."

"Oh, I dare say I shall keep you busy scurrying about. I can't send you back, can I? Lord knows where your brigade is now; stuck along the road somewhere well out of it. No, no, you'll stay attached to my staff for a few more days and earn your keep. You may also learn something about soldiering . . . that it isn't all walking Buck guard, seducing women and playing cards."

Church bells tolled for early Mass, but that was the last peaceful sound to be heard that Sunday morning. Fenton slept fitfully in the schoolroom, hunkered down at a desk. He woke to the sound of the bells and the distant clatter of rifle fire. Mess orderlies brought dixies of tea into the rooms for the sleepy-eyed staff officers. The field telephones began to ring.

"The Fourth Middlesex report contact with the enemy at Obourg Bridge."

A map pin was placed on the spot. Other reports came in and the sound of distant small arms fire became more rapid and intense . . .

"The West Kents and the Royal Fusiliers are heavily engaged . . . Two Fritz battalions attacking Le Bois Haut . . ."

By ten in the morning German artillery began to open up and the telephone network to the line battalions started to break down as shell fire cut the wires. Messengers and battalion runners came and went. More dixies of hot tea were brought in, along with bully beef and bread. Fenton sat in a corner of the operations room, drinking tea and smoking cigarettes. He felt out of things, a useless mouth to feed. He walked out on to the school playground in the afternoon and watched the pall of smoke which lay heavily along the northern skyline. The towering slag heaps of the area chopped off visibility to a few hundred yards in any direction. A drab and miserable landscape, but people lived there, built homes, married, raised children and sent them off each morning to this little dark brick school. Now shells were screaming out of the hot sky and thundering into the earth a mile from the village. The little houses stood waiting for the storm to reach them. Their occupants were gone or leaving, bundles of belongings piled on to carts, into ancient, wheezing motor cars, in perambulators and two-wheeled dog carts. The shells inched closer to the village and a haze of red dust from blasted houses obscured the sun. Chunks of debris splattered the playgound and the schoolhouse windows were starting to shatter under the heavy concussions. It seemed foolish to stand in the open with a good part of Frameries falling about him, so Fenton walked casually back towards the school, aware that a platoon of Highlanders at the far end of the playground, and prudently under cover, were watching him. It would not do, he thought grimly, for a captain in the Coldstream Guards to run. A piper with a sense of humour blew a few notes of "Johnnie Cope" "*Hey, Johnnie Cope, are ye wauking yet?*" The platoon laughed in appreciation and Fenton doffed his cap to the piper when he reached the school building, a gesture that brought a burst of cheers – followed by a German howitzer shell which turned the centre of the playground into a volcano. The platoon of Royal Scots ducked, a swing and a see-saw were blown into lethal fragments and Fenton dived head first through a door.

The headquarters staff were still working efficiently, despite the broken glass and fallen plaster that littered the rooms. A medical orderly wrapped a bandage around Fenton's cut head, handed him a tot of rum and then hurried off to aid the more desperately wounded, who were being brought into the schoolhouse in increasing numbers. Colonel Blythe, hollow eyed and grim faced, spotted Fenton nursing his head in a corner and came quickly over to him.

"Are you all right, lad?"

"Fine," he said thickly. "Just a knock on the head."

"Because we've got a job for you. We've received orders to disengage and pull back five miles, set up a new line by nightfall. This bloody artillery is getting to be too bloody accurate."

"What does the general feel about that?"

"Woody wants to stay and fight. He sent a message to G.H.Q. asking for ten machine-gun teams. They won't send them, of course. I doubt if there are ten Vickers guns to spare in the entire army. Anyway, machine guns won't stop cannon and the Huns are moving batteries of 'em on to our flank. We've got to pull back, but Woody's afraid that once we start retreating there'll be no end to it. He's sure we'll just keep sliding back to the coast."

"What do you want me to do?"

"We've lost all contact with Fifth Division H.Q. at Elouges. Get in your car and hurry over there, make certain they know we're pulling back to Sars La Bruyère. I'll give you the timetables for the withdrawal. We must coordinate our movements or there'll be frightful gaps in the line." He shoved a packet of papers into Fenton's hand. "Hurry along. There's a good chap."

Fenton gave Webber the choice of staying or going along with him. Like any devoted batman, Webber elected to stay with his officer. He sat in the front with Lance-Corporal Ackroyd, a loaded Lee-Enfield held between his knees, convinced by rumours he had heard that hordes of Germans were on the roads disguised as Belgian nuns.

192

The pattern of the roads forced them due south for a mile before they could hope to turn west towards Elouges. It was a slow mile. The road was choked with artillery and transport turning to go back. Some artillery officers were refusing to turn their teams around, cursing the fact that they had yet to fire their pieces at the enemy. Squads of Tommies from the Wiltshire Regiment were acting as military police and soon the jam of horses, wagons and guns was broken and the retreat became an orderly and steady flow to the south.

The road to the west was narrow and twisting, meandering through fields, woods, nameless little villages and past slag heaps and coal dumps. Streams of infantry crossed the road at a dozen places, moving away from the battle which still cracked and thundered along the horizon. They were tired men, their uniforms torn and filthy, their faces black with coal dust, but they all appeared cheerful and full of optimism. A lieutenant in the Royal Irish, who flagged the car down to ask directions, told Fenton that they had stopped the Germans in their tracks at the canal.

"Shot them down in droves, five rounds rapid all along the line. Didn't have to aim; came on in masses, shoulder to shoulder. I hear the Kaiser called our army contemptible. Wonder what he thinks now?" The lieutenant felt they were on the verge of a major victory even though they were, in his words, giving up a bit of ground. It seemed to Fenton that more than just a "bit of ground" was being given up. The army was turning its back on an advancing enemy and it would be a logistic nightmare to get it turned around again. The lieutenant had assumed that the hundred yards or so of his platoon's front was the entire conflict and he had seen the German attacks on that front wither away under the murderous rifle fire of his marksmen. He had not seen the big map at H.Q. that revealed the action at Mons as being only a tiny part of a huge battle raging from the Swiss border to Brussels. A battle is more than the sum of its parts. Even a stupendous victory at Mons would mean little or nothing if the French armies were falling back from the frontier, which they seemed to be doing. The tiny British Expeditionary Force was way out on a limb and if it didn't pull back in a hurry that limb was going to be chopped off. There was no point in trying to explain any of that to a euphoric young Irishman who felt he had just won the war. Fenton gave him some cigarettes, the directions to Sars La Bruyère and told Lance-Corporal Ackroyd to drive on.

No one at Fifth Division H.Q. gave a damn about the withdrawal timetable of the Third Division. The pressure on Fifth Division's front necessitated their own timetable for retreat and that pressure was severe. Shells were thudding closer and closer to Elouges and turning the roads into interlocking craters. German troops were across the canal in force and the rearguard action was becoming desperate. Most of the bridges across the canal had been blown up, but large formations of German cavalry, supported by infantry, were sweeping around the canal east of Condé and taking the division in flank. Co-ordinated withdrawal was impossible. Each battalion had to pull back when it could.

"Tell Sir Julian that we'll try not to leave any gaps, but we can't possibly guarantee it," the division commander's A.D.C. said a bit testily. "After all, this isn't Salisbury manoeuvres."

Lance-Corporal Ackroyd was pacing restlessly beside the car as Fenton left the H.Q. building in the town square. A battery of eighteen pounders in a seedy little park was firing shrapnel at a not too distant hill, and firing as rapidly as the crews could load the shells. Webber sat rigidly in the front seat clutching his rifle, head turned, watching the shells splatter the skyline with bursts of black smoke.

"Where to now, sir?" Ackroyd said as he opened the car's rear door. He had to shout to be heard.

Fenton looked at his watch. Four twenty-five. It would be dark by the time they got back to Frameries and the chances were that the division would have pulled out by then. They would have to catch up with it on the road to Sars La Bruyère. He sat on the running board with Ackroyd and went over the map with him. The main road south was starting to clog up badly, transport wagons, gun teams and troops already backing up into the town square. To drive into that crush would be folly.

"We can easily go around, sir," the corporal said. "This is a big, powerful car and the fields are as dry as stone. We could cut across country and be at this Sarlabrewer in two hours."

It sounded reasonable to Fenton and he made a mental note to recommend Ackroyd for another stripe.

The car ploughed through fields of oat and barley, leaving a wake of bent grain, but after a few miles the landscape changed from flat fields to a thickly-wooded country, interspersed with slate quarries and coal works. A labyrinth of narrow dirt roads, none of which could be found on the map, headed in all directions. They took one that looked promising, but after two miles of steady travel to the south the road ended abruptly at a coal mine and they had to turn back and try another. The new road wandered haphazardly south, then west, then south again, going through dense woods, the branches of trees forming a gloomy canopy. At one point Ackroyd had to brake in a hurry to keep from slamming into a troop of French dragoons who suddenly emerged from the shadowed woods at a trot, the horses lathered, the riders gaunt-faced with fatigue, moving across the road in a flood of foam-flecked horse hide and glittering accoutrements. Part of General Sordet's corps screening the B.E.F.'s left flank, clattering past in the fading sunlight like ghost cavalry on the way to Waterloo. The woods on the other side of the road swallowed them up.

"Blimey," an awed Ackroyd murmured. "They don't 'arf look a sight."

There was more cavalry further down the road, British Hussars, a hundred or more walking their tired horses. The khaki-clad troopers looked less splendid than their French counterparts, but more warlike with their Lee-Enfield rifles jutting up from the saddle holsters. Fenton recognised the major in command, one of the better whist players at the Marlborough Club, and called out to him. The man walked slowly up to the car, leading his horse.

"Hallo, Fenton," he said. "What are you doing out here all on your lonesome?"

"Trying to reach Sars La Bruyère."

"Well, this road will take you there, eventually. But the place is an unholy mess, jam-packed with transport and all of it moving back into France. What's happening up north?"

"Damned if I know exactly. Big fight this morning all along the canal from Mons to Condé. We did well, I think, but the corps is in full retirement none the less."

The major's smile was thin. "Talk about the fog of war. The right hand hasn't a clue to what the left hand's doing. I don't like this groping around in the dark one bloody bit, I can tell you. Got any whisky?"

"Afraid I haven't."

"Pity."

There was a crackle of rifle fire in the distance, the sound distorted by the wall of trees. The major cocked his head to one side like a hound. The rifle fire slacked off, to be replaced by the unmistakable chatter of a machine gun.

"Trumpeter!" the major shouted as he swung up into the saddle. "Mount! At the canter! . . . Forward!"

A bugle blared and the troop mounted and followed the major across the road and into the trees. They were soon out of sight, swallowed by shadows as the French dragoons had been. There was something forbidding about the woods that brought a shiver up Fenton's spine. They might not have seemed so ominous at noon, but the sun was almost down now, the sky, what could be seen of it, a blood red. The faint light that filtered through the beech trees had the same sanguinary hue.

"Drive on," he said. "Fast."

The road curved east, then due west and the woods began to thin out. The sun was a grossly enlarged scarlet ball that seemed to touch the road ahead of them. Shadows flickered across it.

"More bleedin' horses," Ackroyd muttered as he stepped on the brakes.

"Lancers," Webber said, squinting into the glare from the windscreen.

Fenton caught a glimpse of the riders' headgear silhouetted against the sun. Not English cloth caps nor French brass casques, but small helmets with a flat projection on top.

"Uhlans," he said with remarkable sangfroid, considering the chilling quality of that name. "Back up."

Private Webber was only a batman, but even the lowliest

guardsman went through the regimental training depot and its extensive musketry course. He stood up, braced his body against the windscreen, raised the Lee-Enfield to his shoulder and squeezed off a shot. One of the shadowy figures toppled to the road and a riderless horse careered wildly past the car. His second shot went wide as Ackroyd threw the gears into reverse and floored the accelerator, the car roaring back down the road, weaving from side to side. There was a burst of machine-gun fire from the fringe of the woods ahead of them and bullets splattered the car, shrieking through metal, rubber and glass. The front tyres blew and the car lurched violently off the road into a ditch. Fenton caught a glimpse of Webber toppling backwards with blood sheeting his face and then he was flying out of the back of the car, crashing through branches and landing heavily in a drift of summer-dried leaves.

He blacked out from the fall and when he opened his eyes he could see nothing but dancing red lights. He struggled to breathe, but something seemed to be pressing against his face, holding his mouth and nose with a suffocating grip. He began to struggle and then a mouth pressed against his ear and the barely audible voice of Lance-Corporal Ackroyd said: "Don't move, sir . . . don't move."

The grip on his nose slackened, but Ackroyd's hand was still over his mouth. His eyes came into proper focus and he could see that the red lights that had been darting and flipping about had turned into billows of flame shooting up from the car. He was lying a good thirty yards from it, well into the woods, his view of the fire fragmented by slender black trunks. Surely, he thought, he had not been thrown thirty yards through a beech forest. Lance-Corporal Ackroyd must have dragged him. By Harry, he'd see that the man was made sergeant, and was awarded a D.C.M. to boot. He nodded slowly, an assuring signal to Ackroyd that his restraint was no longer necessary.

"Where are they?" he whispered.

"Fuckin' everywhere, *sir*."

He could hear them now, the soft thud of horses' hooves, the crack and splinter of young trees and undergrowth, the cursing of men – gutteral German curses. There was a clatter of hob-nailed jackboots on the road, the *Jäger* unit of infantry who followed along behind the German cavalry to support them with expert rifle and machine-gun fire. Someone shouted, *"Achtung! Die Engländer kommen!"*

A bugle call from far down the road, the distant thunder of galloping horses. The Uhlans who were searching the wood crashed back towards the road. A machine gun began to clatter from a position near the still-blazing car. Rifles joined it and the firing was sustained and intense. Fenton could see nothing of the action, but he could visualise it all too clearly – the Hussars coming back at the gallop, drawn by the fire – pyre more than likely, because poor old Webber was probably being consumed by it. Horses and men would be going down in a heap.

"Oh, God."

"Shhh. Quiet, sir, quiet. Can you walk, sir?"

"I . . . don't know."

"Try, sir, *try*." There was an edge of desperation in Ackroyd's voice. Fenton got slowly to his feet. There was a dull pain in the small of his back, but nothing seemed to be broken.

"Keep low, sir, and run like hell."

The direction seemed unimportant at the moment, the only factor being to get as far away as possible from the German lancers and the *Jägers*, the latter being, as Fenton knew, born hunters and foresters. Bending nearly double they began to run, Ackroyd in the lead, racing through the closely-grouped trees, stumbling and plunging through the thick undergrowth. The firing continued behind them, but no shots came their way until they broke out of the woods into a small clearing. Dark shapes moved and a voice cried out, *"Wer da?"* Then rifles barked and Ackroyd dived for the tall grass with Fenton right behind him. They lay flat and crawled as bullets hissed through the grass around them. Once among the trees again they stood up and kept running, dodging from trunk to trunk, not stopping until total exhaustion brought them panting and sobbing to the ground. Fenton vomited and rolled on to his back under a hawthorn bush. Ackroyd lay on his face as though dead. They were deep in the forest and there was no sound but the gentle rustling of leaves, a nightingale's lilting notes and their own tortured breaths.

*

They hid by day and moved by night, working their way slowly southward. The German army was all around them, but not in a solid mass. There would be hours during the day when they would not see even one enemy soldier and they would debate whether to leave their hiding place – be it copse or haystack, abandoned mineshaft or reeking pigsty – and walk on more quickly than they could at night, but invariably Germans would appear some time during the day; a solitary squad scouting a road, or an entire battalion swarming across a field. And then there was always the lurking menace of Uhlans, Death's Head Hussars or less exotic looking cavalry to worry about. So they walked south by night, travelling by the map, using kilometre road markers as points of reference and avoiding the villages. They ate apples and wild berries and what little food they could find in the many abandoned cottages. The weather was good, hot by day and balmy at night, with cloudless skies and enough moon and star light to make walking cross-country easy. A sudden and violent thunderstorm struck during the second night of their journey and forced them to seek shelter in a barn. The rain stopped at dawn but a different thunder continued – the thump, thump, thump of heavy shell fire. The artillery bombardment was nearly due east, ten miles or so away, at or near Le Cateau as far as Fenton could judge. It continued from dawn to dusk and was obviously a major battle, but when the firing ceased there was no way of knowing who had won.

"I suppose we could walk to Le Cateau tonight and see who's in possession of the place," Fenton said, studying his map and eating an apple.

"We could, sir," Ackroyd said dubiously. "If we're awful ruddy careful about it."

It was impossible to maintain a strict officer to man relationship with Lance-Corporal Ackroyd, considering the circumstances. Men who had spent hours together half submerged in the stinking wallow of a pigsty while Uhlans foraged their horses nearby, learned a great deal about each other's qualities as human creatures. Fenton had only the greatest respect for Ackroyd. He was uncomplaining, resourceful, cautious and brave. The type of indomitable soldier any officer would want

199

at his side when a situation became rather sticky.

"You don't think it's a good idea, Ackroyd?"

"Beggin' the captain's pardon, but no, sir, I don't. If there was a battle over there it would seem to me that both sides'll be a bit touchy and we could get crumped by either of 'em if we got spotted blunderin' about in the dark. Fritz or Tommy, we'd still be feedin' the crows."

"A sensible deduction." He squinted at the map in the fading light. "Well, then, what say we keep going south until we reach the railway line from Cambrai, then follow the track towards St. Quentin? If the Hun is that far south then we know it's all up and we might just as well toss in the towel."

That met with Ackroyd's approval and they set out as soon as it got dark. The moon rose early and they made swift progress through fields and woods, reaching the railway lines before midnight. They rested in a culvert for an hour, eating the last of their apples, then walked along the edge of the tracks in a south-easterly direction. Fires ringed the northern horizon, a dull glow as though some strange dawn was about to rise. They could only speculate as to the source of the fires. Villages and fields going up in flames? The bivouac fires of some uncountable host? Either thought was chilling and drove them on without further rest. At four in the morning they reached the first scattered houses of a small town, a railway sign beside the tracks revealing the name – St. Petit Cambresis. A narrow road leading to the town came into view, a white ribbon under the dying moon snaking over a low hill and through vineyards. Transport wagons were parked along it, the draft horses grazing in a field.

"Ours, by God," Fenton said as he spotted the distinctive field cookers.

The two men paused to dab at their mud-caked, bramble-torn uniforms then marched on smartly, Ackroyd whistling "Tipperary" to alert any sentries. They were not challenged when they walked along the station platform nor when they went through the deserted ticket office on to the street beyond.

"A bit queer," Fenton said. "There should have been a sentry posted."

"Ruddy town seems to be empty, sir."

"Impossible."

They walked on, their boots ringing loudly on the cobble-stones. The street curved and led to the town square which was dominated by a stone fountain in its centre. Around the fountain and spread out across virtually every inch of the paved square were the sprawled figures of soldiers, three hundred or more, lying like dead men. They were not from one unit. Fenton noticed the badges of half a dozen regiments. A sergeant in the Gordon Highlanders lay on his back in the gutter with his head resting on his pack. His left hand was swathed in a dirty, blood-caked bandage. Fenton nudged him gently in the side with his foot.

"On your feet, sergeant."

The man stared stupidly at Fenton for a moment and then stood up with a groan.

"What the hell is going on?" Fenton said sharply. "It looks like a beggars' army."

The sergeant's red-rimmed eyes moved from Fenton's face to his regimental cap badge and then down to the pips on his stained and muddy sleeves. He pulled himself to rigid attention.

"All the lads is just worn down, sir."

"I can understand that, sergeant. But why are there no pickets out? Good Lord, man, Fritz'll be here by dawn."

"Yes, sir. Colonel told us to stack arms and get some sleep, sir. Told us we were out of the war, sir."

"*Your* colonel, sergeant?"

"No, sir. From the Winchesters, sir."

"How many Gordons are here?"

"Twelve of us, sir."

"Wake them up. Send six out along the railway line and six down the road. Find the transport drivers and wake them up, too. I want those horses in the traces. Where is the colonel?"

"Town hall, sir, just across the square."

"Do you believe you're out of the war, sergeant?"

The muscles in the tall sergeant's jaw tightened. "I cannae argue with a colonel, sir . . . even a colonel in the bloidy foukin' Winchesters, *sir*."

201

The foyer of the town hall and the central corridor were crowded with badly-wounded men being attended to by a couple of medical orderlies and a French civilian. The wounded were well bandaged and all of them appeared heavily anaesthetised. Fenton was impressed by the efficiency.

"You men are doing a good job here."

"Thank you, sir," one of the orderlies said, then nodded towards the Frenchman. "Thanks to 'im. He's the local vet. Brung over bundles of 'orse bandage and plenty of morphine."

"Can any of the men be moved?"

The man rubbed the side of his face and looked thoughtful. His eyes were sunken and there were deep shadows under the sockets.

"A dozen maybe, if they're kept flat. Most are in rum shape, sir. Them bloody shells tear 'ell out of a man."

"Sort out the men you can move, then you and your mate decide which one of you will stay behind with the rest. Toss a coin if you have to, but one of you must stay, I'm afraid. It won't do for the Germans to say we abandon our wounded."

The man nodded gravely. "Right you are, sir, only Colonel Hampton's been sayin' we're all chuckin' it in."

"Not so. Where can I find Colonel Hampton?"

The orderly pointed vaguely down the corridor. "One of them rooms, sir."

"Any other officers present?"

"Yes, sir, two lieutenants and a major. The major's over there on a stretcher. Fractured leg, sir. The lieutenants are with the colonel." He lowered his voice and looked earnestly into Fenton's face. "There's something a bit odd about the colonel, sir. I been in the R.A.M.C. for twenty years, sir, an' I've seen it happen before, more than once I can tell you."

"Seen what happen, sergeant?"

"Why, sir, a man losin' control of himself. I think the colonel's half 'round the bend."

Oh, God, Fenton thought, what a bloody awful situation. The sight of the stuporous men in the square, the drug-deepened sleep of the wounded, made him realise how deathly tired he was himself. It would have been the simplest and most natural act in the world to lie down on the floor and close his eyes – and if a German boot woke him in a few hours so be it. And there was a colonel down the hall, a regimental commander, most probably an elderly man who had seen long and honourable service, who was just as tired but was unable to cope with it, had let exhaustion dictate his decisions. He must, somehow, relieve that man, assume command as senior officer capable of duty and lead the rag, tag and bobtail conglomeration of troops out of the town by dawn. It seemed like an impossible undertaking at the moment, like being asked to scale an insurmountable cliff stark naked.

"I respect your comments, sergeant, but kindly keep them to yourself from now on. Is there anything you can give me that will keep me awake?"

"Sorry, sir. We don't even have a coffee bean or a palmful of tea." He smiled wryly. "I can put you to sleep in a jiffy."

"Thank you, sergeant, but I can do that quite well on my own."

He found the three officers quickly enough in the mayor's office, the two lieutenants lying on the floor and the colonel stretched out on a leather couch. There was an oil lamp on the desk, glowing feebly. Fenton turned up the wick, but no one moved a muscle as the sudden light fell upon them. He kicked the two younger officers until they stirred, groaning and mumbling, then shook the colonel vigorously. The colonel was white haired with a long, cadaverous face. Sixty at least with a faded ribbon from the South African War stitched to his tunic. Off the reserve list, yanked from his London club to lead a regiment to France and into battle. He could almost feel sorry for the man.

"Wake up, sir. Wake up."

The colonel stared at Fenton, slack jawed and glassy eyed.

"What? What's that you say?"

"Wake up. Time to move out."

The colonel struggled feebly to sit up and Fenton helped him by pulling on his tunic.

"Move out?" the old man said bewilderedly. "Move out, you say? What the deuce you talkin' about, sir? What the devil do you mean?"

Fenton glanced at the lieutenants who were now on their

feet, rocking slightly from fatigue. They were both Ninth Brigade men, one from the Winchesters and the other a Royal Fusilier.

"Had enough beauty sleep?" he said icily.

The Fusilier lieutenant rubbed his face vigorously. "God, what time is it?"

"Time to move along," Fenton said. "Go out on the square and start getting the men on their feet."

"What the devil d'you think you're doin'?" the colonel muttered thickly. "Get the men on their feet? By Harry, they've earned their rest, sir . . . earned their rest . . . fifty-two hours without sleep . . . two battles . . . they've done all they can do."

"Not quite, sir," Fenton said quietly. "Not quite enough yet."

The lieutenants seemed unsure of what to do, tensely aware that some sort of clash was developing between two superior officers.

"Stay for a moment," Fenton told them. "I'll need you as witnesses. I am about to request that the colonel should place himself on the sick list."

The colonel's face turned a mottled shade of purple.

"Sick list? What the deuce you talkin' about?"

"There must be something the matter with you, sir, to permit your command to fall asleep and be captured by the enemy."

The elderly officer opened his mouth several times, spittle drooling from a corner of his lips. He was staring up at Fenton with the pop-eyed fixation of someone on the verge of apoplexy.

"What's that you say, sir? What? Good God . . . jetsam . . . not *my* command . . . flotsam . . . found 'em here . . . tired to the bone . . . can't expect 'em to go on . . . too bloody much to ask of any man . . . not fair . . . not . . ."

Fenton interrupted coldly. "No colonel of the Winchesters would give up without a struggle unless he was an ill man. I needn't remind the colonel of his regiment's history."

The man's face became darker, the eyes more protuberant.

"Coldstream," he said thickly. "You bloody Guards are all alike, arrogant bastards every man Jack of you. Who the hell d'you think you are talkin' to me like that, tellin' me what to do? Ill? I'm not *ill*, sir!"

"You are either ill or a coward, sir. If you refuse to place yourself on the sick list then I have no other recourse but to leave this room, come back with a rifle and blow your head off."

The colonel seemed to stop breathing. His mouth worked soundlessly, then the staring eyes rolled back and he slumped forward, Fenton putting out his hands to keep him from pitching to the floor.

"Poor old duffer," the Fusilier scoffed.

"Watch your tongue," Fenton said sharply. "Fetch the medical orderly and be damned quick about it."

The young officer darted from the room while the other lieutenant lurched almost drunkenly towards the couch.

"Is he all right?"

"Yes. Get out on the square. Rouse the men. Blow bugles, ring bells, kick posteriors, but get 'em on their feet."

"I'll try, sir."

Fenton glared at him. "Not *try*. I didn't ask you to *try*."

He glared the lieutenant out of the room and then pressed his fingers firmly against the colonel's wrist. The flesh was clammy, but there was a faint pulse. He would be all right. Or would he? No, how could he ever be *all right* again? The man might live to be a hundred but he had died in France just as surely as poor old Webber had died. He let go of the wrist and eased the colonel on to his back. The orange, yellow and black South Africa ribbon looked a bit frivolous on his chest.

Some progress was being made in the square. Roughly one quarter of the men were standing up, but there was nothing martial in their attitudes. They had ceased to be soldiers. They looked like tramps crawling out from under bridges in a cold dawn. Lance-Corporal Ackroyd was helping the two lieutenants get men up, swearing and pleading with them, tugging at their belts and straps, kicking them. Some men rose, others lay half stupefied, muttering curses and threats. It looked to Fenton like a hopeless task and time was running out. The Germans would be stirring smartly at dawn and moving on towards St. Petit Cambresis in a grey-green tide. He spotted three Cameronian privates buckling on their equipment near the fountain. One of them had a canvas sack slung over one shoulder, bagpipes jutting up from it.

"You there!" Fenton shouted at the man. "Blow us a tune."

"He dinna 'ave the breath, sir," one of his mates called back.

"He'd better bloody well find some!"

The piper grinned sheepishly and took his pipes from the bag. There was a slow howl like a dying cat and then the skirling of "*Blue Bonnets Over the Border*" issued forth, clear and stirring with just that hint of sadness which all pipe music seemed to contain, a vision of gallant men doomed on bleak moors in lost causes. The Bonnie Prince had listened to those same notes before Culloden.

"Walk around, man, walk around."

The piper moved slowly among the exhausted men, picking his way carefully to avoid stepping on anyone's face. Soldiers began to stand up. A few cheered feebly. A Royal Fusilier corporal cupped his hands to his mouth and shouted, "Bugger the Jocks!"

There was some laughter here and there. More men got up and began to buckle on their equipment.

"If you don't like Jock tunes," Fenton called out, "let's hear it from the Londoners!"

A mouth organ appeared from one man's pocket; a small concertina from a pack. "Who's Your Lady Fair?" and "The Old Kent Road" competed with "Blue Bonnets". Singing began and the troops started to form fours and move slowly out of the square. There was a distant neighing of horses and the clatter and creak of the transport wagons. The men knew which way to go – south across the railway and a small bridge, dark poplars marking the road.

Fenton remained in the square until the last man, wagon and horse had left the town. It was dawn, the dark stone of the church steeple turning to a pale rose. Swallows dived from the sun-tinged belfry into the dark folds of a chestnut tree. It reminded Fenton of Abington on any summer morning. He turned to go, pausing for a moment to look at the medical orderly who was staying behind with the wounded. The man stood on the steps of the town hall, smoking his pipe, seemingly unconcerned. Perhaps he was relieved that he wasn't marching out with the others, that the war was over for him.

"Good luck, sir," the orderly called out.

Fenton raised his arm in a pointless gesture of farewell and walked away, limping slightly, the cobblestones painful to his feet, following the droning bagpipe out of the little town.

Over by Christmas . . . That was what everyone had been saying, *Home before the leaves fall*. He pondered the truth of it as the first shells howled out of the dawn, the German gunners searching for the St. Quentin road and the troops they knew would be on it. The shells were fifty yards off target, air bursting black and crimson, ripping shrapnel paths through a vineyard.

Home before the leaves fall. A damned good joke that.

3

THE MORNING CRACKLED WITH FROST, THE GRASS SNAPPING
under Jupiter's hooves as Lord Stanmore cantered out of a leafless copse and headed back across the fields towards Abington
Pryory. A black February day with slate grey clouds lowering
against the frozen earth. The earl could feel the chill penetrate
to his bones and he was grateful when the stables came in sight,
an elderly groom, well scarfed and wrapped up against the
cold, waiting to take the horse.

The earl left the stable area in a hurry. It pained him more
than anyone knew to see the rows of empty stalls, the shuttered
cottage where George Banks had lived, the deserted sleeping
quarters that had once been noisy with the shouts and laughter
of grooms and stableboys. All of the horses, with the exception
of Jupiter and a twelve-year-old brood mare, had been given to
the army in October. Cavalry losses had been heavy at the
Marne and during the many clashes following the epic German
retreat. The call had gone out for remounts and the earl had
been generous. He did not regret his gesture of patriotism – it
was, after all, the least he could do – and yet, seeing the empty
stalls brought a lump to his throat. The call to the colours had
not stopped there. Banks had taken a commission in the
veterinary corps and the grooms and stableboys had joined the
Yeomanry or the Regulars. No one was left at Abington Pryory
but the middle-aged and the elderly, the halt and the blind.
And not just men either, the earl reflected bitterly. The last of
the young maids had departed after Christmas, answering
their country's call for women to take over the jobs that men
were leaving. Men and more men. Kitchener had asked for one
hundred thousand volunteers to form the nucleus of his New
Army. Over a million responded.

YOUR COUNTRY NEEDS YOU

Kitchener's likeness on posters, grim faced, steely eyed, pointing his finger directly at one's face. Advertising the war, selling it like Pears' soap or White Manor Tea Shops. And of course the men would go, hurrying to the flag for a bit of excitement and adventure. The girls, too . . .

WOMEN OF BRITAIN ANSWER THE CALL

. . . to train as nurses in Queen Alexandra's Imperial Military Nursing Service, the Q.A.s, or the Red Cross, or to learn the tricky business of stuffing lydite into shell cases. Much jollier than waiting on table or polishing the banisters. The result of this exodus being that fully two-thirds of Abington Pryory was closed off, the furnishings covered with white sheets. A house embalmed and awaiting resurrection. Dust settling gently in deserted corridors. Weeds peeking up through the flagstones on the terrace. He complained of neglect, the lack of help.

"*It's the war, Tony,*" Hanna's only reply. As if he had to be told! Charles in uniform, Roger Wood-Lacy as well. Not in France – yet. *In France.* What an ugly sound . . . ominous as the sounds he had heard in late October and during the first weeks in November, early in the mornings when the air was still, the rumble of artillery bombardments across the sea in Flanders. And then the casualty lists on the first page of *The Times* to be scanned over breakfast. Fifty-eight thousand names of the dead, wounded and missing after Ypres alone. So many names that he recognised, could put faces to, the names of men he had hunted with, played cards with, but mainly the names of their sons. No, he didn't need Hanna to remind him that there was a war going on.

The chill lingered even after two cups of strong tea, the final cup laced with a dollop of Jamaica. There was a permanent frost on his spirits and he felt incapable of dispelling it. God knows the paper was of no help. Nothing in *The Times* but the war, the lengthening number of names in the Roll of Honour. Not too many wounded and missing listed. The fighting had bogged down in the snow and freezing sleet. Many of the dead would be those poor devils who had finally, perhaps even mercifully, succumbed to wounds received in the summer and autumn at Mons, Le Cateau, the Marne, Messines and Ypres.

He glanced at the list with a heavy heart. Two names stood out. Gilsworth, R. T., Col. 1/Hampshire; the Earl of Maidhurst, Capt. Royal Horse Guards.

He remembered Andrew Maidhurst as a boisterous fifteen-year-old, taking every jump with a wild, blood chilling yell, like a Red Indian. Damned fine horseman. He must send the marquess and his lady a letter of condolence. The eldest son. Christ, what a terrible blow. And poor old Ronnie Gilsworth. How many times had they tramped through the fields above Pately Bridge after snipe? Some good news from the Dardanelles. Admiral Carden's ships had successfully bombarded the Turkish forts on the Gallipoli Peninsula. Royal Marines had landed and poked about in the rubble without being fired on. The Turk had fled from the power of British naval gunnery. What they hoped to achieve in that remote corner of the world was not clear, but something was afoot. Strictly a navy show. Give the poor bloody devils of infantry a rest for a change, and yet the military seemed divided. The army very much against it. Article by Repington on page four.

Defeat of the Central Powers in 1915 can only come by a decisive victory in France . . . in the spring . . . combined French and British offensive in Artois and Champagne . . . overwhelm German trench structure . . . power of the British cavalry to exploit infantry gains . . . the First Lord of the Admiralty is misguided in believing that sea power alone can bring the Turks to their knees . . . vast numbers of troops needed . . . consolidate peninsular and Asiatic shore . . . troop deployment to the east would seriously undermine the plans of Sir John French and Marshal Joffre.

Dash it all! So much bickering back and forth between the services, not that he cared very much if young Winston Churchill was raked over the coals. Too bloody big for his breeches, that fellow. Father died a lunatic.

Coatsworth shuffled in with scrambled eggs and lamb's kidneys. He set the dish before the earl and removed the silver cover.

"Ross is leaving us, m'lord," he said, looking vaguely pleased.

"What? Ross? Oh, I say."

"Yes, m'lord, just told us in the servants' hall."

"Send the chap in after I've had my breakfast. Ross leaving; what a bloody bore."

The earl lit his first cigar of the day after first offering the humidor to his chauffeur who preferred one of the earl's Abdullah cigarettes from the tin of fifty on the table.

"Well, Ross, I hear you're rushing off to take the king's shilling."

Jamie Ross looked pained. "I wanted to join the army, m'lord. Nothing would have given me greater pleasure than to wear a khaki uniform, but, the fact of the matter is I received a letter this morning by special post. From the Rolls-Royce company."

"The Rolls-Royce company?" Lord Stanmore's incredulity showed on his face.

"Yes, m'lord. With regard to a patent I took out on a carburation system. The Rolls-Royce company had been interested, but felt it wasn't necessary for their cars. But now they're going to make aeroplane engines, m'lord, up at Enfield, m'lord, and they think that my system will make their engines run much more efficiently."

Lord Stanmore drew the cigar slowly from his mouth and allowed the smoke to bubble out. He was quite mystified.

"*Aeroplane* engines?"

"Yes, m'lord," Ross said with great patience. He felt as though he were talking to some slow-witted child. "The army has ordered a great many aeroplanes, m'lord, for observation purposes and artillery spotting. What they have now are terribly slow and the engine conks out if the machine turns upside down . . . drains all the petrol from the carburettor, m'lord. Same basic sort of trouble we used to have driving up Box Hill, a tendency for the engine to stutter or even stall on steep grades."

"Upside down? Why on earth would they want to fly upside down, Ross?"

"I suppose they can't help it sometimes, m'lord. Strong

winds, or evasive action." The ash was growing on his cigarette, but he couldn't quite muster the nerve to lean across the table and deposit it in the earl's silver ashtray. He placed his hand behind his right leg and dropped the ash on the carpet, smoothing it into the nap with his foot. "Well, m'lord, I received this letter and the Rolls-Royce people want me to come up to Enfield to work with their engineers. They say I can do more to crush the Hun there than by enlisting in the ranks."

The earl studied him through plumes of grey-blue smoke. Curious. *Ross* of all people, *his* Ross getting a letter from Rolls-Royce. Quite incredible. Of course, he had known that the lad was mechanically clever, always tinkering with the cars and making them run better than when the factories had delivered them. Still, it was curious. The chap probably had little education and yet he was considered too valuable to go to France. Charles had left Cambridge with first-class honours and yet no one could find a greater use for his services than a second lieutenancy in the Royal Windsor Fusiliers.

"I suppose these engines are quite important, Ross."

"Oh, yes, m'lord. I was reading just the other day in *Mechanics and Journeymen* . . ."

"In what?"

"*Mechanics and Journeymen*, m'lord, a periodical I subscribe to, very popular in the machinists' and mechanics' trade, m'lord; well, there was an article that caught my eye. The editor of the journal wrote that it was going to be machines that would win the war, m'lord; better weapons, faster and more reliable aeroplanes, and that the men who produced them were more valuable, or, anyway, *as* valuable, m'lord, as Tommy in the line."

"Yes," the earl mused, eyes half closed, "yes, I dare say."

"In fact, m'lord, they're weeding out machinists from the army and sending them back to their lathes."

"Quite so. It was in *The Times*. When are you leaving us, Ross?"

"They want me as soon as possible. Within a few days at the outside."

"Dashed inconvenient for me, I must say. Where on earth shall I find another driver?"

Jamie Ross shifted his feet uncomfortably. The cigarette had burned down to his fingers and he was forced to crush it out in the earl's gleaming ashtray.

"There's always Maddox in the village, m'lord."

The earl made a scoffing sound deep in his throat. "Man must be eighty if he's a day."

"Or young Fishcombe, m'lord. He's only sixteen, but he drives his father's van."

"Yes, I suppose I could hire him."

"Or, begging your lordship's pardon, why don't you do your own driving? I could teach you in just a few hours. It's really quite simple."

"I'm sure it is, Ross," he said stiffly, "but I prefer to be driven."

He was struggling to prevent the patterns of his life from being irrevocably washed away. *It's the war, Tony.* It explained the giving up of his stable, the shutting down of most of his house, the gradual turning of his gardens into an unpruned wilderness. It explained the departure of his chauffeur and the difficulty of finding a suitable replacement. One had simply to accept it all as a fact, an idea against which there was no possible argument. It was childish not to consider Ross' proposal, but, surely, the war would be over by spring and everything would return to normal.

He took a glass of neat rum and felt better for it. Sleet seethed against the library windows. Hanna on the telephone to Mary Dexford for an hour. She hung up and dabbed at her eyes with a lace handkerchief.

"She's taking it so wonderfully. Andrew died of wounds but was in no pain. Mary read me the letter his colonel sent. The boy was terribly brave, led his troop against a machine gun that was holding up an advance. Terrible . . . terrible . . . and yet Mary seemed so resigned, so fatalistic about it. And she has no fears for her other sons. John and Timothy are in France and Bramwell is in an Officers' Training Corps at Oxford. She told me that she senses an aura of invincibility around them. A holy shield."

"I never thought of Mary as being a religious person," the earl said moodily, staring at the windows, the icy sheen across the leaded glass.

"She isn't. She believes there is a greater force than our modern conception of God, an ancient spirit that the Druids knew well. She told me once that she had felt that spirit surround her when she stood in the centre of Stonehenge long ago."

"Utter rot," the earl muttered.

"Perhaps, but it comforts her."

"The *holy shield* did damned little good for Andrew."

"She said only his body died. I'm not certain what she meant by that." She twisted the handkerchief into a lace string. "Alex told me this morning that she has a surprise for us. The child sounded quite excited."

"Alexandra is always excited."

"Quite bubbly, in fact."

"Did you tell her that Winifred's brother is dead?"

"No, not yet."

"Ronnie Gilsworth was killed also. You remember him, Colonel Gilsworth, we used to go hunting together."

"Yes," she said vacantly. "So many are gone in such a short time. Ours and theirs. I wonder if any of the Rilkes . . .?"

She could not complete the thought. She could expect no words of sympathy from her husband over the fate of her relatives in Germany. Anti-German feeling ran like a virulent fever throughout the entire country. There was even talk in Parliament of suggesting firmly to the Crown that the name of the royal house be changed from Saxe-Coburg to something more English. Mr. Koepke, the baker who had sold his bread and cakes in Guildford for the past twenty years, had been interned, taken away without a moment's notice. Poor Adolph Koepke, who had always kept a small barrel of broken biscuits and jam tarts by the door for passing children to take free of charge, hauled off in a police van like a common criminal. The same children who had filled their pockets with old Koepke's generosity had stood in the street and jeered, then scrawled DIRTY GERMAN across the windows of his shop with paint. Mrs. Kenilworth, sister of the Bishop of Stoke, lived in Abington and had the misfortune to own a dachshund bitch. A boy hurled a stone at it and she no longer dared take the poor little beast out of the house except at night. Madness.

She pulled and twisted the handkerchief abstractedly. There was a twelve-page letter from her Great Aunt Louise, Baroness Seebach, locked in her sitting-room desk. Martin had delivered it to her after visiting Germany in September. He had spent two weeks with the Rilkes and the Seebachs, the Grunewalds and the Hoffman-Shusters in Lubeck, Koblenz, Hanover and Berlin. The baroness, ninety years of age and, in Martin's words "sharp as a tack", had entrusted the letter to him. It contained an up-to-the-second family tree painstakingly compiled by the old woman. The Rilkes and all their Germanic branches. So many names listed, so many young men, tiny asterisks beside the names of those in uniform. Cousin Frederick Ernst von Rilke's two sons, Werner and Otto, Werner the same age as Charles, Otto two years older. They had been in the reserve officer corps at the University of Lubeck. Martin had met them and liked them. They were in active service now, the infantry. Were they alive or dead? The cold rain hissed against the glass and gave no answer.

"Quite a remarkable country, Aunt Hanna," Martin had told her. He had been impressed by the efficiency of the modern German state, impressed by the things that had always impressed her when she used to visit Germany every spring, the absence of extreme poverty, the slumless cities, the school system and the working conditions in the factories – a nursery school for the children of women workers at the Rilke chemical plant in Koblenz, the sunny, well-ventilated electric motor plant at Potsdam – so unlike English factories which were like dark, airless caves.

"Werner and Otto showed me around. Very nice guys."

She glanced at her husband who was staring into nothingness, brooding at the bleakness of the day, thinking no doubt of Andrew Maidhurst and Colonel Gilsworth. Tony had been fond of Werner and Otto. Otto had stayed at the Park Lane house for seven months in 1912 while studying chemical engineering at the University of London. He would not be fond of them now.

She had always been proud of her German blood and proud of what Germany had accomplished in less than half a century.

215

The Germany that her father had known had been a land of peasants and artisans, a plodding, early rising, thoughtful, God-fearing folk who spawned out of their lean soil great thinkers: Goethe, Kant, Heine, Schiller, and then under Bismarck great doers. *Aus dem Lern-folk soll ein That-folk werden*, Bismarck had promised and now German industry was second to none in the world. Their steel production dwarfed that of England. Their merchant ships challenged the British flag on the sea lanes. The roots of the war lay there: British fear of German expansion and German arrogance. Yes, German arrogance. Not a perfect society by any means. Not Utopia. A rigid caste system dominated by Prussian militarism. No, not perfect, but not a nation of red-eyed monsters either. German soldiers did not rape Belgian nuns on altar steps, did not spit Belgian babies on swords and bayonets and tie Belgian virgins by their hair to the clappers of church bells. All of that talk was propaganda nonsense, but it was believed as gospel truth, the ugly rumours spawned by the factual brutality of the German army's march through Belgium. Martin had witnessed some of that brutality. Werner had been posted to a regiment in occupied Brussels and Martin had travelled with him as far as Louvain. Soldiers there, infuriated by snipers, seeing *francs-tireurs* hiding in every alley, kneeling behind every wall, had lost their heads and run amok, shooting a few innocent civilians and setting fire to a few buildings. The fires had spread out of control until large sections of the old town, including the medieval library, had burnt to the ground. An appalling incident, but that was war. One terrible incident after another. Martin had explained it all very well, seated at the dining table the night of his return to England, the centre of everyone's attention . . .

"Some troops went berserk. I suppose you could say that the burning of Louvain is similar to the burning of Columbia, South Carolina, by Sherman's troops during the Civil War. But, gosh, it was a shocking sight. Werner was horrified. We were all horrified. A colonel who travelled with us from Berlin wept at the sight of the – "

"A Hun colonel?" one of the guests had asked incredulously.

"A German, yes," Martin had replied quietly. "The man

had visited Louvain long before the war when he had been a student at Heidelberg."

"A student of what? Butchery?"

There was no point in trying to speak rationally or objectively about the war, or about the Germans. Any chance of that had fled during the terrible weeks in November, buried for ever with the British dead at Ypres.

"Mamma, Papa, close your eyes!" Alexandra's voice from beyond the library door. It was easy for Hanna to comply. Her eyes were already closed, her lips moving slightly in a soundless prayer, *Ach du lieber Gott* . . .

The door opened. "You can look now!"

Alexandra in a nurse's uniform, pirouetting so that the long white skirt swirled, the white veil floating from beneath a white headband, red crosses on the sides of it.

"How . . . *summery* you look," Hanna said slowly, not trusting her voice.

The earl looked bemused. "What on earth . . . ?"

"I've joined the Voluntary Aid Detachment of the Red Cross," Alexandra blurted happily. "Jennifer Wiggins, Cecily, Jane Hargreaves, Sheila and I all joined up together." She made another mannequin's turn. "Do you like it? Summery, yes, Mamma, because this is the summer uniform. The winter one is a pale blue serge with accents of red, but it doesn't fit properly in the bodice. I shall have to return it to Ferris for refitting before they make the others."

"Others?" the earl muttered.

"Three of each. Three summer, white, three winter, blue. And a couple of heavy woollen cloaks for cold weather. And I must get the proper type of shoes. We shall be doing so much walking, you know."

"What on earth do you know about nursing?" the earl asked.

"Oh, we shan't be doing that awful bedpan and dressing type of thing. They have proper nurses for that, elderly women. Our jobs will be to look after men who are convalescing . . . push them in their wheelchairs, write letters for them if their hands are bandaged or their arms are in plaster, read to them if the poor dears have been blinded. That sort of thing. There will be ever so much to do."

217

"Will you be leaving home?" Hanna asked.

"Yes, in a way. We shall be living in a dorm. But I shan't be far off. The Hargreaves gave their house at Roehampton to the Red Cross as a convalescent hospital for officers. They're jolly glad to be rid of it, such an awful barn of a place. They moved into a perfectly darling house in Portman Square." She made a final pirouette. "Do you like me in it? Isn't it chic?"

"Dashed smart," the earl said without conviction. "Are you sure you can do that sort of work? Some of those poor fellows will be quite badly off, you know."

Alexandra glanced at her image in a mirror and couldn't help but smile at what she saw. An angel of mercy. The headband and veil suited her. Made her look like an especially pretty young nun. Not too concealing, though. One could still see her blonde hair.

"I shall do quite well, Papa. I can feel it in my heart." She drew herself up proudly. A Nightingale figure in the glass. "It might be difficult at first, but this is war and one must be prepared for some degree of travail and self-sacrifice."

The rain seethed on the drill ground, turning the churned turf into a morass. The platoon moved across it, ankle-deep in mud. Barely half of the men were in uniform, the rest struggled along in cheap mackintoshes. A bowler hat or two; cloth caps mostly. The working poor, working at soldiering for a shilling a day. Only ten men had rifles.

"Platoon, halt! Dis-miss!"

They streamed towards the barracks in a sodden mass.

Second Lieutenant Viscount Amberley watched them go. He was properly dressed for a soldier of King and Country – a well fitting uniform, decent boots, a British Warm. The uniform was not provided by the government. They merely gave him a token amount of money towards its purchase. The uniform came from Hanesbury & Peeke, Military and Clerical Tailors, The Haymarket, London. It had cost a great deal of money and was worth every farthing.

Strangely enough, the men did not resent his martial magnificence in the least. When he stuck his head through the barracks doorway they all grinned at him.

"You chaps all right?"

"Right as bloody rain, sir!" a gangly young man said, warming his backside by the pot-belly stove. "Are we downhearted?"

The platoon answered with fervour, "NO-O-O-O!"

So much for that. First Platoon, D Company, Second Battalion the Royal Windsor Fusiliers, was right as rain. Charles walked on to the mess, hurrying his steps in anticipation of a whisky and hot water; a double whisky, come to think of it.

The mess was crowded, the barman hard pressed to keep up with the demand. The Royal Windsors shared the mess with a new battalion of the London Rifles – "Quite unthinkable before the war", the Royal Windsors' adjutant had remarked sourly when the London's officers had first entered the mess. The breaking of tradition didn't bother the younger officers of either regiment. They were all civilians in uniform, a few short months removed from Oxford, Cambridge, Eton, the Inns of Court, budding business careers. Sharing the mess gave them the opportunity to share their uncertainties at what they were doing, or trying to do. They were all candidly aware of their shortcomings.

"I wish to hell I had just one N.C.O. who knew the ropes," a London Rifles lieutenant remarked moodily. "I feel such a bloody fool drilling the men with a book in my hand."

Second Lieutenant Roger Wood-Lacy, the Royal Windsors, took a sip of his ginger beer.

"The men don't mind. I told my chaps straight out that I didn't know the first thing about drilling and we muddled through together. I must say, in all modesty, that we're first-rate now."

"When are they going to instruct us on trenches?" a downy-cheeked subaltern asked.

"When we get to France," Charles said as he joined the group at the bar. "I understand they're building a training base at Harfleur and they'll run us through it for a week or two before sending us up the line."

"With half our lads in macks, bowlers and brollies," Roger scoffed. "Fritz'll die from laughing."

"All of the men will be in uniform by the middle of next week, and they'll have Lee-Enfields and bayonets by then, too. The Colonel told me this morning. That goes for the Londons as well."

"I hope you're right," a London Rifles officer said. "The lads find it difficult to feel like soldiers when they don't look like soldiers. I marched my platoon over to Datchet Common the other day and some horrid chap standing outside a public house wanted to know where I was going with *a mob of bleedin' navvies*! If there'd been a man among us with a working rifle I'd have ordered the blighter shot."

"He'd only have missed," Roger said. "I doubt if there are ten men in your battalion or ours who know which end of the rifle does what."

Charles smiled sardonically and ordered his hot whisky. He recalled Fenton telling him that the Guards never talked shop in the mess. That might well have been a tradition in the Royal Windsor Fusiliers too, before the war, before the First Battalion, the regulars, had been destroyed at Ypres. New traditions were being formed at the depot in the shadow of Windsor Castle that were no doubt shocking to those who had known the regiment in peace-time. It was said that Queen Victoria used to watch the men drill from her sitting-room window. She would have been dismayed if she had watched them now. But there was no point in reflecting on the past. There wasn't an enlisted man in his platoon who could have told him what the regiment had done at Blenheim, Oudenarde, Badajoz, Vittoria, Quatre Bras, Inkerman or Tel-el-Kebir. Those battles meant nothing to them, faded lettering on the regimental colours, half-remembered names from dimly-recalled school lessons. They were eager to make their own history, singing "Tipperary" as they marched in the rain in their wretched clothes.

"What are you up to this afternoon?" Roger asked.

Charles looked at his wristwatch. "Meeting Lydia at Charing Cross, if I don't miss the train. I've got noon to midnight off."

"Lucky devil! Where are you taking her?"

"Lunch at the Piccadilly, perhaps the theatre. I don't much

care what we do. Lounging around on a sofa with a brandy and soda would suit me fine."

"Typical thinking of the active service officer." Roger scowled at the bubbles in his glass. "I suppose you heard the news about poor Winnie's brother."

"Yes. Bad luck. Barely knew the chap . . . yet . . . well, it's rotten. I'll send her a letter."

"Got a note from Fenton this morning. They upped him to major."

"Still on staff?"

"No, back with the Guards. In trenches near Bethune. He says they're quite snug and enjoying the winter sports. Only a hangman would appreciate Fenton's humour."

"Well," he said lamely, glancing at his watch again, "you know your brother."

Did he? He wondered, seated in the train as it skirted the freezing Thames, if they would ever know Fenton again. Not the old Fenton, surely. *In trenches.* Those two words separated Fenton from the majority of mankind as completely as though he were on the far side of the moon. Being *in trenches* was an experience that only those who had been in them could possibly imagine. Those few survivors of the First Battalion who had drifted back to the fusilier depot at Windsor never talked about their experiences at Wytschaete in November. Never in fact even talked to each other, although they all shared the same memories of that hellish place. They kept what they had seen and done on White Sheet Ridge to themselves. There was a veil drawn about each man that was totally impenetrable. They had glimpsed purgatory and were not whispering its secrets to Dante or anyone else. Fenton would be the same, withdrawing behind his gift for sardonic understatement to blot out the horrors. The official communiqués from France told of heavy artillery exchanges from Aubers Ridge to the La Bassee canal. Fenton would be somewhere in that area, *quite snug and enjoying the winter sports.* He tried to imagine what it must be like to huddle in an icy trench while shells slammed into iron-hard ground. He could not bring any vision into focus. It was a mystery that must await his own initiation.

221

"How grand you look," Lydia said as he pushed his way through the crowded station to meet her.

"You look rather grand yourself," he said with a grin of pure joy. She looked so beautiful in a Russian sable coat that he felt like sweeping her into his arms and kissing her right there in front of a thousand people – not that anyone would have cared or even noticed. There were soldiers kissing girls everywhere one looked, a battalion waiting to board a train for Folkestone, their packs and rifles stacked in momentarily neglected rows down the platform, and yet he pecked at her cheek almost furtively.

"How demonstrative you are, Charles." Her smile was cryptic. "Have you missed me terribly?"

He took hold of her gloved hands. "You know I have."

"I would never know by your letters."

"Sorry." He squeezed her hands as though to prove his sincerity. "It was almost impossible to write. We've been on the go eighteen hours a day, trying to learn soldiering and teach it to the men. It's been the blind leading the blind, but we're starting to form into shape now and I'll be able to come up to London more often." He was about to add, "Before they ship us to France", but thought better of it. There was no point in putting an immediate damper on the afternoon.

She kissed him squarely on the mouth. "There! That's a proper welcome. Kindly make a note of it, Lieutenant." He hugged her to him, but it was awkward, so much fur and wool and khaki between them. Her perfume made him giddy. How exquisitely marvellous was the smell of woman! He thought of the dankly rancid odour of his platoon in the tar-paper and wood barracks. The haze from sodden cloth as they ringed the stove.

"It's so marvellous to be with you again," he murmured, brushing his lips against her neck. "It seems like an age."

It seemed that way to her too. This tall, uniformed, lean-faced man seemed almost a stranger in some ways. Not that he had changed that much in a physical sense, a bit thinner perhaps, but so much else had changed. The span of time between October, 1914, and February, 1915, could not be measured in months. It seemed like the gap between one century and another. She clung tightly to his arm as they walked out of the station. Ambulances were drawn up all the way along the Strand, waiting for the hospital train from Southampton. They hurried past them in silence into Buckingham Street where she had parked her car.

"I thought we might have lunch at the Piccadilly grill," he said as she handed him the car keys.

"It's terribly dull there. Nothing but grim-faced matrons and retired brigadiers. I took the liberty of reserving a table at the Café Royal, far from the orchestra so we can talk, talk, talk."

Talking was out of the question except at a level of near shouting that Charles found irritating. The Café Royal was jammed with men in uniform (most of them with the red tabs of staff officers on their lapels), businessmen, high government officials and droves of elegant women (most of them considerably younger than their escorts). An orchestra played ragtime and the dance floor was so densely crowded that couples could barely go through the gyrations of the "Grizzly Bear" or the "Temptation Rag". The menu was extensive and the prices outrageous. It was not a place where second lieutenants took their girls on a second lieutenant's pay. But he had left those modest trappings back at Windsor along with his muddy boots. In the Café Royal he was the heir to an earldom, and to hell with expense.

The food was ambrosial after regimental boiled beef and greens, the Pouilly Fumé pure nectar, but the orchestral thumpings and wailings, the squeal of the female dancers doing the maxixe became too much to bear. He smiled ruefully and raised his voice above the din.

"Rather difficult to talk here."

"Yes," Lydia agreed. "Shall we go?"

"Please."

It was raining again, an arctic drizzle from a black, sullen sky. They drove to a house her father owned in Grosvenor Square, twenty rooms of Regency elegance, one of Archie's many London residences.

"Don't you feel cramped?" Charles asked, eyeing the domed ceiling in the foyer with its skylight of stained glass, the long marble corridors, doorways framed in the Ionic order.

"We do a great deal of entertaining lately," she said handing her coat to a maid. "This place is really more for Daddy's friends at the ministry than it is for us."

"Archie in the government! I couldn't believe it when I saw the announcement in *The Times*."

"Yes, on a war committee and enjoying every minute of it. He and the minister are very much alike."

"Langham, is it?"

"Yes. David Selkirk Langham, whirring like a dynamo, the Lancashire bantam cock, sharp of spur and tongue, soothing half of Parliament and irritating the rest."

"What exactly is your father doing?"

"Applying the Foxe Ltd. method to the war effort: the three pillars of the company, advertising, efficiency and quality. He started by criticising the recruiting posters. Kitchener sticking his fat finger in one's face will be replaced by more subtle inducements. And then there's the problem of army rations. The system is quite inadequate for the million or so men Kitchener wants. Food distribution is Daddy's game, you know. The whole purpose of Langham's ministry is to get experts to handle the planning problems of the war. He believes that war is far too complex a matter to be left to the military. He just recruited Lord whatever-his-name-is, you know, the London omnibus tycoon, to help solve the army's transportation problems."

A fire burned in the drawing room, reflecting off highly polished wood, silver and glass. It was an eighteenth-century room, large but warmly intimate. The maid drew the velvet curtains to shut out the bleakness of the afternoon, while a butler in livery brought brandy in a cut crystal decanter.

"And yourself?" Charles asked. "What are you doing to keep busy?"

"Oh, a rather ambiguous rôle in the war effort. I'm serving as Daddy's social secretary. Langham's too, in a way. I arrange small dinners here. Dining-room politics, Liberal and Conservative, capital and labour breaking bread and resolving to pull together for a change. I suppose it sounds rather silly and frivolous to you, but more things are accomplished over a good dinner and a fine port than one could possibly realise."

"What do you think can be accomplished after a fine lunch and a bottle of Pouilly Fumé? Not to mention a rare old brandy."

"That's really up to you, isn't it?" she said, sitting on a divan and patting the cushion beside her.

Charles waited until the maid and butler had left the room and then sat next to her.

"I know what I'd like to accomplish – and will."

She looked at him intently and placed a cool hand against the side of his face.

"Please, Charles. Don't spoil a perfectly wonderful day by making promises that you're in no position to keep. It isn't fair to me, or you."

He drained his brandy in one swallow and set the bulbous glass on a side table.

"That's all in the past, Lydia. I know it is, I can sense it. Don't you feel a great change in the air? A fresh wind? Oh, I don't know how to put it exactly. A paradox. I mean to say, I rather dread the thought of going to France and having shells tossed at my head, and yet I'm glad we're at war and happy to be a part of it. Something new and marvellously exciting is taking place in our lives. A clean start for a tired old world. The ranks are aware of it too – all those ex-clerks, delivery boys, apprentices – they know that the war will change their lives utterly, break the moulds, the ruts; that's why they're so cheer-ful and uncomplaining. Their uniforms, when they have them, are shoddy, the food is dull, the barracks damp and draughty, and yet they act like schoolboys on holiday." He took hold of her hand and kissed the palm of it. "We'll be going across soon – at least that's the talk in the mess – drive the Boche to the Rhine this spring and summer. When I get back I shall marry you, and if my father doesn't like it he can lump it, and if he threatens to disavow you I shall shame him in front of the peers. I shall go to the House of Lords and condemn him for his actions."

"Oh, Charles," she laughed. "That's nonsense."

"I mean it," he said fiercely. "I mean every word. Or, anyway, I'd threaten such action and he'd back down in a hurry. By God, it's young men who are fighting this war and it's young men who must benefit from the victory. *I* shall not back off on *my* rights. *That* I promise you, Lydia."

He made an attempt to get down on one knee in front of her, but stumbled in doing so. The rich food of the Café Royal, the wine, the brandy, the glow of the fire, the fact that he had been up before dawn, conspired to rob him of grace. His head spun and he sat at her feet and rested his brow against her knees.

"Lord," he muttered, "I feel as if I've been drugged."

"Poor darling." She bent forward and kissed the top of his head. "You must be exhausted. Would you like to take a nap?"

"Yes, I think so. For an hour or two."

She stroked his hair, idly, unconsciously sensual. "We don't have to go to the theatre. You can rest, and then we'll have supper here."

"I have to be back by midnight."

"I know. I arranged with Daddy to have Simmons drive you. The car will be here at ten thirty. The night train is so horrid."

He nestled his head in her lap and sighed with contentment.

"Oh, Lydia, I feel such peace with you."

"And I with you, my darling. But come on, don't go to sleep on the floor. You can stretch out in a perfectly luxurious bed."

"I haven't been in a perfectly luxurious bed in months. I'll never get up again. No, I'll just take an hour on the couch."

She helped him out of his jacket, laughing at the complexities of the Sam Browne belt which resisted both their efforts to detach. Finally he was lying down, jacket and shoes off, head resting on a cushion. She covered him with a rug and kissed him on the brow.

"I feel such a fool," he muttered drowsily. "With the prettiest girl in England and I . . . take a nap on her couch."

She kissed him again. "I shan't breathe a word to your brother officers. It would ruin your reputation."

He fell asleep almost instantly and she stood for a moment looking down at him, so blissful in sleep, so boyishly vulnerable. She felt a purely maternal emotion and tucked the rug gently around him, brushed a lock of hair from his eyes and tiptoed from the room, closing the door quietly behind her.

Would he do it? She thought about it, seated in the morning room, staring through the tall windows at the green oval of the square. How dark and forbidding the iron railings looked, how bleak the sodden, leafless trees. A man crossed the road towards South Audley Street clutching a wind-whipped umbrella with both hands. *Would he?* She lit a cigarette and puffed on it, drawing the smoke into her mouth and then blowing it out again rapidly. Yes. She had the feeling that he would. That *this* time he would. It was the uniform, being part of something that his father was not part of. *In the war.* His father might be Lord Stanmore, ninth Earl, but he was Charles Amberley, Second Lieutenant, The Royal Windsor Fusiliers. The importance of their respective statutes had flip-flopped, at least for the time being.

> Oh, we do love the soldier boy,
> The lads in khaki proud,
> And jolly Jack Tar and the bold marine
> Who guard the Empire 'round . . .

A silly music-hall ditty but one that captured the public mood. Nothing was too good for the men who served King and Country. She half closed her eyes against the caustic smoke of the cigarette and envisioned Charles standing in the House of Lords – his right arm neatly bound in a sling, a bandage about his Shakespearean brow – pleading his case with passion . . .

My father is an honourable man, but I am not without honour of my own . . . the honour of shedding my blood for England . . . and to have the woman I love denied my father's blessing . . . Shame, I say . . . shame . . .

She almost laughed at the vision. It was so impossibly romantic, like a scene out of one of Alexandra's trashy novels.

There was a rumble of voices in the corridor and then the door opened and her father stepped into the room followed by a short, slender, dark haired man of forty-five.

"Good weather for ducks." Archie Foxe growled, peeling fur-lined leather gloves from his pudgy hands. "Is that Charles sleepin' in the drawing room?"

"Yes," Lydia said, snuffing out her cigarette. Archie did not approve of women smoking.

227

"Anything the matter with the lad?"

"No, just tired."

"The rigours of army life, eh?"

"Something like that," she said.

"I have some telephone calls to make. Will you see to it that Mr. Langham gets a double brandy and soda to ward off the chill?"

"Of course. How are you, Mr. Langham?"

"Wet, Miss Foxe. Quite damp to the bone."

He was not, of course, wet at all, having stepped from a motor car to the front door under a large umbrella. His dark woollen overcoat with the astrakhan collar was unblemished by rain. Archie Foxe went off down the corridor towards the stairs and his office-bedroom on the second floor, the minister's overcoat was taken by the butler and a large brandy and soda brought in on a silver tray. David Selkirk Langham, neat as a pin in striped trousers and morning coat, walked slowly about the room, his dark, piercing eyes taking in every detail.

"Sumptuous. There is no finer combination than a great deal of money and faultless taste. Did you choose the furnishings?"

"Yes," Lydia said.

"In all of your father's numerous abodes?"

She smiled faintly. "Those that I know of."

"Ah, yes," he chuckled. "I dare say the sly fox has his secret den or two."

"Complete with vixen."

"I detect a note of disapproval in your tone, Miss Foxe. One should not begrudge a man his amusements."

There *was* something devilish about his face, Lydia decided. The Tory papers often caricatured him as the Prince of Darkness whispering into Asquith's ear, or Lloyd George's. He had a narrow, spade-shaped face with a long, sharp nose, thin eyebrows like a pencil line and a trim Van Dyck beard. The devil's countenance, but there was no hint of evil about him, only a quality of restrained amusement as though he were always on the verge of breaking into peals of mocking laughter. David Selkirk Langham, born in a Liverpool slum, self-educated solicitor, advocate for the Mersey dock workers, member of parliament, cabinet minister. A married man with five children, but there had been salacious stories whispered about him since the day he had entered Parliament in 1908. Women, it was said, were hypnotised by his eyes and his air of blunt, forceful virility. Tory lies, her father had said, but she wasn't so sure. She had heard too many stories to dismiss every one of them as false, and she had merely to look into his eyes to read the challenge there.

"The young man on the couch, is that Charles Amberley?"

"Yes."

"The earl referred to me as a blackguard once during a speech in the House. Of course, there was nothing personal in the remark. He was merely angry at the way the election had turned out. Is the son as Tory as the father?"

"No. He has no political feelings one way or the other."

Langham raised one eyebrow in a sharply quizzical arch. "Is that so? Doesn't he know it's politics that make the world go round? That it's politics that have him in a uniform and politics that're likely to keep him in it for a long time?"

"He doesn't look upon the war quite that way."

"Foolish of him. It pays to be realistic in this day and age. The way some of these soldier lads talk, you'd think they were going off in suits of armour for to fight the King of France. It's going to be a long war and a bitter one, a war of political ideologies, a war of . . ."

Her laugh interrupted him. "Mr. Langham, you're not in the Commons making a speech."

He bowed slightly. "My apologies. It used to be my fame that I would make a speech on any street corner or in any public house for no better reason than to hear the sound of my own voice. Those are days long gone. There are more enjoyable things to talk about with a young and beautiful woman than the turmoil of European politics."

"Such as?"

"Why, the pure pleasure of your company, as just one example." He eyed her boldly, a smile lurking behind his dark eyes. He reminded her of a ferret toying with a rabbit. She could understand why many women would find him intriguing. There was nothing subtle or circumspect about him

229

in any way. Totally sure of himself and his power over the weaker sex. And he was such a little man. So trim and dapper, one would have taken him for a tailor if he wasn't so obviously a cabinet minister whose star was on the rise. She felt a vague excitement, a small knot of tension in the pit of her stomach. How many women, she wondered, had experienced that sense of excitement and succumbed to it? Her hand went idly to her throat and she looked away from him. Rain drummed against the windows.

"Where are you and Father off to this afternoon?"

Langham smiled at the huskiness of her voice and took a sip of his drink. "A meeting with the prime minister at Number Ten. Kitchener will be there to discuss this Dardanelles business."

"What do you think about it?"

"Brilliant in concept, just what one would expect from young Mr. Churchill's fertile mind. My own mind is not made up about it. Should the enterprise fail, the political repercussions could be disastrous."

"You don't strike me as a man who would be afraid of risk."

There was a sound in his throat, like muffled laughter or the purring of a cat. His hand brushed her arm, gentle as silk.

"Some games are always worth the candle and some are not. Don't you think that's true, Lydia Foxe?"

She ignored his touch, her eyes fixed on the cold glass window panes.

"I'm not certain, Mr. Langham. It's not candles I care about in games, only prizes."

4

MARTIN RILKE SAT IN REGENT'S PARK, TOSSING PELLETS OF bread to a flotilla of ducks. It had been a long, hard winter and the ducks were celebrating the approach of spring by eating everything that was cast upon the waters. Martin sprinkled what remained of four slices of bread among the reeds and then stood up and walked slowly along a broad gravel path towards Clarence Gate. His hands were in the pockets of his overcoat, one hand curled around a crumpled letter from Chicago. The letter had arrived in the morning post and had contained a cheque from the *Express* for eighty-five dollars and some words of advice from Comstock Harrington Briggs:

Dear Rilke:

The enclosed check does not reflect your worth but does measure pretty accurately the extent of your usefulness to us at this time. The good folk in the midwest are getting a bit irritated at old Europe and her wars. Sympathy along the lake front from Milwaukee to Gary is pretty evenly divided. Many German-Americans are becoming vocal in their condemnation of England, France and Russia – especially England – for conducting what they feel is a crush-German-trade war. The British naval blockade is certainly playing havoc with the grain merchants and the iron ore shippers. Folks in these parts can't understand why they should be prevented from selling to the Central Powers. Even Washington is irked at the blockade so you can well imagine how feelings run in certain sections of Chicago and everywhere in Milwaukee.

Your Belgium sketches were good and fair, but your current things on war-time Britain are becoming too overtly Anglophile to suit our readers. Never lose sight of the fact that the redcoats burned the White House – although I can think of a Republican or two who would gladly burn it down today as long as Mr. Wilson was inside. No, Rilke, I can't think of any good reason for you to stay in London any longer. Joe Finley had one bottle of rye too many so there is now an opening on the police beat. The job is yours if you'll send me a cable. A simple yes or no will suffice. If you're short of the fare, say so.

P.S. I have to go with the Phillies this year for the pennant. Cliff Cravath and Grover Cleveland Alexander ... too tough a combination to beat.

He removed the letter from his pocket, wadded it into a tight ball and sent a hard fast one curving out and away from Cliff Cravath's knees. The paper hit the water and brought a flurry of ducks to the scene.

Jacob Golden was stretched out on the living-room couch staring at the ceiling. It was a position he had been in, almost without interruption, since returning from Servia in January. He had said little and written less about his experiences there with General Putnik's armies. Some rift had developed between Jacob and his father, but Martin had not tried to nose out the cause of it.

"Enjoy the April sunshine?" Jacob drawled as Martin hung up his coat in the tiny hall.

"Yes, went up to the park and fed the ducks."

"Reach any firm decision?"

Martin shrugged and slumped into a chair. "Go back to Chicago, I guess."

"Turning your back on the war, eh?"

"It's being turned for me."

Jacob yawned and sat up. He had lost a good deal of weight and looked skeletal, the skin stretched across his face like parchment over a bone frame.

"Why don't you join the *Daily Post*? The guv'nor likes your writing and he's sending me to Egypt to cover the Dardanelles expedition. You could take my spot. I intend to leave the old paper."

Martin mulled that information over for a few seconds. There was a clatter of dishes from the restaurant below. The Hungarians were gone, innocent victims of the war, replaced by a large Italian family, verbose and operatic.

"When did you decide that?"

"Been considering it for months."

"What happened in Serbia, Jacob?"

Golden ran his hands through his hair. "Christ! Nothing that I hadn't expected to happen. I told you that there was an unholy amount of hate in that part of the world. The war gave it an impetus and an outlet. Rape, torture and butchery are simply words until one has seen the victims. I saw what the Austrians did to Servian villagers and I saw what Servians did to Austrians after Putnik counter-attacked across the Save River. My dispatches detailed the atrocities on both sides, but only the Austrian outrages were printed."

"That shouldn't have come as a surprise."

"No, of course it didn't. I hardly expected gallant little Servia to be vilified in the press." He smiled sardonically. "War and truth do not blend very well. I suppose I have an obligation as a journalist to bear witness to events even if the new censorship regulations prevent me from publishing all the facts, but I can't do it. There's something hideously wrong about this war. It's going to be a mindless, pointless, chaotic slaughter and I don't wish to be involved in it."

"It's going to be difficult not to be involved, isn't it? Where will you go?"

"Why, into the army, of course. Best place in the world to avoid emotional involvements of any kind. Chap I knew at Oxford is in the Royal Signals Corps. Gave him a ring the other day and he offered me a commission. Back-room job in Whitehall, thinking up codes and ciphers. Cryptography has always been a passion of mine since I was six years old. How do you think I'll look in a uniform?"

"Gaunt."

He winced and ran a hand across his jaw. "Quite right. A bit on the lean and hungry side. I miss all that sour cream and paprika from downstairs. I suppose I'd better develop a taste for pasta and put some flesh on my bones."

233

"You seem to be a bit more cheerful all of a sudden."

"It's getting it off my chest, old boy. You're a marvellous chap, Martin. You let people speak without clucking your tongue or acting pontifically. I truly think you'd have lent a sympathetic ear to Attila the Hun."

"I suppose that's a compliment," Martin said with a dubious air, "but I'm not without some strong views."

"Of course you're not, it's just that you're far more objective about things than I am, and more truly tolerant of mankind's insanities than I could ever hope to be. This war is going to need a few unbiased witnesses and you should definitely be one of them. Would you like to go to the Dardanelles?"

"If I can, sure."

"Right! I'll get on the blower and fix it up. Pop a cork of bubbly while I mend a fence or two with the guv'nor."

Jacob was on the telephone to his father when Martin came back from the kitchen with a bottle of champagne and two glasses.

"It just seemed the decent thing to do," Jacob was saying, his tone unctuously patriotic. "No reasonably healthy Englishman should be out of uniform and so . . . Yes . . . Royal Signals Corps . . . a full lieutenancy . . . their need for me is rather desperate . . . codes, ciphers, decoding . . . that sort of thing. Yes . . . posted here in London . . . top-hole sort of job in Whitehall . . . yes, should make Mother happy . . . quite right . . . they don't use code experts in the trenches. Glad you understand, Father . . . that's why I've been so moody and out of sorts lately . . . trying to make up my mind as to the best thing to do . . . thank you, Father . . . I appreciate your saying that . . . Now then, as for this Mediterranean business, I can't think of anyone more suited to take my place than Martin Rilke . . ."

He stayed apart from the other newspaper correspondents, an outsider, "that American chap", tolerated but resented. The number of press representatives allowed to join the Mediterranean Expeditionary Force was limited to a scant half dozen. Kitchener would have preferred none, but General Sir Ian Hamilton, commanding the expedition, had permitted a few select men to come along as observers. Most of them were elderly men who had covered military affairs since the Boer War and even beyond. They were on a first-name basis with all the staff officers and fitted neatly into the social order of the mess. They could, in fact, have been colonels or majors in mufti, so complete was their grasp of military procedures and ethics. Martin's very presence had been subject to doubt almost up to the hour of sailing from Southampton. The advisability of a neutral coming along had been questioned by the War Office, but Lord Trewe's arguments had prevailed in the end. It was his contention that Martin Rilke should be allowed to accompany the expedition precisely *because* he was a neutral. America, he had stated in a strongly-worded note to the War Office, must be made aware of the scope and grandeur of the British adventure to the east. American sentiment towards the British war effort was at a low ebb and British newspaper accounts of it were looked on as biased reporting . . . "Let the truth come out in American papers, documented by an American whose sympathy and understanding for the English people in this war is beyond question."

And so he was part of the host gathering in Egypt for an assault on the Gallipoli peninsula, a lone American strolling the gritty, crowded streets of Alexandria in an open-necked shirt, Kodak slung over one shoulder, notebook and pencil in hand. Little of what he wrote was passed uncensored by G.H.Q. and none of his photographs had been stamped with the censor's seal. It seemed curious to Martin that the British would be so touchy about what could or could not be sent back to London. The smallest and most ragged Egyptian shoeshine boy knew that the English were preparing to sail for Gallipoli by the last week in April. Fishing boats from Greece drifted with impunity through the vast armada of ships anchored in the roadstead. It was common knowledge that at least half of the Greek fishermen were either Turkish sympathisers or Turkish spies, and yet the censors sliced out the most innocuous comments from the newsmen's copy, as though a remark, such as, "The Australian and New Zealand soldiers appear to be very much at home amid the rock strewn desolation of the Egyptian desert," was of prime military importance.

"Oh, can't have that, sir. Might tip off to the enemy where the troops are to be sent. Gallipoli is desolate and rock strewn, you know."

Martin wondered whether Jacob, in the brilliance of his mind, had not foreseen all this official fantasia and had neatly outwitted him into taking his place. He could imagine him laughing himself silly as he lolled about the flat in his silk pyjamas, drinking champagne and renewing his friendship with Shaftesbury Avenue chorus girls. Still, he didn't care. It was Jacob's loss. London was fine, but it was only a city, not unlike Chicago or New York. Alexandria was the threshold of the East. Alexandria was time caught in mellow limestone. The city of Alexander. Al-Iskandariyah. A city that was ancient when Euclid studied in its library. A city where Cleopatra dozed in the arms of Antony. He strolled along the broad avenue flanking the crescent-shaped bay, the Mediterranean blue-green to the west, yellowish brown to the east, stained by the soil of Africa in the Nile flood. There was a café near the docks which officers of the Royal Navy and the French *Armée de Mer* had taken as their own, hooting away any khaki-clad officer who dared to enter, but tolerating the unobtrusive presence of a solitary newspaperman from Chicago who took the farthest table on the terrace and spent his time over a beer or two writing in a journal and not bothering a soul:

Alexandria. April 10th, 1915

Observations and reflections. It is curious here. An air of almost unbearable excitement permeates every aspect of the expedition as though nothing but laurel leaves and great honours wait over the horizon for every man bound to go there. What the Turks are thinking at this moment no one can say, but I doubt if they are filled with the same euphoria. I have tried without success to find out more about this peninsula where the armada is soon to head. It is waterless and desolate, I know that much, a spit of land dividing Europe from Asia, rock strewn, mountainous, scrub covered, bleak and inhospitable. Are there many beaches? No one seems to know . . . or, rather, not say. Maps of the place are impossible to find. What

236

few existed here in Alexandria and in Cairo have been bought up by the British and are securely in the hands of the top brass. Will it be heavily defended by the Turks? A month or so ago marines and sailors from the fleet walked among the ruins of Turkish forts and gun emplacements after Admiral Carden bombarded the place. The British and French fleets attempted to force a passage through the Dardanelles into the Sea of Marmara, sail to Constantinople and knock Turkey out of the war. A bold stroke. The Turks are uneasy about casting their lot with Germany and Austria. The sight of battleships like the *Queen Elizabeth*, with her fifteen-inch guns steaming through the Golden Horn, would no doubt have been the final straw to break their nerve. But the battleships never reached the Sea of Marmara. Admiral Carden . . . or so the rumour goes . . . suffered a mental and physical collapse. Admiral De Robeck, who replaced him, tried to force the Narrows, lost three or four battleships in one day and gave up the attempt. It was decided that the navy would not try again until the peninsula was in British hands so that the Turks could no longer enfilade the warships from batteries on shore or float mines out against them. I know nothing of military strategy, but that seems to make sense. I had a few drinks with an English colonel and a colonel in the French contingent, the commander of a regiment in the *Legion d'Étranger*. They were both of them quite glum. We sat on the balcony of a fine French restaurant in El Fuwa over-looking the Nile and they explained their anxiety by pointing out that the Turks and their German military advisers have had a month of uninterrupted work to fortify every possible landing site. Barbed wire on the beaches and machine guns on the bluffs will play hell with soldiers trying to wade ashore. They don't like one thing about this upcoming operation – a feeling not shared by the rank and file.

Charles Amberley is here! We met by accident in the lobby of Shepheard's Hotel in Cairo and I spent a day with him and Roger Wood-Lacy, Rupert Brooke and some other officers. Drove over to Gezira and watched a cricket match and then out to Giza in the late afternoon to see the pyramids in the sunset. Brooke is a fine fellow with the ability to talk for hours without boring anyone. The most mundane, even shabby things fill him with poetic delight – the narrow, crowded, dirty streets of Cairo, the tents of the army stretching for miles along the Nile, flags stirring lazily against the white sky, a frieze of palms along the horizon, the *fellaheen* working their fields, drawing water from the river, oblivious to the distant boom of guns as the artillery send practice rounds howling across the desert. The troops – French *légionnaires*, Senegalese, Sikhs, Gurkhas, British in khaki and pith sun helmets, Australians and New Zealanders in their broad slouch hats – *Now, God be thanked Who has matched us with His hour, and caught our youth, and wakened us from sleeping* – Everyone in Egypt seems to know that poem of his. Don't care for it myself. Too romantic in concept. I can't look on war as being a blessing. Keep thinking of those poor bastards of infantry dying on that hillside near Hannogne-St. Martin.

Brooke is in the Naval Division, a marine unit that saw a little service at Antwerp last September. Roger Wood-Lacy was disappointed that he had not been able to enlist with Brooke, for some reason, but he's happy now that they are together in Egypt "A happy band of brothers" – his words. *Everybody*, with the exception of my two glum colonels, is happy, all caught up in the magic of three words – Dardanelles, Constantinople and Hellespont. Literary allusions abound. Keats and Byron are constantly being quoted, as is Homer, and the legends of Helle and the golden ram, Hero and Leander, are constantly being invoked. Men who a few months ago read nothing but the *Sporting News* and *Punch* now speak of "wine-dark seas" and "The winds are high on Helle's wave". Brooke is writing a poem about the expedition, so is Roger Wood-Lacy and, I assume, ten or twenty thousand other men. Even the commander of this invasion force is a poet and writer of note. The sole occasion when General Hamilton condescended to meet the press corp en masse, turned out to be rather like a literary tea. There is something professorial about Hamilton anyway and when he opened his remarks by saying, "Gentlemen, we shall shortly be embarking for the peninsula of Gallipoli, or, as I prefer to call it, the Thracian Chersonese …", I had the uncanny feeling that I was back at the university. The poor Turks are about to be bombarded not only by fifteen-inch shells and field howitzers but by storms of anapests, dactyls, Alexandrines and couplets as well.

April 12th, 1915

Rupert Brooke is ill . . . a touch of the sun. Charles came up here and told me about it. Brooke assures everyone that sunstroke is not as terrible as it sounds, but his commanding officer thinks otherwise and he's being taken aboard one of the many hospital ships that have assembled at Alexandria. He will miss the Gallipoli landings which must be a blow to him. I then went with Charles and the second-in-command of his battalion, a Major Thursby, to the Royal Navy dockyard to see a ship that three companies of the Royal Windsor Fusiliers will board next week. We took a venerable Victoria drawn by four white mules and a pleasant and quaint trip it was. On the way, Major Thursby told me a good deal more about the history of the Royal Windsors than I cared to know, this battle and that campaign and what "the ever glorious Captain Pikestaff" did at the storming of Badajoz. At one point in the narrative Charles leaned close to me and whispered, "He's really a dreadful old bore of a man", and I quite agreed with him.

The ship that the Windsors will board for the Gallipoli landing muted even the garrulous Thursby. It's a rusty old collier called the *River Clyde*, the type of ship that chugs about the sea lanes of the world carrying coal in her bunkers to feed other ships. A sad-looking scow, paint flecked and forlorn amid a cluster of new destroyers. Two square openings are being cut in her hull on both sides and wooden ramps are being built that will be swung out on the cargo booms over these sallyports when the ship is run close to shore. Two thousand men will be aboard her for the assault, the Windsors, Dublin Fusiliers, Munster Fusiliers and two companies of the Hampshire Regiment. Officers from those units were on the dock and they seemed no happier at the prospect than Thursby and Charles.

"Rather a seamy way to go to war," Major Thursby said.

S.S. *Lahore*, April 18th, 1915

Received a cable from Lord Trewe informing me that not one dispatch of mine has reached London. Discussed this with

239

Ellis Ashmead-Bartlett, a morose and faintly eccentric London newspaperman, who was not in the least surprised. He plied a censor with a few drinks one night in Alexandria and discovered that all civilian accounts of the military preparations for the Dardanelles expedition were being held back. He also expressed grave doubt that any press representatives would be allowed to go in with the assault forces. We are all being encouraged to stay in Egypt, but he is determined to go, so am I, and a myopic guy from Reuters. That's it, the entire press corps. The others are on the beach. One elderly war correspondent told me that he was staying behind so "as not to interfere with the army in any way", implying that I was simply being American and "pushy" for wanting to go along.

The S.S. *Lahore* is a P. & O. liner commandeered a few weeks ago to serve as a headquarters ship. Accommodations and service are the finest, Lascar servants abound, all dressed in sparkling white mess jackets with brass buttons. I sit on a deck chair sipping a planter's punch and watch the armada steam out of Alexandria. Horns blow, steam whistles toot, signal flags whip up the halyards, lights flicker back and forth among the two hundred or more ships sailing from Egypt. We are heading for the Aegean, to the island of Lemnos fifty miles off the southwestern tip of Gallipoli. A ship's officer tells me that Mudros Bay on Lemnos is large enough and deep enough to contain every vessel in sight with a good deal of room left to spare. I assume the final sorting out for the assault will be done there. Everything appears to be so smoothly handled, so efficiently worked out that success must be assured.

Charles Amberley stood in the bows of the *River Clyde* and watched the men of his platoon fill and stack sandbags to form a loopholed wall, four feet high and many layers thick, turning the fo'c'sle into a small fort where twelve machine guns could be emplaced. The collier drifted slowly at anchor in the dead calm waters of Mudros Bay, the sun hammering down on the deck plates.

"Like old Vulcan's forge," Roger Wood-Lacy remarked, wiping sweat from the back of his neck with a soiled handkerchief. He leaned against the rail and squinted towards the harsh, treeless hills of the island. "Vulcan lived here, you know. His little paradise. One wonders what he saw in the place. Still, I rather like old Vulcan, solid type of chap. Never could understand why Jupiter kicked him out of heaven. Remember your Milton? *'From morn to noon he fell, from noon to dewy eve, a summer's day; and with the setting sun dropped from the zenith, like a falling star, on Lemnos, the Aegean isle.'* Makes one think, doesn't it? The proximity of the past. Vulcan up there in the hills looking down on us all. Wonder what he thinks?"

"That we're a bunch of damned fools I expect," Charles muttered. "Don't you have anything better to do than hang about quoting *Paradise Lost*?"

Roger tipped his sun helmet to the back of his head and then pointed off across the bay.

"Not till A Company arrives. That's them now, just crossing *Swiftsure's* stern."

Troops had been coming out all morning from the transport ships. There were twelve hundred men aboard the collier now, fretting in the stifling hold. Eight hundred more were due – B and C Companies of the Windsors and two companies from the Munsters.

"You don't seem very happy about things," Roger said. "Anything the matter?"

"No, just tired. Talbot's supposed to be battalion machine-gun officer, but he's done bugger all since we came aboard."

Roger put his hands to his ears in mock horror. "My, my, what dreadful language. Haven't heard such speech since Aunt Mary caught her tits in the wringer!"

Charles laughed. "Hop to it and get your chaps stowed away."

He watched his friend go off down the deck towards the boarding ladders at midship. Not walking with languid grace any longer, the poet's stroll, but moving with a cocky swagger, a seasoned subaltern more than capable of keeping his platoon of tough South Londoners in line. He looked away and scrutinised the sandbag revetment.

"Pack 'em down hard with the flat of a spade, Corporal."

"Right you are, sir."

"Then start setting up the guns, and place bags on the tripod feet."

"Very good, sir."

He watched the Fusiliers and some Royal Marines clamp the Vickers guns to their mounts and unpack the boxes of belt ammunition. The men knew what they were doing and needed no further direction. He leaned against one of the sandbag walls and gazed out at the host of ships in the vast harbour. Lemnos in the Aegean! The phrase rang through his head like poetry. Looking at the warships and the myriad transport ships floating so serenely on the bluest of water under the bluest of skies he thanked God for his mercy at not sending him to France. He could have conjured up a hundred images to dwell upon – Xerxes and his fleet sailing towards Salamis, Jason and the Argonauts seeking the Golden Fleece, Ulysses and Achilles tarrying here on their reluctant journey to Troy. And Byron, of course, seeking Hero's tower overlooking Homer's wine-dark sea. Well, the blind bard had been wrong about that. An ocean like any other, blue or grey, depending on the sky. But it *was* the sunlit Aegean and not the muddy wastes of Picardy that he looked at over the sandbag rampart. He whispered a silent prayer.

"Lieutenant Amberley, sir." The megaphoned voice of Lieutenant-Colonel Askins. "Kindly come up to the bridge."

The colonel stood timber straight on the bridge wing, one large brown hand toying with his sun-streaked moustache. Charles faced his commanding officer with a clear conscience.

"Yes, sir?"

"Ah, Charles. Damned fine job of sandbagging there."

"Thank you, sir."

"What the deuce is wrong with Captain Talbot? That's his bloody job, y'know. Told me he had the cramps. Don't believe a word of it. Shirking, I call it. That's the trouble with the special reserve, too much time on civvy street and they go soft on you. I'm putting him ashore and making you acting captain and battalion chatter gunner."

"Thank you, sir."

The colonel's eyes became distant and he looked away towards the nude brown hills of the island.

"You're a friend of that poet chap, Rupert Brooke. You and Wood-Lacy."

Charles felt his stomach contract. "Yes, sir."

"Wood-Lacy more than you."

"He knows him better, yes, sir."

"Chap died yesterday. Sorry to be so blunt about it, but the message from General Hamilton was as brief as that. It was directed to Wood-Lacy, but I thought I'd better tell you about it. We up anchor at midnight and draw into V beach at six in the morning, as planned. Young W.-L. has a damned important job to do tomorrow and I don't want his thoughts to be wandering about. You can break the news to him after we're safely ashore at Sedd el Bahr. I'm sorry about this, Amberely. I know what it is to lose a friend."

The sun seemed to lose its heat as though a great deal of the light had gone from the sky. The sea had turned sullen and oily. Charles stood at the bridge rail and looked down at the lighters coming alongside with their dense cargoes of men. Two thousand troops for V beach. Only the Lord and General Hamilton knew how many for W, X, S, Y and the ANZAC landing at Gaba Tepe. There seemed little point in grieving for one dead poet.

It lay ahead of him in the darkness, unseen except in the mind's eye, the sharp, semi-circle curve of Sedd el Bahr bay. Memorised map statistics: four hundred yards of narrow sand just west of the ruins of the medieval castle, the land rising gently behind the beach in a series of terraced slopes, a village of stone huts beyond the old fort. He peered through a narrow embrasure, his cheek resting against the cold metal of a Vickers gun. Nothing to be seen but the dark bulk of the land, nothing to be heard but the throb of the *River Clyde*'s engines and the rush of water past the prow. He straightened up and glanced towards the stern. The two empty lighters that would form a causeway to the shore were trailing in tow, dark shapes in the phosphorescent wake. Behind them, only dimly seen, were twenty cutters manned by naval crews and filled with Dublin Fusiliers. They would secure the beach while the *River Clyde* grounded herself in the bay and the lighters were warped around from the stern to make the bridge. Fifteen minutes after grounding the whistles would blow and the two thousand men in the collier's hold would pour out of the sallyports, race down the wooden platforms suspended against the hull, jump on to the lighters and run on to the beach without getting their feet wet.

One hour to morning. A bell clanged and the ship slowed. From out of the dawn behind them came thunderclaps and chain lightning, stabs of intense orange and red light along the horizon. Then the heavy shells of the fleet roared overhead and screamed in their plunge to the land. The half moon coast from Sedd el Bahr to the tip of Cape Helles exploded in flame.

"Stuff it to 'em!" someone called out in the gloom. "Bugger the Turk!"

The pale sky was sullied by sheets of dun-coloured cloud. Grit settled on the deck, the dust of Gallipoli borne on the wind, the soil uprooted by the hammering shells. Explosions blinked and twinkled, sharp points of fire beneath fountains of yellow earth. Squinting over the sandbags, Charles could see the village on the high point of the cove disappear under the shockwave blasts of the navy guns. He held his wrist close to his face and looked at his watch. Six o'clock. The guns of the fleet had been firing steadily for nearly an hour. Nothing, not a mouse, not a bird, could be alive in that boiling, churning, cordite-reeking stretch of land.

"God pity them," he murmured.

CLANG, CLANG! CLANG, CLANG!

The ship trembled as the engines went full speed. The hazy sunlit bay drew closer.

"Load all guns!" he called out.

There was the clatter of ammunition boxes being opened, the sharp snap and clang as the coiled belts were locked into the breeches.

"Open sights, one hundred yards!"

They would fire at ghosts, at pulverised bone.

The shelling ceased as suddenly as it had begun. The shore drew closer, palled in drifting smoke and dust, heavy with silence. He could hear the sigh of debris strike the waters of the bay like a gentle rain.

"Away all boats!" an impetuous midshipman called out, his boyish voice thin as a curlew's cry. "On to the beach!"

The navy cutters slipped their tow ropes from the small steam launches that had pulled them in clusters from the transports and headed in a long line for the shore. The Dubliners were standing, bayonets fixed, the early sun catching the blades.

"Up the Irish!" A Munster Fusilier shouted from the shadowed well deck of the *River Clyde*.

Five hundred yards to the loop of sand. The cutters drifted apart, regrouped slowly, fighting a strong current that boiled beneath the placid surface of the bay. Charles stared at his watch as interminable minutes ticked away. The collier was battling the currents now, surging with added power against the force of the Hellespont flood.

"Blimey," a machine-gunner said as he glared past the barrel of his gun, "the shellin' didn't touch the wire."

Charles bent his head to a loophole in the sandbag wall. The man was correct. Thickets of barbed wire stretched the length of the cove and up the slopes. It was dew wet, like a spider's web.

"The Dublins will have to cut it," he said. "I hope they . . ." The keel grated against the bottom and the ship trembled and groaned then came to a stop thirty yards from the beach. Footsteps hammered on the deck as sailors ran towards the stern to haul the big lighters around to bridge the gap of deep water. Charles looked through one of the side embrasures. The cutters were back in line and moving steadily towards the shore. It was so quiet he could hear the Dublin Fusilier officers and sergeants relaying commands. Thirty yards to go . . . twenty . . . ten. A bluejacket clutching a boat hook jumped into the surf.

Was that a bugle? A faint, brassy, two-note call coming from the ruins of the village? Charles couldn't be certain.

"Did anyone hear . . .?" he started to ask and then a haze of smoke sheeted the entire curve of the bay and the surface of the water was suddenly whipped into a white froth by the first blast of Turkish rifle and machine-gun fire. The soldiers packed into the boats began to scream as the bullets scythed into them.

"Fire!" Charles yelled. The Vickers guns jolted and buckled on the mounts, their noise drowning the cries of the dying Dubliners. Spouts of sand and clay traversed hillside and beach but the Turkish fusillade didn't slacken for an instant. There were no targets, Charles thought wildly. Not a Turk could be seen. There must be trenches all along the slopes, narrow, well concealed. How in God's name had the men in them escaped being blown to pieces by the bombardment? They had probably stayed back in the hills until the shelling had ceased and then had rushed down to the positions. There were only five beaches on the entire peninsula where troops could land. The Turks knew that and had had a month to fortify them and to rehearse their defence strategies. They had learned them well. In the water there was only death, the boats broadside to the beach, splinters flying from the wooden hulls, men tumbling into the sea or lying in heaps across the thwarts. A few soldiers managed to reach the beach and lay huddled behind a low embankment. A handful rushed the wire only to die among the strands.

Bullets clanged against the steel plates of the *River Clyde* and thudded ceaselessly against the sandbags. The sailors trying to drag the lighters around from the stern were shot off the decks and catwalks. Other men took their places to haul on the tow ropes for a few seconds before the shrieking bullet storm dropped them where they stood or sent them flopping over the side. A few bullets were coming through the embrasures in the bags and two machine-gunners fell backward. Other men instantly took their places and the guns kept firing, belt after belt uncoiling from the ammunition boxes, the water starting to boil in the cooling-jackets.

Charles slammed a fist against a bag and cursed under his breath. Why the hell didn't they back off and signal the fleet to start shooting again? He tapped the broad back of a Windsor Fusilier sergeant and shouted loudly to be heard. "Going to the bridge. Take charge."

He dropped down the fo'c'sle hatch into a fetid gloom, skinning one knee badly on the iron ladder. Bullets slapping the hull made the interior of the ship ring like a bell. He stumbled through the fo'c'sle which was stacked high with wooden boxes of cartridges and the belted rounds for the machine guns, brushed past the sweating ammunition handlers and half ran, half stumbled out on to the well deck. A platoon of the Hampshires were kneeling in tight masses against the high iron sides as bullets passed over them cracking like steel whips.

"What the bloody hell's going on?" a white-faced subaltern said.

There was no point in answering him. He'd find out soon enough for himself. The wooden ramps were being lowered over the sides, the operation directed by Lieutenant-Colonel Askins and a navy commander standing on the bridge, both men exposed to the fire storm and totally oblivious to it.

"What the hell are you doin' here?" Colonel Askins said as Charles reached the bridge. The colonel was staring at the shore, lips compressed to bloodless slits.

"We can't dampen that fire with the machine guns, sir. Can't make a dent in it."

"I know. I can see that."

"Need artillery . . . the fleet . . ."

"Too late for that . . . committed now. Bloody ship's fast on the sands. Second wave coming in now." He moved his right arm in a jerky fashion, pointing over his left shoulder.

Charles glanced aft. A string of launches and cutters packed with men were fanning into the bay.

"Signal them to bloody well stop," the colonel said in a flat, tired voice. "General Napier's leading 'em in. Thinks he's Admiral bloody Nelson and turning a blind eye. Every damn one of them wants the V.C. today."

The navy commander suddenly leaned over the totally inadequate barricade of boiler plate and sandbags that lined the bridge, roared orders to the sailors on the steam winches, then darted for the ladder.

"Have to do it myself, damn it!"

"Dear Mr. Unwin," the colonel remarked drily. "He'll get his cross today, or a pine box, or both." He looked at Charles with distant eyes. "It's a bloody balls up, Amberley, but we have to stick it. Get the men ashore, bayonet the Turk up the beach. No other bloody way to do it now. Understood?"

"Yes, sir."

"Good lad. Get back to your guns and keep –"

And then he was dead, the top half of his skull spinning away towards the ship's funnel, hair and cap neatly together, brains splattering the wheelhouse with a pinkish-grey slime. Charles dropped to his knees and pressed his hands to his eyes to shut out the horror. There was no point to it. He knew that. Anyone seeing him would only mistake his cringing attitude for cowardice. He wasn't afraid. He was far beyond fear. Terror created its own unique form of courage. It was just that the colonel's death had come with such explosive suddenness he hadn't been prepared for it. The death itself was meaningless. What of it? He could have died at Tugela or Spion Kop during the South African War. Boer bullets had missed him. Turk bullets had not. He glanced at the long, sprawled, blood-draining body and stood up. A navy signaller crouched with his back against a slab of boiler plate and stared at him with hollow eyes.

"Keep signalling the boats to stop," Charles yelled.

The man's stare was fixed, like an epileptic's. There was no point in telling him to do anything. He ran humpbacked from the bridge to search for the adjutant and tell him that the colonel was dead. He found the man at the bottom of the starboard bridge ladder, flat on the deck with Mauser holes across his chest.

The broad, flat lighters had been lashed together in front of the bows, the debarking platforms sloped down along the ship's sides from the sallyports cut in the hull. Whistles blew and men of the first platoon, A Company the Royal Windsor Fusiliers, started down for the beach, running hard, the starboard platform rattling at their pounding feet.

"Stick it, the Windsors!"

Charles caught a flashing glimpse of Roger, revolver in hand, whistle in his mouth, leading his men down. Bullets slapped against the ship or ricocheted off with a whirring howl. It was like standing in a blizzard of lead, the ferocity of the storm increasing as the troops ran down to the lighters. Charles flung himself to the deck and lay flat behind the slim protection of a lifeboat davit, the boat long gone, rifled to dangling shards. He looked over the side under the bottom rail and saw to his horror that the ramp was empty, the platoon gone, a few men lying in the lighter in a bloody heap, the others in the water, motionless clumps of dark brown, sinking slowly, trailing plumes of scarlet. A whistle blew. The second platoon of A Company ran the gauntlet and withered away to six lone men before they reached the lighter. A platoon of the Munsters followed instantly and died as they ran, tumbling head over heels into the sea.

Dead. Roger was dead. The realisation materialised slowly. Dead and gone. One of the corpses in the lighter, or one of the bobbing sacks of khaki in the water. Gone. Vanished without a goodbye, a parting word. The insanity numbed him. He became oblivious to the fire and stood up, made his way slowly back to the fo'c'sle and took his position again amid the steaming, clattering Vickers guns.

"Blimey," the Fusilier sergeant said, "I didn't give you a snowball's chance in bloody 'ell of makin' it."

They were snug and safe here, Charles thought dully. The wider embrasures had been plugged with bags. The gunners were no longer bothering to aim their weapons because there was simply nothing to aim at. They lay on the deck and pressed the triggers while Turkish bullets cracked and hummed or thudded into the heavy sacks of white Egyptian sand.

A major in the Hampshires crawled up from the well deck and shouted to Charles over the stuttering roar of the machine guns.

"No more chaps going in . . . Waiting till nightfall. Keep the Vickers . . . firing."

Charles nodded and rested his head against the sun heated bags. Through a peephole he could see the bay, the drifting boats of the second wave filled with dead, countless bodies rolling in the surf, blood staining the water a rose pink, a Burgundy red. God, he thought, old Homer had been right after all. It was a wine-dark sea.

5

THERE WERE SIX OFFICERS SEATED IN THE FIRST-CLASS CARRIAGE when Martin Rilke got on the train at Southampton. All of them were back in Blighty after months in France and they eyed Martin with icy contempt, taking in at a glance his age, state of health, the tanned colour of his skin – and his civilian clothes.

"Back from a nice holiday?" a major in the Durham Light Infantry remarked with stiletto politeness.

"No," Martin said as he struggled to place his bulging brief-case in the netting above the seat. "Gallipoli."

The thaw was instant. Cigarettes and stories were exchanged. Martin told the officers about conditions at Cape Helles and Anzac Cove; they in turn told him about Neuve Chapelle and Aubers Ridge – a sombre discussion of massacres as the train rumbled through the summer countryside of southern England.

London sweltered in the July heat, but it felt cool to Martin after Lemnos and the peninsula. There were more travellers than taxis outside Waterloo Station and as he waited impatiently on the kerb for an empty one, a young woman in a pale green dress approached him, eyed him disdainfully and handed him a white feather.

It was odd. Nothing had changed. The message capsules hummed over the ceiling wires and plummeted down on harassed editors and rewrite men, the teletype machines chattered away, copy boys raced back and forth between the multitude of desks and the presses rumbled in the distance like the engines of some great ship. It had been a year since he had sat at his desk in the glass-walled cubicle writing glib copy about English manners and pastimes. He wondered if the theatre reviewer still came in each evening wearing white tie and tails.

No, little had changed. A few new faces, another man at Jacob's old desk.

There were still shilling maps pinned to the walls of Lord Trewe's sumptuous office, a map of the Western Front next to a landscape by Constable, a map of the Mediterranean pinned beside a Turner. Lord Trewe was as burly as ever, but his face was no longer bronzed. Ocean yacht racing was not a possible sport in war-time England.

"Well, Rilke, I'm glad to see you back."

"I'm glad to be here, sir." He sat in an antique chair and placed his briefcase on the oak dining table that served as the press lord's desk. "I have quite a few things for you to read, sir. Journals I've been keeping . . . observations that would never have passed the censors in Mudros."

Lord Trewe settled back in his Biedermeier chair and folded his heavy hands across his waistcoat.

"I don't like reading personal journals, Rilke. I like to read your writing in print, on the fourth page of the *Daily Post*, along with millions of other readers. Let me tell you something that you may not know. Those who wish to read about generals and the high strategy of this war read Repington in *The Times*. Those who wish to read about the flesh and blood men who are doing the dirty, dangerous jobs at the front read the *Daily Post*. Specifically, they read 'Gallipoli Sketches' by Martin Rilke, as do the readers of five American newspapers, three Canadian, two Australian and *Leslie's Weekly* magazine. You have been away three and a half months and you've come back a famous man, an innovator. I do not hesitate to say that you've invented a new journalism, a new form of war reporting, not so much the story of great battles, but the stories of men. Human interest, Rilke, human bloody interest, that's your forte. Now you're back and I take it you don't want to return to Gallipoli. I can understand that. A sideshow, Rilke. The main blows will come in France this autumn. Sir John French and Joffre have a master plan in the works and I'd like your next byline to read 'Western Front Sketches' by Martin Rilke."

Martin opened the briefcase and removed his notebooks. The knowledge that he was known around the world, read in a dozen newspapers, had not sunk in yet. Even if it had, he didn't

251

feel like basking in the glow. His reason for leaving Gallipoli was contained in the notebooks that he pushed across the table.

Lord Trewe rested a hand on them for a moment and then pushed them away.

"I know what's in these, Rilke. They contain everything that the censors would have tossed out had they read them. I'm sure that you depart from sketches and try your hand at comment."

"Lord Trewe –"

"No, Rilke, not Lord Trewe. You've more than earned the right to call me Guv'nor." He leaned forward and folded his arms on the table. His eyes had a sailor's direct gaze. "I know what's happening out there. Nothing you can tell me could possibly outrage me. A brilliant concept bungled very badly. The landings were a disgrace, a waste of brave men. Hamilton sitting on his arse in a battleship far at sea and allowing two thousand men to stand around brewing tea at Y beach while a couple of miles away men were dying in droves at Sedd el Bahr, and Hunter-Weston doing the same damned thing with the landing force at Eski Hissarlik, permitting them to loll about instead of pouring more men into that spot and sending them on the double down to V beach to take the Turk in the flank. Botched! The entire enterprise mangled. And the insanity of the Anzac corps! All those men jammed on a cliff not fit for goats. It will take brilliant high command thinking to pull a rabbit out of that dark hat, Rilke, and there is no brilliance out there above the rank of bloody major! Now, what can you teach me in your journals that I don't already know?"

"Apparently nothing. But tell me, what does the average man on the street know?"

"What he reads in the newspapers."

"Then let him read this, *Guv'nor.*" He tapped the journals with stiff, persistent fingers. "Run this on the front page. My observations and the comments of officers and men that I've interviewed over the past three months. This is the *real* story of Gallipoli: a general staff that thinks the best way to go through a brick wall is head first, a government that's playing politics with the battle, feeding just enough men into it to keep it going but not angering the Western Front generals by shifting all effort there. It's a bloody mess and the public have a right to know just how bloody and hopeless it is. If you people expect to win this war – "

The press lord's fist came down on the stack of journals like a hammer.

"We *will* win. We'll win because if we do not we cease to exist as a nation, let alone as an Empire. The man in the street wants this war to be won. There is firm resolve on that point, and neither this newspaper nor any other will print stories that serve to undermine that determination by castigating our military leadership and eroding the people's faith in the army to win through, eventually."

Martin smiled wryly and took from his pocket the tiny white feather and let it drift to the table.

"Part of that resolve you're talking about, I suppose. It was shoved into my hand outside Waterloo Station by a very pretty girl."

"It's symptomatic, yes. I can't say that I approve of that kind of badgering, but it does reveal what the civilian population feels about this war. They want an all-out effort, every young man of fighting age in uniform, the Boche and the Turk on the run no matter what it takes. They read the casualty lists. No one draws the wool over their eyes on that bloody score. They know how many lads died at Aubers Ridge, Neuve Chapelle – and are dying now in the Dardanelles – and they would hang any newspaperman in effigy who told them that those men died for nothing." He leaned back in his chair and toyed abstractedly with his gold watch chain, threading the heavy links through his fingers. "I'll tell you something, Rilke. Great changes are in the wind. This Gallipoli fiasco will topple many men and bring others to the fore. Asquith's days are numbered as prime minister, in my opinion. Churchill's career has been ruined, Kitchener's powers are being blunted, Lloyd George and David Langham are on the rise. The conduct of the war will be taking a new turn; more statesmen and less generals calling the shots. I don't know if that's good or bad. We're all feeling our way. There has never been a war to compare it with, no lessons of the past to guide us at all. I do know this, the war will go on until one side or the other breaks. This newspaper will report the war and that is *all* we will do.

The day-to-day business of fighting it, the men and the events, the human drama as it unfolds. You write of those things very well, Rilke. You capture the bravery as well as the pain. I want you to continue, within the limits prescribed by the censorship regulations. Will you?"

Martin touched the white feather lying on the cover of one of his journals, shredded it into downy fragments.

"I guess I must. It has to be witnessed, doesn't it?"

"Yes. Let me read you something printed this morning in the *Telegraph*, dated Mudros, Thursday last, byline a certain Robert Allensworth who did honourable reporting for the *Telegraph* in the Boer War." Lord Trewe shuffled among the papers in front of him and drew out a copy of the rival newspaper. "I shall not read the entire article, just this part. 'The lieutenant laughed gaily, a boyish laugh of pure delight . . . and he was a mere boy, fresh from the playing fields of a great and noble public school. It was a jolly lark, this boy soldier cried, Brother Turk has no stomach for English steel, they ran like hares when we charged them with the bayonet. It was a jolly half hour and gave us all quite a hearty appetite for breakfast.'" He folded the paper carefully and then dropped it into a wastepaper basket.

"I know Allensworth," Martin said, watching the feathery fragments drift across the table-top like lint. "He never went near the fighting. Came over from Egypt for three days and made up stories out of his own head."

"There are many men like him; not too many like yourself. You may not be writing *all* the truth, but by God you're writing enough of it so that you should feel no shame. Your descriptions of the attack on June 4th made every Englishman who read them weep at the bravery and the heartbreak of it. The censors barely cut a word. It was good, honest reporting, Rilke, and you did a service for every poor Tommy who died on those bloody slopes. You may criticise the high command's handling of that attack in your journal, I don't know, but such criticism, printed now, would only give comfort to our enemies." He pushed the slim stack of books towards Martin. "Keep these to yourself, and don't look so glum, lad. A man can do only so much and no more in these times."

*

254

He took a seat on the upper deck of a bus going along Fleet Street towards the Strand. The crowds that he looked down upon from the open-topped bus were anything but glum and dispirited. That a war was on was evident by the number of men in uniform, the recruiting posters on every letter box and the white-feather girls prowling outside the cinemas, but the atmosphere in the city was one of lightness, as though the most pressing problem on this sunny afternoon was in buying the right article in a shop or finding the best place for tea.

The briefcase felt heavy on Martin's lap. Lord Trewe . . . *Guv'nor* . . . had been right, of course. The war had to go on even if it shambled forward at the moment, overburdened with inept and unimaginative commanders. Things would change in time, he supposed, fresh minds rising to the top. Doubt of that gnawed at him. He had had the chance to observe the command structure of the army at first hand on Lemnos: the tight clique of brother officers above the rank of colonel, an esoteric fraternity that resented and feared outsiders. They had refused – politely, for politeness was inherent in their bones – permission for war correspondents to visit the battle front until three weeks after the landings and then only for limited times. He and Ashmead-Bartlett had ignored those restrictions when they finally reached the peninsula by the simple method of going directly to the front-line trenches – a spot where staff officers were loathe to follow. A kind of vacuum existed between the men at the front and the men at headquarters. Operations were planned on maps at Lemnos without the staff officers having any clear idea of what those operations entailed for the men ordered to carry them out. Fifty yards looked a tiny distance on a map, a distance easily covered, if one ignored the fact that every inch of those yards was barren of cover and under the sights of Turkish artillery and machine guns. The staff never talked of *the men*, that is the tired, dirty, lice-infested, fly-plagued soldiers weak from diarrhoea, but always in terms of *the regiment*. "The Royal Windsors can do it . . . one can always rely on the Lancashire Fusiliers . . .", as though those dun-coloured ranks living like moles were scarlet-clad phalanxes of immortals.

He tapped the briefcase and stared sourly at the crowded

pavements. The holiday atmosphere irked him. Why? It was Friday afternoon and people who had worked hard all week had a right to look forward to the weekend. Many of them probably had sons, fathers, brothers, husbands or lovers at the front and felt the presence of the war keenly. That didn't mean that they should walk around in mourning or not walk around at all. He was annoyed at them because he felt a pang of guilt for sitting in perfect safety on top of a London bus holding on his lap journals of anguish and fear. The men he had written about, the English, Indians, Frenchmen, Australians and New Zealanders, the sun-scorched, thirst-plagued infantrymen clinging to their toehold in the Aegean, might at this moment be corpses turning black on the dead-ground below Achi Baba or Chunuk Bair – Charles among them. That thought made his palms sweat. He had sought out Charles on his first trip over to Gallipoli from Lemnos, not knowing whether he were alive or dead, knowing only that his cousin's battalion had been badly cut up leaving the *River Clyde*. "By Gad, we can all be proud of the Windsors," an elderly staff officer had said the day after the landings, seated on the terrace of a café in Mudros, drinking Greek wine. "Those chaps know how to die."

The face of a woman in the crowd as the bus turned off the Strand into Charing Cross Road, a slim, ivory pale face, thin, delicate features, slender nose, black hair. She had been in a uniform when he had seen her last, she was in a uniform now, the blue and red uniform of an army nurse. The bus slowed as a torrent of pedestrians crossed the street, heading for Trafalgar Square. He spotted her again, walking slowly, drifting along with the crowd. There was no point in yelling. She wouldn't hear him and quite possibly, it wasn't her at all. Clutching the briefcase to his side he dashed down the aisle and half ran, half fell down the narrow, curving steps to the bottom deck and then leaped past an astonished conductor into the street.

"Get killed that way, mate," the man yelled after him.

He lost sight of her in Trafalgar Square, hemmed in by a crowd watching a recruiting drive of the London Scottish, kilted pipers parading under Nelson's Column. He darted up

256

the steps of the monument in order to see better and spotted a blue and red figure at the far edge of the square walking slowly towards the Haymarket. A recruiting sergeant made a grab for his arm.

"That's the lad! There's nothing to beat the London Scots!"

"Sorry," Martin said,.pulling away. "Thought you were the Black Watch."

She was standing in front of a dress shop, gazing reflectively at the display in the window. He studied her profile for a second and then walked up to her.

"Ivy Thaxton?"

She looked at him curiously and then smiled.

"Why, if it isn't Mr. Rilke . . . from Chicago, Illinois."

"That's right," he said, grinning broadly. "Railways and Cattlemarkets. I spotted you from the top of a bus . . . knew it was you, or, anyway, hoped it was. How are you?"

"Fine. And yourself?"

"Swell, just swell."

"You certainly look fit. Been at the seaside?" Her violet eyes were innocent enough, but he felt disquieted by their steady gaze.

"Say," he said nervously, "you're not going to hand me a white feather or something, are you?"

"Why, whatever for?"

"Well, it happened once today. I guess I looked too healthy to be out of uniform."

"You should have told her who you were," she said heatedly. "Silly woman." She touched his hand and smiled again. "I'm sorry if I gave you a turn. I was just being face-tious. We've all read your articles in the *Post*. The men in the ward say you're the only one who knows what the soldier goes through. I'm terribly proud of you, Mr. Rilke, and I do brag a bit about knowing you. Fancy! I used to make your bed!"

"Golly, that was a long time ago."

She scowled. "Oh, the more I think about it, the angrier I get. All those feather girls are frumps. Nothing better to do with their time than hang about street corners and shame young men."

He touched the soft fabric of her uniform sleeve. "You've sure found something better to do with your time."

"Yes. Joined the Q.A.s last September. Her ladyship helped me get in by writing a letter of recommendation. I'm not a sister yet, of course. It takes ever so much training to become that. I'm a probationer, training at All Souls Hospital in Holborn."

"You'll make it."

"Yes," she said thoughtfully, "I will. I know how to work. And, oh Lord, do they work us hard! This is my first afternoon off in weeks and I doubt if I'll get another one for months."

"When do you have to be back?"

"Eight o'clock."

"It's only four thirty. Had tea yet?"

"No."

"Neither have I. Will you join me? I have great respect for the Q.A.s. I met a dozen of your sisters on Lemnos and I owe every one of them a good cup of tea. There's a White Manor in Charing Cross."

"I understand it's very posh," she said doubtfully. "An orchestra and everything like that. I wouldn't want you to go to any expense. I believe there's an ordinary White Manor on Shaftesbury Avenue."

"Ordinary places are for ordinary people. You're special, Ivy. And anyway, I've got three months' pay burning holes in my pocket."

He talked about Gallipoli as they walked slowly towards Charing Cross and told her how he had met Lord Amberley there, in the trenches at Cape Helles. She listened gravely, keenly aware of death and wounds.

"I'm so happy that his lordship is all right. That must be a hellish place. We haven't received any of the Gallipoli wounded. They send most of them to Egypt and Malta. It's just as well, we have so many coming in from Flanders."

"Will they be sending you to France?"

"Not until I'm qualified to work on a surgical team. That might be nine months to a year from now. I hope the war will be over by then. Do you think it will?"

"No, I'm afraid I don't."

"Oh, dear," she sighed. "Neither do most of the chaps I talk to in the wards. But one lad placed a little sign behind his bed. He lettered it himself very cleverly with a coloured pencil. It reads, 'Peace be with us in 1916'. Not that it will make much difference to him. He lost both legs and an arm at Festubert."

Her sombre, reflective mood changed as they walked into the plush elegance of the Grand Tea Salon on the second floor of the White Manor. An orchestra was playing a tango and many couples were dancing.

"Oh, my, isn't it grand!"

The tea was lavish, petits-fours and éclairs, slices of Madeira cake and ices – too rich for Martin. He toyed with a piece of cake and watched Ivy eat.

"A welcome change from hospital food, I bet."

She nodded and bit into a petit-four. "Yes, they boil everything. I missed Abington Pryory at first. They had such good cooks there, didn't they? I'm very fond of food, in case you haven't noticed, but I never gain an ounce. Must be glandular."

"Just youthful energy burning it off. How old are you, Ivy?"

"I turned eighteen in March. Getting on in life. Oh, dear, there are so many things I'd like to do, places I'd like to see. Do you know, this is the first time I've ever been out to tea with a man? Think of that!"

"Make the most of it then. Would you care to dance?"

"I never learned how. I'd hate to make a fool of myself in front of all these people."

"Watch the dancers. None of them are very good, just having a good time. Come on, they're playing foxtrots now. That's easy to do. Just walk backwards while I hold you."

"It doesn't sound easy," she said dubiously, "but I'll give it a try."

The first touch of her slender body made his legs feel weak. It seemed incredible how neatly she fitted against him. He marvelled at that revelation and held her tightly.

"Am I doing it correctly?" she asked.

"Oh, yes," he said, brushing his cheek against hers. "You're doing just swell."

They danced until *thé dansant* ended at six thirty and the

orchestra played its final number. It had been the most enjoyable couple of hours Martin had spent for a long time, the most enjoyable she had ever spent, a fact she made a point of telling him as they walked towards St. James's Park.

"Oh, I did like that! I can't wait to tell the other girls. And, oh, how beautiful some of those women looked in their gowns!"

"None as beautiful as you, Ivy."

She stared ahead as though she hadn't heard the compliment.

"Do you go dancing with lots of girls, Mr. Rilke?"

"Martin. Please call me Martin. And no, I've been too busy to go dancing."

"Did you go dancing in Chicago?"

"Sometimes."

"I never went to a dance. Da didn't approve of them. My Da is a bit straitlaced."

"Your father, you mean?"

"That's right."

"What does he do for a living?"

"Works in a shoe factory. He's doing very well now. His establishment is making boots for the army. Queer, isn't it? Times were so hard for him before the war and now he's making ever so much money. Quite odd, if you stop to think about it."

It would be light until nearly ten o'clock and this hour was the loveliest of the day, the sun catching the tops of the trees and all the buildings along Whitehall, the air cooling after the heat of the long day. The park was crowded with soldiers and their girls.

"I feel kind of silly carrying this briefcase, like some sort of door-to-door drummer."

"I think it makes you look distinguished. I'm sure people think you just left Parliament and are on your way to see the King."

"Taking my nurse with me, I suppose."

"Yes. You're subject to seizures and fits, like my Uncle Arthur, only Da says he only has fits when he suspects the publican of watering the beer." She suddenly spread her arms wide. "Oh, I do love green parks! London would be such a lovely town if they'd only allow grass to grow in the streets."

He took her hand and led her away from the path towards a grotto of trees.

"You're such a happy soul, Ivy."

"Do you think so? I'm not really. I'm a bit on the glum side most of the time. It's being around so much pain. Oh, you have to keep cheery, matron insists on that, but inside, around the heart, there's always a dull ache."

"Do you feel it now?"

"A little, yes. I mean to say, I'm enjoying myself and I'm awfully glad to be with you, but I have to be on duty in an hour and part of my mind is back in the ward. I'm in the amputation ward, you see, have been for the past nine weeks, and there's such a terrible amount of sadness there."

He dropped the briefcase and took her impulsively into his arms, pressing her to him, his hands strong against her back. There were couples all around them, seated or lying on the grass, under the trees, strolling by the dark green lake. No one paid the slightest attention as he kissed her firmly on the lips, as she kissed him. All the horrors of Gallipoli lay in the leather case at his feet, but all thought of them vanished for a moment in the sweetness of her mouth.

Hanna Stanmore lingered over her tea on the terrace of Abington Pryory, a high tea, watercress sandwiches and thinly sliced ham and smoked Scotch salmon. She avoided large, heavy meals in the summertime believing it conducive to gout in later years. Across the stone balustrade she could see William and four of his friends making a mockery of a tennis game, slamming balls into the well-rolled and clipped grass to see how high they would bounce, or using their racquets as cricket bats and slapping the white balls into the trees. High-spirited lads, happy to be down from Eton for the holidays. Seventeen. A difficult age, not quite boys, not yet men. She knew that her son and his house-guests smoked cigarettes behind the stables and sampled the sherry: Coatsworth turned a blind eye to the latter while keeping the better casks firmly under lock and key.

The heat lingered, rising from the terrace stones. She fanned herself with a Japanese silk fan and watched the boys, leaping over the net now – back and forth, back and forth – like sheep over a fence. William was growing so tall. He would be taller than Charles. A fine, strapping boy and the apple of his father's eye. So much like Tony; fine rider, good shot.

She felt a sense of dread the moment she saw the footman walk on to the terrace from the conservatory. His very age was disquieting. He moved so slowly and painfully on his old feet that it was really high farce to dress septuagenarians in livery. The poor man's leaden countenance foretold doom. The pale blue envelope on the small silver tray he carried confirmed it.

"By special post, your ladyship," the footman said.

"Thank you, Crawshay."

She held the envelope in her hand until the man had gone. War Office stationery. Addressed to her, but then they always addressed the letter to the mothers. She slit the envelope with a knife, her hand calm and sure, only her heart racing, a throbbing pain behind the eyes.

July 17th, 1915

Dear Lady Stanmore;

It is with regret that I have received word today that your son, Capt. Viscount Amberley, 2/RWF, has sustained wounds during the recent fighting at Cape Helles. Accounts of the extent and severity of his injuries are necessarily sketchy at this time, but it is known to us that he has been evacuated from the Peninsula and taken aboard a hospital ship.

We wish him well.

Yours sincerely,
T. Pike, Brig. Gen.

There had been a great many men wounded or taken sick during the July battles at Cape Helles and Anzac Cove. Finding the exact particulars about one man was next to impossible. Lord Stanmore haunted the War Office and Martin sent messages through the press channels to Alexandria and Lemnos. Nothing. Captain Lord Amberley was simply one of a multitude evacuated from the Aegean on hospital ships. No one was quite sure which ship had received him and there was no way on earth of finding out until the ship docked somewhere and disgorged its sick. At that point hospital orderlies would write down the particulars of each man and forward that information to London. It took two weeks, fourteen days and nights that moved in a timeless vacuum of nightmare for Hanna. Her husband's assurances to her that Charles was bound to be all right, *probably no more than a flesh wound*, sounded hollow and forced. She spent the days working on needlepoint to try to keep her mind occupied, but there was nothing she could do at night except lie in bed in a cold sweat and imagine her son lying on an antiseptically white bed, his body shattered and mutilated ... limbless ... faceless ... a hollow-mouthed creature that could no longer even scream. She felt on the verge of madness. And then the afternoon came when William ran whooping into her sewing room yelling, "Old Charlie's all right! Only a fractured hip and pelvis. They took him to Toulon on a French ship . . . that chap from the army just rang up Father and told him!"

She burst into tears and was weeping uncontrollably when her husband came into the room. The sight of his mother's hysteria embarrassed William and he was moody for the rest of the day.

August 9th, '15

My dearest Mother, Father, William and Alex,

This short letter is for you all. I was almost literally hit by a Turk shell, the great ugly thing landed right next to where I was lying but failed to explode. Broke my right hip and pelvis in several places, but the bones are mending well. I am quite wasted from dysentery, but that condition is on the mend so I should be back to passing normal in a few weeks and fit for active duty within three to four months.

I am in the French naval hospital in Toulon, a great stone barn of a place built by Napoleon with a magnificent view of the docks from the windows in my room, long, cool passageways, very pretty French nurses, first-rate food and a doctor who believes that half a litre of good red wine a day never hurt any man. Bless the chap in your prayers! I could not ask for better or more sympathetic care and will be evacuated to a hospital in England in about three weeks' time. It will seem odd coming home. I don't quite know how to put it, but I am not the same man who left just a few short months ago. So much has changed. So much more will be changed. But we shall talk about that when I arrive.

My warmest regards to Coatsworth, Mrs. Broome and all the staff. Also, please convey to the vicar that God has been kind to me and I much regret filching pears from the vicarage garden when I was eleven. All my love . . .

Charles

The earl scowled at the broken top of his soft-boiled egg.

"What do you think he means about change? Of course he's changed. Can't get hit by a shell and not be affected by it somewhat."

"I suppose he means . . . many things," Hanna said quietly. She read the letter through again silently and then placed it on the polished surface of the breakfast table. "I could weep."

"Oh, Mother, *please*," William muttered, then glanced quickly towards his father. The earl did not admonish him. They both shared a horror of emotional outbursts.

"Sounds cheerful enough, my dear, considering the circumstances."

"I was thinking of poor Roger," she said. "If only God had showed a little kindness to him as well."

She was not being entirely honest. She grieved for Roger Wood-Lacy, but what truly distressed her was Charles's assurance that he would be *fit for active duty within three to four months*. An unexploded shell. Would God grant any man two miracles in a lifetime?

"I would like us to go to France, Tony."

The earl dabbed at his mouth with a napkin. "That might be quite difficult. Restrictions on civilian travel to the Continent are severe. I might possibly be able to arrange it, but it could easily take a few weeks and Charles could well be on his way here by then. There's really nothing we can do for the lad by going. In fact, I think it would only distress him knowing we were crossing the Channel on a passenger ship with all those blasted U-boats skulking about. He must, surely, have heard about the *Lusitania* going down."

"I suppose you're right," she sighed. "Yes, it would worry him, I'm sure."

Her instinct to protect and cherish her first born was being thwarted by the dictates of the war. Civilian travel to France was not encouraged in the least. Visas would be required, skeins of red tape to cut through. Tony was right, it would be an unnecessary gesture at best. Charles would be in England in a matter of weeks to convalesce. She had read that soldiers were often sent as close to their homes as possible and there were several war hospitals within half an hour's drive from Abington.

"Patience, my dear," the earl said gently. "You must have patience."

She reflected on her husband's attitude, and that of William, as she sat in the music room working on a tapestry. She worked swiftly with the needles and the many strands of coloured thread, shading and highlighting the spire of Salisbury Cathedral in petit-point. William she dismissed with a sad smile. He was at an age that ignored tragedy utterly. His brother had suffered an accident, no worse than that, like a crash in a motor car or a fall from a horse. Fear, death and mourning were not words in his vocabulary. As for Tony, she felt a grudging respect. She knew how he had suffered for the past two weeks, had noticed what no other eyes but her own would have seen – the hint of pain in his eyes, the paleness at the corners of his mouth. Once, unable to sleep, she had opened the door to his room and had seen him standing in front of a window in the darkness, his head pressed against the glass. He had been weeping, very quietly, an insular sadness that she had not dared to intrude upon.

Men did not cry, only in their hearts or in the aloneness of midnight rooms, away from prying eyes or the unmanly comfort of a woman's arms. She understood that well enough even if she questioned the code men lived by. It seemed unnatural to be so restrained, but she supposed it was precisely that code which had permitted Tony to function during a stage of crisis.

All during the ordeal of the past two weeks, not knowing whether Charles was alive or dead, mildly injured or horribly mangled, he had been following his normal routines to the letter: riding in the morning, inspecting the estate, going up to London for debates in the House, visiting his clubs. "Life must go on, Hanna," he had said. To the casual observer his attitude might have appeared cold, uncaring, but she understood his inner torment and knew that the only way he had been able to cope with it had been to pretend that it didn't exist. But it *had* existed and his repressed suffering must leave some mark on him, alter him in some way. There had been a hint of it after breakfast. He had remarked casually, "Hanna, what's the name of that book dealer in Guildford who Charles dealt with all the time?"

"Clipstone . . . small shop in the High Street. Why?"

"Oh, thought he might know the books Charles'd enjoy reading. Poetry, I suppose, history, stuff like that. Make up a parcel to send the lad."

The last book he had bought for Charles had been *Captain Haxwell's Tales of Great Hunts*, given on Charles's sixteenth birthday and left unopened to this day.

"Miss Foxe on the line, your ladyship."

"Thank you, Coatsworth."

She carefully finished a stitch. Lydia had obviously received a letter as well and she had a strong feeling that she knew what Charles had written her. Change. Yes, many things would change.

"I didn't mean to disturb you, Lady Stanmore," Lydia said, her voice faint over the crackling wires. The telephone service from London to Abington was abysmal. "I thought that you'd like to know I received a very long letter from Charles this morning."

"We received one, too, my dear."

"Yes, I felt certain you would have. Are you and Lord Stanmore intending to visit him in France?"

"We would certainly like to, but I understand that it is much too difficult . . . visas . . . special travel permits from the French military."

"That's really why I called. I can arrange it. You could leave

266

this weekend via army transport from Portsmouth and then by train to Marseilles."

Hanna held the receiver very tightly. "How easily you can manage things, Lydia."

"It's really not at all difficult, Lady Stanmore, but it can be terribly frustrating if one tries to go through the regular channels. Shall we say Saturday morning? That way you and Lord Stanmore could be in Toulon by Sunday afternoon."

"I should very much like to discuss it. Could we have luncheon tomorrow? Say at the Savoy? One thirty?"

There was a moment's pause. The wires hummed and snapped. And then Lydia's voice, accepting at that time and place, a calm, self-assured voice, the tone of a chess player who knows the exact number of moves to checkmate.

She had not been up to London for months, not since the winter, and the size of the crowds amazed her, as did the sight of women porters at Charing Cross. An elderly cabbie drove her the few blocks to the Savoy.

"So many people," she said, "and so many women working at such odd occupations."

"It's the war, ma'am," the driver replied sourly, half turning his head towards the little glass partition behind him. "All the young lads takin' the king's silver so the girls is fillin' in like. Can't say as I likes seein' it. Why, you can go to any public 'ouse and see the women liftin' their pints right alongside the men."

"You don't say so."

"God strike me if it ain't the truth. Seen it with me own eyes any number of times, ma'am."

"And the streets are so crowded."

"Why, bless you, ma'am, it's the war, see . . . the munition works down Woolwich way and all them bullet-makers and what-not out Ilford and Epping. Everyone's makin' good money and ol' London's the best place to spend it."

There were lorry-loads of soldiers all down the Strand, inching towards Charing Cross Station. The men were in full kit, heavily loaded packs, rifles, all of them waving their caps and cheering.

"Goin' over," the driver said gloomily. "I was at Mafekin'. It ain't no bloody picnic, war is, I can tell you."

The lounge of the Savoy had always been so quiet, so sedate, now it was bedlam, a swirl of officers and young women. Many of the officers were from the Canadian divisions, tall, boisterous, back-slapping men with flat, almost American accents. It was like being back in Chicago. At last she spotted Lydia and moved imperiously through the throng like the countess she was.

"How lovely you look, my dear. Your dress is most becoming, so chic. Not Ferris, surely."

"No, from Worth. I'm glad you like it."

"Very much. The shorter skirts suit your figure." Her compliments were genuine. She had certain reservations about Lydia, but none for her taste in clothes. "How hot it is here. Must be the crowd."

"I meant to warn you," Lydia said with a laugh. "The Savoy these days is rather like Waterloo Station on Bank Holiday, but I did manage to reserve a table on the terrace. It's relatively quiet and there's a lovely breeze off the river."

Waiters hovered. They ordered consommé and cold lobster, a dish of fruit and a bottle of Liebfraumilch – now labelled, the *sommelier* remarked patriotically, Alsatian White.

Hanna removed Charles's letter from her handbag. "I thought you might like to read this. If I remember correctly, you used to help him raid the vicar's pear trees."

"I'd almost forgotten. Yes. I stood as lookout for Charles and Fenton." She read the short letter and handed it back. "I brought my letter along. You can read it if you'd like."

"You want me to, don't you, Lydia?"

"Yes," she replied evenly. "I want very much for you to read it. I . . . I think it might explain a good deal."

"About you and Charles? I don't think so. He loves you and I'm sure his letter expresses that love. Such letters are not meant to be read by a third party. They lose flavour in the transition."

The consommé and the lobsters came and the two women ate, talking of generalities – the hot weather, the war. When the coffee arrived Lydia poured two coffee-cups from the silver pot.

"Was Lord Stanmore pleased at the thought of seeing Charles by Sunday?"

"I didn't mention our conversation," Hanna said, sipping her coffee. "He would only resent special treatment. No, we will wait until Charles is sent home, but I am most grateful for the gesture. Could you really have arranged things so effortlessly?"

"Yes."

"Might I ask how?"

"Through David Langham."

Hanna looked away and watched the river traffic moving under the span of Waterloo Bridge. One of the boats was a steam yacht with a white funnel. Highly polished brass glinted in the sun and reminded her strongly of regatta days at Henley before the war. Only a year ago, and yet every aspect of life had changed utterly.

"Mr. Langham has become a most powerful man, or so I gather from the newspapers."

"Yes," Lydia said. "His ministry has become quite vital."

"What precisely is its function?"

"Military appropriations, the co-ordination of supply to need. The shell shortage at Neuve Chapelle spurred the importance of the ministry. As my father remarked at the time, no White Manor ever ran out of meat pies at a crucial moment. The ministry sees to it that if the army projects a need for a million rounds of machine-gun ammunition in September, those million rounds will be available. The same holds true for everything from tinned stew to bootlaces."

"Fascinating," Hanna murmured. "The ministry must employ a great many people."

"Yes, both civilians and military."

"Might I have some more coffee?" She averted her eyes from the peaceful tableau on the river and studied Lydia as though seeing her for the first time. Charles's infatuation with the woman was easy to understand, but she doubted if he had ever looked much beyond the shiny chestnut hair and the faultless skin. Lydia's beauty was beyond questioning, but it was a surface loveliness, an enchantment of bone structure and ivory flesh. There were depths in the green eyes that were impenetrable, a labyrinthine murkiness that Hanna found disquieting. But then she was a woman. A man gazing into those eyes would feel no qualms whatever. Certainly not Charles, not even the Honourable David Selkirk Langham.

"Charles is determined to marry you, Lydia, come what may. That's the crux of his letter, isn't it?"

"Yes."

"I can understand his feelings. He's seen so much death. Now he's determined to embrace living, if . . . if only for a little while." She looked down at her cup and ran a finger around the thin porcelain rim. "It appears to be an almost universal attitude these days. So many marriages. The registry offices are crowded with young men in uniform and their girls. I find it difficult to understand why a man would take a bride today only to leave her a widow tomorrow."

"No man believes it will happen to him. If there's a chance at happiness before going to the front . . ."

"He grasps it. I can sympathise with that, and yet I can't dispel the distress I feel at the idea of a young man being married one minute and torn apart by a shell the next."

"I share that concern, Lady Stanmore. When I think how close Charles came . . ." She let the thought dangle and took a sip of her coffee.

"Both Lord Stanmore and I want Charles to be happy. That is uppermost in our thoughts. I understand my husband very well and I know that he would be willing to make concessions, to soften certain inflexible attitudes that he once had towards you and Charles. To be blunt, I could induce him to give his blessing."

"And would you?"

"No. Never. Not if it means seeing Charles go back to the front a mere three or four short months after his honeymoon. I'm sure that you find that just as painful to contemplate as I do."

"Yes, I do."

"Charles has shed his blood . . . nobly and with honour. He's done, as they say, *his bit*."

Lydia set down her cup and glanced around for a waiter. "Would you care for a brandy, Lady Stanmore? Daddy keeps a private stock here of some wonderful fifty-year-old cognac."

"He must dine here often."

"Late suppers mainly, with Mr. Langham."

"I'd enjoy a glass. I find brandy settles the nerves."

The waiter caught Lydia's eye and moved to the table like a dancer. She told him to ask the wine waiter for a bottle of 1865 Otard and to bring a pot of fresh coffee.

"I was talking to Mr. Langham this morning and I happened to mention Charles. It was Mr. Langham who told me how to go about arranging clearance papers and offered to facilitate things."

"That was very kind of him."

"Well, today, he was telling me about a new branch of the ministry that's being formed. It will be known as N.S.5 and will deal with the testing and procurement of new equipment for the army. Major-General Sir Thomas Haldane will head it and he's looking for bright men to staff it, preference going to officers who have seen the war at first hand and understand the army's needs. I thought of Charles right away."

"Yes," Hanna said, speaking slowly so as to keep any tremor of emotion from her voice, "he would certainly qualify, wouldn't he?"

"Of course. Not quite as much scientific background as General Haldane might like, but that obstacle can be overcome easily enough. Charles has a quick mind. He can learn anything if he has to."

"Would he take such a job? Leave his regiment?"

"He would have no choice. Mr. Langham has given General Haldane top priority on this. He can order the transfer of any line officer he wishes to have."

"It sounds like a satisfying and worthwhile task."

"Very. The prime minister and Lord Kitchener are terribly enthusiastic about it. So much of the army's equipment and weapons are antiquated. Charles would be doing far more for his country in Whitehall than he could ever do in the trenches."

Hanna felt faint as weeks of unending tension suddenly left

her body. She was grateful for the brandy when it arrived and inhaled the heady fumes before taking a sip.

"To Charles," she said. "And to you."

Lydia smiled and reached across the table to touch Hanna lightly on the arm.

"Thank you, Lady Stanmore. I know everything will work out for the best. I shall make Charles a very good wife."

"I'm sure you will, my dear," Hanna said with the barest trace of a smile. "He's a fortunate young man."

And she meant that to the very bottom of her heart.

6

NUMBER SEVEN RED CROSS HOSPITAL AT CHARTRES OCCUPIED A limestone château overlooking the River Eure. It had been conceived as a centre for the convalescence and rehabilitation of severe fracture cases, but the heavy casualties in Artois during the spring offensive had flooded it with every conceivable type of injury. Wooden barracks had been erected in the once lovely gardens and the stables and coach house had been turned into wards and living quarters for nurses. The expansion barely kept pace with the flow. Fortunately, there had been minimal activity on the Western Front during the summer, but the *médecin-chef*, Dr. Gilles Jary, had just received notice from Paris that he could expect a marked increase in patients by the third week in September. The notice had arrived by ordinary post and the contents infuriated him.

"Such stupidity!" he stormed, pacing his small, crowded, untidy office in what had once been a garret room for lackeys. "*Merde!* That is all I can say, *merde!*" He held the offending message between two fingers and then let it drift to the floor. His matron of nurses, a stout, middle-aged Englishwoman watched him impassively.

"May I read it, doctor?"

"Why not? Why should you be an exception?" He kicked at the paper. "But I shall save you the bother. We are to prepare for many casualties by the third week in September. Identical messages have no doubt been sent to every other hospital. Perhaps they also sent the message to Boche headquarters! My dear Fritz, as you can see by the enclosed notice we are preparing to attack you on or about the twenty-second day of next month. Cordially, *Maréchal* Joffre."

The doctor lit a cigarette from the butt of another smouldering between his lips.

"You shall set your beard alight one day," the matron said.

"Perhaps. It does not matter in the least."

"Where do we put more wounded?"

"A question for which there is no answer, matron, no answer at all. Clear beds, I suppose. Any *blessé* capable of standing must be moved out, sent down to Moulins, Lyons, Valence. I don't know. I will have to make enquiries as to available beds. Then there is the Hôtel Marcel in town. We could requisition it for the ambulatory."

The matron smiled faintly. "You see, doctor, there are answers to everything."

"I suppose," he growled, running a hand through his shaggy hair. "Now then, what problems do *you* have for me this morning?"

"None . . . a small pleasure. Three V.A.D.s have arrived from England, very eager to serve, anxiously awaiting their first meeting with the *médecin-chef.*"

"All of them blonde and willowy?"

"Only one is blonde and rather more *voluptueuse* than willowy, I would say."

"Ah," he sighed, "English girls. Aromatic as their tea. They stir the dead ashes of my youthful lechery."

"How Gallic you are today, doctor. Shall I send them up?"

"No, I shall meet them in Ward D. They can follow me on rounds."

Alexandra Greville walked gravely behind Dr. Jary, the English matron and a French nurse. The other two V.A.D.s stood as close to the doctor as they could, both of them jotting down what he said in notebooks. Their eagerness pleased the doctor and he complimented them extravagantly after the rounds of Wards D and F had been completed. He then turned to face Alexandra.

"You do not keep notes, Miss . . . Miss . . . ?"

"Greville. No, I have a very retentive memory."

"You seem, if you will pardon me, abstracted. Is anything the matter?"

"No, just a bit disappointed."

Yes, Dr. Jary was thinking, *voluptueuse* was certainly the word to describe this blonde beauty. Most English girls he had known were virtually breastless and hipless. This one was superbly endowed with both. She reminded him of the opulent nudes of Ingres. It was quite easy to visualise her naked and he felt a momentary regret at not being thirty years younger.

"Disappointed? With our little hospital?"

"Oh, no, doctor," she said quickly. "Not at all. It's just that I had hoped to be sent to Toulon, to the naval hospital there."

He squinted at her through plumes of tobacco smoke. "Ah, you perhaps have a lover who is a wounded sailor. Is that it?"

"No," she said, blushing hotly. "My brother, he was wounded at Gallipoli. The moment I found out where he was I volunteered for duty in France. I requested the Red Cross to send me to Toulon, but I ended up here."

"Well, one must make the best of it, no? *C'est la guerre.* Come with me, child, we shall walk through Ward C together."

Ward C was a fracture ward, rows of beds, fifty men in plaster casts, limbs suspended by weights and wires.

"Half a hundred *blessés*. All of them, as you can see, gravely injured. All far from their loved ones." He stopped by a bed. "Young Rialland here, nineteen years of age, wounded at Lens. He is a long way from his home in Bordeaux. Think of *him* as your brother."

The young man on the bed was staring at Alexandra as though a vision had appeared before him.

"*Une belle ange,*" he whispered.

"*Merci,*" she murmured shyly.

"You see!" The doctor patted her affectionately on the shoulder. "You are an angel to him, and a pretty French nurse will be an angel to your brother. You will be happy here and we will certainly be happy to have you."

She looked older. Only two weeks in France and yet, studying her face in the dressing table mirror, she could discern subtle changes in her appearance. She had seen true suffering – that was reflected. And she had worked hard, harder than she had ever worked in her life, and done disagreeable, even repugnant tasks, and that was reflected also.

"Yes," she whispered, bending closer to the glass and running her fingers across her cheekbones. "The war is changing you."

She felt a sense of pride in herself. She had stuck it out and had come through with flying colours. The hospital in Chartres was quite unlike the convalescent hospital for officers in England. Her duties there had been, looking back on it, quite laughable. A companion, no more than that. A sympathetic female. Someone to joke with the recuperating men, play cards with them, lead them into the garden for walks, perhaps push them in a wheelchair. The staff at Chartres expected a great deal more from their V.A.D. girls. They were understaffed and the trained nurses had enough to do without having to bathe the bedridden or cater to their bodily functions. Her first bed-pan had made her retch. The second had made her gag. The third, fourth, fifth had done no more than wrinkle her nose in disgust. Now the duty was commonplace and automatic. And she could bathe men now without feeling squeamish about touching their naked flesh with a soapy rag.

"I am altered," she murmured. "I've become a woman."

It was as though she had suddenly walked through a door, crossing from one room to another with no possibility of ever going back. She doubted if her mother and father would understand the change in her and her letters to them were filled with the type of formal observations that had distinguished her letters from boarding school:

> . . . Chartres is a beautiful old town and the cathedral is quite magnificent, a purity of Gothic art. I have not been to visit it yet as we are quite busy, but hope to do so soon. However, one can see its towers rising above the trees. I am allowed one afternoon off a week – rather like being a house-maid! – and may request, and probably be refused, three days' "leave" a month. I am quite happy and the food is plentiful, although lentil soup can become quite tiresome.

She reserved her innermost thoughts for Lydia Foxe, filling page after page with a hasty scrawl, a tumultuous outpouring of intimate reflections. These letters were written in the room that she shared with four other girls, in the golden light between daylight and dusk, the sun sinking late in early September . . . sleep measured from sunset to dawn.

276

Dearest L.,

The *blessés* never talk about their experiences. Why this is I do not know, but the fact remains that they are quite mute regarding the circumstances which brought about their injuries. Places may be mentioned, which draw nods of understanding from their fellows in adjacent beds, the names of villages, woods, crossroads, trenches, but never a word about the actual event that crippled them. They keep that awful moment secret, fearing perhaps that we gentle girls will be shocked by the description of it. I want so much to be able to comfort them, to understand thoroughly all of their agony, but when I ask them to tell me about the trenches they shake their heads and mutter that I would not comprehend it.

Oh, Lydia, I know now why God placed women on this earth. It is to be a comfort to men . . . a balm, a solace. Our cool touch on a fevered brow does more than all the medicines in the world! I yearn to give so much more of myself than I do, body and soul. I know I am capable of it. The silly schoolgirl that you knew, the child with visions of sugarplum fairies dancing in her head has been changed utterly.

Her nightly letters to Lydia were never posted because she did not wish to share her feelings with the censors, but putting her thoughts on paper made her feel in harmony with her friend. There was no one else she could confide in. The other V.A.D. girls were not unfriendly, but they were drab, reserved little creatures and Alexandra had the feeling that they resented her. She was friendly with one of the trained nurses, a woman from Normandy who had taken her training at Guy's Hospital in London, but the woman had no illusions about the art of nursing. "It is a business like any other. We are not angels of mercy, my pet, we are technicians pure and simple."

Alexandra rejected that definition. The woman was quite wrong. She sensed the rightness of her own feelings every time she walked through the wards and the men murmured to her, their golden angel who could comfort them with a touch, a smile, the merriness of her laugh. *Les blessés* who could walk on crutches or with canes brought her flowers from the fields or apples from the orchard. And after supper, when the ambulatory sat on benches in the courtyard, they would argue good-naturedly as to who would have the privilege of playing a game of draughts with her. A tall, ebony-faced Senegalese with great plaster casts on both of his arms followed her everywhere. Yes, she thought, I am loved, loved for what I am capable of giving . . . loved – and the thought made her tingle with the awesome presumption of it – the way a saint is loved!

They all saw the airman fall. It was on a Saturday morning and the aeroplane flew low over the hospital, its motor stuttering and making sharp barking sounds. The windowpanes rattled and everyone who could move rushed out of doors to see the fragile machine clip the top of a tree and go spinning towards the ground like a bird with a broken wing.

"Well, he's dead, poor man," matron said.

Ambulance drivers, orderlies and soldiers ran across the fields towards the wreckage and brought the airman to the hospital on a stretcher. The man was unconscious from a blow to the head and both legs were twisted at unnatural angles, but he was very much alive and Dr. Jary and an orthopaedic surgeon went to work on him immediately.

"Young bones are a miracle," Jary remarked as he emerged from the operating theatre two hours later. Alexandra helped him remove his blood-specked apron and filled a basin with hot water. The *médecin-chef* lit a cigarette and then washed his hands. "Yes, Miss Greville, a miracle. Clean breaks, like good wood, no splinters to complicate matters."

"Will he walk again, doctor?"

"Walk? He will run, fly. A lucky young man, I might add. Clever of him to crash next to a hospital. But then you English are a clever race, no?"

"He's English?"

"Royal Flying Corps. They have a field near Maintenon. I must telephone them and tell that their Lieutenant Dennis Mackendric will be as good as new. Perhaps they will be grateful enough to send me some of their excellent cigarettes and a bottle of whisky."

Lieutenant Mackendric shared a room with Captain Morizet, a gloomy officer who had been shot through the lungs in May. He soon had the captain out of his depression and it was not long before the twenty-year-old airman was known as "Merry Dennis" by all the English nurses and "The Crazy One" by the French. He was not English but Scottish, from Lochgelly, sandy haired and ruddy faced. He was of medium height with a lean and wiry body and incredibly strong hands and arms. An athlete's torso that was always on display, for he refused to wear a nightshirt. He had a rich, melodic voice with just a trace of a burr to make it that much more interesting. Alexandra fell in love with him on the spot, as did every other nurse in the hospital from matron on down. He did not suffer from inattention by the staff, nor did he lack visitors. A steady stream of R.F.C. officers and French airmen came to see him and Dr. Jary's supply of cigarettes and whisky overflowed.

One morning, a week after the accident, Alexandra sat rolling bandages at a table in the cool entrance hall of the château. It was monotonous work and her thoughts were drifting in a dozen more pleasant directions. She did not hear the man as he crossed the tiled floor from the front door and his voice startled her.

"Excuse me. I'm looking for a Lieutenant Dennis Mackendric."

A tall, gaunt faced officer with the emblems of the Royal Army Medical Corps on his lapels stood facing her. He was perhaps thirty, but could have been older or younger. The mouth had a youthful quality, but the eyes, dark brown and deeply recessed in shadowed sockets, were ageless. He smiled slightly, a mere twist of the lips.

"*Parlez-vous anglais, mademoiselle?*"

"Yes," she stammered. "Of course. I *am* English."

"I rather thought you might be. I'm Major Mackendric, the lieutenant's brother. He is a patient here, is he not?"

"Yes, he is. And you say you're his brother?" Her surprise was registered in her tone of voice. No two men could have been more opposite in looks and manner.

"Half brothers, to be precise. May I see him?"

Visitors were not permitted during the morning hours, but

the R.A.M.C. badges excluded him from that category.

"If you'll follow me, I'll take you to him."

"Thank you. By the way, who's in charge of this hospital?"

"Dr. Jary."

"Gilles Jary? Burly man with a beard, chain smoker?"

"That's right."

"Thank heaven for that. Some of these Red Cross surgeons couldn't set a watch, let alone a fracture."

"We're an extremely capable hospital," she said coolly. "Perhaps the best in France."

"No doubt, no doubt." His gaze wandered, taking in the marble walls, the broad staircase curving gracefully to the second-floor landing. "Certainly grand enough. I do my work in a tent."

She could not have cared less if he did his work in a field. He seemed an arrogant, caustic man. Even his own brother did not appear to be overjoyed at seeing him.

"Oh, Lord, Robbie!"

"Hallo, Dennis. Took a tumble, I gather."

"Oh, aye, dinna have the sense to watch the petrol gauge."

Major Robin Mackendric eyed him sourly and then turned his cold eyes on Alexandra.

"Do you permit all your patients to lie about half naked?"

"No," she blurted. "It's just that . . ."

"It's bluidy hot, man," Dennis protested.

"One is as liable to catch pneumonia on a hot day as on a cold one. Put a flannel top on him, nurse."

"Now, look here, Robbie . . ."

The major ignored the outburst as he walked to the end of the bed and glanced at the chart. "Slight fever last night. Must be mad to let you lie about uncovered."

"I take the bluidy top off on ma own. I won't wear the scratchy thing. Don't go about blamin' the lass."

"If you kept taking your top off in my ward I'd have the sisters tie your hands to the frame." He nodded curtly at Alexandra. "Not blaming you, of course. Probationer or V.A.D.?"

"V.A.D.," she said, a quiver of rage in her voice. "And we happen to have the best – "

"I know," he interrupted. "The best nurses in France. Your loyalty to this hospital is admirable. Where will I find Dr. Jary?"

"In his office. Down the corridor to your left and then up the garret stairs."

"What you want to see him for?" Dennis asked. "Don't go leapin' on the poor man because of my bluidy flannel!"

"I want to study the X-ray plates."

"He did a bluidy fine job of it, mon."

"I'm sure he did."

"And if he didn'a, you'd bust my bluidy legs again, I suppose!"

"Exactly right. And go easy on the word *bluidy*. Makes you sound like a Clydeside riveter."

Dennis flopped back on his pillow with a groan of exasperation.

"Christ! Wasn't there enough to keep you busy up at Ypres?"

"Yes," the major said with a quiet intensity. "More than enough."

The younger Mackendric sucked in his breath and looked quickly at his brother.

"I didn't mean to say that, Robbie. You know I didn't."

"I know."

"And I'm really awfully . . . *damned* glad to see your ugly mug."

"And I yours. Put your pyjama top on, that's the lad. I'll be back shortly." He strode off, boots clicking briskly down the marble corridor.

"Well!" Alexandra said, letting her pent-up sense of outrage underline the word. "Well! What an exasperating man!"

"That he is," Dennis said with a grin. "He'd drive a saint to drink. The annoying thing about Robbie, though, is that he's always right." He sat up and held out his arms. "Slip the smelly old flannel on. There's no point in sendin' him into a bluidy blitherin' rage."

She saw Major Robin Mackendric later in the day as he toured

F Ward with Dr. Jary and Dr. Lavantier. He smiled at her, but she made a point of ignoring him.

"There are two or three cases you could help us out with," Dr. Jary said. "Abdominals, foecal abscesses . . ."

"I only have a few days' leave."

"I can have them prepared right now, cut after lunch. You were Sir Osbert's pupil, after all, your cup of tea, *cela est dans votre cordes*. Shall we say yes?"

"It's meant to be my holiday, but – oh, what the hell!"

They wheeled the last patient from the operating room at one o'clock in the morning, matron told them during breakfast.

"He was marvellous to watch. Very sure of himself. Took nine feet of intestines from number eighty-seven and snipped more than that from the Turko and Papa Celine. Better a short bowel than a rotten one, he said!"

"I had to laugh," an Irish surgical nurse said. "Dr. Jary was leaning over his shoulder and ashes fell from his fag into the cavity. I'm used to that, of course, but I thought, oh-oh, the Scotsman is going to spin like a top, but he kept on cutting cool as you please and said, well, at least there's somethin' sterile in the poor man's gut!"

"He must have been very tired by the time it was over," Alexandra said.

The Irish woman nodded. "He was that. Quite the colour of paste. Dr. Jary pressed a bottle of whisky on him and sent him into town in an ambulance."

"He could have slept here."

"That he could, but he said he'd be damned if he'd spend one night of his leave on a canvas cot." She winked broadly at Alexandra. "The British are a grand race. I wonder why I hate them so!"

She felt a compulsion to see him again, volunteering for double duty in order not to miss him. He arrived late in the afternoon looking pale and drawn.

"Your brother's sleeping," she said, meeting him at the top of the stairs.

"Good. Best thing for him."

"In a pyjama top," she added pointedly.

"Sorry I made such a strafe about it."

"You were quite right to do so. It's just that your brother has a talent for getting his own way."

He removed a handkerchief from his pocket and wiped a sheen of sweat from his forehead. "Do you have such a thing as a cool drink, Miss . . . I'm sorry, I don't know your name."

"Alexandra Greville," she said simply.

"Robin Mackendric, now formally introduced." He shifted the handkerchief to his left hand and held out his right. The palm was damp, the fingers icy.

"Do you feel all right, major?"

"A bit under the weather. I could use that drink . . . and a couple of Aspirin tablets."

"Of course. I'll fetch you a glass of lemonade."

He was seated in his brother's room talking quietly to the wounded French captain when she brought the glass to him. He took the Aspirins from her hand and drank the lemonade almost without pause.

"Thank you. Very refreshing."

"The service here is as good as at the Crillon," the Frenchman said.

"And cheaper," the major added. He handed the glass back to Alexandra and stood up. "I shan't wake Dennis. He's sleeping too peacefully. Tell him I'll drop by in the morning before I go."

"Is your leave over?" she asked.

"No. I can take a few more days if I want it, but I'm feeling a bit guilty staying away."

"Where is your hospital, *commandant?*" Captain Morizet asked.

"Number twenty C.C.S. near Kemmel."

The captain nodded, his expression grim. "Hellish up there. Yes. I know what it is like. My battalion was in reserve at Messines in April. A bad place for soldiers that salient, I can tell you. *Très pouilleux!*"

She walked beside him down the hall to the stairwell.

"In case I don't see you again, Major Mackendric – "

"Tell me," he said, interrupting her, "what time do you get off duty?"

She looked at him blankly. "Get off?"

"They don't chain you to your post, do they? Aren't you permitted free time?"

"Yes, of course. My shift is over at six thirty."

"Will you have supper with me in town? Say, seven o'clock?"

She could only stare at him. The invitation was totally unexpected. The man was at least ten years her senior. What on earth did they have in common? What could they talk about? Her instinct was to murmur a polite but firm no, but there was a look in his eyes that made her hesitant. She saw pain there, an almost desperate appeal.

"All right. Will you pick me up or shall I meet you somewhere?" Her voice sounded alien to her.

"It's a pleasant walk. I could meet you by the river."

She nodded gravely. "Yes. That would be better than coming here."

They walked slowly along the towpath in the orange light of early evening, the sun turning the poplars to slim columns of brass. Barges moved up the river, pulled by plodding horses while the bargemen sat cross-legged on the narrow decks, munching bread and onions and drinking wine from dark green bottles.

"France is such a beautiful country, don't you agree, Major Mackendric?"

"Yes, quite lovely."

"And so historic. Chartres, such an unspoiled old town. The cathedral is certainly one of the finest examples of Gothic architecture to be found anywhere. I developed a passion for Gothic architecture when I was about eleven. It didn't last, of course, one of those stages that one always outgrows, but I can remember looking at stereoscopic views of Chartres. We had thousands of stereoscopic views, every country on earth, all in colour . . . I think the views of Chartres and the cathedral were my favourites among all the sets – those and the ones of Japan, the cherry trees and the Geisha girls – but I did love Chartres so, and here I am, practically living in its shadow. Curious, isn't it?"

She was talking too much and too rapidly. Lydia had once told her that rapid and garrulous speech was a form of hysteria. She took a deep breath in an attempt to calm herself. She found the taciturn doctor disconcerting. She sensed complexities in him beyond her ability to unravel and depths to his moodiness that she didn't feel capable of probing. He paused for a moment to light a short briar pipe. She noticed that his hand holding the match trembled slightly. That only disconcerted her more and loosened her tongue again.

"I do love your brother. He's such a . . . bonny Scot!"

"He's really more English than Scottish, but he can turn on the burr when he feels like it. Dennis is a bit of an actor."

"And oh, the pranks he pulls! One day he stuck his thermometer in his tea and nearly scared one of the girls out of her wits when she read it."

"Yes," he remarked drily, "he's quite the cut-up."

"You . . . you're a bit older than he is, I take it."

"I'm thirty-two. Dennis is twenty."

"I'm nineteen."

"A very good age to be."

"But I feel a good deal older. I suppose it must be the war. Have you been out here long, Major Mackendric?"

"Since last October . . . first Ypres."

"What a dreadful battle that must have been. And you're assigned to a Casualty Clearing Station?"

"Yes."

"It must be quite dangerous being so close to the front."

"Only the longer-range guns bother us once in a while." He stopped and faced her. "Let's not talk about it." He turned his head slightly to one side. "No matter how still it is, no matter how hard you listen, you can't hear the guns. So let's forget the war."

"What would you like to talk about?"

"You, good food, barges and barge horses. In roughly that order."

"Food then," she said a little too brightly. "All I've eaten for weeks is lentil soup and something grey and stringy boiled with turnips. Matron said there are some fine restaurants in Chartres."

"So they say. Did you tell matron that I was taking you to supper?"

"No, of course not."

"Why *of course not*? Would she have disapproved?"

"I . . . I don't know," she said, flustered. "I just didn't think it was anyone's business."

That was a lie. Had Major Mackendric been one of those merry-eyed, dashing young Royal Flying Corps officers who came to visit his brother, she would probably have told quite a few people that she was being taken out to supper. Her socialising with such a man would have been understandable, and enviable. Major Mackendric was not so easily explained.

There were several elegant restaurants in the town, all of them with staff cars and limousines parked in front. He took her to an inn that had a garden at the back which sloped down to the river. There were tables in the garden under the trees, Japanese lanterns suspended from the lower branches, their soft lights glowing yellow on the placid waters of the Eure. He ordered roast duckling, a bottle of Montrachet and fresh fruit. He ate little, toying with his food as he watched her eat. He drank some wine, picked absently at a dish of strawberries.

"You don't eat very much, do you, Major Mackendric?"

"Sometimes. Right now I prefer looking at you to staring down at roast duck. It's a matter of momentary preference. You're a remarkably beautiful young woman, Miss Greville. So vibrantly alive. Are you always so buoyant?"

"I'm usually accused of being too talkative, too *bubbly*. I'm not sure if those are desirable qualities in a woman."

"It reveals an enthusiasm for life that I find captivating."

He had an *interesting* face, she decided, certainly far from handsome, or at least far from her concept of what constituted male beauty. It was the face of a man who had seen much and had suffered a good deal.

"Have you always been an army surgeon, Major Mackendric?"

"No. I am a Fellow of the Royal College of Surgeons and I had a practice in Liverpool. Still have, I suppose."

"Do you come from a medical family?"

"My uncle's a professor of anatomy at Edinburgh. That's as

286

far as it goes. My father was a shipbuilder. Dennis shows no inclination towards medicine, or anything that involves studying, if it comes to that."

"I'm sure he's a fine airman though."

"I hardly think a fine airman would fly into a tree. Dennis's problem is that he has no patience for minor details, like petrol gauges."

They walked back towards the hospital along the river, barges still moving, cabin lights twinkling in the darkness.

"Thank you so much, Major Mackendric," she said when they reached the lane that led up to the château. "I enjoyed the meal thoroughly."

"And I enjoyed your company, thoroughly."

"Perhaps we can meet again, sometime."

He stepped closer to her and placed a hand on her upper arm, his fingers firm and sure.

"Miss . . . Alexandra . . . I believe in being candid with people. I know no other way of behaving. I've become rather obsessed by you from the moment I saw you rolling bandages in that sepulchral entrance hall. I lost an entire night's sleep just thinking about you, conjuring up your face."

"Major Mackendric . . ." she said haltingly. "I'm sure I . . ."

God knows, she had been kissed before, any number of times, the last occasion being a hearty peck on the cheek by Sir Carveth Saunders, Bart., on the platform of Victoria Station the morning she left London for France; altogether too brotherly a kiss, she had thought at the time, when one considered the fact that she had practically promised to be engaged to the man. There was nothing brotherly about the way she was being kissed now. Major Robin Mackendric's lips were firm against her own and the hand that had been on her arm was now centred in the small of her back and pressing her body against his. She was acutely aware of her breasts against his chest, but made no move to pull away. A warmth she had never felt before swept through her veins and her legs felt waxen. Her lips, which had been rigid and unresponsive, parted slightly and remained parted for some seconds after his lips had been withdrawn from them.

"I'm leaving for Paris in the morning. Will you come with me?"

"Impossible," she said weakly. "You must be mad, Major Mackendric."

He bent his head slightly and kissed her throat. "Mad as a March hare, as a hatter. All right, not tomorrow morning, then. Wait a day. Come up on the Friday train, the one that leaves at noon. I'll meet you at the Gare Montparnasse. You can take the evening train back on Sunday."

She tried to laugh, but only an odd, husky sound emerged.

"Really, quite impossible, major . . . really . . ."

"Dr. Jary encourages leaves now and then. He told me. All work and no play. I agreed with him wholeheartedly." He took hold of her arm again, a brief, taut-fingered squeeze. "I ask only that you think about it. Will you do that much?" *His eyes burned with lust* . . . She had read that line in a novel and it ran crazily through her head as she stared at Major Mackendric. But she saw no lustful burning in his eyes, only the pain she had noticed before.

"I . . . I'll think about it."

He let go of her arm reluctantly. "Thank you, Alexandra. The noon train Friday. I shall be at the Gare Montparnasse when it arrives. I hope very much that you'll be on it."

The train covered the eighty kilometres to Paris in less than three hours, but it seemed like an endless journey to Alexandra. She felt feverish and light headed. The train made an unscheduled stop at Rambouillet for a few minutes and she thought of rushing from the compartment, but was so hemmed in by *poilus* returning from leave, jamming the corridor, standing and sitting everywhere, loaded down with packs, rifles and greatcoats, that getting past them in a hurry would have been impossible. So she remained, feeling sicker, her heart pounding and her throat constricted. *Clickity-click* . . . *clickity-click* . . . the wheels rattled over the rails, drawing the train closer to Paris, closer to Major Robin Mackendric who loomed in her thoughts in mosaics of conflicting emotion.

She had tried as discreetly as possible to find out all she could

288

about him, asking his brother oblique questions and receiving answers that had only left her deeper in quandary and confusion.

"Robbie and I were never very close, too much difference in our ages for that. He was at University when I was in prep school . . . more like an uncle than a brother. But after he got married . . ."

"Married?"

"Oh, yes," Dennis Mackendric had said, not noticing the note of dismay in her voice. "The poor sod. A bluidy laird's daughter, doesn't take kindly to Robbie's views on medicine, didn't like him workin' down in Liverpool in a charity hospital, not a bit she didn't. I was in Liverpool, too, then, got expelled from my school and was thinking of running off to sea. Old Robbie took me under his wing and tried to knock some sense in my skull, wanted me to go back to school, try for university. Got sick to death of his naggin' at me so I crammed for Glasgow and managed to get in. They had an aero club there which I joined, so it wasn't a total waste. No, I'll never have Robbie's brains, but I've got more raw sense. I'll never marry some blue-nosed, thin-lipped Aberdeen woman and I'll never let this bluidy war get the best of me."

"Meaning?"

"Why, the man's half round the bend. Coiled up like a steel spring about to snap. I was at Ypres in May with Number Sixteen Squadron. Dropped by to see Robbie one day and he looked like death warmed up. Told him to chuck it in and go back for a month. But no, wouldn't think of it. Figured it might be the thought of spendin' time with Catherine . . ."

"Is that her name? His wife's name?"

"Yes. Catherine the bluidy Great. But, no, it wasn't that, it was the idea of leavin' the wards. I said, mon, you're not the only sawbones in Flanders, you know, but he said . . . oh, what's the bluidy use! Robbie is Robbie. It took breaking my legs for him to act human, an' then he only stays for a day and a night. Any normal person would try to grab as much time as possible. Only common sense. He won't do anybody any bluidy good if he goes stark raving bonkers."

*

Clickity-click, clickity-click, the wheels sang to the rails, the whistle blew sharply, the outskirts of Paris whipped past the window, the scattered fields and dingy houses of Vanves and Malakoff. And then the great, sprawling city itself. She had been to Paris many times as a girl – to visit the Louvre, the Luxembourg, the shops on the rue St. Honoré with Mamma. Now she was coming to Paris alone to confront a man, a *married* man thirteen years older than herself! Her heart sank and a fine dew of icy sweat formed on her upper lip.

She felt like a sleep-walker as the crowd of passengers propelled her along the platform. And then she saw him. He stood with his back to a kiosk, anxiously watching the flow of people and she knew, watching him, that she had been right in coming. What would he have done if she had not been on the train? If he had stood there until the last passenger had walked down the platform leaving nothing in view but open carriage doors and bits of scuffed newspaper drifting in the wind?

"Good afternoon, Major Mackendric."

He had not seen her approach. He looked at her, startled, and then let out a sigh and pushed his cap to the back of his head.

"And a very good afternoon to you. I was starting to give you up."

"I was a bit wedged in. The train was terribly crowded."

"Yes, I could see that."

She was wearing a pale blue uniform with a short, darker blue cape trimmed in red. One of the gowns made for her by Ferris. It made her look like a stage actress playing the rôle of a nurse.

"How nice you look," he said. "May I carry your suitcase?"

She handed him her small, leather overnight bag. "Are you somewhat surprised that I came?"

"A bit, yes. But delighted."

"I debated about it, but then I had a long talk with your brother."

"Ah. And what did Dennis tell you about me?"

"That you're married, among other things."

His eyes had a vacant look. "Yes. Been married for several years."

"Dennis is quite concerned about you. He has the feeling that you're . . . well, reaching the end of your tether, so to speak. That was the impression I had when we first met. You made me think of a man clinging to a cliff by his finger-tips."

"What picturesque imagery."

"I think you're just horribly lonely and need companion-ship, someone to talk to, to share a good meal with."

"A chum, in other words."

"Yes, something like that."

"That's very kind of you."

"It's really no trouble at all. We can be together until Sunday evening, visit the Louvre, go out to Versailles. I can stay at the Y.W.C.A."

"Yes," he said thoughtfully, "I suppose you could at that."

She had been rehearsing what she would say all the way up from Chartres, going over and over her lines and trying to anticipate his response. She had expected a more volatile reaction, disappointment at least, possibly even anger. His bland acceptance threw her a little off balance. She felt vaguely nauseous.

"Is it terribly hot? Or do I have a fever?"

He placed a hand on her brow, then sought her wrist, fingers pressing softly against the pulse.

"A bit rapid, but you're not feverish. It's very humid today . . . chance of rain."

"Perhaps if I walk for a bit, get some fresh air . . ."

"Just the ticket. Hold on to my arm if you feel the least bit faint. You need a cold glass of Chablis with a splash of soda in it. I know just the place."

She went with him meekly, holding lightly to his arm. He seemed taller than she remembered him being. Slightly stoop shouldered. Surgeon's stoop, matron called it. All doctors seemed to have it. Came from bending over things for years: books, cadavers, patients in operating theatres. His uniform hung loosely on his thin frame, Sam Browne belt unpolished, cap visor slightly cracked. An officer in name only, but two English sergeants striding briskly along the Boulevard Pasteur snapped him stiff-handed salutes, their eyes fixed not on the crown emblems of his rank but the R.A.M.C. badges of his worth.

There was a pavement café on the rue de Vaugirard, green-painted iron tables and chairs under brightly-striped umbrellas. The place was crowded, but three young men, wearing soiled white jackets over their shirts, stood up with their glasses of beer and empty saucers.

"Kindly take our table, *docteur*," one of them said in halting English.

"*Merci.*" He watched them stroll off into the crowd, table hopping. "Students. There's a first-rate training hospital around the corner on the rue de Sèvres. I attended a seminar there. Your Dr. Jary conducted it."

"How interesting."

"He was a professor of orthopaedics. That would have been in the spring of 1910."

That comment made her painfully aware of the difference in their ages. She had been a plump schoolgirl in the spring of 1910, struggling with Latin verbs. He had been a doctor attending a seminar.

"Did you visit this café then?" she asked.

"Oh, yes."

"Rather like going back in time, isn't it?"

He watched the students impassively. "A bit, but from the wrong side of the looking glass."

The Chablis and soda was icily effervescent and she drank her glass quickly.

"It's mostly wine, you know," he cautioned.

"I don't care. A moderate amount of alcohol can be a boon to the spirits. That's a rather silly pun of my brother Charles. Do you enjoy puns?"

"Not particularly."

"Neither do I." She rolled the cool glass between her palms. "Why are you so reluctant to go on leave? Your brother's afraid you'll work yourself to death."

"I'm reluctant because there are far more wounded up the line than there are surgeons to care for them."

"No one man is indispensable, major."

"I am."

*

292

A gendarme strolling past the café told them that the Y.W.C.A. hostel was in the rue Poliveau near the Gare d'Austerlitz.

"Oh, dear," Alexandra said. "That's quite a long way from here, isn't it?"

"Yes," Major Mackendric said. "But we can take a taxi."

"It's so pleasant now, I thought we might go for a walk. Do you mind awfully carrying my bag?"

"Not at all. It isn't heavy."

"Could we go to the Eiffel Tower?"

"If you'd like."

"I always loved watching the sunset from the observation landing when I was a child. You see, one is quite capable of going back in time."

He was so unlike any man she had ever known that it was pointless to even try to find points of similarity. To begin with, he didn't try to impress her, no stories of great deeds done on the cricket field, in point-to-point races or rowing against Cambridge, or Oxford, as the case may be. And no funny stories to make her laugh, or conjuring tricks, or riddles. He was simply . . . himself. Moody, introspective, and yet capable of breaking out of his thoughts from time to time to tell her one thing or another . . . the history of that building, how such and such a street they crossed had received its name. He had a student's knowledge of Paris and spoke French flawlessly, but with a hideous accent that made Frenchmen smile. He knew a great deal about architecture, engineering, music, literature and botany and touched on all of those subjects as they walked slowly through the gardens of the Champs de Mars before and after visiting the tower. It was dark by then and he took her to a restaurant by the Seine near the Pont de l'Alma.

"One thing you have not talked about," she said, spearing a truffle with her fork, "is medicine. One has the feeling that you're ashamed of being a doctor."

"I'm ashamed of our limitations. I'm ashamed at the burden mankind has thrust upon us during the past year. No. Let me retract that. Not ashamed, angry."

Yes, she thought, studying his face across the table in the glow of the candles, it wasn't pain that she had noticed in his eyes at all, but anger – deep, smouldering fury. The realisation shocked and puzzled her and she was unable to finish her meal.

"You don't eat very much, do you?" Alexandra said.

She stared at his eyes. The brooding rage was gone for a moment. She recalled her own comment to him at the inn by the river in Chartres.

"Tit for tat." She looked down at her plate. "I feel a bit tired, all of a sudden."

"Let's go then. I'll call for a taxi."

"Is a taxi necessary?"

"Lord, yes. The rue Poliveau is miles from here, the other side of Paris."

She shifted a sautée tomato with her fork, moving it from one side of her plate to the other. "I don't think I wish to stay at the Y.W.C.A. hostel. No, I don't want to at all. I . . . I'm certain that where you are staying is far more pleasant. Is it?"

"It's . . . a nice old hotel, yes."

"Can we walk there?"

"I suppose so. It's on the Right Bank, rue Tronchet. But are you sure you want to walk? Are you *absolutely* sure you want to go at all?"

She nodded and looked up, meeting his eyes, holding her gaze without flinching. "Yes. Quite sure. But not in a taxi. There's something rather . . . *sordid* about going to an assignation in a taxicab."

His smile was slight, almost sad. "It's not an *assignation* if we go together."

Her face was burning and the realisation made her angry. She hated to appear so disgustingly virginal.

"Oh, very well, call a taxi if you wish."

"No. We'll walk. A quiet, leisurely *unsordid* stroll."

She had no possible way of knowing what to expect. Every novel she had ever read had concluded the seduction scene with a series of dots. At school she had pooled her ignorance with the other girls. Once she had seen a drawing in Gray's *Anatomy* of a penis – a tubular thing, reminiscent of a flayed eel. She had always suspected that Lydia knew, but Lydia had never told her anything except, "*You'll find out in time.*" The time was now. She lay naked in a wide bed on the fourth floor of a hotel in the very shadow of the Madeleine. Naked, vulnerable to violent assault by a man as naked as herself. But of course she wasn't being assaulted and knew that she wouldn't be the moment they had entered the room. He hadn't *pulled her passionately into his arms* the way Elinor Glyn would have described it, he had simply looked at her after closing the door and had said, *"Well, this is my room, and I'm overwhelmingly happy you're in it."*

His hand moved slowly over her body in the darkness, fingers stroking the hollow of her throat, straying across her breasts, abdomen, the petal softness between her thighs.

"How lovely you are, Alexandra," he said in quiet wonder. "A miracle."

She wanted to tell him that she loved him for his gentleness and for the pleasure he was giving her with his firm, sure touch, but she was incapable of speech. Nothing emerged from her throat but low moans and tiny whimpers. She moved her hands and touched her breasts. They seemed to be larger, swollen, the nipples thick and taut. She touched his body, clinging to him, pulling him closer to her, legs parting to embrace him totally.

"I shan't hurt you," he whispered.

She didn't care, barely was aware of the sharp stab of pain as he entered her. The pain flowed upwards, dissolved, ended – replaced by an agony that was beyond her powers to describe. She dug her fingers into his heaving back and smothered her gasps against his shoulder. She felt consumed, every nerve drawn out of fiery tendrils, molten wax coursing under her flesh. It was a torture so exquisite that she felt she must scream if it continued for another second and then the fever peaked, subsided, and she felt limp, drowsily exhausted. Normal senses returned. She noticed the patch of light on the ceiling, heard the trumpeting klaxon horns from the street below. Her hands lingered on Major Mackendric's long body.

"Robbie," she murmured. "Robbie."

The thought of leaving him filled her with dread. The world seemed bleak on Sunday morning, despite the sun flooding the room. She wouldn't allow him to leave the bed but clung wantonly to him, the frothy silk, outrageously seductive, night-gown she had bought on Saturday afternoon sliding provoca-tively off one shoulder.

"Take me with you."

"No," he said, kissing her breasts through the silk. "Quite impossible."

"Why is it impossible?" she pouted. "I'm a nurse, I can work by your side."

"You're a volunteer girl, fluffing pillows and sponging fevered brows."

"And bedpans, and working the autoclave machine. I'd be useful." She kissed the top of his head and ruffled his hair with her fingers. "And there would be nights when we could be together in some charming country inn."

He moved away from her and sat with his back against the headboard.

"There are no charming country inns in the salient. Nothing up there but shelled-out villages, shelled-out woods, shelled-out roads. And troops, troops everywhere, coming up to the line, moving back. There's no privacy at all, not for anyone. No, you'll go back to Chartres and I'll take the night train to St. Omer." He cupped her chin in both hands and bent forward to kiss her softly on the lips. "I shall miss you, Alex. These have been the most wondrous two days of my life. When things get too bad, I'll hold on to my sanity by remembering you."

It was over. She had known it would have to end. The realisation of it had struck her on Saturday when they had left the hotel for a few hours. She had walked with a singular sense of pride, head back, chin up, telling the world by the jauntiness of her step that she was no longer a virgin. Her buying of the nightgown in a small, elegant shop on the Petis Champs – Major Mackendric waiting patiently outside – had been no more than a gesture, the acquiring of a talisman that through its magic of silk and lace might bind him to her. But as the salesgirl had folded the flimsy garment into a box she knew that she would have only that one night to wear it, that on Sunday they would part, most probably for ever.

"May I write to you? I write marvellous letters."

"I can't stop you, Alex, but do you think it's wise?" He took both of her hands into his and pressed them gently. "Alex, you're a beautiful, passionate, nineteen-year-old woman. When you step off the train in Chartres you will probably meet a handsome, gallant twenty-year-old man. You'll be married in a church and forget all about me. That's as it should be. You shared two days of your life with me and you could never comprehend how much it's meant to me. I said that one can't go back. I was wrong. For just a little while I was back in a time where there were no unending horrors and for that I shall always be grateful."

"Oh, Robbie," she whispered, kissing his hands. "We must see each other again."

"That would be next to impossible. It might be months before I could manage even a few days' leave."

"Oh, damn this silly war! Maybe it will end tomorrow."

"Yes," he said tonelessly. "Maybe it will."

It was impossible to get him out of her mind. If there had been someone to confide in, someone to share her thoughts with, it might have been halfway bearable, but there was no one. Even her only link with him was gone. Dennis Mackendric moved to Number Eleven Stationary Hospital in Rouen. The days dragged and the nights became eternities. She yearned to plunge herself in work, to drown the image of Robin Mackendric in soapy water and mountains of rolled bandages, but the hospital was half empty now, entire wards barren and the staff increased by the arrival of seven more V.A.D. girls from England and three French nurses. The great offensive was beginning in this last week of September, the British striking from Ypres to Loos, the French attacking in Champagne with thirty-five divisions.

"It will take a little time before the *blessés* filter down to us," Dr. Jary told the staff. "From aid posts to casualty clearing stations, corps dressing stations, base hospitals, but we shall get our share, never fear."

She took French leave, an impulsive departure, catching the train at five in the morning for Paris and then the train to St.

297

Omer. A British military policeman walked up to her when she stepped off the train and asked to see her papers. She was wearing her heavy winter cape because the weather had turned sour and looked suitably like an army nurse. The man barely glanced at her identity papers and handed them back.

"Going to Number Fourteen General, sister?"

"No, Number Twenty C.C.S., near Kemmel."

He whistled softly through his teeth. "Been up there before, have you?"

"No, I haven't, as a matter of fact."

"Well . . . might be a bit difficult. Terrible amount of traffic on the roads. There'll be a hospital train leaving in the morning as far as Bailleul, or you could try your luck with the ambulance transport officer." He pointed his baton in the general direction of the town. "He's in the rue Hericat. Little white-washed stone house; can't miss it."

The narrow, dingy streets were clogged with British soldiers marching through on their way from Calais to the front, silent streams of rain-darkened khaki, the men hunched under their heavy packs. They reminded her of cattle plodding wearily through a market town.

There was a convoy of thirty empty ambulances leaving for Flanders, six of them marked for the Kemmel C.C.S. The ambulance transport officer, an elderly, hollow-cheeked captain, didn't question her right to go there and rubber-stamped her papers without so much as saying one word to her. The ambulance she got into reeked of carbolic and the driver, a dour little Welshman, compounded the vile odour by smoking one cheap cigar after another.

She began to experience a growing sense of dread, a cold feeling that settled in the stomach and became more pervasive the closer they came to the low, treeless hills of the Messines ridge. The countryside was grey, waterlogged and squalid. On the crest of a hill that evening she could see the distant skyline of the front, stabs and flickers of flame, and when they stopped in a village for tea and cold bully beef sandwiches she could hear the continuous thumping of the artillery. They were only a few miles from Kemmel, but a Royal Engineer officer sloshed through the muddy village street to tell the drivers that the road to Kemmel and Ypres had been heavily shelled that morning and would be impassable until daybreak. She huddled in the ambulance, not able to sleep, listening to the Welshman snore and the muttering thunder of the guns. Her depression deepened with the night.

It was eight in the morning when the ambulances pulled into the C.C.S. compound. "I do my work in a tent," he had told her. She had imagined him standing under white canvas, perhaps in a wood or a meadow. What she now gazed at were long rows of wooden buildings with dirty brown canvas roofs, half an acre of dismal sheds connected to each other by duckboards laid across a sea of mud. Beyond a sagging barbed wire fence lay the remains of an orchard, a few stumps of shattered trees amid interlocking craters. A landscape of misery.

A tall, sharp-faced English nurse eyed her coldly.

"V.A.D.? What on earth are you doing up here?"

"I . . . I wish to see Major Mackendric. He is stationed here, isn't he, sister?"

The middle-aged nurse studied the forlorn-looking girl standing in front of her desk and her expression softened. She stood up, her starched uniform making a crisp, rustling sound.

"He's in surgery at the moment. Have you had your breakfast?"

"No, sister."

"Well, come along and I'll take you to the mess tent. Did you drive up from St. Omer or come by train?"

"I drove, sister."

"You must be quite at the end of your tether then. We shall soon fix that with a good cup of tea. You're a friend of the Major's, I take it?"

"Yes. I . . . I nursed his brother."

A tiny smile tugged at the woman's firm mouth. "Oh, you nursed him, did you? Well, I never."

A thin, fair-haired officer, wearing a white jacket over his uniform, almost collided with them in the narrow passage outside the nurse's office.

"Hallo!" the doctor said cheerfully, leering at Alexandra. "What have we got here?"

"A friend of the major's," the nurse said.

"Oh, I say! A friend of Mac's? How absolutely topping! Have you been assigned to us?"

"She's a V.A.D., " the nurse said. "We never get that sort, as well you know, captain."

"Yes, worse luck. Nothing but you old curmudgeons." He kissed the woman on the cheek. "Look after her, sister, and tell her that Captain Ronald David Vale is by far the nicest chap in the army."

She sipped her tea, holding the mug tightly with both hands to keep it from spilling. A battery of heavy British guns a mile away were firing and the salt and pepper shakers on the mess table bounced and slid at every sound. The noise was nerve jarring, but none of the dozen or so nurses, orderlies and doctors in the long tent seemed to be paying any attention to it.

And suddenly he was seated across from her, his uniform jacket hastily buttoned, his tie askew. He folded his arms on the table and looked at her with a slightly bemused expression.

"What on earth am I going to do with you, Alex?"

She stared into the murky depths of her tea, not trusting herself to look at him. She felt close to tears.

"I shan't go back."

"But you can't stay here. Surely you can see that."

She shook her head like an obdurate child. "I'll be useful."

"All of the nurses here are Q.A.s, some with fifteen or twenty years of service. Even the probationers have had at least a year's training at a teaching hospital. There are no V.A.D. girls beyond St. Omer and none are needed. You don't have the slightest conception of what we do here."

She set her tea down and looked at him for the first time, her longing for him so evident in her eyes that his firmness wilted.

"Oh, Alex . . . Alex . . ." He reached across the table and touched her hand. "You're making this so difficult for me."

"I don't mean to, Robbie. Really I don't. But it's partially your fault. I'm not very *experienced* at this sort of thing. Perhaps there are some girls who can have a . . . a love affair with a man and then forget all about it. I can't. I tried very hard. Believe me, Robbie, I did. Perhaps if you had been less kind . . . less gentle and loving with me I could have done so. But the fact is . . . the fact is . . ."

He squeezed her wrist and glanced away. Two X-ray orderlies at a nearby table were casting sidelong looks at them. A casualty clearing station was like a village. Everyone knew everything about everybody and anything not known for certain was grist for endless speculation. The sudden arrival of a young and beautiful nurse's aide so soon after the Major's leave would have the whole place buzzing; her bursting into tears in the mess would provide enough material for months of gossip.

"Don't cry," he said firmly. "Please don't cry."

"I won't. It's just that I'm so happy to see you and I want so badly to stay. I know I can be useful, I just know it – and I won't be an embarrassment to you in any way."

He signalled one of the mess orderlies to bring him tea and then took out his pipe and filled it, being very slow and deliberate with his movements so as to give himself time to think.

"I was quite wrong in making love to you, Alex, and I regret having done so. Making love, falling in love . . . those are such gentle acts, such fragile emotions. There's no room for them now. I'm sorry that you've been unhappy. I've had a few rough moments myself. I suppose I'm like you. I can't have a love affair and then walk away and forget about it. I wish I could. It would make saying goodbye so much easier."

"I can't say goodbye, Robbie."

"But you must. We shared a speck of time together and it can't be enlarged or expanded into anything more than that. A moment. No more. You'll have many moments, Alex. You have a lifetime ahead of you."

"I can't think about that, Robbie. Can't think ahead. I'm with you and that's all that seems to matter. My heart's out of my throat for the first time in days and days."

"Look, Alexandra, be sensible. You say you wish to be useful . . ."

"To you, Robbie, yes . . . yes, I do."

"And you have some sort of romantic notion of playing nurse to my doctor. Your ingenuousness captivated me in Chartres. But it's an entirely different matter here. There are no pillows to fluff, no lemonade to make. If you're serious about wanting to become a nurse then join the Q.A.s and in ten months or so

301

you might be qualified to be sent here as a probationer. It takes time, like becoming a doctor; a day-to-day process of learning, a slow building of experience, a . . . Oh, Lord, here comes Vale."

Captain Ronald David Vale walked towards their table, smoothing his moustache with one finger. He drew up a wooden chair without being invited to sit down.

"Ta-ta, major, Parsons needs your touch in Number Six right away. It's the Gurkha sergeant. Gas gangrene in the right leg."

"Damn."

"Jenny's talking to him in Nepali, but not making much headway, I'm afraid. Oh, well, can't be helped, can it? Have to chop-chop quick-quick or the poor fella's done for."

Robin stood up with obvious reluctance. "I suppose you want a formal introduction, Vale?"

"Yes," he said, grinning at Alexandra. "If you don't mind, old chap."

"Alexandra Greville, Captain Vale. Captain Vale, Alexandra Greville." He tapped out his pipe in a shell case ashtray. "I'll be an hour. Show Miss Greville around the place, will you, Vale?"

"Be delighted, dear man, positively delighted." He took a sip of the major's tea and then lit a cigarette. "Curious chaps these Gurkhas. Damned good fighters. Give the Boche cold sweats, but we have no end of trouble with them. Rather die than have an amputation. Believe in reincarnation, you see. Won't tolerate the idea of going into the next life missing a limb. I say, you're a smashing-looking girl. Don't mind my saying so, do you?"

"No." He reminded her of Carveth Saunders, only she assumed his Mayfair tone to be nothing but a pose.

"Care to see our little carnival?"

"Yes, I would, thank you."

"A bit on the empty side at the moment. We cleared shop by six this morning, ready for the next batch. Rather like old Waterloo Station. Chappies come and go."

"Go where?"

"Oh, by hospital train to St. Omer, Calais, Rouen – or down

the road to the graveyard. We do more than our best, but we lose quite a few."

Her nagging sense of trepidation returned when Captain Vale showed her through the wards. They were coldly functional. No white sheeted beds, simply row upon row of canvas cots with brown army blankets folded neatly at the foot of each. Wheeled carts piled high with dressings, bottles of anti-tetanus serum, hypodermic needles and morphine capsules were next to every fifth bed. The sisters and R.A.M.C. orderlies looked at her with frank curiosity.

"It's your uniform," Captain Vale said. "Obviously not a regulation issue. Leave it to the sisters to note *that*. As for the orderlies, it's what's *in* the uniform that they're gaping at." He opened a door and led the way across a duckboard past a drystone structure that might once have been a stable. "That's where we operate, move the chappies in, move 'em out . . . cut, cut, cut. Tommy calls this place Mendinghem; Number Fifteen C.C.S. over at Neuve Eglise they call Bandagehem. The French hospital at Hazebrouck is Endinghem. Tommy has a droll sense of humour."

"Is Major Mackendric in charge here?"

"Oh my yes, the top doctor wallah. It's a colonel's job actually, but surgeons are spread thin these days. Even have some Yank chaps coming over to us from Harvard Medical School. Should be here any day now, God bless their colonial socks."

A bell rang, four loud clangs . . . pause . . . four more.

"What's that?"

Captain Vale's expression hardened slightly, a tense thinning of the lips.

"Staff call. Get the news of what we're in for today. Nasty bit of firing since dawn. Won't be a pleasant afternoon, I'm afraid. Oh well, can't have sunshine and flowers every day, can we?"

Alexandra stood at the far end of the mess tent, out of everyone's way. Doctors, surgical and ward nurses, orderlies and various other assistants stood about in silent groups. Finally Mackendric came into the tent, a surgical gown over his uniform.

"All right," he said. "Brigade just rang through. The

303

Bedfords and Suffolks were in it this morning up at White Sheet and got scuppered. Half their wounded are on the way down to us now, three to four hundred of them, sitters and stretchers – stretchers predominate, I gather. They were badly shelled so prepare for extreme multiples. The bearers found thirty or so Cameronians who had been lying out in the wire since Wednesday. We know what to expect there so be sure to have chloroform handy." He glanced at his watch. "Should be arriving by sixteen hundred hours so get your suppers out of the way and prepare for a long night. I want as many as possible on the train by dawn."

She had hoped he would find time to talk to her again, perhaps even have supper with her, but although she wandered about the hospital she never caught so much as a glimpse of him. Then the elderly sister she had met that morning came up to her as she sat dejectedly in the mess tent.

"Feel a bit lost, do you?"

"Yes, a bit."

"Well, can't have that, can we? Have you been taught anything useful?"

"Yes," she said bridling, "of course."

"Can you insert a catheter?"

"No . . ." she said hesitantly.

"If I told you to inject a man with five hundred units of A.T.S., would you know how to go about it? Or how much morphine to give without killing him? Or set up a Carrel drip?"

"No . . . I . . ." She could feel her face burning. The woman's grey eyes seemed to bore right through her.

"I'm matron here," she went on, not unkindly. "Major Mackendric asked me if there was any possibility of my using you. I'm afraid there isn't. You'll have to go back to St. Omer tomorrow. But you look like a strong, healthy girl and I can certainly find something useful for you to do this afternoon. We'll be receiving casualties shortly and you can give the orderlies a hand. Find a smock to put over your uniform so that you don't get it messy. You can report to Corporal Hyde in Number Five admitting; that's the building over there with the *green* cross on the tenting. We had a very nice soldier do a bit of painting for us and he turned out to be quite colour blind."

304

The orderlies were tense but friendly, offering her sweet, milky tea and some practical advice.

"Speed's the ticket," Corporal Hyde said, a cigarette pasted to his lower lip. "It's like a ruddy factory when we get movin'."

"What exactly do we do?"

"Turn the lads over to the sisters as unmucky as possible so's they can get to work on 'em. They'll have all kinds of rags and tatters about their wounds. Cut the old dressin's off and toss 'em in a bucket. If there's lots of mud we wash it off with green soap and antiseptic solution. There'll be three sisters with us, givin' A.T.S. jabs and morphine, an' they don't take kindly to hold-ups. Fast but thorough is the bloomin' motto around here."

At three forty-five the first ambulances and army lorries came rocking and swaying up the deeply-rutted road that led to Wytschaete and the front. Gears ground and the vehicles lumbered into the compound and drew up in front of the admitting tent. Orderlies and stretcher-bearers ran to open the ambulance doors and to get the wounded from the back of the lorries even as more ambulances, some of them horse-drawn, came up the road.

There was a sound that Alexandra could not associate with anything she had ever heard before – a muttering, moaning, muted howl of a noise coming from the mud-encrusted conveyances parked in front. She glanced at the sisters standing by two dressing carts. Their faces were impassive, their eyes devoid of any expression at all. *Stretchers* and *sitters*. The words were self-explanatory. "Stretchers" were the men who had to be carried in by the bearers; "sitters" were men capable of stumbling into the tent with minimal aid. All brought the sound with them, a continuous groaning, a stifled shriek, deep body-convulsing sobs. All had been hastily bandaged at their regimental aid posts, given morphine pellets, but the effects of the drugs were wearing off. Pain beyond comprehension gripped many of them and they threshed about on their stretchers or clung kneeling to the wooden benches along one wall of the tent.

"Hop to it, girl," one of the sisters said in a taut voice.

She had been among the wounded. All the *blessés* at Chartres

305

had been hit, but that had been weeks before they had arrived at Number Seven Hôpital Croix Rouge. She had seen them only as clean, well-bandaged men, aware, many of them, that further operations might be necessary. But *further* operations held no terror for them. Body casts and bandages might be uncomfortable, but their beds were clean, the food was wholesome, there were flowers in the wards.

"Arterial haemorrhage, sister!" an orderly shouted out.

Alexandra saw a stream of blood pump upwards from a sodden khaki bundle lying on a stretcher. The sister knelt quickly beside the groaning man and clamped off the flow. Alexandra could only stare as more and more men were brought into the large tent, horror piled on horror: a man with his eyeballs blown out, dirty cottonwool stuffed into the sockets; sheared-off legs and arms, the stumps wound with blood-caked bandage or soiled puttees; a man screaming and twisting like an animal in a trap, hands pressed against a bulge of intestines that were slipping through his fingers. Her legs shook and an icy chill clutched her head and made her scalp crawl.

Corporal Hyde thrust a pair of scissors into her limp hand and whispered fiercely, "Come on, miss, don't stand about."

She sank to her knees beside a stretcher, not from choice, her legs giving way beneath her. She stared down at a blackened, muddy bandage covering the man's upper thigh and hip, dirty grey flesh beneath the slit trouser leg. As she cut hesitantly at the bandage the man screamed and cursed and tried to sit up. Corporal Hyde held him down.

"Cut them bloody rags off, miss!"

She cut, her hand shaking so violently she almost dropped the scissors. Beneath the bandage lay a bloody puddle with bits of hip bone jutting up from the ooze. Vomit rose in her throat and she clamped her teeth to hold it back. The vomit scorched and choked her as she swallowed.

"Keep them moving along, for God's sake," a sister called out in exasperation. "They're beginning to pile up outside."

Nausea came in wave after wave. Her jaws ached and her throat was on fire. Sweat clung in cold beads to her pallid face. There seemed to be no end to the writhing, grunting,

306

animal-like creatures who were laid in front of her by the stretcher-bearers. The bucket of filthy bandages she had snipped away overflowed and another was quickly brought – then another and another. She did not become numb to the ghastliness revealed when each rag of a dressing was removed: splintered ends of bone, loops of gut, the red hollow where a lower jaw had been; each revelation seemed worse than the last. The nightmare only deepened.

"Cameronian," an orderly muttered to her as a mud-encrusted form was set down in front of her by the bearers. The orderly placed a dark brown bottle of chloroform and some cotton dressing on the floor beside her. "Just douse the little bastards."

It was a Cameronian sergeant, four days in a shell hole between the wire, four days of sun and rain. The letter "T" had been painted on his forehead with iodine. They had done that much for him at the aid post, anti-tetanus serum, no more than that. A self-applied dressing under his right armpit bulged over the festering wound beneath. She cut the dressing away with difficulty, dried blood holding the edges like tar. Pus flowed yellow-green and then, boiling up out of the suppurating depths of the shell-chewed cavity, a mass of living things, a churning, undulating ball of fat, white maggots, creeping on to her fingers along the blades of the scissors, up her fingers, squirming blindly along the back of her hand.

She screamed and could not stop screaming. She screamed as she stumbled to her feet, kicking the bottle of chloroform. She screamed as she staggered, retching, towards the door. A sister grabbed her arms and then slapped her hard across the face . . . once . . . twice . . . stiff-fingered blows. She felt nothing, saw nothing as she slipped down into a misty, comforting darkness.

It was peaceful in the back of the ambulance. Around her in the blackness were silent forms, drugged, still as death. She pulled her warm cloak up to her chin. Someone was calling her name, she could hear it softly, softly . . . "*Alex, Alex* . . ." out there in the inky night. She stared fixedly at the bottom of a stretcher laid on the brackets above her.

307

Alex, Alex . . .

The ambulance began to move, creaking and lurching slowly across the compound. Taking away the wounded. Yes, she thought dully. Taking them away. And she was one of them . . . just one of the wounded. Perhaps even one of the dead.

Book Three

God knows 'twere better to be deep
Pillowed in silk and scented down,
Where love throbs out in blissful sleep,
Pulse nigh to pulse, and breath to breath,
Where hushed awakenings are dear . . .
But I've a rendezvous with Death
At midnight in some flaming town,
When spring trips north again this year . . .

ALLAN SEEGER (1888-1916)

I

LADY WINIFRED SUTTON WALKED SLOWLY UP FROM SLOANE
Square, her Bedlington terrier no longer tugging at the leash
but plodding wearily ahead, eyes half closed against the granu-
lated snow that swept up from the pavement. It was a clear
morning, but cold and blustery, the leafless trees in Cadogan
Place swaying crazily. She had been walking for two hours or
more through Chelsea and along the river on this December
day of arctic winds and pale, heatless sun. The wind whined
through the iron railings enclosing the strip of garden flanking
Sloane Street. No nursemaids pushing prams along the paths
today, only the wild trees and the sleet-scoured grass.

The dog perked up, sensing the nearness of home and its bed
near the kitchen fire, but Winifred approached her house with
the usual feeling of dread. She hated London, but her father
had donated Lulworth Manor to the Red Cross for the duration of the war. Life had always seemed less complicated in the
country and problems more easily coped with. She knew for
certain that her mother would have been better off, less
frenetic, more reconciled to the finality of death. The war was
too pervasive in London, the daily newspapers, with their
endless stories of battles and lists of casualties, the soldiers
everywhere, the infrequent but unnerving Zeppelin raids. She
yearned for the quiet fields, the ordered landscape of Dorset.

She had hoped to avoid her mother's "group", but the front
door opened as she came up the steps and there they were, half
of them reluctant to leave, still orbiting, keyed up and vocal,
about the exotic figure of Madame Nestorli, Princess Pearl.

"Oh, Winifred," the Duchess of Ascombe said, still dabbing
at her tear-filled eyes with a lace handkerchief. "Oh, my dear,
it was so wonderful today. Too marvellous for mere words to
express."

Winifred moved to one side, pulling the terrier closer to her leg to keep it from being stepped on as the ladies began to descend to the pavement, the Dexford family butler hurrying ahead of them to whistle for their cars, which were parked up and down the street. At last only Princess Pearl was left, talking to Lady Dexford in the hall, her voice whisper soft. A dozen gold bracelets jingled as she moved her hands to emphasise her words, words that Winifred had no interest in hearing. She wished it were possible for her to move past the two women and go up to her room unseen, but that was clearly impossible. Lady Mary blocked the way to the stairs, her bird claw hands gripping the cold fur of her daughter's coat.

"I do so wish you had been here, Winifred. We made such a significant breakthrough. Both of my dear boys were in the room, and Clarissa's young George moved the counter to say he was content."

She looked away from her mother's impassioned, gleaming eyes. The eyes of Princess Pearl were inscrutable stones. The most sought-after medium in London reached into a pearl-encrusted bag and removed a gold and jade cigarette-holder and a cigarette. A Capstan, Winifred noticed. Raising spirits for twenty pounds a corpse had made the woman rich, but she had not lost her plebeian tastes.

"We were successful, yes," Madame Nestorli whispered in her odd, difficult to define accent. Rumanian? Greek? Welsh, perhaps. "But no, we have not broken through the veil quite yet. We have not touched the outer reaches of the void."

"But we shall, we shall!" Lady Dexford cried. "I know you have reservations, Winifred, but had you only been with us today!"

She managed to break away and hurried up to the second floor; her terrier trailing its leash, scampered down the corridor towards the kitchen stairs.

Her bedroom was a private refuge and she shut the door, then leaned against it for a moment as though barring it from assault. Anger and bitterness choked her and it was a struggle to draw a deep breath. Her mother attended three or four séances a week, most of them in the mahogany panelled dining room downstairs, a room that Madame Nestorli, the great Princess Pearl, had found to be unusually conducive to reaching her personal spirit, her envoy to the realm of the dead, a Nubian prince named Ram who had been sealed alive in a wall at Thebes one thousand years to the day before Christ's birth. Ram spoke amazingly like Madame Nestorli, but no one seemed to question that in the least.

"Oh, God! Such rot." She removed her coat and tossed it over the back of a chair, then flopped on her bed and stared at the ceiling. Her rage slowly subsided into a dull pity for her mother and all the other pathetic women who tried so desperately to bring back their loved ones. Two of her brothers were dead. Andrew buried somewhere in France and Timothy in the family plot at Lulworth churchyard. She could understand to some degree her mother's refusal to accept the finality of Andrew's passing. She had not seen him die nor talked to anyone who had. A short letter from his colonel was all the proof she had. But Timothy was another matter. He had been hit in the throat by a shell fragment in June and had died in a London hospital in September, kept alive for a while by rubber tubes inserted in the mangled cavity of his neck. But then it wasn't the *body* that mattered according to Madame Nestorli. The body was nothing, a mere shell of common clay containing the elusive spirit. The spirit never died. It was simply released when the body gave it up and the spirit could be enticed back from eternity if one knew how to go about it. It was merely a question of time, patience, fervent belief – and money.

There was a gentle knock on the inner door that led to her sitting room and then the door opened a crack and one of the maids peeked in.

"I drew a nice warm bath for you, m'lady."

"Thank you, Daphne."

There was nothing she could do about her mother's obsession. She had always been inclined towards the mystic and the war had given it impetus. She lay back in the warm tub and touched her heavy breasts with soapy hands. She was pleased with her body. Long, brisk walks and a total abstinence of sweets, cakes, custards and other fattening foods had slimmed her hips, flattened her tummy and firmed her legs. Only her breasts left something to be desired. They were so big and round and pink-nippled. Perhaps Robert Herrick would have found them enchanting, she thought wryly, recalling the amorous poet's hymn to the nipples of his Julia.

> Have ye beheld (with much delight)
> A red rose peeping through a white?

But large breasts were out of fashion. Women flattened them now for the new styles coming out of Paris. She had found binding them uncomfortable. Not that it did much good anyway.

She had dried herself and was slipping on a silk dressing-gown when Daphne tapped on the door and said, "Colonel Wood-Lacy on the telephone, m'lady. Shall he ring back?"

She drew the robe around her body and fastened the cord. "Tell him I'm . . . indisposed and that . . . yes, he may ring back in half an hour."

Fenton in London. She hadn't seen him since the war started . . . fifteen months. He had never taken a leave in England, but her brother John, who had enlisted in the Rifle Brigade, had told her that few regulars had been able to get back to England unless carried on a stretcher. He had written to her once in a while.

She sat at her dressing-table and idly brushed her hair, soft brown waves touching her shoulders. The slender pile of his letters was in her dressing-table drawer. They were letters that were suitable reading by the entire family. Informative letters . . .

> Today we moved up to the line and took over trenches recently held by the French. Quite messy, I'm afraid, with the wire in a shocking state of neglect . . .

Not love letters by any means, and yet she had kept them neatly together as though they were. They all began *Dear Winifred* and were signed *Affectionately, Fenton*. Like letters from an uncle who was travelling abroad.

His portrait in pastels and charcoal looked down at her from the wall, her portrait beside his. Done so long ago. Not just in time, although a year and a half was a long time – she had just turned eighteen then – but almost a different era. Mario's in King's Road in July of 1914; painters and writers, actors and poets; wine bottles and candles . . . It was all gone now. Shuttered and padlocked. Closed by the police because pacifists and radicals had been suspected of gathering there. Captain Fenton Wood-Lacy looked at her, dressed in mufti . . . a striped blazer, straw boater in his right hand. Now he was Lieutenant-Colonel Fenton Wood-Lacy, D.S.O. She had read of his new rank and his decoration in *The Times*. One always read the lists – the dead, the wounded, the missing – and the promoted. Lieutenant-Colonel F. Wood-Lacy would call back within half an hour. Whatever would they talk about?

His voice was the same as she remembered it, a deep, throaty timbre.

"Ah, Winifred, I hope I'm not inconveniencing you by calling."

"Not at all, Fenton. How nice to hear your voice."

"I got in last night . . . staying at the Guards' Club."

"Oh? Did you give up your flat?"

"Yes, a long time ago. Let it to a brigadier at the War Office. He's a major-general now so I can hardly boot him out of the place, can I?"

"No," she said, forcing a tiny laugh. "Hardly. Do you have a long leave?"

"A few weeks."

"And then back to France?"

"No, up to Yorkshire." There was a slight pause. "I thought we might have tea together somewhere . . . that is, if you're free this afternoon."

"I would enjoy that, yes."

"Shall we say four thirty?"

"That would be fine."

How correct and proper he was, she thought bitterly as she hung up the telephone. Honour-bound to at least see her. After all, he had taken the first step that long-ago July in the ritual of courtship. That ritual was now as archaic as the pavane, one of the lesser casualties of the war, but he was too much of a gentleman to totally ignore it. So he would take her to tea – not to dinner and the theatre, with dancing afterwards at the Café Royal, but to *tea*! Ices and petit fours and an apologetic, avuncular pat on the hand.

The Guards' Club was crowded and it was depressing to Fenton to see such a vast number of men whom he didn't know. So many of his friends and brother officers had gone west that he felt uncomfortably conspicuous for still being alive. A lone survivor of some dreadful catastrophe, pointed at, whispered about: "*There goes Wood-Lacy, last of those who passed out from Sandhurst in 1908.*"

Well, hardly. He finally bumped into enough of his peers in the bar to assure himself that his mortality wasn't unique. But he found their conversations to be morbid. All shared the same experiences in much the same places at the same times – rue du Bois and Festubert, Auchy and the dismal approaches to Loos. Their words nagged at old pains and still raw nerves.

"Must be off," he said draining a whisky and soda after glancing at his watch. He walked briskly out of the club and along Pall Mall towards the taxi stand in St. James's Square. Tattered sheets of grey cloud scudded overhead. The streaming fragments reminded him of shrapnel bursts and he could see his last command in the wind: B Company struggling through cratered ground, whizz-bangs and machine guns catching them, the First Platoon lurching towards the ridge, stopped by the German wire, dozens of them hanging in the rusty thickets for days, ragged husks, blackened clods against the skyline . . .

The taxicab door closed with a comforting chunky sound. Sealed from the counter-barrage by solid Austin walls, he sat stiffly on the edge of the seat all the way to Cadogan Square.

The war had touched half a million English homes, an avalanche of letters or telegrams pushed through letterboxes telling of dead or wounded men, missing men, captured men. Number Twenty-four Cadogan Square was such a home. Two dead sons. Two living sons anxious to get over to France and . . .

"Scupper Boche," Lord Dexford remarked heatedly as he

poured whisky into two glasses. "By Gad, Fenton, that's all young John and Bramwell think about, getting up to the line and killing the blighters."

He had never met them, but they were probably like Andrew and Timothy had been – recklessly brave. Their father's sons. He glanced past the portly, red-faced man. A full-length portrait of him hung on one wall of the library, the young Marquess in Hussar uniform, the painter capturing that look of zeal and arrogance that had sent Victorians galloping heedlessly towards the guns, *into the jaws of death . . . into the mouth of hell . . .*

"It pays to be cautious in France," he said quietly.

If Lord Dexford heard him, he paid no attention to the remark.

"A mere splash of soda water. Too fine a whisky to spoil. Pure malt, sir. From my own distillery in Kinlochewe. No contaminating *neutral spirits* which I wouldn't rub on a horse." He handed Fenton a glass and raised his own. "To your decoration and your rise in rank. I suppose this means you'll be commanding a battalion now, eh?"

"Yes, sir. One of the New Army mobs. I'm to train it and have it in France by next spring."

"As part of which regiment?"

"The Green Howards."

"I was with the Eleventh Hussars, Prince Albert's Own . . . the Cherry Pickers, sir!"

He was not really looking at him, Fenton realised as he sipped his drink. The eyes were glazed and fixed on some point in the distant past. They were the eyes of a man who was fortunate to have his own distillery. He talked ceaselessly, leaping from one disconnected subject to the next, until Lady Dexford entered the room and then he sat down and lapsed into a moody silence.

"Ah, my dear Fenton! Most noble heart!" She came towards him like some gaunt, predatory bird. Her hands never stopped moving and long ropes of jade and jet beads swung from around her throat. "Dear little Winifred will be ready shortly, fussing with her hair, poor child. I am quite vexed with her today . . . quite vexed, really I am. Her own brothers crying out from that awful void, anxious to come home, and she won't lift a finger to help them. But of course you understand, I'm sure."

He listened with growing apprehension to Lady Dexford's talk of the spirit world, of ouija boards and Ram the Nubian. He pitied Winifred living amid such irrationality. She'd always been under her mother's thumb and her refusal to take part in this nonsense was bound to have its repercussions. He expected a mousy, half-beaten creature to come into the library. He barely recognised the tall, beautiful woman who did.

"Hello, Fenton," she said.

He couldn't keep from staring at her as they drove towards Mayfair in the back of a taxi. The change in her was dramatic. He had remembered her, with twinges of shame, as a schoolgirl of touching eagerness whose gratitude for his attentions had been almost embarrassing. And yet there had been a quality about her even then that had intrigued him. He had truly enjoyed being with her and he felt that same sense of ease now.

"Why are you staring at me?"

"I'm sorry," he said. "I was trying to recall the Winifred I knew."

"Have I changed that much?"

"Well, you're older, of course."

"So are you, for that matter."

"Yes, about a century older." He didn't want to appear rude and so he deliberately looked away from her and stared at the back of the driver's neck. "You're a very lovely young woman, Winifred."

"Thank you, and you're still a very . . ." A smile barely teased her lips. "I was going to say *lovely* looking man. But that's hardly the correct word, is it? The word to describe a colonel would be *distinguished*. Yes, you're very distinguished." She glanced out of the side window. It was getting dark and crowds streamed across Hyde Park Corner towards the underground station in Piccadilly. "Must we go to tea?"

"Don't you feel like having tea?"

"Not especially."

"What would you like to do?"

"Oh, go to Madame Tussauds. I've always wanted to see the

317

Chamber of Horrors . . . Sweeney Todd cutting throats and Jack the Ripper. Father would never take me to see that section of the waxworks, but I had a friend in school, Rose Collins. She's seen it several times. Her uncle used to take her."

His hearing was not so numbed by shell fire that he couldn't detect sarcasm when he heard it. He leaned forward and tapped on the glass.

"Stop here, driver."

They walked along Piccadilly in silence, not because they had nothing to say to each other, but because the wind had picked up and was driving grains of ice into their faces. He took hold of her arm and led her into Half Moon Street and into the warm, spacious lobby of the Torrington Hotel.

"Did your friend's uncle ever buy the child a pink gin?"

"He may have," she said thoughtfully. "But I doubt it."

"May I buy you one, or will it alter your growth?"

"You're angry, aren't you?"

"Don't you think I have a right to be?"

"Yes, and no. Let's just say, for the sake of fairness, that we both have a right."

The saloon bar was crowded with officers and well-dressed women. There was a tiny dance floor – every hotel saloon bar had a dance floor now – and a four-piece ragtime band was playing the Castle Walk. Winifred cast a stony glance at the women and a wildly cavorting Canadian second lieutenant.

"Could you find some place quieter?"

He escorted her upstairs to the main salon where more sedate couples sat taking tea or cocktails. An elderly waiter in livery showed them to a table on the glassed-in balcony with a fine view of Green Park. Fenton ordered a pink gin and a whisky and soda and the drinks were quickly brought out on a silver tray.

"You feel that I'm being patronising, don't you?" he asked.

"No," she said. "I think you're just being noble . . . the honourable thing to do. A less considerate man would have simply ignored the situation entirely and not called on me at all." She took a sip of her gin. "Quite tasty. Odd. Us having a drink together in a public place. Quite unthinkable a year and a half ago, but *tempora mutantur* and all that."

"Yes, times change, but human emotions do not. If I've hurt you, Winifred, I'm deeply sorry."

"You have nothing to apologise for. The war has changed everyone's plans. I suppose we'd be married by now if Germany hadn't marched into Belgium. I wonder if we'd be happy? Probably. I would have a handsome husband and you would have . . . what? Why did you choose me, Fenton? It wasn't love. I wasn't under that illusion even then. Fundamentally monetary, I suppose. Or is that an uncalled-for remark?"

"No. You deserve to know why. It's true I needed money to stay in the regiment. It was either marry well or resign my commission. Your father understood my motive, so did Andrew. Their feelings were that I'd make you a good husband. That was my rationale as well. And I would have. But it wasn't just money . . . I wasn't that cold blooded about it. I would have sought out some simpering daughter of a Sheffield millionaire if I had been. God knows there were enough of that sort fluttering about Mayfair ballrooms. I liked you, enjoyed your company. I enjoy it now."

She toyed absently with her drink, turning the slender glass between her fingers.

"What would you do if I held you to your obligation to at least ask me to marry you?"

"I would propose, of course."

"Of course. I hardly needed to ask the question, did I?" She set her drink on the table and looked at him, her face expressionless. "I have difficulty sometimes in remembering what I was like that summer, or what you were like. We're different people now, aren't we? Not just in a physical sense. I mean to say, too much has happened in our lives for us not to have been altered quite drastically. But I recall how infatuated I was, how utterly giddy I felt. I knew in my heart that you couldn't possibly be in love with me, but I was desperate to be engaged by the end of July. I felt I owed it to my mother for all her efforts to see me wed. She made me feel that it was all my fault Charles hadn't dropped on one knee . . . that, somehow, I'd made a mess of it. But then she never had to walk in the garden with Charles as I did, knowing that every time he looked at me he was comparing me with Lydia Foxe. That was

319

cruel. I couldn't possibly compete. I felt such a frump. And then, out of the blue, you strolled into my life with a box of chocolates under your arm. No man's timing could have been more perfect, or more deliberately planned."

He took a hefty pull at his drink and then dug into his jacket for a tin of cigarettes.

"I hope you don't mind if I smoke."

"Not at all."

"This is rather like hearing a story about two unattractive strangers. You're an exceedingly beautiful woman. You don't need to feel grateful if a man looks at you."

"And you don't need a rich wife in order to stay in the army. The slate has been wiped clean, Fenton. It's like meeting for the first time."

"My feelings exactly. What say we make a proper evening of it? Dinner at Romano's or upstairs at the Café Royal . . . ."

Her smile went unnoticed as she took a sip of her drink.

"Sounds like fun, but I really don't feel up to celebrating. Will you be in London long?"

He felt a twinge of disappointment and a sense of having been deliberately cut by her. How deeply did she resent him, he wondered? He blew a thin stream of cigarette smoke from the corner of his mouth.

"On and off for the next two weeks. I'm going down to Abington for the weekend. May I telephone you next week?"

She looked at him without a flicker of emotion, a cautious, deliberating gaze.

"Yes," she said with a slight nod. "If you really want to."

There was a bleakness to the countryside that Fenton had never seen before during all the many winters he had spent in the North Downs and the Weald. A shabbiness and neglect that was not solely attributable to the weather. The lack of able-bodied men, he supposed, as the train lumbered slowly past one neglected-looking village after another: Effingham and Horsley, Clandon and Merrow. Roofs needed repair, walls thirsted for whitewashing, orchards were unpruned. The train was delayed at Abbotswood Junction to permit a battalion of New Army troops to double time across the tracks. The West

Surreys, he noticed, catching sight of the flag-bearing lamb badge on an officer's cap. The officer was grey-haired and rode his horse with taut-bodied fury, mentally cursing the shambling mob of soldiers who were obviously in the first stages of their training and could not run across a railway line without stumbling into each other or tripping over the rails. The West Surrey officer saw only a thousand green troops foisted on his ancient and noble regiment to meet the needs of the war. Fenton saw one thousand bricklayers, house-painters, carpenters, well-diggers, tree-pruners, butchers and butchers' boys and God knew what else. The heart's blood of the shire running across the embankment and on into the misted, sleet-covered fields beyond.

Charles had warned him that there might not be a taxi for hire in Godalming and to telephone the house when his train got in. There was a taxi, if he cared to wait an hour for it, but Mr. Pearson, the brewer, was driving his lorry into Abington with six barrels of ale and offered Fenton a lift.

"Like when you was a young 'un," Mr. Pearson said jovially. "You and young ·Lord Amberley and your brother, God bless him, 'opping on the wagon when I'd slow them old Percherons o' mine on Burgate Hill."

Summer fields and dray horses. Fresh in old Pearson's memory. Beyond recall to Fenton. He got out at the iron gates that marked the mile-long road to the house and walked the rest of the way, his kit bag slung over one shoulder. The Pryory looked as weathered and bleak as everything else he had seen, the house stretching away in the afternoon gloom like some abandoned relic. The once manicured quadrangle of the Italian garden seen beyond the weed-dotted terrace was a tangle of unpruned cypress. The stables, he knew without seeing, would be empty, the horses given to the cavalry. They might just as well have stayed in their warm and comfortable stalls for all the good they were doing in France.

But the house only looked abandoned. There were a number of cars parked at the end of the drive and when Coatsworth opened the door he was in full livery.

"Why, Mr. Fenton, sir, good to see you."

"Thank you, Coatsworth. Did I walk in on a party?"

"Just a few of his lordship's friends. Last gathering for some time, sir." He took Fenton's trenchcoat and kit bag and whispered, "They're closing the Pryory after Christmas, sir. We all move to the Park Lane house. Only forty rooms there, much easier to keep up."

Only forty rooms, Fenton thought wryly as he walked down the corridor towards the library. Well, everyone had to make sacrifices in war-time.

The candles in their silver holders were reflected in the highly polished surface of the long table. But for the lack of footmen – only three, old, older even than Coatsworth – it could have been any gathering for dinner at Abington Pryory at any time. The war was snugly tucked away as Lord Stanmore sliced the roast mutton and Coatsworth uncorked the wine. It seemed to Fenton that he had but to close his eyes for a second and when he opened them again Roger would be arguing with Charles about current trends in modern poetry and Alexandra would be chattering away about Paris frocks or what was playing at the cinema in Guildford. But time did not come back, no matter how familiar the surroundings. Roger was dead. Charles was a married man and Alexandra hadn't opened her mouth all evening, except to say hallo. Some things never changed, however. Mr. Cavendish, squire of Dilton Hall and the second largest landowner in the district, still bore his grudge against the Liberal party, although Lydia's presence at the table caused him to keep his comments to a near inaudible mumble.

Lydia Amberley. Fenton was seated opposite her and it was impossible for their eyes not to meet. What did he see there? A hint of triumph? A veiled smugness? Perhaps. It had always been difficult to tell what Lydia was thinking. When toasts had been offered he had raised his glass to her and she had smiled at him as though saying, "You see, I told you I would do it." The future Countess of Stanmore. It seemed incredible, but there she sat, looking to the manner born – and almost excessively lovely.

"So the fighting has wound down for the winter and I would like to know what we've got to show for it." Brigadier-General

Sir Bertram Sturdee, long retired, tapped his wine glass with a spoon. "1915 is not a year I would ever like to see again."

"Must we talk of the war, Bertram?"Hanna said.

"It's on everyone's mind, Hanna. *Non* war conversation always seems to flounder somewhat. And with Fenton's D.S.O. ribbon staring me in the face I can't quite keep my thoughts on local matters."

Hanna rose majestically. "You may talk of the war all you wish over the port. We ladies would prefer to be spared."

Alexandra stood up with the other women and then walked to the head of the table and kissed her father on the temple.

"Goodnight, Papa. I'm going to bed."

"Still feeling under the weather?" he asked.

"Yes," she said. "A bit." She turned to Fenton and placed a hand on his shoulder. "Goodnight, Fenton. It's so good to see you again."

He touched her hand. It was cold and her face had a waxen appearance.

"Alexandra not well?" he asked after the women had left the room.

"One bout of 'flu after another," the earl said, passing a box of cigars to his right. "Caught a chill of some sort in France and can't shake it."

"Alex was in France?"

"Thought you knew. Yes. Went over with the Red Cross, came back in October quite ill."

"Mustard and vinegar," Mr. Cavendish said. "Rub it thickly on the child's chest, wrap it in flannel and keep her in bed. Works wonders."

Brigadier-General Sturdee lit a cigar and waited for Coatsworth to pour the port.

"So Sir John French is out and Sir Douglas Haig is in. So much for the politics of the high command. You're in Whitehall these days, Charles. What sort of wild tales filter through the War Office halls?"

"Not too many filter down to my office," Charles replied, scowling at his glass of port. "I'm rather a new boy and not on the grapevine. But I understand that Haig would like to end the war next year with one huge blow in late summer, up at

Ypres. Joffre would prefer having our offensive launched closer to the French build-up in Champagne, perhaps along the Somme. Either way, it's going to be a big push and 1916 might just be the victory year."

"Don't bet a quid on it," Fenton said. "They're just getting lightheaded up at G.H.Q., seeing all these New Army battalions come into being. A million men under arms. They're mesmerised by the figures, but it doesn't change the formula. *Ten* million men could have gone over the top at Loos and they still would have been stopped by the wire and the Boche machine gunners. The Hun formula for defence is basic, simple, and works like a bloody charm. We have to make a radical change in our strategy and Haig isn't the man to do it. He thinks the infantry's sole function is to find a path through the wire and punch a few holes in the trench system so that the cavalry can pour through and win the war with sabre and lance. That's lunacy and every Tommy knows it."

Mr. Cavendish cleared his throat loudly. "Dash it, Fenton. That sounds defeatist, like an article in one of those damnable pacifist broadsides one finds scattered about in railway stations or on the street. I am quite surprised at your attitude, sir."

Sturdee chuckled softly. "You said the same thing to me once, Tom, when I came back from the Transvaal. I said Buller's an ass and you nearly shoved the Union Jack down my throat."

Lord Stanmore coughed discreetly. "Let's open a bottle of whisky and play some snooker. I agree with my dear wife . . . must we talk of the war?"

The old general walked slowly and stiffly beside Fenton towards the billiard room, the Boer bullet that had terminated his career still embedded deeply in his right hip.

"Your uncle was kind enough to take the time to write me a letter. He's damned proud of you, Fenton. He predicts you'll be commanding a brigade before summer. I assume you intend to stay in the army, make it your career?"

"I don't know anything else."

"You have all the qualities it takes to make field-marshal one day. That is to say, all the qualities but one. You're too quick to express an opinion. You're bound to rub the mossbacks the wrong way, and there are a great many mossbacks above you in rank. Believe me, I know. I would have retired a major-general instead of a brigadier if I had been less vocal about the débâcle of the Tugela River crossings. If you will permit an old man to utter an old saw . . . a word to the wise, dear fellow . . . a word to the wise.''

By midnight, only Fenton and Charles remained in the billiard room, playing in a desultory fashion. Fenton poured two whiskies and watched Charles miss an easy shot.

"You haven't said much about Whitehall.''

Charles glared at the tip of his cue. "Not in Whitehall actually, small building of our own in Old Pye Street. Just started really so I don't quite know what it'll be like. We're an odd group, officers and N.C.O.s, mechanical engineering and chemistry dons from London University, mad scientists with Viennese accents, a whole gamut of eccentrics talking to other eccentrics and crackpots. Strange people come to us with mad ideas on how to win the war – death rays, stuff like that.''

Fenton sunk the blue ball and scanned the table. "Don't exaggerate.''

"Well, they've come up with some good ideas: steel helmets, all the troops will have them by spring; a truly decent gas mask; an improved trench mortar and more powerful grenades that always work, so I suppose they've justified their existence to date.''

"Sounds like a very worthwhile place to be.''

"I suppose it is. We used to make our own grenades at Gallipoli, jam tins stuffed with guncotton filched from the navy. One out of six actually exploded. It's just that . . . well, dammit, I feel I should be with the Windsors. The regiment's back in England, what's left of it. Seventy-five per cent casualty rate, almost all of the officers either dead or in hospital. I should be on the square helping to drill the new battalions, not talking to farmers about their experiences with caterpillar tread tractors. Someone, somewhere, came up with the whimsical idea for a land battleship, a sort of enormous, armoured tractor with naval cannon in gun turrets, its iron-sides bristling with machine guns. Bound to be a washout. We simply don't have the technology to develop something that exotic, and even if we did develop it, we don't have the generals who would know what to do with the bloody thing. Generals hate machines, you know that. If they can't saddle it or boot it in the arse they don't want it in their commands. I have the sinking feeling that I'm devoting my energy to a doomed enterprise."

"If you feel so strongly about it you shouldn't have volunteered for the job."

Charles flubbed another shot and watched in disgust as the cue ball drifted into a corner pocket.

"I was picked right out of the hospital, ordered to report to General Haldane as soon as I could walk without crutches. He told me that he wanted me to work in N.S. 5, shoved a mass of technical journals at me and that was that. It's only a temporary assignment, of course. When the medical board finally gets around to certifying me fit for active duty I can say goodbye to talking to Hampshire farmers and looking at moving picture films of muddy old tractors crawling over muddy old ditches."

"Well, at least you have a lovely young wife to go home to every night. Count your blessings."

"I do," he said gravely. "In fact, I feel guilty about having so many to count."

"Remind me to send you a hair shirt. Be sensible, old boy. I've been watching you. You walk rather painfully."

"All the breaks have knitted well," he said defensively.

"Perhaps they have, but you'd be bloody useless marching around for hours, drilling troops. Any sod can do that. Keep working on your death ray, or land battleship, and remember that there's a chap just like you in Berlin trying to beat you to the punch."

He became full awake before the first pale light tinted the windows in his room. It was from force of habit, the morning stand-to of the trenches, the men alert and tense, bayonets fixed, waiting for the sun to rise behind the German lines. A machine gun or two would tap out a few rounds, a signal rocket might hiss upwards into the dawn sky, a flurry of rifle shots as men sensed movements in the mist-cloaked no man's land between the belts of wire. The time of greatest tension. Then the day would break with no sign of the Germans coming across. The men would stand down and listen for the comforting rattle of the tea dixies being carried along the communication trench from the cookers in the rear. His heart was beating faster and he felt sweaty under the eiderdown. He sat on the edge of the bed and lit a cigarette, wondering if he would ever be able to enjoy dawn again, or even enjoy sleep for that matter. His dreams had been bad ones. Nothing specific. No faces, no vivid images of the war, only feelings of dread and raw terror. There was a tremor in his right hand, a spasmodic movement of the thumb. He cursed it softly, held the cigarette in his left hand and slapped his right sharply against his leg. He lived in dread that one day his body would betray him and he would suddenly begin to tremble all over, or lose the use of his legs, or bolt screaming into the vomiting earth of the barrage as his Company Sergeant-Major had done so unexpectedly at Auchy.

The cooks had tea brewing and were fixing breakfast for the staff – only twelve now where once there had been forty. The servants' hall was closed off and the staff were seated in the kitchen when Fenton walked in among them. He was given a massive country breakfast of bloaters, eggs, ham and fried bread and held the servants in awe with the type of stories civilians liked to hear about the fighting. When he had finished eating, one of the bell boards emitted a tinkling sound and a small white disc popped into view, revealing that Lord Stanmore was awake and calling for his tea. Coatsworth sighed and poked his feet into a pair of carpet slippers.

"I'll inform his lordship that you're up and dressed, sir. He hasn't been riding lately, just hasn't had the heart for it, I suppose."

"I assumed that the horses were gone."

"That they are, sir, except for Jupiter and one of the mares, Rose O'Fen, corking good jumper in her day and still full of mustard."

"Yes, tell him I'm up and that I'll be in the stables."

The old groom was happy to have company and the horses were eager to be saddled. They frisked about, kicking their heels and snorting. Missed the companionship of the other horses, Fenton felt sure. There was something almost sinister about the rows of empty, shuttered stalls. The two men had just finished tightening the saddle girths when the earl hurried towards them, his jacket only half buttoned.

"Why in blazes didn't you tell me you weren't going to sleep late? Thought a returned soldier would lie abed to all hours."

"Rather hoped I could, to tell the truth. But here I am. Anything I should know about the mare?"

"She's going on fifteen and has a sensitive mouth."

"I'll be gentle with her if she'll be patient with me. Haven't been on a horse in a year and a half."

Time seemed to slip backwards in the exhilaration of the ride. Memories of the past rushed to the surface, brought vividly alive by the rhythmic thudding of the hooves on the frosty ground. But the illusion faded quickly. There was nothing to sustain it. His horse was old and in poor shape. The earl was old and embittered. They rode slowly and in silence, past the fringe of a leafless wood and then along a rutted path that led to the back of Abington Pryory. When the roofs of the house came into view the earl reined in and lit a cigarette.

"Giving it up, Fenton." He waved his cigarette at the distant house. "Moving up to London."

"Yes. Coatsworth told me."

"I'm lending all this to the army. Not sure what they'll be doing with it; officers' training school, I expect. Well, I shan't miss it. It's only a house now, you see. It's not the house I loved so much as the life I lived in it. That life's gone and all I'm left with is a ruddy big building, impossible to maintain. I shan't come back here until the war's over and I can re-stock the stables, lay out some new gardens, perhaps turn the flat land near Herons' Copse into a first-class polo field." He smoked silently for a moment, staring out across the meadows and the evergreen woods that screened his house. "Deluding myself, Fenton. A door's been slammed shut and it will never open again."

"That's nonsense, sir."

"No, Fenton. All of this is as dead as a dodo bird. Even if the war should end tomorrow nothing would ever be the same."

The earl went in for his breakfast and Fenton walked slowly

along the terrace, slapping his riding crop against his right boot. It had been a mistake to come down to Abington. A mere force of habit, or perhaps a yearning to recapture something that he knew in his heart was irretrievably gone. There had been no point in telling the earl that the giving up of his house and manner of living was not the greatest loss to be suffered in 1915. He would, no doubt, have agreed but not truly believed it. After all, it was the greatest loss for *him*, and it was not an easy matter to visualise two hundred thousand graves.

The door to the conservatory opened and Charles hurried out. He was in uniform, a Burberry slung over one shoulder, and he looked harassed and irritable.

"I have to grab the eight forty to Salisbury. My so-called commander just rang down and ordered me to Wiltshire, to see some farmer who owns a ruddy big steam tractor."

"A what?"

"Steam tractor! The fellow bought it in Canada before the war. I have to commandeer the bloody thing and arrange for its shipment to Newbury."

"Want me to come along?"

"No. Just drive me to the station. Father's latest chauffeur can't get out of bed. He's seventy-six, so that's hardly surprising."

With Charles gone, there didn't seem to be much point in staying for the rest of the weekend. Fenton thought up various excuses for going back to London as he drove the Rolls-Royce back to the house. Lydia and Hanna were having coffee in the breakfast room.

"Did he make his train?" Lydia asked.

"Just. He asked me to tell you that he'll get back to London some time Monday afternoon." He made a show of looking at his watch. "And speaking of London, I'll hop the three forty-two for Charing Cross. Sorry to cut my stay short, but I've got a devil of a lot of things to do. Seeing Charles rush off made me feel guilty for neglecting the war."

Hanna sipped at her coffee. "We love having you, even for a few brief hours."

"No point in your taking the train," Lydia said casually. "The service is atrocious. The three forty-two will end up being the four thirty-five and you'll be forced to stand in the corridor. I'm driving up in an hour."

"Oh?" Hanna said.

"Yes. I thought Charles told you. The upholsterer's man is due in this afternoon to measure the windows and bring the swatches." She glanced at Fenton over the rim of her cup. "Charles and I have bought a house in Bristol Mews. I'm in the middle of redecorating it. A horrible amount of work, I might add."

And that was that. He was grateful to be gone. So was Lydia. She no longer dared drive a German car, but her Napier Six was suitably rakish and powerful. She drove at her usual breakneck speed and said nothing until the house was far behind them.

"I can't tolerate being there without Charles."

"No upholsterer's man?"

"A small white lie, but I couldn't face being alone with them. I could stand it if Alex was up and about, but she's pretty much taken to her bed."

"What's the matter with her?"

"They say it's the 'flu, but I'm not so sure. Something happened when she was in France but I can't get a word out of her. Very curious. She used to overwhelm me with confidences."

She concentrated on the road. There was very little civilian traffic but a good deal of army transport, most of it horse drawn. She passed the long columns slowly so as not to frighten the horses.

"I find you a bit curious as well," she said. "You haven't said anything. Not one word."

"About what?"

"Charles and me."

"You seem to be a happy couple. What am I supposed to say?"

"You never thought it would happen, so you must have some degree of inquisitive curiosity."

"I gave up being inquisitive about anything that happens these days. I wouldn't have raised an eyebrow had you married the Prince of Wales."

"Please don't play the bastard with me, Fenton. We've known each other too long for that."

"Very well, I'll be suitably brotherly. Are you happy?"

She hesitated slightly. "Yes."

"Do you love him at all?"

"He loves me. That's all that matters."

"Did you get him his job with N.S. 5?"

She stiffened. "What makes you ask that?"

"Because I know how the army works. General Haldane's a Royal Engineer. There must have been any number of R.E. officers he could have picked with more technical training than Charles. I suspect a bit of string-pulling by you or Archie."

"All right. I talked to a few people. Is there anything wrong in that?"

"No. I would gladly have done the same. He probably realises it, but he thinks he's only doing this until he's fit for duty in the line. Is that how it works, or is there something he doesn't know yet?"

"He's locked in for the duration of the war," she said flatly.

"He'll hate you for it when he finds out."

"How regimental you sound. He might just be grateful for being spared the trenches."

"Most men would be, but not Charles. As long as you're married to him you might take the trouble to understand his class."

"God! The peerage have their little ways, haven't they? Duty, self-sacrifice, stalwart resistance to change. One wonders sometimes if they'll emerge from this war with their coronets intact."

"I assume they'll survive," he said quietly. "They always have."

"Charles will survive. That's all I care about."

"With coronet in place?"

She brushed a loose strand of hair from her forehead and smiled wryly.

"England will always be England. The power may rest one day in the hands of an ex-Liverpool solicitor, but the people will bow at the sight of a coronet be it tarnished or not."

Bristol Mews was a short, brick-paved street near Berkeley

Square. Lydia parked the car in front of a narrow, three-storey house that had been built during the reign of George II. The windowsills had been freshly painted white, shutters and front door a gleaming black.

"Handsome-looking place," Fenton said.

"It's quite charming on the inside, too. Care for a drink?"

"I could do with a whisky, yes."

There were painters' ladders in the foyer and a strong smell of turpentine, wallpaper paste and wood shavings throughout the first floor.

"It takes for ever," Lydia said. "It's so difficult finding good workers and those you do find are unbearably independent. It's more ordered on the upper floors."

She led the way up a gently curving staircase to the second-floor landing and into a large room furnished in the Oriental manner, with black and red lacquered cabinets and tables, a huge Chinese screen and low divans covered in pale green silk.

"Like it?"

"Yes," he said, after giving it some thought. "A change from Burgate House."

"Daddy told me to take furniture from there, but there was nothing in the old place except Sheraton and Hepplewhite. I wanted something different."

"Very exotic. I feel out of place in khaki."

"There's whisky and soda in the teak cabinet. Help yourself while I change."

An elderly maid came in to light the fire while Fenton poured himself a whisky. No neutral spirits . . . which made him think of Winifred. He was still thinking of her when Lydia came back into the room, her travelling suit of heavy tweed replaced by a flowing silk hostess gown in shades of blue and dark green. Yes, he thought, it had been cruel of Charles to compare Winifred to Lydia. Comparison between them was not as marked now as it had been then, but there was certainly an air of chic about Lydia that Winifred would never acquire. She closed the doors and walked over to the fire, the glow of the flames turning her loose hair a shimmering copper. He poured her a brandy and then sat beside her on a divan facing the fire.

332

"How long will you be in England?" she asked.

"Four or five months. I must go up to Leeds after the New Year and start training a battalion. One of those chums and pals conglomerations, all the lads enlisting together. I'll feel a rank outsider."

"I'm sure they'll be proud having a Guards officer commanding them. I know I'd be."

"I can just see myself ordering *you* about."

"I don't know," she said tautly. "That would depend on what you ordered me to do."

She set her drink on a low table and turned to him. He moved his arms around her, feeling the warmth of her body beneath the silk gown.

"I want you, Fenton."

"You *have* Charles."

She undid the middle buttons of his shirt and slipped a hand through the gap.

"His love is ethereal. Passion shocks him."

"You'll have to teach him. One doesn't learn much about women at Winchester and Cambridge. Be patient."

She kissed him on the mouth, her tongue gliding against his teeth.

"I don't feel very patient at the moment," she whispered. "Please, Fenton . . ."

He could take her to bed. Or he could take her on the divan. A pleasant afternoon's rutting in Bristol Mews, the first step to becoming her lover. She might talk to a few people and he would find his orders mysteriously changed. Staff job in Whitehall. Nothing to be ashamed of. Brother officers would say that he jolly well deserved it after Mons, the Marne, Festubert and Loos. Her tongue sought the deeper recesses of his mouth. Lingered . . . drew back.

"Please . . ."

She was warm, vibrant, passionate. Infinitely desirable. But there was a taste of brass in his mouth. The taste of tarnish.

"No." He pushed her gently away from him and stood up. "We're much too late for this, darling Lydia. We quite missed the boat."

She lay back against the cushions, staring at him, her eyes reflecting the fire.

"You're not serious."

"Yes, as a matter of fact, I am."

"Why? Charles would never know. You wouldn't be hurting him or ruining his marriage in the slightest."

He buttoned his shirt and straightened his tie. "I wasn't thinking of Charles, actually. He never crossed my mind. I was thinking of myself. Everything is becoming so shabby these days. So lacking in worth. I just don't feel like joining the trend."

"You bastard," she said quietly as he walked out of the room.

2

MARTIN RILKE STRUGGLED ALONG OXFORD STREET, THE WIND yanking at his umbrella and threatening to tear it from his hand. A middle-aged woman waiting at a bus stop stared at him without sympathy.

"Slacker," she said in a strong Cockney accent. "Strong chap like you."

He was used to it, the insults and the white feathers. Quite a large number of men whose work was vital to the war effort or who had been judged medically unfit for service had taken to wearing armbands to avoid being harassed. He had considered the idea of wearing one with a small American flag stitched to it, but had thought better of it. It would only have led to other snide remarks, "Too bloody proud to fight, eh?"

He entered the White Manor at Marble Arch, removed his raincoat and hat and handed them to a cloakroom attendant, along with his battered umbrella. An orchestra in the second-floor dining salon was playing a waltz, the soft strains fragmented by the clatter of plates and teacups in the crowded and plebeian first floor. He looked around and finally spotted Ivy Thaxton seated at a small table next to a travertine column. He felt like shouting at the sight of her – he hadn't seen her for three and a half weeks – but suppressed the urge.

"Ivy!" He slid into the chair opposite her and reached across the table to touch her hand. "Gosh, it's good to see you. I hope you weren't waiting long."

"No, just a few minutes." She smiled warmly, her hand clenching his. "Have you been all right?"

"Of course."

"You look pale."

"I'm fine."

She frowned slightly. "I mean it. A bit wan under the eyes."

"I know you've been capped, but don't play nurse with me, sister. I'm just weak from hunger."

"So am I."

He looked around. There were tables almost on top of them, two hefty, kilted Highlanders within touching distance.

"Wouldn't you rather go upstairs? Maybe we could get a better table, and dance."

"It's horribly crowded up there, too. And besides, the food's the same up or down. Let's just have our tea and talk about dancing later."

She could eat, bless her. He felt almost paternal, watching her devour what was placed before her – a pork pie, tea sandwiches of ham and cress, a slice of Dundee cake and cup after cup of tea. And yet she was as thin as a waif. She amazed him.

"Stop staring at me."

"I like to watch you eat."

"It's rude."

"Sure, but you know how we Yanks are." He took a cigar from his pocket but didn't light it. She frowned on his smoking while they ate. "I have a little something for you. A Christmas present."

She looked at him sternly. "That's not fair. We made a promise not to exchange gifts."

"Okay, I welshed on the deal. But I saw this certain item in Regent Street the other day and I knew you'd like it so I bought it for you."

"You shouldn't have."

"Ah, but I did and they won't take it back." He toyed with the cigar. "You'll be going to France, won't you?"

"Yes." She looked down at her plate and crumbled a bit of cake between her fingers. "My group leaves on January 3rd . . . Number Nine Stationary Hospital in Boulogne."

He fished for a match and lit the cigar. "So soon?"

"Afraid so."

"Will I be able to see you before you leave?"

"I doubt it. We go down to Portsmouth for an orientation course right after Christmas. The twenty-seventh, I believe. Sorry, Martin, but this is our last get-together . . ."

"Date," he said, forcing a grin.

"Yes, *date*. I must remember that word."

"I could come over, write an article or two about Number Nine Stationary Hospital in Boulogne and Sister Ivy Thaxton of the Q.A.s."

"Please don't. It's going to be a difficult time for me, adjusting to the type of cases we'll meet there. I would only be terribly distracted if you were hanging about."

His grin was genuine this time. "Would you really?"

"Don't look so pleased with yourself." She frowned at the demolished fragments of cake. "I shall miss you, Martin. Miss you very much."

"I'll sure as heck miss you. Funny, come to think of it. We hardly see each other, maybe once every month or so, and yet just knowing that you're in London is a comfort to me. When I got back from France last trip my train got shunted around a lot coming up from Folkestone and we pulled into Euston Station instead of Waterloo. I took a taxi down Gower Street, past the University, and there was All Souls. A couple of guys from the *Journal-American* were with me and I pointed the place out. I said, there's the best training hospital for nurses and army doctors in England. One of them said, Jesus, looks like the biggest and oldest brickyard in the world. Well, it sure didn't look like that to me because somewhere in that maze of buildings was my best girl."

Ivy blushed and poured herself another cup of tea. "Is that what I am to you, Martin?"

"Why do you have to ask? I've told you enough times. Sure you're my best girl. Heck, you're the only girl I know."

"You must meet so many girls in . . . well, Paris, places like that."

"I only meet generals in Paris, drinking port at the Hôtel Crillon."

"And Cairo. They say that Egyptian women are the most exotic women in the world."

"Who told you that? You can't even see them. They wear black sheets over their heads." He stubbed out his cigar because the smoke was drifting into her face. "Look, you're a daisy and my heart jumps into my throat whenever I see you. Okay? Do you believe that?"

"If you say so, yes."

"You don't seem very pleased about it. Anything the matter?"

"No, I suppose not."

He reached across the table and touched her cheek. "You've got the blues because you're leaving soon. I feel the same way about it, but it won't be for ever. After you're used to the hospital and sure of yourself I'll come over. Maybe you'll be able to get a few days' leave and we could go to Paris and I'll show you the sights. And anyway, I'll be writing to you all the time so we won't get out of touch, not for a minute."

"Perhaps it would be better if we did get out of touch, at least until the war's over."

"I don't see any reason for that, Ivy." He leaned back in his chair and lit his cigar again. "It seems to me that a war's the best time to hang on to friendships, not abandon them. Why don't you finish your tea and we'll go over to the flat and I'll give you your Christmas present. Okay?"

Something was troubling her and he wasn't sure what it was. Simple anxiety and depression, he hoped. That was to be expected. She had never been out of England before and the idea of going across the Channel to France, to work as a regular nurse in a huge base hospital, must be unnerving to her. He held her hand tightly as they left the restaurant, but she seemed unresponsive to his touch and she barely said a word in the taxi as they drove to Soho.

The flat was tidy for a change because Jacob rarely spent any time in it. The first time he had brought Ivy there she had been appalled by its disorder and had spent half an hour, over his protests, picking things up.

"How about a glass of sherry?"

"No, thank you." She sat stiffly on the edge of the sofa. "Sherry makes me feel tipsy."

"Do you good. Make you relax a bit."

"I'm quite relaxed, thank you."

"Well," he said lamely, "have it your own way." He clapped his hands and said with a forced cheerfulness, "Santa Claus has come to town, so close your eyes and don't open them until I say so."

338

He ducked into the hall and brought out a large package from the hall cupboard. It had been wrapped in bright paper and tied with a red ribbon. He placed it on the cushion next to her.

"You can open your eyes now."

She had never received a present in her life, at least not one that came wrapped in a parcel. A rag doll and three penny-worth of rock in a Christmas stocking were the only presents she had ever been given. She looked at the parcel in awe and could do no more than touch the ribbons.

"Open it. Go on."

She undid it carefully so as not to tear the paper. A large white box with the name of the firm embossed on the lid was revealed.

"That's such a fine shop," she said. "What on earth did you buy me?"

"You'll never know until you lift the lid. It's practical, I'm sorry to say. I wanted to buy you a whole raft of things . . . you know, feminine things, but I figured there was no point in getting you stuff you couldn't use right now."

"No," she said, touching the crest on the lid. "That's true."

She opened the box gingerly and stared in awe at a large, glove-leather carrying bag, IVY THAXTON stamped in gold on one of the many flapped compartments. It was as sturdily constructed as a cavalry saddle but amazingly light.

"Oh, my," she whispered, stroking the leather. "It must have cost a fortune."

"You bet it did. Nearly beggared me." He sat next to her and put one arm about her waist. "There are all kinds of things inside – brush and comb, nail kit – you can carry all your gear in it."

"It's beautiful. Just beautiful."

He kissed the side of her neck. "So are you, Ivy."

She half turned and seemed about to say something, but he stopped her with his lips. She resisted at first, her mouth hard, unyielding, and then she suddenly responded with a degree of passion that left them both a little shaken.

"Oh, Ivy, Ivy . . ." he whispered hoarsely, his lips against her cheek, one hand lightly stroking the curve of a breast felt through the winter serge of her uniform.

She moved his hand away with regret. "No, we mustn't . . ."

"Marry me, Ivy."

She drew away from him, shaking her head firmly. "No. You shouldn't ask me."

"Why not? You know how I feel about you and you knew I'd ask. I've done everything but advertise in the papers that I love you."

"And I love you, Martin, really I do, but it wouldn't be right. You'd only regret it after a while."

He tried to read the meaning of that remark in her violet eyes. Her eyes were usually so expressive, but they were fathomless now.

"I don't know what you mean. Why would I regret it? Does insanity run in the family, or something? That doesn't make any sense, Ivy. Only the world's biggest fool would regret marrying a girl like you."

"And what would your family think?"

He sensed a bitterness in her tone as she looked away from him and stared down at the leather bag.

"My family? Boy! I know what my Uncle Paul would say if he saw you. He'd say that I'd finally done something really smart for a change."

"And what would . . . Lady Stanmore say?"

So that was it. He understood clearly now. The upstairs maid. He put an arm about her shoulders and gave her a hug.

"Aunt Hanna would love you as much as I do. She's a fine woman. Don't let her English airs throw you. Underneath it all she's Hanna Rilke from Prairie Avenue. She wouldn't bat an eye if I told her you were the girl for me."

"I saw her this morning," she said quietly. "The Duke and Duchess of Brendon came to visit the convalescent ward in D wing, to hand out little Christmas presents to the men. There were several other people in their party: Lord this and Lady that . . . and Lady Stanmore. Lady Alexandra was with her. I tried to be as inconspicuous as possible, but her ladyship spotted me right off."

"And?"

340

"Oh, she was very gracious, held out her hand and asked me how I was . . . things like that . . . how was I getting along and all and how pleased she was to see me. I don't know what I said; just stammered a few words. I felt awkward somehow. And Lady Alexandra just stood behind her mother, staring at me, not saying a word. I think perhaps she was a bit shocked to see me, Ivy Thaxton, shaking her mother's hand. She kept on staring at me even after they moved down the row of beds. There was something in her eyes, a coldness . . . I don't know how to explain it, Martin. You just wouldn't understand."

He attempted to draw her closer to him, but her body was rigid.

"Look here, Ivy. That's got nothing to do with us. If we got married we wouldn't be moving into the same house with Alexandra."

"Perhaps not, but you'd still be marrying her maid. And think how awkward it would be if we were invited to dinner. Can't you just see Mr. Coatsworth's face if he had to serve me at the table?"

"The butler, you mean?"

"Yes. And all those stuck-up footmen. I know one of them would trip on purpose and dump soup on my head."

She smiled to herself and then turned to Martin and rested her head on his shoulder.

"Oh, I know I'm being silly. I really shouldn't care about that. We'd live in America, wouldn't we, Martin? In Chicago, Illinois, on Lake Michigan."

"Anywhere you wanted to live," he said, stroking her hair. "Any place in the world. The Associated Press want me to leave the *Post* and work exclusively for them. They're dangling a lot of money in front of me and I'm seriously thinking it over. A.P. men go all over the world: China, Japan, the South Seas. And any place they sent me you'd be right there with me."

She nestled closer to him and was silent for a time, content to lie against him while he stroked her hair. Then she said, "I'm going to France, Martin. I could never marry you until this horror is over."

"I know," he said quietly. "I know that."

"I've been nursing gas cases the past five weeks. I never told

341

you. It's frightful working with them. There's so little you can do. They sit propped up in bed and cough themselves to death, and they're so terrified."

"Shush," he whispered, holding her tighter. "Don't talk about it."

"We lost sixty per cent. And they're not the worst ones. The really bad cases are left in Boulogne. They're the ones my team will be nursing. They need me more than you do at the moment, Martin."

"I understand," he said, thinking of the stumbling, retching men he had seen at Hulluch in late September. Chlorine gas, the brass buttons of their uniforms turned a vivid green, the stark terror of death in their eyes. He held her closer. "I understand."

She felt like walking even though it was dark and the wind was bitter. It wasn't that far and the rain had stopped and they enjoyed striding briskly side by side along Old Compton Street and Charing Cross Road and Great Russell Street, past the black, looming hulk of the British Museum and then up Gower Street to the sprawling hospital, lights glowing from myriad windows – no black-outs tonight, no fear of Zepp raids in this wind. The leather bag hung from Ivy's right shoulder on its broad, sheepskin-padded strap and, looking at her out of the corner of his eye, at the smartness of it and her obvious pride of ownership, he couldn't have felt more pleased if he had bought her a diamond ring – although he would have much preferred *that* expense.

"Well, here we are," she said, facing him. The brick structure of the main building rose behind her like a cliff. "I shall write you when I get settled and give you my address."

"Number Nine Stationary, Boulogne."

"Yes, but it might be Number Four in Salonika for all we know. Nothing can be relied on these days, can it?"

"No." He wanted to embrace her, but a great many people were walking past them in and out of All Souls. He bent forward and kissed the tip of her nose. "Take care of yourself."

He was gone. She stood for a moment watching him walk away and then she turned and entered the building. A group of sisters passed her on their way out. A tall, red-haired girl stopped and touched the bag.

"I say, Thaxton. Wherever did you get it?"

"It was a present. From my young man."

The red-head leaned closer, swaying forward like a sapling.

"The Yank chap?" she whispered.

"Yes. Isn't it grand?"

"Lovely! Mine gave me a rather smallish box of sweets – but that's a Welshman for you! Oh, by the way, Thaxton, your friend has been waiting for ages. I let her sit in the sisters' lounge in D wing."

"Friend? What friend?"

"Blonde lass, very pretty."

"Oh," Ivy said, momentarily stunned. "Thank you."

It was the only blonde girl she could think of, but it couldn't be, could it? Why on earth . . . ? But when she reached D wing after hurrying along what seemed miles of corridors and peered through the glass panel in the door of the sisters' lounge there she was, Lady Alexandra Greville, seated on a shabby leather couch in the empty room.

"Hallo, m'lady," Ivy said, walking up to her. Her face burned. Alexandra had been staring down at her lap. She looked up and Ivy noticed how blank her eyes were. Then she smiled slightly.

"Hallo, Ivy. I suppose you're surprised to see me."

"Yes." She stood stiffly, not knowing what to say. "Have you been here long?"

"A couple of hours I suppose."

"I was off duty."

"So I discovered."

"I go back on at nine."

Alexandra glanced at a wall clock. "That gives us about an hour. That is, if you can spare me the time."

"Time for what, m'lady?"

"To talk." She reached out and took Ivy gently by the hand. The well-manicured fingers were icy. "And please don't keep calling me m'lady. You're not my maid any longer."

No, not a maid any longer, and yet she suddenly felt awkward. She could almost hear Mrs. Broome whispering over

343

her shoulder, "Stand up straight, Ivy, and for heaven's sake don't fidget or stammer. A good maid is both at ease and respectful when talking to her betters." She felt vaguely sick to her stomach. How terribly wrong Martin was. But how could an American possibly understand?

"Do sit down, Ivy."

"Yes, ma'am." She sat stiffly on the very edge of the couch. Alexandra still had hold of her hand and so she couldn't sit as far away as she would have wished.

"I was surprised to see you this morning, Ivy. I had quite forgotten that you had joined the Q.A.s. How smart you look in your uniform! You're a nursing sister now, aren't you?"

"Yes."

"You must be very proud." She released her grip and folded her hands in her lap. "I haven't been very well and I didn't want to visit All Souls, but mother insisted that I should come with her."

"Not well?"

"A bit under the weather."

"I see." She looked up at the clock. The second hand had never moved so slowly. "Are you living down at Abington?"

"No. We just moved to the Park Lane house."

"That's nice."

"I've always liked being in London."

It was not the same Alexandra Greville, Ivy was thinking, watching her. Certainly as pretty as ever, and as smartly dressed, but the manner had changed. The bubbling, talkative girl had turned into a sombre, introspective woman. The eyes looked troubled. The hands were restive, fingers clenching and unclenching. Bloodless. Cold and white.

Ivy cleared her throat. "I was quite surprised to see you and her ladyship. Quite . . . happily surprised, I should say."

"Were you? That's nice. I was happy to see you. So was Mother. She made a point of telling Mrs. Broome when we got home."

"How is Mrs. Broome?"

"Her nephew was killed at Cambrin in September which upset her very much, but she's quite her old self again. An indomitable woman, Mrs. Broome."

344

"Yes, she is."

It felt horribly hot in the lounge, but Ivy resisted the urge to stand up and remove her heavy cape. Alexandra was wearing a coat with sable collar and cuffs. She looked as cool as marble.

"Mother and the Duchess of Brendon were quite upset after touring the wards. We had lunch at Claridges and they cried all the way through it." She looked at Ivy and her eyes were bitter. "Odd they would be so moved. It was merely a nice ward, wasn't it?"

"A . . . nice ward?"

"I think you know what I mean, Ivy. A show ward. All the lads so cheerful, despite their wounds. And all the wounds so trivial and so neatly bandaged."

"They . . . the chief of staff, that is . . . doesn't like to upset important visitors."

"I can understand the point. It would have upset Mother and the duchess dreadfully to have seen a man with his face blown off, especially before lunch."

Ivy's mouth went dry. "That takes getting used to," she said with difficulty.

"Does one ever get used to it? Is it possible to cope with a sight like that?"

The intensity of Alexandra's stare was disquieting. Ivy shifted slightly on the seat and rubbed the back of her hand across her lips.

"It takes time."

A young doctor wearing a white jacket over an obviously new uniform stepped into the lounge.

"I say, are you on duty, Sister Thaxton?"

"No, sir. Not till nine."

"Have you seen Sister Jones?"

"Which Jones, sir?"

"Number Sixteen Jones."

"She was assigned to Abdominals this afternoon by Captain Mason."

"Mason? Do I know him?"

"Regular, sir, Indian army – purple nose."

"Ah, yes," he said, as though that took care of his immediate problem. "Thank you, Thaxton."

345

"They're becoming younger every day," Ivy said after the doctor walked off. "Barely qualified for surgery, but they do a very good job despite their lack of experience." She had been grateful for the slight interruption.

"One gains experience very quickly these days, I would imagine."

"There's no lack of patients here."

"Nor in France," Alexandra said quietly.

A dozen probationers carrying notebooks followed their nursing instructor down the corridor and into the lounge. The probationers were all young and gaunt with fatigue. They stared at Alexandra as though she were a creature from some alien world. The nursing instructor was a tall, jolly woman of forty who took everything in her stride.

"Hallo, Thaxton! Entertaining visitors, are we? Well, not in here, my girl. We were right in the middle of wet dressings and got kicked out of Room Fifty-six by the jaw and plastic lads."

The two women walked into the corridor.

"Is there anywhere private where we could talk?"

"No," Ivy said stiffly. "This is a very crowded place."

"You resent my coming here, don't you?"

Well, Ivy thought, an honest question deserves an honest answer.

"Yes. I don't wish to hurt your feelings, but I don't have the time for small talk. And after all, we really don't have that much to talk about, do we?"

"The reason I came, Ivy, was simply to ask you a few questions. You see, I want to join the Q.A.s."

Her stare was rude, frankly incredulous. "You?"

Alexandra flinched. "Why not me?"

"I don't know exactly. I just can't see you going through the training. It's a lot of hard, dirty, exhausting work. The maids at Abington Pryory were never worked as hard. There's a Red Cross V.A.D. unit here for ladies of good birth – mornings or afternoons, writing letters, reading to the men, rolling bandages – why don't you join that?"

"Oh, dear," Alexandra said, drawing in her breath sharply. "What an awful little snob you turned out to be."

And she was gone, half running down the corridor. Ivy

346

stared after her in bewilderment. Her hidden anger and resentment turned to cheek-burning shame.

"Wait!"

She ran swiftly, dodging nurses and orderlies. She caught up with Alexandra near the end of the corridor, grabbed her by one arm and propelled her towards a narrow green door which she opened and closed after them with the quickness of a conjurer. They were in a blanket storage room lit by a low watt bulb dangling from the ceiling. Ivy slid a bolt into place and leaned back against the door.

"I'm not a snob," she said in between deep breaths.

Alexandra stood stiffly, her face taut and pale. "Yes, you are. It would be like my saying that all *you're* suited for is making beds and carrying tea trays!"

"I was only speaking my mind. I just can't imagine you as a Q.A. probationer, that's all. If it's a question of wanting to do your bit . . ."

"I joined the Red Cross at the beginning of the year. A convalescent home for officers in Wimbledon – writing letters, fluffing pillows, all the things that ladies of *good birth* do as volunteers."

"There can be more to it than that."

"I know. I went to France after my brother was wounded and mastered the art of emptying bedpans!"

They studied each other like two strangers. But there was a bond of sorts. Alexandra Greville had always been kind.

"I'm sorry," Ivy said. "I'm sure you didn't wait hours just to tell me that you wanted to join up." She waved a hand at their cramped surroundings. "You asked for a quiet place to talk."

"Thank you, Ivy. Something happened to me in France – a kind of breakdown, more emotional than physical – and although I want very badly to become a military nurse, I have this fear, you see . . . this feeling of inner panic that under similar circumstances I might break down again. It's not a fear I can express to the director of recruitments."

It was so quiet in the closet that Ivy could hear the thumping of her heart.

"Tell me about it."

347

She kept her eyes on Alexandra's face, seeing pain and honesty and truth mirrored there. She could visualise the Alexandra she had known, romantic and vain, play-acting the rôle of a nurse in her elegant and expensive uniforms from the House of Ferris. *Alexandra Nightingale, Saint Alexandra* – the girl mocked herself without indulging in self-pity. Ivy knew the inevitable outcome of her folly as she told of her trip in the ambulance from St. Omer to the casualty clearing station at Kemmel. Reaching out, she took Alexandra by the hand and pressed firmly.

"You don't have to tell me what happened there. I can guess."

"They needed help so badly," she whispered. "Hundreds of men, Ivy, men without arms, legs, faces. I could do so little for them, and what little I began to do . . ." She paused, running her tongue over her dry lips. "I failed them so completely . . ."

"You didn't fail anyone," Ivy said sternly. "You can't fail at something that you weren't equipped to do in the first place." She turned to the door and opened it. "For God's sake let's get out of here before we suffocate."

They walked slowly down the corridor towards the main entrance. Nurses, orderlies and doctors passed them, some nodding in recognition to Ivy, all eyeing Alexandra with varying degrees of curiosity.

"I look out of place," Alexandra said.

"Do you feel out of place? That's what's important, you know."

"I'm not sure I understand what you mean."

"I meant, will you be comfortable in the Q.A.s? Is it what you *really* want to do. Or are you just trying to prove something to yourself?"

"I want to be useful," she said flatly.

"Fine. We can use all the help we can get. And as for your fears . . ." She stopped and faced her. "We all have a certain amount of fear every time we walk into a ward. Do you see those two girls standing by the dispensary window? One of them is the daughter of a parson in Ludlow, the other was a teacher in Wales. A cut finger or a broken ankle were the worst injuries they'd seen before coming here. Now they work ten

348

hours or more a day with men who are coughing up their lungs bit by bit. They don't have some special kind of bravery that you lack. What they have is the assurance that twelve months of training has given them. The only courage you need is the courage to begin that training and the courage to stick it out."

The bells of University College chapel pealed the first stroke of nine.

"I must go," Ivy said. "Perhaps we can talk again tomorrow."

Alexandra bent quickly forward and kissed her on the cheek. "I'll be joining up tomorrow. Goodnight, *Sister* Thaxton."

"Well, I never," Ivy murmured, holding one hand to her cheek. She stood in the corridor and watched Alexandra cross the vast entrance hall, crowded now with departing visitors, frescoes of famous healers on the walls and, stretched above the door, a twenty-foot sign lettered by the ambulatory patients: PEACE ON EARTH, GOOD WILL TOWARDS MEN.

> God rest ye merry, gentlemen:
> Let nothing you dismay.
> Remember Christ, our Saviour,
> Was born on Christmas Day.

"The carol singers are not quite what they used to be," Lady Wood-Lacy whispered. "Jim Penny, Will Adams . . . oh, all the best baritones are in the army."

They sounded harmonic enough to Fenton. He invited them in for hot whiskies or punch, but they gracefully declined and moved off down the lane towards the Shaw house where Mr. and Mrs. Shaw and their five children waited expectantly.

> It came upon a midnight clear,
> That glorious song of old . . .

Fenton closed the front door and followed his mother down the hall and into the drawing room. An aroma of roasting goose filled the house.

"I'd better see how Jinny is coming along," Lady Wood-Lacy said. "She gets forgetful sometimes."

Jinny was eighty years of age and was the only servant Sir

349

Harold and Lady Margaret had ever had, or needed, living most of their married life in cottages at the various job sites – Balmoral, Sandringham, Abington Pryory. But the small, exquisitely constructed house in Suffolk – an architect's house, after all – had always been waiting for them with Jinny puttering about in the kitchen.

He poured a whisky and stood by the bay window. The last glow of the pale winter sun glinted off the cold, wind-stirred waters of the River Deben. Home for Christmas, but his thoughts were far from carol singers, holly and roast goose. The second Christmas of the war and far different from the first one. He had celebrated that Christmas in France, quartered in a château near Bethune. All conversation in the mess had been of peace, perhaps not on earth, but surely in France. They had all believed that the war would be over within a month. Astonishing reports had come to them of British and German troops meeting in no man's land to exchange gifts and to sing carols.

"It means the end, you know," Captain Jarvis had remarked sagely. "Our lads have lost the fighting spirit and the Boche are as exhausted as we are. It's up to their politicians to work out something with our striped-trousered brigade. There'll be a general cease-fire within a week. You mark my words."

He had buried Captain Jarvis three months later at Neuve Chapelle with one hundred and sixty of his men.

One year.

Not just men had died. War destroyed more than human life. It nibbled away at the spirit, corroded the senses, mocked all the old values. It was what the French liaison officer at Laventie, in the wisdom of a cognac haze, had called *le cafard*. It was empty stables and unpruned trees at Abington. It was a thousand men in sodden khaki who could have been better employed than stumbling across a railway line with rifles in their hands. It was Lydia Amberley half naked by a fire.

He looked in on Roger's old room before going to bed. It was exactly as Roger would have expected it to be, had he suddenly come bursting into the house. The bed made. A notebook and pencil on the bedside table. His books, well dusted, on the shelves.

"It's not a shrine," his mother said quietly, seeing him standing there in the hall. "And I have no illusions about him being a prisoner of the Turks. It's just that I hated to put away all the things that he had loved. He wouldn't have wanted his Wordsworth and Shelley sealed in a box."

There would be unfinished poems in the notebook, Fenton knew. Lines for an unfinished life.

Le cafard.

His mother was on a dozen committees of one kind or another in Woodbridge, and certainly did not lack for friends. She enjoyed being with her son, but did not need him for comfort.

"You seem restless, Fenton," she remarked on the Thursday before New Year's Eve. "Thinking about your new job?"

"And other things."

He took the train that afternoon, a slow train crowded with sailors from Harwich going to London on leave. It was dark when the train pulled into King's Cross. He shared a taxi with five naval officers who insisted on buying him a drink at the Army and Navy Club. Conversation in the bar ranged from the merits of oil-fired ships *vis-à-vis* coal, to the bedroom antics of French women. He had one drink, excused himself and left.

It was a familiar route that he walked – along the Mall, past Buckingham Palace and into Lower Belgrave Street. He strode past his old flat without glancing at it and continued to Sloane Street and across Pavilion Road into Cadogan Square. Number Twenty-four.

If the butler was surprised at the lateness of the call he did not show it by so much as a blink of the eye.

"Lady Winifred, sir? I do believe she has retired for the night?"

"Who the devil's at the door, Peterson?" A testy voice called down from the corridor, and then Lord Dexford emerged from the gloom in maroon smoking jacket and carpet slippers.

"Fenton, by Gad! What the devil you doin' here at this hour?"

"I was . . . in the neighbourhood," he said lamely. "Sorry if I woke up the household."

"Nonsense." The marquess dismissed the butler with a

gesture. "It's good to have company. Close the door before you freeze us out."

"I didn't realise it was so late."

"It isn't. We retire early, except for me. Just goin' to have a nightcap or two."

A slender shaft of light fell on the dark stairwell from the upper floors, the light widening with the full opening of a door. Fenton looked up at the figure standing by the second-floor balustrade.

"Hallo," he said.

"We still have a telephone," Winifred said.

"I'm sorry. I intended to call but one thing and another came up, and then I went to Suffolk for Christmas . . ."

"There's nothing to explain, Fenton."

"I think that there is."

Lord Dexford scowled at Fenton and then glared up at his daughter.

"Either come down or go back to bed, Winnie. As for me, I'm going to the library and closin' the door."

"Well?" Fenton asked after the marquess had done just that.

She came down the stairs clad in a long, quilted satin dressing-gown, her hair loose about her shoulders. She did not descend to the foyer but sat on the third step from the bottom.

"What an odd man you are, Fenton."

"Impulsive . . . also a bit reflective." He leaned against the banister post below her, hands shoved into the pockets of his trenchcoat. "I've been doing a lot of thinking the past few days. You said that we're different people now. I know I'm not the same, but I can't say that about you. You're older and wiser, but essentially the same. I don't think anything will ever change you radically, Winnie."

"Everyone changes."

"I suppose they do. It's a matter of degree, isn't it? Some people tarnish more quickly than others. You will always have a polish, a certain lustre."

She folded her arms about her knees. "You came to propose, didn't you?"

"Yes."

352

"That'll make Father very happy."

"It's not your father I care about pleasing."

"It'll make me happy, too. I love you, Fenton. I fell in love with you when I was sixteen and Andrew brought you down to Lulworth for my birthday party. Or was it your scarlet jacket I fell in love with then? Difficult to say. I don't love you for your jacket now. In fact, I love you in spite of it. I hate this war. If you marry me, you'll be in the odd position of having a pacifist for a wife."

"General Davenport's wife is a suffragette. She chained herself to a letterbox once. It didn't ruin his career."

"I pray for the day when *your* career is unnecessary."

"So do I."

She looked at him in silence for a moment and then hugged her knees tighter to her body.

"One thing has been left unsaid. Father will be happy, I'll be happy. What of yourself? Do you love me?"

"If wanting to be with you is loving you, if feeling at peace is loving, then, yes, I love you."

She nodded sombrely. "How blunt and honest you are. Shall we go in and tell Father?"

"I would like that, yes."

"Shall we be married in London? Or would you prefer Suffolk?"

He rubbed the side of his jaw. "The fact is, I have only ten days' leave left. I thought we could . . . well, go up to Scotland tomorrow and get married in Gretna, stand in line with the other couples. That is, if you don't mind."

"Oh, Lord," she laughed. "Gretna Green! What will mother say?"

"She won't have a chance to say anything." Lord Dexford stepped into the hall, a bottle of champagne under each arm. "Knew how the wind was blowin' when you knocked on the door, Fenton. Put the bottles in your kit bag. Mumm's 1910. The Royal Mail leaves Euston Station at midnight. You have plenty of time to make it if you can hurry your packin', Winnie."

She stood up slowly. "We can miss the train, Fenton, if you have any doubts at all, any second thoughts."

353

"Why would he have doubts?" her father blustered. "I'll ring round for the car."

"I mean it," she said.

He reached up and touched her hand, his eyes steady on her face.

"No second thoughts, Winnie."

She turned quickly and hurried up the stairs.

The marquess gazed after her, then handed the bottles of champagne to Fenton.

"I'd crack one of these with you, but there ain't time for it. I'm glad to see her leave this house, Fenton, and I think you know why. She's a good girl. Clever. Strong in body and mind. And she's a Dexford – she'll bear sons.

The wind came in a flood off the Irish Sea to churn the waters of Luce Bay and rattle the windows of the inn. Putting one hand on the glass, Fenton could feel the chill power of it. The wind had chased the mist and the hills of Cumberland were like banks of green cloud across the Solway Firth. He drew his robe tighter around him and then lit a cigarette, draught through the windows spiralling the smoke behind him.

"What are you thinking?" she asked after a time.

"Oh, one thing and another. It's New Year's Day and a bright, cold day it is, too."

"A good beginning."

"Yes. To see the sun in Wigtownshire on January 1st is cause for celebration."

"You've been here before, haven't you?"

"Port William, you mean?"

"This inn."

"Oh, yes, several times. A friend of mine kept a boat at Stranraer and we used to sail these waters: Islay, Mull, the Hebrides, and up and down the Solway, of course. Tricky seas and bloody dangerous at times."

"Ever bed a girl here?"

He puffed on the cigarette. "What a question! Downright Elizabethan phrasing. The answer is no. I never bedded a girl . . . *here*."

354

"I do love you, Fenton. I think you're quite incapable of lying. Even your white ones have the ring of truth."

His feet were numb with cold. He ground the cigarette out in a saucer and got back into bed. Winifred opened his robe and pressed the warmth of her body against him.

"I'm not a disappointment, am I?"

"You're an astonishing revelation," he said.

"It's being a country girl," she said, stroking his hip. "I know all the natural acts."

He turned on to his side and kissed her forehead. "And a few naughty ones, too. A sweet doxy."

"Who's being Elizabethan now?" Her arms enfolded him. "May I ask you something that you don't have to answer?"

"Yes."

"Was there someone you would rather have brought here than me? Someone you couldn't have?"

"That was an age ago," he said quietly.

"Do you find yourself comparing us?"

"There's nothing to compare. You are Winifred. Uniquely yourself."

"The colonel's lady."

"Yes. A lady to your fingertips."

Her hands glided up and down his back. "Not all the time."

He did not think of Lydia, nor had he while making love to her during the night. The act was beyond the objective comparing of one woman to another, one body to another. It was even beyond the seeking of pleasure. It was life that he sought in her, and creation. The war kept its hold of him even in bed; his thrusts into her warm, living body, her gasps and cries, became the antithesis of death and pain to him. He sensed her understanding of that, her awareness of his need, and it set her uniquely apart from any other woman he had known. The wind tugged at the windows, rattling them in their frames, howled and shrieked under the eaves, reminding him of the demented sound of shells. He pressed his face into the soft hollow between her breasts as she clasped him tightly – as though shielding him on this first day of the year from all the days to follow.

355

3

CHARLES LEFT THE WAR OFFICE AND WALKED BRISKLY ALONG Whitehall to Charing Cross. It was an almost too perfect April day, the type of day to inspire a poet to rapture. The wind was gentle out of the west and carried with it a heady perfume of spring rain. Soft, impeccably white clouds drifted across a flag-blue sky and a shaft of sun, as though arranged by the Almighty, fell directly on Admiral Nelson standing on his column. At the base of the monument, clustered like grey pigeons, were old women selling violets.

He crossed Trafalgar Square and strode as though in a great hurry up St. Martin's Lane until he reached a four-storey, nondescript building in Shelton Street. There he paused to straighten his uniform, dust his shoes with a handkerchief and allow his heart-beat to return to normal. He then entered the building and walked slowly up the stairs to the second floor. There were half a dozen officers ahead of him, standing in the corridor or seated on the two wooden benches that flanked the door marked NO. 7 MEDICAL BOARD. One or two officers carried canes, but most of them looked fit and not altogether overjoyed at that fact.

"Don't I know you?" a major in the Rifle Brigade asked, puffing on a cigarette.

"I don't believe so," Charles said.

"Thought I did. Sorry. Name's Merton and I'm fit as a fiddle, worse luck. Bound to be sent back to the Salient and I won't be as bloody lucky next time, I can tell you."

Charles turned away from the man and slowly paced the corridor. At last his name was called. A grey-haired lance-corporal seated behind a desk checked his name off a typewritten list.

"Major Lord Amberley? Colonel Beaumont would like to see you in his office – third door down that hall, sir."

Colonel Beaumont had been a prominent Harley Street surgeon before the war. Now, at seventy, he found himself a colonel in the R.A.M.C. assigned to a medical board whose job it was to certify wounded officers fit for duty in the line.

"Ah, Amberley," he said warmly as Charles entered his small, cluttered office. "How's the pelvis?"

"Better than new."

"And the leg?"

"The same. One hundred per cent. I walked very quickly all the way from Whitehall and don't feel a twinge."

"Good, good. And all the Asian bugs out of your system?"

"I hope so." He smiled to warn the old man that he was telling a joke. "Haven't seen one of the blighters in weeks."

"Quite so." The colonel looked down at his desk and shifted a few loose papers around. "Your coming here today is rather academic. I am personally delighted to know that you feel as good as new but you are no longer the responsibility of this board."

"I'm not sure I understand you, colonel."

"We received a directive from General Haldane yesterday, informing us that your name is to be struck from the list of wounded officers awaiting certification for active duty. It would appear that you are part and parcel of N.S. 5 and something calling itself the Landship Committee. Just what a *land* ship could be is quite beyond me, sir, but there it is." He leaned across his desk and extended his hand. "Good luck, Amberley. I'm glad I'm not sending you back to the trenches."

He took a taxi to his office in Old Pye Street, to the building that had housed a variety of governmental functions since the days of Pepys. The sentry there opened the front door without asking to see his credentials. He was well known now, he thought with a twinge of bitterness. One of the old hands in N.S. 5. He took the narrow stairs two at a time and went up to the room on the third floor which he shared with three other officers, two of them from the navy, and two civilian engineers. Only Lieutenant-Commander Penhope, R.A.N.S., was at his desk, leaning back in his chair and reading the afternoon edition of the *Daily Post*. A headline screamed, VERDUN COUNTERATTACK – LARGE FRENCH GAINS.

"Fisher's been looking for you, Amberley," the naval officer said without glancing away from his newspaper.

Charles sat on the edge of his desk and lit a cigarette.

"Oh? What did he want?"

"The usual strafe. Big Willie failed to impress some brass again. Low on power. He wants you to go up to Yorkshire, or some other heathen place, and check out the specs on a new engine. You're to take Bigsby with you."

He blew a savage stream of smoke. "Why the hell doesn't he just send Bigsby on his own?"

"You know why," Penhope drawled.

Algernon Bigsby was a civilian, a consumptive looking middle-aged man who dropped his "h's" when speaking. He also chewed cigars and spat a good deal. Algernon Bigsby knew everything there was to know about engines, but staff officers detested him on sight. It would be Bigsby who would check out the specs on the engine in Yorkshire and Charles who would pass on that information – "sell it" in the argot of N.S. 5 – to the brass.

"Did he say where in Yorkshire?"

"His girl has all the information and the travel vouchers."

A messenger boy. No more than that. His contribution to the caterpillar tread landship, now called "tank" MK 1, or "Big Willie", as opposed to "Little Willie" which had been a washout, was limited to his ability to be articulate – and, of course, his immediate acceptance in any mess. Algernon Bigsby might have the know how, but he did not wear a smartly-tailored uniform with the badges of the Royal Windsor Fusiliers on the jacket lapels.

There was a cocktail party in progress when he reached home. He had promised Lydia he would be there but had forgotten about it completely. Archie found the warm yet elegant atmosphere of Bristol Mews conducive to business, to getting disparate elements together, and his daughter the perfect hostess. Odd types conversed in the first-floor drawing room – a Manchester mill owner cheek by jowl with a Labour M.P., General Sir William Robertson nodding his head to whatever David Langham was telling him; scientists, engineers, red-tabbed Whitehall brass, politicians, business leaders and beautifully dressed women blended harmoniously. Archie met Charles as he came up the stairs and pressed a drink into his hand. Archie Foxe, the perfect host, treating every house he was in as his own.

"Langham is talking to Wully Robertson," he whispered. "The general would like to meet you. He's expanding his staff and Langham's been telling him what a fine job you've been doing with N.S. 5."

"It's nice of Mr. Langham to look after my interests," he said tautly, "but I'm not suited for a staff job at such a high level."

Archie's gaze was dyspeptic. "You're too self-effacing, Charles. Thump your bloody chest once in a while and people will sit up and take notice."

There was no point in trying to explain to Archie that he didn't want to be noticed. Ambition was the banner under which Archie Foxe had always marched. He had carried it proudly out of a Shadwell workhouse to the marble halls of power and there was no reason for him to think that all other men did not share his belief in it. Sir William "Wully" Robertson certainly did. He had come up from the ranks in Victoria's army to become Chief of the Imperial General Staff and he had not done so by being modest. Robertson liked ambitious people because they were more inclined to get the job done than the stick-in-the-muds.

A job on the general's staff. Red tabs on his lapels . . . perhaps a Lieutenant-Colonelcy to boot. It was his for the asking – if he impressed the general with his zeal, his eagerness to get ahead.

"Yes, sir, I like N.S. 5, but I find it constricting. My job there is pretty much routine and I'd like to be involved in broader aspects of the war effort."

Langham would stand on the sidelines, smiling that faintly mocking smile of his, and General Sir William Robertson, Wully to his intimates, would smile knowingly and nod his head and say, in effect, "Can I trust you? Will you do as you're told? Will you aid me in kicking Lord Horatio Herbert Kitchener of Khartoum into a cocked hat?" The politics of the war were being fought in the drawing rooms of London. The

359

unseating of Sir John French, the rise of Sir Douglas Haig, the battles between the Minister of War, Lord Kitchener, and the Chief of the Imperial General Staff – Wully. It was all going on in this particular drawing room on this particular afternoon in Bristol Mews. Should Kitchener be dethroned – in a polite way, of course – there would be a vacancy in the cabinet and David Langham might just be the man to fit the empty chair. He would get along well with Robertson and the high brass, but it wouldn't hurt to have a friend on the general's staff.

Good reasoning, Charles thought as he sipped his drink. The only thing wrong with it was that he didn't like David Langham and he had no intention of approaching General Robertson. He drifted to the opposite side of the room, turning his back to the crowd and gazing through the tall windows at the narrow, brick-paved street below.

"You're not being very sociable," Lydia murmured, coming up beside him. "Don't you feel well?"

"I feel fine. Like new, in fact." He took another pull on his drink. "The medical board informed me that I'm not fit for duty in France, but not for physical reasons. Too bloody important for such crass pursuits as shooting Germans. I'm locked into N.S. 5."

"Oh, dear." She kissed him lightly on the cheek. "I had a feeling that would happen. You proved to be too useful to them." She kissed him again and ran a hand across his back. "Don't fret, my darling. Did Daddy tell you about General Robertson?"

"He mentioned something."

"A staff job liaison between the general staff and Haig's headquarters in France. You'd be in Montreuil as much as you'd be in London. And knowing Wully, I'm sure he'd have you poking your nose into the divisional headquarters to get the type of information he requires. You'd be right in the thick of things and not spending your time with all those eccentrics in Old Pye Street."

"They're not such bad chaps."

"Of course they're not, darling, but you do feel a bit out of place. On staff is much more like being in the army. And being across the Channel would be more satisfying to you than trudging about farms or visiting factories."

Her perfume was exquisite. Her silk gown caressed his hand as she pressed against his side. Her touch lingered on his back. He thought of Algernon Bigsby squirting tobacco juice at the oily base of a turret lathe.

"I suppose you're right."

Her fingers dug into him. "I know I am. Come on, talk to Wully just for a moment, just an hallo."

He fought to keep a straight face. General Sir William Robertson dropped his "h's" just like Algernon Bigsby.

They had separate bedrooms. Hers was frilly and feminine, cream and gold, his richly masculine, mahogany and brass. He came to her room as his father had gone to Hanna.

He slumped beside her, feeling sweaty in his nightshirt. He had found it impossible to make love to her. He felt too keyed up, too pressured. He had done no more than move her satin nightgown up to her hips and touch the warm dampness of her thighs.

"Sorry," he said. "I should have left you in peace."

"It doesn't matter." She bent over him and kissed his brow. "Poor tired soldier."

"I feel such a fraud, Lydia. Too important to be sent to France, and yet anyone could do my job."

"Perhaps. But not anyone can be on Robertson's staff. He uses his own judgment on that. Did you know that he told the Duke of Chatsworth that his son wasn't fit to shoe cavalry mounts? It's true! Percy! You know him, captain in the Blues. His father could get him that commission, but not a staff job with Wully."

She stroked his chest, her palm light on the flannel nightshirt. No more than that. It distressed him if she became too bold. Men initiated acts. Women did not.

"I have to go to Yorkshire tomorrow," he said after a long silence. "To Huddersfield, to look at some engines. I take the seven ten from St. Pancras."

"I'll get up early and drive you to the station."

"No. A car will be here to pick me up." He turned away

from her and sat on the edge of the bed. "I thought I might drop in and see Fenton. He's at Flockton Moor camp, just a short drive from where I'll be."

"Give him my best," she said, staring at the ceiling.

"Of course." He was standing now, ready to go back to his room. He leaned across the bed and kissed her. "When I get back we'll take off a few days and go down to Lyme Regis. We can rent a cottage, bathe in the sea. Would you enjoy that?"

"Very much."

"And I'll seriously consider that staff appointment . . . if I get asked, that is."

"You'll get it. He was impressed with you."

"After a little nudge from Langham?"

"No," she said tonelessly. "You get everything on your own."

She parked her car and walked along the Embankment, the Thames at low tide, birds pecking in the mud flats. She entered the ministry from the river side, the lone sentry on guard there telephoning up to Langham's office before allowing her into the building. She did not get lost in the maze of corridors and stairs and entered the inner chamber of Langham's suite through a side door. It was a dark, musty room lined with law books and great, cloth-bound volumes on economics and vital statistics, coal output, railway tonnage, steel production and all the dry facts of national functions. She sat on a leather couch and after ten minutes David Langham came into the room from the outer office, closed and locked the door.

"I'm glad you came," he said, barely glancing at her. He removed his coat and began to roll up his sleeves as he walked into the small lavatory to wash his hands. "The general called me this morning. He was impressed with Charles . . . well, why wouldn't he be? The archetype of young peers. Wully admires nobility, but then, don't we all?"

"I doubt if you do."

"Quite wrong, my dear. I'm a firm believer in the preservation of relics and national treasures of all sorts." He came out of the lavatory wiping his hands on a towel. "So, a joyous morning for you. Young Charles will get red tabs on his collars and will no doubt become a brigadier before the war's over. And after the war? Well, who knows? Governor of some speck of the Empire, a firm but just hand on the native throat, the governor's lady by his side, dressed in imperial white, a parasol shielding her lovely head."

"You do enjoy baiting people, don't you?"

"I enjoy foretelling futures. You would enjoy yourself immensely. And it would be a charming spot. Bermuda, perhaps, or Malta." He rolled the towel into a ball and tossed it through the open lavatory door. "I have spent all morning foretelling futures, none as pleasant as yours. The French are being bled white at Verdun and are demanding that we should begin our offensive on the Somme immediately. The P.M. is quite upset at the demand and Kitchener is in a dither. Sir Douglas Haig claims that he won't be ready to jump off before the end of August, but the French might cave in before then. We will attack by the end of June, a compromise that will please neither Haig nor the French. I sent a strong letter to Poincaré suggesting that the best way for them to cut their losses would be to withdraw across the Meuse and let the Germans have Verdun. It has no strategic importance whatever. Why treat it as a holy shrine? But of course it isn't up to poor Poincaré. After all, he's only the president. Joffre and the generals don't give a damn about losses. Men are mere digits to them. Eighty-nine thousand dead *poilus* so far, and God knows how many maimed for totally useless ground. A mere bagatelle when weighed against the glory of France. *Ils ne passerent pas! Vive la gloire! La voie sacrée!* Schoolboy rhetoric."

He stood facing her, hands on his hips, his slim body taut as a bent bow. A fiery little man, his dark eyes burning.

"How spell-binding you are, Mr. Langham. I would hate to be a Frenchman debating with you."

He waved a finger under her nose. "War is far too complex a matter for the military mind to grasp – but then you've heard that speech before, haven't you? Why must I always make speeches when you come here? Such a terrible waste of time." He sat beside her on the couch and cupped her chin in one hand, turning her face towards him. "You're much too beautiful, Lady Amberley. If I had married a woman with your face I would still be a Liverpool solicitor."

"Is that why successful politicians have plain wives?"

"It's vital on the hustings. Men will never vote for someone with a beautiful wife. They feel he has achieved enough. Why grace him with further rewards!"

"I could ask the same question."

He let his hand drop to the top of her dress and began to undo the buttons with nimble ease.

"One wonders who is being rewarded the most by these brief encounters. Your appetites for the pleasures of the flesh match my own stroke for stroke." His hand was inside her chemise, pressed firmly against a naked breast. "You see? Your heart races, the breath catches in your throat."

"Please hurry.",

"We shall make haste slowly, if you don't mind. Savour it as always."

"Hurry . . ."

"My, my! What a passionate little whore we are today."

"Please . . ."

It had been raining steadily in Yorkshire and the factory on the outskirts of Huddersfield was surrounded by a lake of mud and standing water. A tall chainlink fence topped with barbed wire enclosed the place and there was no signboard to say what kind of factory it was or to whom it belonged. Only when the army car which had brought them from Leeds pulled up in front of the main building did Charles see a small sign on one of the doors: ROLLS-ROYCE MOTOR WORKS – EXPERIMENTAL.

A gangly young man wearing a blue work smock stepped outside to meet them.

"Lord Amberley? Mr. Bigsby?"

"Aye," Bigsby grunted. He spat a stream of brown saliva into a puddle. "Bloody 'orrible bit o' country, Yorkshire."

"Dampish," the young man said. He directed his attention to Charles. "My name's Wilson. I'm plant manager here. Our Mr. Ross is over in shed Number Four, next to the railway siding."

"The package arrived, I hope," Charles said.

"Oh, yes. It was delivered early this morning. Ugly looking thing, isn't it? We pulled the engine out already." He pointed off into the swirling drizzle. "Just keep to the duckboards. No point in driving there, your motor would only sink below the wheels."

"Big Willie" was inside the large corrugated iron building, electric lights shining off its steel-plated sides, a great, rhomboid-shaped monster, the six-pounder naval cannons jutting from the sponsons on the sides. Men in overalls were crawling all over it and there was the dull boom of heavy hammers from inside the hull. Charles and Bigsby climbed on to the back of the tank and peered into the open engine hatch.

"Is Mr. Ross there?" Charles yelled.

The hammering ceased. An oily-faced workman looked up at them.

"Aye, he be that. Mr. Ross, sir, coomp'ny callin'."

A tousled-haired man in grease-stained overalls emerged from the inner gloom of the hull. Charles stared at him in disbelief.

"But . . . you're *our* Ross!"

Jamie Ross grinned and pulled himself out of the hatch.

"Not exactly *your* Ross any longer." He wiped his fingers on a cloth and held out his right hand. "It's fair good to see you, m'lord. Indeed it is."

"I'm quite flabbergasted, Ross. I knew you'd gone with the Rolls-Royce company, but to find you here . . ."

"Oh, they've moved me back and forth a bit. I've been at this factory the past three months." He folded his arms and looked Charles up and down. "Major, now. My, my. You look right smart in the uniform, m'lord. You one of the chaps responsible for this clanking dragon of a thing?"

"Not really. Just sort of an overseer."

"I talked to one of your bunch in London . . . telephoned up here the other day. He said the machine was underpowered. That's a bit of a laugh, you know. This must weigh thirty tons and it's got a one hundred and five h.p. engine in it. Doubt if you'd get more'n three miles to the hour on a dead flat, hard-paved road."

"That's about it," Bigsby said, spitting over the right side track.

Ross stepped down to the ground and gazed reflectively at the tank's engine which hung in chains from a pulley.

"Daimler. A good engine, but not for this *thing*."

"Do you have a better one?" Charles asked, stepping off the tank and standing beside him.

"Oh, yes. Two hundred and fifty h.p. in line ready for production. A proper beauty. We also have a three hundred and fifty h.p. in the testing stage. Aircraft engines. But as I tried to explain to that sod in London, we don't have them on the factory line. Won't have 'em either for at least four months. Now, these one hundred and five h.p. Daimlers must be bulging out of the warehouses."

"Right," Bigsby said. "That's the bloody rub."

"We can fit one of our prototype Falcons in this hull so you could see how it'd move with a hundred more horsepowers inside, but if time's the problem I don't much see the point of it."

"Neither do I," Charles said. "They're prepared to build fifty hulls now and they can't wait four months for engines to go in them."

"If we could coax more bloody power from what we've got . . ." Bigsby said.

Ross closed his eyes and clasped his hands behind his back. He rocked slowly on his heels for a minute and then said, "The gear ratios seem wrong to me somehow, and the carburation and exhaust systems are inadequate for the amount of stress the engine's going to be put to. She's goin' to be fuel starved and she'll vapour lock sure as hell takes sinners."

Bigsby squirted juice again. "The gear box is a bloody 'orror. I been tellin' 'em that all along. I know what it needs."

"Yes," Ross said. "I think I do, too. If you could give my lads three days around the clock . . ."

"Of course," Charles said.

"Modifications with available parts. Shouldn't hold up your schedule by more than a week or two and it would make a ruddy big difference in performance."

"Sounds good," Charles said.

"Fine. We'll get on with it then. Like a mug of tea?"

"Yes . . . I would, please."

"Mr. Bigsby?"

"I'm not much for tea." He chewed on his cigar and squinted at the dangling engine. "Bloody 'ot water's bad on the 'eart."

It seemed odd to be walking beside Jamie Ross, odder still to be seated across from him in the tiny engineering office. Ross poured two mugs of sweet, milky tea from a tea urn and then sat behind a battered desk.

"Funny us meeting like this, isn't it?"

"Yes," Charles agreed. "It is rather."

"I read about Mr. Wood-Lacy dyin' at Gallipoli. Sorry. He was a nice chap. How's his lordship and her ladyship?"

"They're fine, thank you."

"And Lady Alexandra?"

"She's training as a nurse . . . at All Souls Hospital in London . . . the army nursing service."

Ross shook his head in disbelief. "Hard to believe. She was tango-mad last time I saw her. The old world do change a bit, don't it?"

Charles stared into his tea. "Yes, it does."

"Been changin' a bit for me, too. I got seven patents on this new engine. It's really my idea and I'm responsible for its mass production. The company's sendin' me to America at the end of the month, to Cleveland and Detroit. The Yanks are going to build the bulk of 'em under licence for us. Lor', think of it, me, Jamie Ross, goin' to America." He sipped reflectively at his tea. "That Algy Bigsby's a wonder, he is. I used to read his articles all the time in *Mechanics and Journeymen*. Quite an inspiration to me when I was a nipper. I never knew you to be much interested in mechanical things."

"No. I'm still not terribly interested."

Ross smiled. "I get the picture. I've had to deal with the army chaps on a few occasions. They turn deaf when a man with grease on his hands speaks to 'em. I suppose old 'spittin' ' Bigsby tells you and you tell the brass. Is that it?"

"Something like that." His face felt hotter than the tea.

"Gor', the bloody army. They think they're fightin' in the

bleedin' Crimea or in India's sunny climes. Must be a strain on you. Still, as long as the job gets done, that's the main thing, isn't it? Get the better equipment out to the lads. Anything to that land fort?"

"Some people seem to think so, but most of the generals are dubious. One of them called it a pretty toy. I'm sure it's more than that."

"Looks like it could crush barbed wire and deflect bullets easily enough. That is, if it has enough power to move across no man's land."

"That's your job now, isn't it?"

"Yes. And it can be done. It won't be perfect by any means. You can expect twenty per cent breakdowns at least. The ratio of weight to power plant is ridiculous. It needs at least a three hundred horse power engine to give it momentum; eight to ten miles per hour on the flat, five on shell-pitted ground. Tell 'em that."

"My job," he said hollowly.

"That's right," Ross said, slurping tea. "Your job and you're bloody welcome to it."

He was too much the outsider. Bigsby and Ross, the grimy mechanics, they spoke an arcane language that set them totally apart from him. They all seemed relieved when he excused himself and went back to the car. He told the driver to take him to Flockton Moor. A fifteen-minute drive, over sodden hills and then, on a featureless moor, rows of wooden barracks, corrugated iron huts and bell tents. A flagpole, the Union Jack whipping in the wind, a sentry box on the side road, men at drill, a skirmish line moving through the gorse. He felt a sense of peace. His familiar element. He thought of Windsor and the Second Battalion, First Platoon, D Company . . . *Right as bloody rain, sir!*

The officers' mess was in a tarpaper and wood shack that leaked in a few spots. There were no battalion trophies to be seen simply because there were no battalion trophies to be displayed. No honours won but the honour of having been formed in the first place. Volunteers all – except for a sprinkling of regular officers and N.C.O.s seconded to the battalion from other units. For the sake of administrative convenience, the War Office had attached this battalion of amateurs to the Princess of Wales's Own Yorkshire Regiment, the Green Howards, but not one man in a hundred knew anything at all about that venerable concern.

"Nor care less," Fenton said, nursing a whisky. "Mill hands for the most part, the wool trade, but they're tough birds and eager to kill Boches."

He looked lean and fit, Charles was thinking, feeling a pang of envy.

"Are you up to strength?"

"Over strength as a matter of fact, except for officers and N.C.O.s. I should have thirty-five officers but have only twenty-six. But it's the same everywhere and they're eager chaps and not afraid to work hard. The senior N.C.O.s are first rate. Seduced a couple away from the Coldstreams and one who had been with me during the retreat, Sergeant-Major Ackroyd. I stole him from the Middlesex."

"Bit of a pack rat, aren't you?"

"Got to be, old fellow. There are just so many experienced men to go round and I want my battalion to have its fair share. It's trench experience that counts, not eagerness to kill Germans. Yorkshiremen love a good fight, but I need calm and steady hands to tell the lads when to shoot and when to keep their bloody heads down."

Charles sipped his whisky and glanced across the room. Two pink-cheeked first lieutenants were playing darts. Their combined ages wouldn't have reached forty.

"They're getting horribly young."

"Yes," Fenton said. "Coming right out of public school. Make them full lieutenants if they've had any O.T.C." He drained his drink. "Winne's with me, you know. We found a roomy old house up the road at Highbury. Stay the night with us. No point in your driving back to Huddersfield."

"No. I shan't be missed."

The Royal Windsor Fusiliers and the Green Howards had fought side by side at Inkerman in the Crimean War and had shared the same marching tune ever since, "The Bonnie English Rose". It was an apt description of Winifred, Charles decided as they walked on the moors after supper. The rain had stopped and the sky flamed with the sunset. He stood beside Fenton and watched Winifred striding through the gorse in muddy boots, whistling for her Bedlington which was off on a rabbit hunt.

"I'm glad for you and Winnie. You seem very happy together."

"She's a fine woman."

"And a downright lovely one."

Fenton lit a cigarette and blew smoke through his nose. "I detect a vague bitterness in your manner, Charles. Are you and Lydia getting along, or is it rude of me to ask?"

"Oh, we get along without strain, considering the circumstances."

"What circumstances?"

"My job. I hate what I'm doing, Fenton. And I feel manipulated, pulled on to an inside track by invisible wires. Well, not so invisible, come to think of it. I've just closed my eyes so far."

Fenton dropped his half-smoked cigarette at his feet and crushed it with the heel of his boot.

"If Lydia is pulling a few wires it's only for your benefit. You came within an inch of being killed at Gallipoli, old boy. She wouldn't be human if she didn't think of that. And you're not skulking in an attic, you know. For every man at the front there are a dozen serving usefully . . . no, *vitally* behind the lines. Only amateurs feel compelled to charge the foe with drawn sword. Professionals take the billets as they come, fair or foul, good job or bad. Make the best of it."

"It's rather a question of my own self-respect, Fenton."

"Bugger that," Fenton said angrily. "You're one of the few men left in the army who went ashore from the *River Clyde*. That ranks with the Charge of the Light Brigade or the bloody stand at Albuera. There isn't a soldier alive who wouldn't touch his cap in respect. Stop sticking needles in your flesh."

"A man should do what he feels is the right thing for *him*," Charles said with a quiet intensity. "If he doesn't, he pays for it in some way. This may sound like an odd paradox, Fenton, but I never felt so alive, so needed, as I did at Gallipoli. My function was simple – to lead and inspire my men. I did that

370

well. I was a damned good officer and . . ." his voice trailed off until it was virtually inaudible ". . . I was happy."

Fenton found it impossible to sleep. Not that it mattered very much. He had told his batman to wake him at four, as always. A quick shave, a spot of breakfast and then up to the camp before reveille. Usually he was in bed by ten thirty, but he had sat up drinking with Charles until two in the morning. No more talk about Lydia or his problems, thank God, just jawing about old times at Abington Pryory. But the man's moodiness had still remained, a dark shadow beneath the surface.

Winifred stirred and moved against him. Her hand created an opening in his pyjamas and drifted slowly across his chest in a loving tracery.

"Thought you were asleep," he murmured.

"No. Just silently respectful. I could almost hear you thinking. Dull army matters, no doubt. How many tins of bully beef per man, boot laces, spare socks. I wonder if Napoleon thought about such things?"

"Probably."

"But that's not on your mind, is it?"

"No. I was thinking of Charles. I have a feeling he's going to do something rash."

"Charles never does anything rash."

"He let you get away. But that was more foolish than rash, I suppose."

"Some people might say it was sensible."

"Some people still think the earth is flat."

She lay silently beside him, listening to the night wind moan and whisper down the chimney. Then she said, "Does Charles know that Lydia was in love with you?"

He raised himself on one elbow. "Whatever gave you that idea?"

"Women can sense those things. I'll never forget the look in her eyes when you were teaching me how to tango. She was dancing with Charles, but watching us. I was only seventeen, but women are born with the instinct to understand other women. Were you in love with her?"

"Does it matter?"

"No. Even if you were, you're not in love with her now. A woman can sense that, too."

He bent his head and kissed her. "You're the only woman I love, the only woman I shall ever love. I'm a disgustingly lucky man, Winnie."

"Like Napoleon?"

"His luck ran out. And besides, I'm taller than he was."

Charles stayed at the factory for the next two days, forty-eight hours with virtually no sleep, watching what Ross and Bigsby instructed the mechanics to do. He kept meticulous notes and drew diagrams of each procedure. When the job was completed to Bigsby's satisfaction, the men from the test centre at Hatfield Park, who had brought the tank, drove it out of the building and on to a wagon on the railway siding. They then covered it with canvas so not an inch of its metal body could be seen.

"And that's that," Ross said. "What do you do now?"

"Follow it down to the test ground and demonstrate it for some generals and war ministers. Rather like selling a terribly expensive motor car to people who don't really want to buy one."

"You handle the test, do you?"

"Oh, no, just the selling part. I mingle with the brass, answer questions, tell a few jokes and talk shop. Above all, I keep cheerful, even when the damned thing runs off its tracks or the engine explodes. Keep cheery about it, make light of the problems with a sort of, Well, sir, we'll jolly well do better next time attitude."

Ross shook his head in wonder. "Queer way to fight a war, ain't it?"

"Yes. I think it is." He held out his hand. "Good luck in America, Ross. It's been splendid seeing you again and I mean that most sincerely. Truly splendid. You know what you can do and you do it to perfection. I admire that. You must be a very happy man."

Ross frowned slightly. "Well, I don't know about that, but I'm satisfied. Is that what you mean?"

"Yes. I suppose it is, Ross. I suppose it is."

*

372

There were more people than Charles had expected. The ground was relatively dry, except for the mud-filled hollow which was one of the test obstacles. The absence of rain and the crisp April air had everyone in a good mood and they strolled about in the sun outside the refreshment tent, downing whisky and sodas or drinking tea and munching ham sandwiches. Army and navy officers, frock-coated civil servants and ministers. The usual type of crowd. General Haldane did not mingle with any of them. General Haldane, Royal Engineers, chief of N.S. 5, stayed as far away from them as possible, his pale eyes fixed on the tank as though examining every bolt, screw and rivet. He was sixty-two, a man who had spent forty years of his service life in India and Burma, building railways and steel bridges from Mysore to the Salween. He had no capacity for small talk of any kind. He was waiting for the driver of the machine to signal that his crew was ready. When he did so, the general turned to Charles and growled, "Tell 'em all to watch. And keep bloody well cheery."

She was dressing for a dinner engagement when he came home, dried mud on his boots and badly in need of a shave. His entrance into her pristine dressing room was almost an obscenity.

"Charles! You could at least have telephoned."

He slumped into a small, velvet chair and looked at her, groggy from fatigue.

"How fragile you look."

She turned back to her dressing-table mirror and applied the slightest amount of rouge to her cheeks.

"Most naked people do."

"Half naked," he corrected. "What do you call those skimpy things?"

"Underclothes."

"Must be more to it than that. Hardly the army manner, is it? Chemise, Mark One. Garter belt, Model 1916, dash seven one two H."

She glanced over a white, powdered shoulder. "Are you tipsy?"

"God, no. Just worn to the bone. Big Willie did himself

373

proud for a change. Even knocked over a small tree. Went seven miles at four miles per hour and didn't break down once. No jammed gears, no stalls for lack of petrol. Everything clicked. General Haldane was so pleased he smiled, at least I think it was a smile. If an iceberg could smile it would look like Haldane's smile. He thanked me and I told him I was chucking it in, resigning from N.S. 5. He wasn't the least bit surprised."

"That's because he already received notice. Someone on the general staff informed him this morning."

"So I got the appointment," he said in a flat, weary voice.

"Of course. You impressed General Robertson favourably, to say the least."

"I'm chucking that in, too. I don't want to be on *Wully's* staff."

She studied an eyebrow in the glass. "Oh? What do you want to do then?"

"Go to Windsor and rejoin my battalion."

She plucked a solitary hair with a pair of tweezers. "That's ridiculous. You don't have medical clearance and you're on staff. Don't make gestures, Charles."

"It's not a gesture. I want to be doing something that fits my abilities for a change – and my temperament. I just won't fit on Robertson's staff. There's too much politics involved, too much spying and skulking about expected. Haig is Robertson's creature and any mutterings about Haig from divisional commanders must be quashed. That's where I would come in, and others like me, hanging about various H.Q.s in France and keeping our ears open. I don't want that kind of employment. I want something clean, manly. I want to be a company commander and take my chances in the line like everyone else."

"Not *everyone* is in the line." She put the steel tweezers down very carefully, as though they would smash if she dropped them on the table, then turned in her chair and looked at him. "I fail to see anything *manly* in wanting to get killed."

"I don't expect to be killed. I expect to serve a few tours in trenches and then be rotated by the winter, given a battalion to train. The same kind of process Fenton went through."

"Fenton's a regular army officer," she said, measuring each word. "What he did in France, what he's doing now, is

374

expected of him. You fulfilled your martial duties in Gallipoli. Nothing further is expected of you except the wearing of a uniform and the performance of some useful task. Being a staff officer is such a task, Charles. There's more to it than *skulking about*, as you put it. It's a job that requires intelligence and tact – two qualities you possess in abundance. Now, why don't you take a bath and a shave, put on some clean clothes and come with me. I'm meeting some people at Claridges and then we're going on from there to the theatre."

"No, I'm going to get some sleep. I want to be at Windsor first thing in the morning."

She stood up and leaned back against the edge of the dressing-table.

"Manly," she said softly. "That's the crux of it, isn't it, Charles? Your periodic bouts of impotency distress you."

He looked away from her. She reminded him of an illustration he had seen once in an erotic novel someone had abandoned in a railway carriage, *La Passion de Marie*: the nearly transparent chemise, the lace belt supporting dark silk hose. "That's only a symptom. I know the cause."

"And you hope to cure it in the trenches?" Her tone was mocking. "I could cure it in one night! You really make me laugh, Charles. Your conceptions of *honour* and *duty* and *good form* and *playing the game* belong to another century! What about your duty to me? And I'm not talking about your duty in bed. That failure is no more than prissy ignorance, not a disease. No, I mean your duty to me as your wife. There are more than enough widows these days without you going out of your way to create another one!"

"There's no point in our talking about it," he said, getting to his feet. "You simply wouldn't understand."

"Why? Because I'm not of your class? Because I wasn't initiated at birth into the code of *noblesse oblige*? For God's sake, Charles, don't turn your *noble heritage* into high bloody farce!"

He left quietly. He did not slam the door, but there was a finality about his departure that she knew to be absolute. She sat down and looked at herself in the mirror. Lydia Amberley, future Countess of Stanmore, German bullets permitting, mistress of Abington Pryory and all it contained. Her child-hood dream. A dream from an age rapidly fading. No, she thought, smoothing her eyebrows with her fingertips, an age already gone.

4

Lieutenant General Sir Julian Wood-Lacy enjoyed speaking to war correspondents. He felt that he owed the breed a debt for their treatment of him after Mons. He had emerged from that débâcle as something of a hero, although he had done nothing to warrant it, had simply handled his division in adversity with calmness and intelligence, fighting when he could, pulling back when it seemed prudent to do so. A competent job of generalship, no more than that, but the London press had been determined to wring glory out of defeat for the sake of civilian morale. The adjective "glorious" was tagged on to the word "retreat" and the old general with his John Bull face and manner was elevated to the military pantheon and promoted from the commander of a division to the leader of a corps.

"I should like to propose a toast to the memory of Lord Kitchener," the general said, raising his glass of sherry. "I hate to think of poor K.'s body floatin' out there in the North Sea. Indeed I do. No way for a *soldier* to die. Served under him in the Sudan, don't you know. A hard taskmaster, but *de mortuis* and all that. Drink up, lads."

The sherry was too sweet for Martin's taste and he merely raised the cut crystal glass to his lips. Fenton Wood-Lacy, standing with a group of battalion commanders, caught his eye and moved his head in the direction of the terrace doors. Martin nodded in acknowledgment and when the general began to pace back and forth in the ballroom, warming to an anecdote about some long forgotten battle on the Nile, he drifted out of the ornate room and met Fenton on the terrace.

"Well," Fenton said with a smile, "you're pretty good at sneaking away."

"Almost as good as yourself. How are you, Fenton?"

"As well as can be expected. Overworked and underpaid, as they say in the ranks."

"Are you in Sir Julian's corps?"

"Hard to say. They keep shifting our brigade about a bit. We're in trenches opposite Thiepval now, so I suppose we're in the old boy's domain. Anyway, I got an invitation to come for supper, so here I am. Did he give you chaps the picture yet?"

"Just that the Fourth Army intends to break through the German lines in one day, and be in Bapaume with the cavalry within two. The *Big Push*. Nothing new in that. This must be the worst kept secret of the war, but he didn't explain the magic formula."

"Just as well," Fenton said grimly. "It's more wishful thinking than magic." He strolled to the stone balustrade and looked out across the neatly trimmed gardens of the château, the River Ancre, narrow and sluggish, curving past the orchards. On the skyline, brown sausage balloons hung motionless in the June heat. "Fifteen divisions in eighteen miles of trench. They say there are no more than six Boche divisions dug in over there, and two of those are in reserve. We've beaten them hollow – on paper."

Martin smiled and leaned against the balustrade beside him. "Pessimistic, as always."

Fenton stared gloomily at the landscape, following the distant flight of some British two-seaters by the trailing puffs of Archie bursts.

"I can recall a similar observation of mine before Loos. Remember? The Café Bristol in Bethune, you and that fellow from the *Daily Telegram* telling me I was wrong because the Germans were outnumbered four to one. Machine gun and wire become great equallisers."

"I hear hints dropped that Haig has found the solution to that."

"No mystery about it – artillery and more artillery. In this case, one gun to every seventeen yards of German trench with a day and night bombardment for a week before Z-day."

"Good God," Martin said quietly.

Fenton's smile was a shadow. "Sounds irresistible, doesn't it? A total pulverising of the Hun positions, destruction of the

378

wire. But I have grave doubts about it and I'm not muttering alone. How much of the front have you seen, Martin?"

"Not much. It's been a controlled tour. No closer to the line than Albert. A German shell or two came over and they moved us back again. Three of us took a hotel room in Amiens. We'll stay there during the offensive and get fed the communiqués – that is, unless we can manage to sneak up for a closer look."

"Won't do you much good though, will it?"

"Well, you know, the censors won't permit anything that deviates too much from the official reports, but I've always managed to get a good story through from time to time."

"Are you still with the *Post*?"

"No. Associated Press. Parted amicably with Lord Crewe. I'm based in Paris now and like it better."

"Jacob must miss your company."

"No one to clear up after him."

A heavy howitzer in a wood a mile away fired a round, the concussion rattling the château's windows.

"Firing for register," Fenton said. "All new guns coming into position are allowed a few rounds to check their range. They'll hear this barrage in England clearly enough when it gets going. Would you like a front-row seat? I can swing a special pass from the old boy."

"I would appreciate that very much."

"I wonder if you'll appreciate it a week from now," Fenton said.

Mesnil-Martinsart, June 23rd, 1916. This village is approximately in dead centre of the British assault line which begins at the Gommecourt salient seven miles to the north and ends eight miles to the south where the British link up with the French in the marshes of the River Somme. The objective of the British offensive is the town of Bapaume, nine miles to the north-east, straddling the straight-as-an-arrow Roman road that runs from Amiens. The timetable calls for a total rupture of the German trench system on day one and the taking of Bapaume by the cavalry on day two. Roads and railways radiate from Bapaume to Arras and Cambrai and a breakthrough there would put the British to the rear of the German armies with a good chance of rolling them up and forcing a major retreat. The optimism of the troops – Fenton and the old sweats excepted – verges on the ecstatic.

"We're going to scupper 'em, old chum," a private in the 13th Yorks and Lancs (Barnsley Pals) told me. This is the New Army for the most part, volunteers, men joining up together, battalions of friends and co-workers; Hull Tradesmen, Sheffield City Battalion, Grimsby Chums, Glasgow Tramways, Tyneside Irish, Liverpool Pals. Pals and chums and post-office workers, even a group of footballers, cricketers and rugby players who formed a battalion. They have been tacked on to the traditional units of the army, but each group has its own particular and unique ties. A people's army if there ever was one, like the army Grant led down the Mississippi to Vicksburg, and they are here on the Somme determined to win the war. The enthusiasm is electric.

June 24th. The barrage began today. Birds flutter in confusion above Aveluy Wood. There is simply no way to describe the power of it. The earth rocks and the air reeks -- battle reporting cliché number 346 – but, dammit, the earth *does* rock and the air *does* reek. Birds fly in erratic patterns across the Aveluy–Hamel road into Thiepval Wood. Not a shred of cloud and the heat is intense. One can see, I'm sure of it, a twinkle of brassy specks far off in the sky as the howitzer shells pause in their arcs before plunging to earth.

June 27th. In a front-line observation post with Fenton and several other officers. They are checking the effect of the bombardment on the German wire. Fenton and the others grim. The belts of wire with their inch-long barbs are a hundred yards deep in some places. A jungle of steel brambles. Artillery using eighteen pounder guns firing shrapnel to cut the thickets. Not too effective. There are gaps here and there, but Fenton explained that the Germans will deliberately leave gaps so as to channelise attacks – men bunched up going through a gap become easy targets for machine gunners. To compound their concern, one of those freak summer storms has swept in and the heavy rains will make the churned-up ground tough going for the infantry.

June 28th. Château Querrieux. H.Q. of Sir Henry Rawlinson, commanding general of the Fourth Army. He has called a meeting of his corps commanders and I have driven here with Sir Julian who is in fine spirits. I tell him of Fenton's concern for the wire.

"Bugger the wire," Sir Julian says.

June 29th. Fenton's battalion H.Q. A comfortable old farmhouse. Excellent meal. Plenty of whisky. Fenton tells it straight to his company commanders. Attack will jump off on the morning of July 1st. Sir Julian's unconcern for the uncut wire is now obvious as Fenton reads a message sent down to all battalion commanders:

> There will be nothing ahead of you but dead or wounded Germans and a few crazed derelicts. Troops may slope arms if they wish while crossing no man's land. The bombardment will roll ahead of you and destroy any semblance of resistance.

"We will exercise full caution," Fenton says tightly. "And we will move at the ready and as quickly as possible."

The barrage grows in intensity. Candle flames sway in the shock blasts. Looking outside, one can see nothing but bolts of flame erupting from the German front lines. It seems inconceivable that so much as a rat could be alive over there.

"Colonel's a bit of a worrier, isn't he?" a young captain whispers in my ear.

July 1st. Thiepval Wood. Men packed into the forward trenches five hundred yards from where I sit in what had once been a fine old wood. Most of the trees cut down, either by German shelling or by brigade artillery so as to give better fields of fire for their guns. Rain has stopped and the sky is clear, sun hot. Barrage has been continuous all night. Suddenly ceases at 7.30 a.m. Silence catches at the heart and I can clearly hear the whistles blowing all up and down the line. One hundred and fifty thousand Englishmen climb out of their trenches and start across. Twinkle of sunlight off bayonets for as far as the eye can see in both directions. Many men with rifles sloped. They are heavily laden and walk slowly, almost casually, in long lines, nearly shoulder to shoulder. I think of an illustration in a history book – 8th grade? – the redcoats marching up Bunker Hill. A Highland battalion off to my right is being piped across.

Machine guns at a distance sound ineffectual, a metallic, rattling sound, like a marble shaken in a tin can. Nothing dramatic takes place as it does with artillery, no scream of shell, no bursting charge and fountain of earth, nothing to a machine gun but that clattering sound and the invisibility of death. The lines of walking men begin to melt away. Some begin to run towards the German wire. They do not get far. Others waver, turn in confusion and drop. The second wave plods on, the third wave follows the second. There may not be many Germans left alive in the ruins of Thiepval or in the shell-pulverised trenches, but there are enough. Their machine guns scythe the middle ground and the Tommies die where they stand. Difficult to write . . . hands shaking badly. The generals were quite wrong . . . battle of the Somme will not be won today – or tomorrow, or the day after that . . .

Alexandra Greville waited with her group on the deck of the small steamer that had brought them up the Seine to Rouen. There were eighty of them and they stood silently together, wrapped in their woollen capes, flurries of rain sweeping the river in the chill September wind.

"All right, ladies," a sergeant in the R.A.M.C. called out cheerfully as he came across the gangplank from the quay. "All off, an' a nice mug o' tea waitin' for you at the canteen."

The quay was jammed with men, mules, artillery pieces, great mounds of unfused shells, new ambulances and a myriad assortment of other supplies. The nurses joined hands to keep from being separated and followed the sergeant past a maze of open-sided storage sheds and giant warehouses into the streets of the town.

"Not far now, girls!" the sergeant said gleefully, grinning at them as though they were all his personal possessions. "Don't wander off. This is France, and you know what they say about Frenchmen!"

France. Alexandra felt a tightness in the throat as memory stirred. It all seemed so long ago, almost a different war. The soldiers in their steel helmets and rain capes looked alien to her; medieval, like the men-at-arms who had burned Joan of Arc in Rouen in yet another war. Lorries filled with troops clogged the street leading away from the docks. Australians, veterans of Gallipoli. One of them leaned out over the tailgate and said, "You'll be washin' me bloody stumps in a month, sister!"

The soldiers in the lorry laughed. The nurses stared fixedly ahead.

A short, bald-headed captain came into the Red Cross canteen and addressed them.

"My name is Captain Jenkins and I'm rather a long way from Harley Street. You are all a long way from other places, your homes, your loving parents. We of the Royal Army Medical Corps greet you fine young women of Queen Alexandra's Imperial Military Nursing Service." He paused for effect. "My, my, takes as long to say *that* as it does to sail to France, doesn't it?"

The nurses, tense with fatigue and trepidation, laughed much too loudly.

Captain Jenkins waited patiently until the laughter subsided. "Well, now. Here you are. No longer probationers but qualified nursing sisters in the Q.A.s. I realise that your training has been cut short due to the increased casualty rate on the Somme throughout the summer, but you will soon pick up any fine points you missed at All Souls. You are greatly needed here. We will work you hard and I know you will do your very best. I salute you, and may God bless you."

She lay in a cot in the nurses' quarters of one of the base hospitals on the outskirts of Rouen, drifting in a vague half sleep. She was riding in the back of an ambulance and Robbie was kneeling beside her holding her hands. "Alex, Alex, Alex . . ."

383

"What? What?" A light was shining in her face. Someone was kneeling beside the cot, touching her.

"It's me, Ivy."

She sat up and embraced Ivy fiercely. "Ivy! How on earth . . . ?"

Ivy Thaxton set her lighted torch on the floor and returned the hug.

"I got your letter last week and I've been checking the draft lists ever since."

"Did you come down from Boulogne?"

"No. I'm based here now, in the hospital train unit. We're getting twenty of your group so I made sure your name was included on our list." She drew back and took a folded sheet of paper from her carrying bag. "We leave at five thirty, running empty to Amiens. Here's the list of girls. You can help me find them."

"I'm glad you did this, Ivy. Glad we're together."

"It helps to have a friend," Ivy said.

The runner from brigade H.Q. came along Ale trench, paused for a second at the corner of Bitter and Stout and then turned into Stout, moving swiftly at a half crouch like a large and wily rat. A bullet cracked loudly as it passed over the narrow trench. Sniper's corner; but he had been this way many times before and knew all the bad spots. Stout was a horrible trench, tumbled in from shelling, full of deep, muddy sumps and broken duckboards. It meandered along the edge of High Wood in the direction of Martinpuich, in and around the shattered trunks of blackened trees. Cadavers had been spaded into the parapet and bony fingers and legs mingled with the snaky roots of the trees. The stench on a hot day was enough to stifle a man, but it was raining now, and cold, and the smell wasn't too bad. He passed four New Zealanders squatting in an observation sap, faces smeared with mud, only their eyes bright, luminous as the eyes of ferrets.

"What's your bloody 'urry, mate?"

He didn't pause for conversation but hurried on, the leather message pouch flopping against his hip. The shriek of a five point nine sent him head first to the trench bottom and he hugged the crumbling sides as the shell exploded ten yards behind the trench. Four more shells followed the first, each explosion further away. The salvo was badly off range, creeping the wrong way. He got up and ran on to Clapham Junction and turned sharply to his right into Watling trench. There he rested and lit a cigarette. Watling was deep and the sandbagging in good repair. He could see men sleeping further down the trench, lying in niches cut into the sides. A sentry kneeled against the parados above him, so caked with mud he blended into the background. The runner didn't see him until the man turned his head and looked down at him.

"Can you spare a fag, chum?"

"Yes," the runner said. He handed up his cigarette and lit another for himself. "This the Second Windsors?"

"You got it, chum. Which comp'ny you lookin' for?"

"Battalion commander."

"First communication trench and back fifty yards. Can't bloody well miss it. Thanks for the smoke."

"Think nothin' of it, mate," the runner said as he scurried on his way.

He was not surprised to find a major commanding the battalion; he had seen captains handling the job and there was a rumour that a lance-corporal had led the ninth battalion of the West Yorks after the Delville Wood attack. It meant nothing to the runner. He handed over his message from brigade and waited.

Major Charles Amberley slit the flimsy envelope with his thumb and read the contents, holding the paper under the hissing pressure lamp which dangled from the ceiling of the dug-out.

"No reply," he said crisply. "Tell the storeman to give you a double tot of rum."

The adjutant stirred on his wire mesh bunk. "What's up?"

Charles stared at the paper. "We're to attack Hanoverian redoubt at 0800 tomorrow with A, C and D. No whimsy about taking the ruddy place. We're to draw fire, I suspect, while the New Zealanders go in on our left."

The adjutant lay back with a groan. "Bloody waste."

"See if you can ring through to brigade."

"No point to it. The wires must be cut in a hundred places after yesterday's strafe. They wouldn't have sent that poor sod of a runner if they could have got us on the blower."

Charles sat down at the table and sipped his tea. It was ice cold and tasted of kerosene. The stupidity of the order caused his hand to tremble with rage. The battalion had lost nine officers and two hundred and sixty men in their last attack, half the casualties occurring as the men went through their own wire. One corporal had managed to get close enough to the German positions to hurl a Mills bomb and he had died throwing it. Five officers and a hundred and fifty men had come up from the reserves during the night, but the battalion was seriously under strength and now they wanted another attack on a totally impregnable position, carried out in broad daylight. He couldn't even inspire the men by telling them they were going to take Hanoverian and clean out that corner of the wood once and for all. No, they were simply to go over the top and give the Boche something to shoot at while the New Zealanders clawed their way up Guinness ravine. No artillery support mentioned in the order. New theory at staff; artillery preps tip off attacks. It was as good a theory as any other, he thought bitterly. All the theories were bloody wrong.

The adjutant swung his legs off the bed and scratched his chest.

"Do you realise something, Charles? We've pushed the Germans four miles since the first of July. Young Baker figured it out last night. By his calculations we'll have 'em over the Rhine by the summer of 1938. What do you think of that?"

"I think Baker's an idiot," he said savagely. "If he had told me, I'd have put him on a charge."

"He's a good lad. I knew his brother at Harrow. We used to rag about a bit."

Charles stood up, took his helmet from a peg on one of the support beams and went up the dug-out steps into the trench. B Company was in reserve, the men squatting in their shallow funkholes eating their dinner, rain capes draped over their heads. At least the food was hot, steam rising from the tinned stew in their mess plates. The three companies in the forward line weren't that lucky. It was bully beef and biscuits for them, with perhaps some hot tea going up after sunset if there was no night barrage.

"Stretcher comin' down!" someone shouted from further along the trench.

"Mind the wire there! Watch your bloody heads!"

He walked towards the commotion. The bearers were lugging a big, groaning man along the communication trench. The bearers were small men and it was taking four of them to carry the stretcher through the mud.

"Who is it?" Charles asked.

"Corporal Thomas, sir," one of the bearers grunted. "Rifle grenade 'it the parados, bounced back an' blew his 'and off."

"Damn." Corporal Thomas was one of the best N.C.O.s in D Company. He was going to be damned hard to replace.

The stump of the corporal's right hand was heavily bound with bloody bandage. There was blood on his face as well, smeared by the rain.

"Is me face gone?" he whispered in terror, struggling to sit upright. "Is me face gone?"

The bearers set the stretcher down for a moment to rest. One of them knelt beside the corporal and patted his shoulder.

"No, Bert, just a few scratches. It's your right 'and. Sliced clean as a whistle. It's Blighty for you, Bert."

"Thank God for that," the corporal sobbed. "Thank God I'm out of it."

"'Ave to diddle the old woman with your left 'and from now on, Bert. Make a nice change for 'er."

"Thank God for it," the corporal said, slumping back on the stretcher. "What's a . . . bleedin' . . . 'and."

The bearer stood up and glanced at Charles with an apologetic smile.

"It's the morphia, sir. Gave 'im two pellets and he's gone out of 'is 'ead. Don't pay no nevermind to 'im."

"Get him down to the aid post," he said stiffly. It wouldn't do to show sympathy for a man who felt blessed being wounded. He made a cursory inspection of the trench and went back into the dug-out, pausing before he did so to glance down the slope behind him at the burned-out hull of an MK 1 tank, a

Big Willie. The tank had come groaning and sputtering and backfiring up the road from Bazentin the week before. Moving at about two miles per hour, lurching in and out of ditches and shell holes like some dying beast. Seeing it that day had made him think of Jamie Ross and how Ross would have shaken his head and muttered something about too little power, not enough bloody engine to crawl through mud. Brigade had rung through and told him to send two companies up the hill into High Wood behind the tank. The tank never came within five hundred yards of the wood. The Germans had shelled it with whizz-bangs and Big Willie had exploded. Not knowing what it was they had shelled and burned, the German gunners had gone into a frenzy and laid down a blanket barrage for two hours, killing sixty men and wounding one hundred and seventy.

The company commanders and seconds in command came to the dug-out that evening for a briefing and a share of the whisky bottle. They listened in silence as Charles explained the order of attack. "D Company at 0800; A to follow at 0810; C to give covering fire with the Lewis guns and then to go across at 0825."

It was all meaningless and everyone in the dug-out knew it. The Germans would see the first men pop up and the barrage would start before they had found the taped paths through their own wire. D Company could be written off. If A Company were lucky, the Germans would spot the New Zealanders moving up Guinness and switch their battery fire to that spot. Then all they would have to contend with would be the machine guns firing from concrete revetments half buried in the earth, the intricate belts of wire and half a dozen *minenwerfers* lobbing high explosive on their heads. C Company had picked the right card. They could justify calling off their attack if the first two assault waves suffered more than fifty per cent casualties – which was almost a certainty. Seventy per cent was more like it. If the two New Zealand battalions got up Guinness from Stout trench and took the Hanoverian redoubt in flank, forcing a withdrawal, then it would be worth any sacrifice – a lofty, patriotic observation which he passed on to the captains and lieutenants, the words greeted by half concealed, sardonic smiles. They would accept the sacrifice because they had no choice in the matter. They did not expect anything to come of the attack.

Dawn came in misty rain. The New Zealanders would have left Stout trench before dawn, using the mist as a cover to crawl as far as possible up Guinness ravine through a splintered wilderness of trees. They would make their rush for the crest of High Wood when they heard the Royal Windsors drawing fire. Charles put a whistle between his teeth and looked at his wristwatch – 0757, 58, 59 – he knew that if he survived the war he would never be able to wear a wristwatch again – 0800. He blew a shrill blast on the whistle, the captain and platoon leaders blew theirs and two hundred men scrambled up the ladders, bunching up as they hurried through the pre-cut gaps in their own wire. Ten yards, twenty; they were scrambling in and out of old craters, bayonets gleaming through the mist; thirty yards now, forty; almost to the German wire which was fifty yards deep. Signal rockets hissed upwards from the enemy lines, bursting yellow and green against the low clouds.

"Damn . . . oh, damn," Charles whispered as he heard the drone of howitzer shells, the drones turning to shrieks, the shrieks to thunderbolts and vomiting geysers of earth and flame. The salvos walked the edge of the German wire. Clods of earth and truncated men hung motionless for a split second against the grey sky. What was left of D Company scattered away from the wire and dived for the steaming shell holes.

0810. Charles blew his whistle with a dry mouth. A Company was slow to leave the trench. Whistles were blowing furiously and the platoon leaders were cursing and shouting. A dozen men went up the ladders and through the wire, keeping low, as the Lewis gun teams from C Company began firing over their heads. The heavy German machine guns started to hammer through slits in the thick concrete revetments, the fire interlocked, catching the men of A Company waist high and ripping along the top of the sandbagged parados. The platoon leaders kept shouting and more men went up the ladders, some only reaching the lip of the trench before tumbling back again. It was a clear washout and Charles yelled at the signallers to send up Very lights, calling for artillery. The trapped men of D Company might make it back under the covering fire of the counter-barrage. If they couldn't, then they'd hole up in the craters and wait for night.

"You rotten little coward!" Lieutenant Baker's voice, high pitched with hysteria. "I should damn well shoot you!"

Charles hurried out of the observation sap into the front trench. A dead man hung head down, one foot caught in the rung of a ladder. He ran past the corpse to where young Baker was standing flourishing a revolver.

"What's the matter?" Charles shouted.

The lieutenant pointed his weapon at a private who sat slumped against the fire step, his rifle beside him, bayonet jammed in the mud. The soldier's face was the colour of putty and blood poured from under his right boot. "Shot himself in the foot! Ordered him up the ladder and he just turned and looked at me, reversed his rifle and gave himself a Blighty." He waved the revolver under the man's nose. "It's a firing squad for you now, without a doubt!"

"Get him back to the aid post," Charles ordered.

"Under guard?"

He looked at the soldier leaning against the trench wall. His eyes were dull, uncaring, oblivious even to the pain of his wound. He was no more than eighteen.

"Yes," Charles said dully. "Under guard, of course."

They would tie him to a post more than likely, shoot him by firing squad; or the Military Police would pistol him in the head without ceremony. Damn, he thought, clenching and unclenching his fists, why hadn't the man been clever enough not to shoot himself in front of his lieutenant! But what was one more corpse? What did it matter? Brigade artillery was firing shrapnel against the German revetment now and the Boche machine-gun fire had ceased. The shrapnel fire was desultory and dwindled to a final burst, the smoke drifting in the wind through a grove of skeleton trees. A Boche machine gunner fired a few rounds, a staccato thumb to the nose. Heavy Boche shelling in the direction of Guinness ravine and that, too, ceased. The men of A Company stood white faced and tense on the fire step of the trench.

"Stand down," Charles ordered. Any further attack would be more than futile.

Out between the wire somewhere, in a shell hole or abandoned sap, a man was screaming, ragged shrieks and sobs. The sound went on and on, rising and falling, dwindling at times but never ending. 0830. When night came he would send out the stretcher bearers. He prayed fervently that the shrieking man would be hours dead by then.

Colonel Robin Mackendric completed his first surgical shift of the day and went to the mess tent for a mug of tea and a late breakfast. He did not wear his colonel's crown and stars on his uniform because he was oblivious to rank. It was purely a by-the-book promotion, the army's obsession with having the proper rank in the proper job. Commanders of casualty clearing stations were supposed to be colonels and so, finally, the War Office papers had caught up with him just as his team was shifted from Kemmel to the Somme. Being a colonel instead of a major had not affected his duties in any way and so he hadn't bothered to remove the old badges and have new ones sewn on to his shoulder straps. Not so Captain Ronald David Vale who had been upped to major. He wore the crown badges on his underwear – or so it was rumoured.

"Had a funny one just now, Mac," Vale said as he joined Mackendric at the table. "Skull furrow, clear to the bone and all the way around. A perfect circle. Bullet penetrated the chap's helmet and just bucketed around inside of it like a buzz saw. He'll go through life with a nice groove to rest his hat on."

Mackendric eyed him sourly and sipped his tea. "You're collecting some marvellous tales for your dotage."

Vale grinned and reached for a plate of buns. "Well, to tell you the truth, it didn't go *all* the way around, but it was quite miraculous."

"We can do with a few miracles."

"Yes," Vale said, suddenly subdued. "I had more than my share of horrors yesterday. You were lucky to be in Amiens."

"I heard all about it."

"Yes, well, the point is, Mac, I don't see how it can get better before it gets a damned sight worse. Are they going to keep on butting their heads against a wall here or blow the bloody whistle and call time?"

"They're going to keep butting." He dipped a bun in his tea and munched on it slowly. "That was the gist of the meeting yesterday. The French medical services have gone to pot, just worn out by Verdun. Haig and Rawlinson are afraid the same sort of wear and tear will break us. We all told them that it wouldn't, and then they began to drop dark hints that we could expect even heavier casualties between now and November."

"Three hundred thousand isn't enough for Haig?"

"Don't be sarcastic, Vale, I pity the man in a way. He's got Joffre on his back like the old man of the sea – attack, attack, attack. It's a war of attrition now, that's obvious. We lose three hundred thousand and the Germans lose four hundred thousand. That spells victory to some minds."

Vale shoved the plate of buns away as though the idea of eating one was repugnant.

"Last man on his feet wins the war, I suppose."

"Something on that order. Don't try to make any sense out of it. Just go on doing your job."

"Oh, I do, Mac, I do. I really love the army, that's the joke of it. I'd rather be a battalion M.O. than a Harley Street surgeon any day of the week. I think that's why I'm more bitter than you are about all this waste – or, anyway, more vocal about it. You hide everything behind that infuriating Scottish stoicism of yours. But, if it keeps you sane, why should I care?"

Afternoons were worse than the mornings. The ambulances bearing the casualties of dawn attacks rolled into Corbie from the battalion aid posts and dressing stations in Albert, Ginchy, Mametz and Bazentin. Number Eighty-five C.C.S. received its full share.

Mackendric was taking his turn as *triage* officer, examining, with three sisters to aid him, each stretcher case that was brought in, sorting out those men who needed immediate surgery and might live because of it; those who needed surgery but would die no matter what was done; and those who could be sent *as is* to the hospital trains and be dealt with at one of the base hospitals in Rouen. The first group was carried to the surgical huts, the second to the moribund ward, where they would be kept under heavy sedation in a clean bed until they died without pain, and the last group was taken back to the ambulances for the short ride to Corbie Junction. It was not a job that anyone wanted, but none of the doctors shirked it. The number of men being sent to the moribund ward seemed to increase daily.

"The men are getting reckless," a battalion medical officer had told Mackendric one day. "They've lost all sense of caution. It's as if they didn't give a damn if they're hit or not."

He was checking his sixtieth case when Captain O'Fallon hurried up to him.

"I'll take over, Mac. Vale's in a bit of trouble. Better take a look-see – Hut Six."

"What sort of trouble?"

"Military Police."

Two sergeant M.P.s and an elderly captain stood in Number Six surgical hut. They were watching, grim faced, as Major Vale worked to close a massive axillary wound. The two sergeants continued to stare intently at the procedure, but the captain turned angrily to face Mackendric when he strolled in.

"Are you in command here, major?"

"Colonel, actually," Mackendric said, fingering his tunic flaps. "Haven't had time to add the pips. But I am in command, yes."

The provost marshal was slightly abashed. "Oh, I see. Well, *colonel*, I shall be forced to register a complaint, sir. I brought in a prisoner for official confirmation of self-inflicted wound, and this man, this *doctor . . .*" His contempt and anger rendered him momentarily speechless.

"Major Vale, do you mean?"

"Yes, if that is his name."

"Bugger off," Vale muttered as he tied a ligature around the axillary artery and prepared to pluck shards of the smashed humerus from the cavity.

"What exactly seems to be the matter?" Mackendric asked politely.

The provost marshal turned his back on the operation and stepped out into the corridor of the tarpaper and wood building.

"I need hardly tell you, sir, that a self-inflicted wound is a

393

most serious matter. The *creature* on that table is suspected of shooting himself in the armpit with a revolver."

"Suspected?"

"No one actually saw him do it, but his platoon leader told us that the edges of the wound were scorched. Powder burns, sir."

Mackendric rubbed the side of his jaw. "Well, now, difficult to say . . . could have been dirt, you know."

The captain stiffened. "Precisely what your Major Vale said when he sliced the evidence away and tossed the flesh into a bucket! I have been in the service for twenty-three years, sir. I know the difference between dirt and powder burns."

"Major Vale is a first-rate surgeon. I can hardly question his judgment. If he claims it was dirt, then I must respect his opinion. I would suggest that you do not pursue this matter any further."

"Quite so," the captain said, eyeing Mackendric frigidly. "May I remind the colonel that it is the duty of the medical service to report all incidents of self-inflicted wounds to the provost marshal's office. This *epidemic* of Blighty wounds done by one's own hand must be stopped. It is un-English, sir, and a disgrace to our heritage. I served in the South African war and not once during that conflict did I hear of a soldier being so craven as to shoot himself."

The provost marshal strode off and the two M.P. sergeants followed him, looking suitably grim faced. Mackendric glanced into the operating room.

"Will he lose the arm, do you think?"

"Oh, hell, no," Vale snapped irritably. "But it won't be worth a damn. Smack in the armpit with a Webley! Stupid sod."

"Take the afternoon off. Go into Corbie and have a brandy or two."

"I bloody well intended to do just that. I might even have three."

It was evening before Major Vale got back to the C.C.S. He was not drunk, but he was far from being sober. His breath, Mackendric noted, smelled like a brewery floor.

"Gave up on the brandy, I take it," he said as the young surgeon came into his room and slumped happily into a canvas chair.

"Met some Australian chaps, marvellous fellows, knew of an *estaminet* near the junction that serves real English beer. None of that pallid French stuff. Sat, talked, watched the trains go by."

Mackendric sat in his cot in his pyjamas reading a book.

"I'm glad you enjoyed yourself."

"One of the Aussies, a colonel, used to be a barrister in Melbourne. He said that he could prove, without a doubt, that the whole bloody war is illegal. Think of that."

"Fascinating. Why don't you go to bed?"

"Yes, might do that little thing – have a decent sleep for a change. Popped in here for some reason . . . had something in mind to say."

"The illegality of it all. In Australia, at least."

"More than that." He got clumsily to his feet, yawning, tugging at one ear. "Ah, yes. Spotted an absolutely smashing Q.A. in the junction off one of the hospital trains. She was buying some apples at the canteen. Blonde stunner . . . seen her before."

Mackendric lowered his book and peered over the wire rims of his eyeglasses. "Oh?"

"Yes. Couldn't be two faces like hers, or two figures when it comes to that. Positive I'd seen her before – but I wasn't sure, you see, didn't want to make a fool of myself. But I'd swear it was the same girl who came up to Kemmel last year, the one who went bonkers on us. Remember?"

"Yes."

"Friend of yours or something, wasn't she?"

"Something like that."

He stayed awake far into the night, trying to read, but forgetting to turn the pages. There were sounds all about him – the rattle of the dressing carts in the wards down the corridor, the rumble of gunfire from the direction of Delville Wood, but he heard nothing. He was miles away, walking hand-in-hand with her along the rue Saint Honoré, window-shopping in the afternoon after that first night. Had that really been him? He felt old and tired. There was a good deal of grey creeping into his hair. His eyes were giving him a few problems, too much straining in the inadequate light of the operating room, and his fingers ached constantly from clenching instruments for too many hours a day, too many days at a time. Burning himself out. Thirty-three and he felt like an old man. She would be what now? Twenty? She had taken his advice and undertaken the training to become a nurse. Perhaps she had taken the rest of his advice as well and had met a handsome man of her own age and forgotten all about him. A possibility. He would never know unless he talked to her. He could contrive a way to do that easily enough. Hospital Trains Detachment. A telephone call to Captain Frazier in Rouen. Frazier arranged the complex train schedules and would know to the lowliest orderly who was on which train and when and at what time. His little corner of the war.

"Greville, Alexandra, Q.A.s. Train 96. Rouen to Corbie via Amiens, Tuesday, Thursday and Sunday runs. Know the woman, Mackendric?"

Yes. Knew her and needed her. But did she need him?

Sister Pilbeam dripped ether on to the nose cone. Vale clutched the rib-spreaders while Mackendric excised a shell-shredded lung. He kept glancing at the wall clock as he finished off.

"You in a hurry to catch a train?" Vale quipped.

"Yes," he said quietly. "As a matter of fact, I am."

She was busy as he knew she would be. The trains came empty into Corbie, were shunted on to a spur at the junction where the ambulances and the walking wounded were waiting. He spotted her among a score of other nurses as he walked along the platform past two hundred New Zealanders lying patiently on their stretchers, bearers and orderlies moving among them, lighting cigarettes, helping the wounded men fill in Field Service Post Cards:

Strike out what does not apply
I am quite well
I have been admitted into hospital
sick   and am going on well
wounded   and hope to be discharged soon

396

"How do I tell my mum I lost a foot?"

"You don't, mate. Save it as a surprise."

She was giving A.T.S. shots with cool proficiency, checking dressings, telling the bearers in which carriage to place the men whom she had checked and tagged. Rain thudded off the corrugated iron roof of the long platform. The train glistened dark olive green, the red crosses bright on a white field.

"Your efficiency is to be commended, sister."

She paused in what she was doing but did not look up at him.

"Hello, Robbie."

"I shan't keep you from your work, Alex. Bit of a surprise seeing you again, a happy surprise."

She nodded, bending lower over a stretcher which rested on two sawhorses, her hands sure and knowing on a dirty scrap of bandage covering a mud-encrusted leg.

He leaned closer to the wounded man. "Calf wounds. Not serious."

"Hurt like ruddy fire," the wounded man said.

"Dare say, but you'll be kicking a football with that leg in three weeks' time."

He watched Alexandra wash an area of flesh around the jagged, blood-clotted holes with green soap solution and then wrap a clean bandage around the leg. She made a motion with one hand and the bearers lifted the stretcher and carried it into the train.

"Next," she said, straightening up. Her eyes met Mackendric's for the first time. It was like an embrace. "You're good to see, Robbie."

"Do you mean that, Alex?" His voice was solemn.

She nodded fiercely. "Yes, yes, I do. Now please go away or I shan't be able to concentrate. If . . . if you can get away this Saturday . . ."

"I will," he said flatly.

"To Rouen . . . Number Fifty-two train. I could meet you at the station."

"I shall be there."

"And no lectures this time, Robbie, no telling me what's best for me."

"No. I've stopped giving advice."

"And there would be nights when we could be together, in some charming country inn."

He could remember her saying that on a Sunday morning in Paris. No country inn, charming or otherwise, in the Ypres salient. But this was Normandy. Apple trees and rich earth between the great loops of the Seine. Clusters of villages with stone houses. Inns with rooms facing the orchards and the banks of the river. Clean linen and feather beds. He held her tightly, watching the sunset through the windows, one hand drifting idly down her naked back. She turned slightly in his arms and moved her lips across his chest.

"I shall never give you up," she whispered.

"I won't talk you out of it, although I should at least try."

"It would only be a gesture. You want me, Robbie."

"Yes. I want you." He held her silently, gently stroking her back, the curve of a hip, then he said, "I didn't tell you about Dennis. He's in Ottawa . . . flying instructor. Got shot down last April near Abbeville and walked away from the crash. He might not be so lucky next time. I'm glad he's in Canada."

"So am I," she murmured.

"He wrote me a long letter about Canada, the people – quite a different world. You know, I'd already decided that I couldn't go back to England. If this war ever does end, I want a new sort of life. I'd go to Toronto, or west to Vancouver. I wrote my wife that and asked her for a divorce; be the best thing for her, too. What she really wants is a respectable sort of chap who stays home, makes lots of money and votes Conservative. We were never a good match."

She pulled back from him, her breasts resting lightly against his chest.

"Will she give you a divorce?"

"I don't know." He began to caress her nipples, tracing the rosy circles with his fingertips, the taut buds. "I hope to God she does, but Catherine could deny it out of pure spite."

"It won't matter," she said, her voice husky. "I don't care. I'll go with you, Robbie, live with you, married or not."

"You might regret that one day, Alex."

"Never."

Never . . . never, she thought, moving her body in a slow rhythm with his. And not because of this, not the feel of him inside of her, the pleasure mounting in gentle spirals. It went beyond passion. Their lives had meshed and become one. She would go with him wherever he went and live with him without shame. And Mamma and Papa? They would never understand why, never comprehend that her need for him was inextricably woven with his greater need for her.

"I love you, Alex . . ."

"Yes," she said, "yes . . . yes."

Martin noticed a certain chill as he walked into the brigade headquarters in Bazentin village. One of the officers who had always been friendly and generous with information pretended to be too busy to say hallo. The H.Q. was located in one of the deep German galleries captured in late August, tunnels and rooms cut into the chalk hill behind the ruins of the village. Two brigades had their headquarters there as well as a signalling company, a Dressing Station and stored supplies of all kinds. It made for a crowded, noisy place, the tunnels and rooms lit by electric lights which burned day and night.

"Is the colonel too busy to see me?" Martin asked.

The officer who was usually so talkative began to shift papers around on his tiny desk.

"Afraid he is, yes."

"All I need from him is a pass to go up to the line."

"Out of the question. Sorry. Perhaps tomorrow."

"I'm sure you know how difficult it is for me to come this far. As long as I'm here . . ."

The officer half turned his back and toyed with a field telephone.

"Look, Mr. Rilke, I'm sorry, but – "

A heavy curtain serving as a room divider parted and Fenton peered through the opening.

"Oh, for God's sake," he said wearily, "you couldn't shoo Mr. Rilke away with a broom. Come on in, Martin."

Fenton's section of the dug-out contained a desk, maps pinned to the chalk walls, one chair and one canvas cot. Fenton drew the curtain back into place and then sat on the edge of the cot and rubbed his eyes.

"I was trying to get some sleep."

"Sorry," Martin said, straddling the chair. "I didn't mean to wake you."

"I said I was *trying*. You didn't wake me. So you want to go back up to Delville Wood, do you?"

"If at all possible."

Fenton nodded slowly and groped for a tin of cigarettes among the disordered blankets.

"I'm afraid you are suddenly *persona non grata*. Received a crisp directive to that effect from Corps yesterday. If you are spotted in battle area you are to be escorted to the rear. Any place beyond Albert is out of bounds to you, old boy."

Martin lit a cigar and then bent forward to light Fenton's cigarette.

"There's nothing in Albert for me to write about, Fenton. The Salvation Army runs canteens in Albert. I might as well be in Biloxi, Mississippi, as far as writing about the war is concerned."

"That might not be a bad idea, Biloxi, Mississippi, I mean. Some of your byline stories in Yank papers came to the attention of our military mission in Washington. They cabled their shock to London, gruesome descriptions of British fighting in August – "

"They weren't gruesome descriptions."

"No, I'm sure they weren't. Just Martin Rilke being graphic about the attacks on Thiepval in August."

"That's right."

"How'd you get them past the censors?"

"Gave them to a fellow A.P. man going back to the States."

Fenton smiled wryly and flipped ashes at his feet. "Naughty boy. Not playing by the rules, are we? The articles were an embarrassment to the General Staff. Thiepval should have been captured on July 1st. Here it is, damned near the end of September, and the place is still a boil in our flanks. Downright humiliating to be reminded of their failures. You are not supposed to mention the names of places, either, just *somewhere on the Somme*. Isn't that right?"

"I suppose so," Martin shrugged.

"And soldiers aren't *blown up*, or *torn apart by a shell*, or *sit screaming in shell holes*. Soldiers simply *fall*."

"I take it you read the articles."

"No. I don't need to read them. I was there, remember? Sir Julian read me the juicier bits over the telephone. He was angrier than a raped baboon. Well, can't blame the gaffer. Wully Robertson raised hell with Haig, Haig raised hell with Rawlinson and Rawly jumped all over Uncle Julian."

"And now you're jumping on me."

"Right. I don't know who you can jump on."

Martin studied the ash on his cigar. A fifty center. One of the few luxuries he permitted himself. He did not disturb the ash, but let it flake away on its own.

"Storm in a teacup, Fenton. I sent those articles out past the censors deliberately. For American consumption only. Tried to bring home to them the reality of this war over here. They may be drawn into it themselves one day and they have a right to know what twentieth-century battle is all about. The fact is, American papers didn't give it much of a play. Everyone in the States is more concerned about Pancho Villa shooting up New Mexico again than they are about a few thousand Tommies dying for fifty yards of French real estate. I guess it just didn't make any sense to them."

There was heavy shelling going on. British eight-inch and French hundred and fives hitting Delville and High Wood a mile away. The volcanic explosions could be felt rather than heard, a trembling in the walls, a fine haze of chalk dust.

"Doesn't make a whole lot of sense to me, either, Martin. Well, what the devil. I'll pretend I never saw you, but stay out of my area from now on. I'm acting brigade commander now, being breveted to brigadier general until they dig up a real one from the reserve and ship him out here – kicking and screaming, no doubt. Anyway, I've got five battalions under my rather loose command: the Royal Windsors, Green Howards and some throw-together battalions with everything in them but the Girl Guides. We're to go over at dawn to the west of High Wood with three other brigades and probe for Flers behind the tanks."

401

"I heard about it. That's why I'm here."

"Of course you've heard about it," Fenton said bitterly. "No one can keep his mouth shut in this army. Every whore in Amiens knows more about high command strategy than I do." He squashed his cigarette out on the chalk floor and drew another from the tin. "They have a few tanks left from the fifty they shipped over, so they're giving them another try. Rotten terrain. Steep and muddy and peppered with old shell holes. Fragile bloody things, these tanks. Break down if you give 'em a sour look. But I can see their potential. If they could move as fast as a man can run and had the power to go up a hill, we'd be on the Rhine in two weeks."

"Americans are interested in tanks," Martin said lamely. "An American invented the caterpillar tread tractor . . . Uncle Benjamin Holt."

"Bully for Uncle B.," Fenton said drily.

Observations and reflections. On the Somme. September 21st, 1916. And a cold wet day it is. My observation point in a sap covered by a camouflaged tarpaulin is reasonably dry, although there is mud on the bottom of the sap up to my knees. Intense British and French artillery fire whacking High Wood, the shell bursts reflected by the rain causing a sheet-lightning effect across the crest of the stump-dotted hill. Same effect can be seen to the east at Delville Wood and Longueval. Appear to be more than four brigades committed to this assault. Have even seen cavalry along the Contalmaison–Bazentin road, troopers and horses black with rain. Cavalry suffer greatly from exposure. Theory behind having these English Hussars and Indian Lancers standing about in the rear must be tied in with morale factor, possibly to give infantry moving up to the line the feeling that a breakthrough is in the works . . . that they have only to chop a few holes through the German trench system and hordes of horsemen will burst through like rockets and ride "into the blue" as Haig so quaintly puts it. No "blue" ahead of me, just dancing flames and muddy, pocked ground. No German return fire. They will be, as always, deep in their bunkers with tons of ferro-concrete and sandbags blunting the blows. When the barrage lifts and the British infantry go

402

forward they will emerge, as they always do, and cut the attack to pieces. This has been the pattern since the first day and no one has yet come up with a plan that alters that depressing scenario.

In trench – 2nd Royal Windsor Fusiliers. Sang-froid not an expression that fits the American temperament – certainly not the American military temperament. Lee may have had sang-froid but Grant didn't, or any other general I can think of. American military men have always been hat slappers, sword benders, tobacco spitters and high cussers. Charles has sang-froid. He stands in exposed position on top of parados and scans High Wood with binoculars. Cool as ice. I feel like shouting, "Hey, that's my cousin standing up there." Brave but dumb. Lots of German stuff coming this way now. Machine-gun bullets crack as they pass over the trench. Charles has sang-froid. He steps down into trench and scribbles notes for the runners. Sending two more companies across, as ordered by Brigade H.Q. Timetable for attack must be met. He is writing out death notices for a few hundred men. His hand doesn't tremble, his face shows no expression at all. Must ask him one day what he was thinking.

German counter barrage heavier than anyone expected. Trench rocks. Bags of sand fly. Bits of wire, bits of men trapped out between wire. Someone shouting, "Tanks are catching it good an' proper." Cockney voice, sounds almost pleased. Shorthand becoming unreadable . . . no point in –

PARIS (AP) December 12th, 1916. Martin Rilke of the Paris bureau of the Associated Press has been released from the Hôpital St. Antoine after suffering severe wounds on the Somme front in September. He is recuperating satisfactorily at St. Germain en Laye outside Paris.

5

JACOB GOLDEN CROSSED THE CHAMPS ELYSÉES AGAINST A SWARM
of traffic, smiled affably at shouting taxi drivers and ignored
the blare of klaxons. On reaching the pavement he straightened his bowler hat, smoothed the moleskin lapels of his
overcoat and strolled into the glittering lobby of the Hôtel
Monceau, swinging his cane with the jaunty air of the born
boulevardier. He ordered a Dubonnet at the bar, speaking to the
barman without the slightest trace of an English accent. A
British colonel standing at the bar drinking whisky asked him
in halting, pocket-dictionary French if he knew of a place in
Montmartre where the *"jeunes filles dansant . . . à nue . . .* don't
you know".

He replied in halting English, giving the man directions to a
place on the Boulevard de Clichy, where the only things naked
and female were the chickens dangling from hooks in the
window. It was the finest poultry shop in Paris and he hoped
the colonel enjoyed the visit.

He had nearly finished his apéritif when he saw the burly
figure of Claude Lenard enter the bar and sit at a table in a dim
corner. Picking up his glass he strolled casually over to him and
sat down.

"Good afternoon, Claude."

Claude Lenard, socialist editor, lifelong friend of Keir
Hardie and Jean Juares, his cause in ruins, his very freedom in
constant jeopardy, looked slowly and suspiciously at every
person in the bar before grunting a reply.

"Let me buy you a drink, Claude."

"It is not necessary, Golden."

"Perhaps it isn't, but it is normal. Men do not come into this
bar just to sit."

The tiny eyes, almost lost in the massive face, the bush of
beard and moustache, flickered. The great head nodded.

"I will take a beer."

"A brandy and soda. This is not a *Syndicaliste* bar, Claude. When in Rome and all that."

The editor glanced bitterly at the cherrywood panelled walls, the elegantly carved rosewood bar with its copper, not zinc, top.

"I do not belong in such a capitalist place."

"No," Jacob replied blandly, "and the special police wouldn't think of looking for you here. This is the safest possible spot for us to talk. This may come as a shock to you, Claude, but you're the image of Ravenot, the munitions tycoon."

"So I have been told," the old man said drily. "Very well, as long as I am Ravenot, order me a brandy and soda, an *Armagnac* and soda."

Jacob snapped his fingers for the waiter. The two men sat in silence until the drinks came.

"All right," Lenard said. "I have found a printer for you willing, for a price, you understand, to undertake what you want. It is not only money; he lost three sons at Verdun and is understandably bitter about it. The man can be trusted, but the price will be high."

"Money is not a factor. I want a quality paper."

"He is capable of it. A master printer."

Jacob removed a thick envelope from the inner pocket of his coat and placed it in front of the other man.

"This should show my faith. Take whatever you need for yourself out of it."

Lenard tapped the envelope with his blunt fingers. "I hope you understand the risks in this, Golden. It is a bad climate for this sort of undertaking. They are sensitive about Verdun. They wish to keep the full truth of that abattoir buried with the corpses. The English, too, with their débâcle on the Somme. Any criticism of the war is looked on as treason."

"I know it."

"However, there are writers here in Paris who worked for me in the old days. Impassioned, fearless men willing to go to prison for their beliefs."

"I don't want impassioned writing, Claude. This is not going to be a tract for the Second International."

"Not spoken as a good socialist."

"I'm not a socialist," Jacob drawled. "Good or otherwise. Politics of all kinds bore me. No, Claude, I am just Jacob Golden swimming against the tide."

Lugging a portmanteau from his apartment on the rue Pigalle, Jacob took the metro as far as Pont de Neuilly and then hired a taxi to take him to St. Germain en Laye, the driver grumbling because it was a long drive and petrol was scarce. He could make more money and use less fuel with short runs. Jacob dipped into his coat again and gave the man double the fare in advance. Money was not a problem – yet. It would be once the paper went into production, but he would contrive some way of getting money out of England. There was no point in worrying about it now and so he leaned back in the taxi and watched the gaunt winter woods flash by. The third winter of the war. The very trees looked tired.

The house that Martin Rilke had rented was set in the middle of a well-cultivated garden, surrounded by dense groves of beech and pine. It was a small, two-storey house of weathered limestone, built at the turn of the century for the mistress of a Parisian banker. It had stood empty since the Germans threatened Paris in the first weeks of the war.

A tall, forbidding-looking woman with iron-grey hair opened the door. She wore a slate-grey uniform with a tiny red cross stitched above her ample bosom.

"It is not a good idea for Monsieur Rilke to have visitors," she said with a strong Breton accent. "I hope you will not stay long."

"Oh," Jacob replied airily, removing his hat and tossing it neatly on to a hatstand, "no more than a week or two."

Martin sat in a small, comfortably furnished room at the rear of the house, propped up on a couch, his canes resting beside him. He was both surprised and delighted to see Jacob stroll into the room, tossed aside the book he was reading and fumbled for his canes.

"Jacob! I don't believe it."

"Ah, how fickle is memory. I sat by your bedside after your second, or was it your third operation? No matter. I was there

406

in your moment of pain and suffering and I wager you can't recall it."

"That's right. I can't." He struggled to get to his feet, but Jacob made a gesture of restraint.

"Don't get up for me, for God's sake. Where do you keep the champagne?"

"In the pantry."

"Well, we shall crack a bottle or two later." He removed his coat and pulled a chair closer to the couch. "Damned fine little house. You own it?"

"No, but I might buy it. The price is cheap enough. The owner still expects hordes of Uhlans to come crashing through the woods any day."

"Come into money, old lad?"

"Back pay and bonuses by the bucketful, and my Uncle Paul was so upset I was hurt, he cabled his import agency in Paris to put forty thousand francs in my account. It pays to get hit by a trench mortar."

"How do you feel?"

"Strong as an ox, until I stand up. But having Madame Lucille nursing me is an incentive to recovery – as rapid as possible."

"Yes, I met the lady. Pleasant as a prison warder."

Martin leaned back against the pillows and looked Jacob up and down.

"How come you're not in uniform?"

"Oh, I severed my relationship before coming to France. I've been here for six weeks, by the way. Rented some digs in Montmartre, but there are far too many distractions there. Haven't lost my penchant for chorus girls of low repute, I'm afraid to say. They take far too much of my money, not to mention creating a severe drain on my energies."

"Wait a second, Jacob. Go back a bit in the narrative. What did you mean by *severing* your relationship?"

"Just that, old fellow. I resigned my commission in the Royal Signals Corps."

"You can do that in the middle of a war?"

"They're beginning to close the loopholes now that conscription is some sort of reality, but, oh my, yes, one serves King

407

and country on a strictly volunteer basis. Ranks might enlist for the duration, but officers, being gentlemen, are under no such obligation. Men of breeding simply do not resign, do they? But I did. I then fulfilled the requirements of the new law and registered with the conscription board. I informed them that I was a conscientious objector and skipped over here before I could be rounded up and put to hard, if worthwhile, labour on some sugarbeet farm in Suffolk."

"You sound awfully damned breezy about it. I never knew you to have strong religious beliefs."

"I don't, but I do have strong, conscientious objections to this war. I consider it to be a foul joke played on mankind. A monstrous deceit. I used to read the battle reports sent in code from Haig's H.Q. It amused me to see how the newspapers elevated the capture of a trench into a major victory. It did not amuse me to read how many lives were squandered for possession of the muddy ditch. I've decided to try and do something about it by publishing a newspaper which will print the unvarnished, unglamorised truth."

Martin whistled softly between his teeth and groped in the pocket of his robe for a cigar.

"You won't get away with it. They close down pacifist newspapers all the time, here and in England."

"I know that, but this won't be a shrill broadside crudely printed on a hand press and tossed around in the streets by young anarchists. This paper will be as sober as the *London Gazette* and as well written as *The Times*. No one who reads it will be able either to dismiss or ignore it. It will contain articles of such documented authenticity that readers will demand enquiries from Parliament or the Chamber of Deputies. It will be published in English and French, by the way. And as for being closed down, once the paper has reached a wide readership, doing so might cause more of a furore than permitting its existence." He scowled slightly and tugged at one ear. "Of course, reaching that readership might be difficult. The initial distribution will be a problem that I have to solve."

"You might solve yourself right into big trouble, for sedition in France, for which you could be shot, and for violations of the Defence of the Realm Act in England, which could land you in the pokey for the rest of the war – fifty years, the way things are going. I'd think twice about this if I were you, Jacob."

"I've thought a thousand times about it. My mind is made up – calm, cool, aware of all dangers – but also aware of the rewards. If I can cause just one person to stop singing "Rule, Britannia" or the "Marseillaise" every time they read an official communiqué from the front, and to begin thinking about this war, to truly ponder the cost of this insanity, then going to gaol would be a pleasure."

"And you want some articles from me, is that what brought you here, Jacob?"

"Yes and no. Yes, I want some articles, unsigned of course, and no, I didn't come just to mine your experiences. I need a quiet place to stay for a while and I value your company."

"I value yours, Jacob, and your friendship. I wouldn't be much of a friend if I encouraged you in this idea. You know, the cost of the Somme offensive has been pretty much tallied up. England lost four hundred thousand men there in four and a half months; nearly half a million dead, wounded or missing for six miles of ground. People want something for that price, Jacob. That's why they believe the official reports that tell them it was worth it, that something great was accomplished there, that the sacrifice had meaning. They'll only reject the truth because it's too damned painful to swallow. No one can stop this war; certainly public opinion won't. It has a life of its own now, like some runaway locomotive. Only one side or the other caving in will stop it. Only victory with a fat capital V will stop it. You're just crying in the wind with this newspaper of yours."

Jacob stood up with a sigh and stretched his arms above his head.

"I surrender to your logic, Martin. I know you're right, but I enjoy crying in the wind on the off-chance that I might just be heard. No, I'll put out a paper and it'll be a damned good one."

"So Jacob the iconoclast has finally found a cause to believe in?"

Jacob clenched his hands behind his back and walked over to

one of the windows. The neatly trimmed hedges in the garden were white with frost.

"Only partially, Martin. There's a side of me that just enjoys running the wrong way in crowds, another side that wants passionately to do something in life that has lasting value. Perhaps I was born to lead an army of pacifists. Perhaps not. I shall soon find out. Now then, to more immediate concerns. Where is this pantry of yours and how good's the champagne?"

Madame Lucille of the *Croix Rouge* was a woman of many objections and not afraid to voice any of them. She objected to visitors, let alone guests, and she objected to the consumption of spirits, the smoking of cigars and cigarettes and the letting in of fresh air. She also objected to Martin's objections to the food that was served him. Martin had hired a cook-housekeeper who had been recommended by the mayor of St. Germain for her gastronomic skills, but he had yet to see any of her cooking except gruel, a watery barley soup and plain boiled chicken. When he demanded that a couple of ducks be roasted, along with potatoes, to celebrate his guest's arrival, Madame Lucille declared that she could no longer be responsible for the health of her patient.

"Good," Martin said, "that's fine with me. Goodbye." And that was that.

"What are you going to do for nursing care?" Jacob asked as he carved the ducks.

"Hell, I don't really need nursing care. I get around okay, and the wound on my hip may look as ugly as sin but it's healed. What I need is strength; roast duck, roast lamb, mutton chops, pork chops, ham and eggs, a litre or two of burgundy and ten good cigars a day. Anyway, I've got a nurse coming to see me in about a week when she gets her leave. Army nurse. You remember her – Ivy Thaxton, you met her at the flat in London a couple of times."

"Slender, dark-haired girl with violet eyes?"

"That's the one."

"Not my type. Too fresh and virginal."

"That's because she is virginal, not like the flappers you race after."

Jacob raised an eyebrow and carved the breast. "Flappers? Right up to date with your slang, aren't you?"

"I keep up with the language. It's my job."

"Is she going to spend her leave here?"

"I'm going to do my best to talk her into it."

"Ah."

"What the hell does 'ah' mean?"

"'Ah' means 'ah'. In this case it means I'll move into that inn down the road while she's here. Three, old boy, is a crowd – although not always to the French."

She arrived four days before Christmas, on the morning train from Rouen to Paris, walking the three kilometres from the station to the house, her leather carrying bag slung over one shoulder. Martin, watching for her through the drawing-room windows, came out to meet her on the path, walking stiffly with two canes, concealing the pain in his hip with a gritted-teeth grimace. Jacob stood a step behind him, ready to catch his friend should he stumble.

"Why didn't you take a taxi?" Martin called out. "You shouldn't have walked."

"I love to walk!" Ivy shouted as she came down the long gravel path from the tree-lined road. "And it was only a mile or two." She stopped in front of him, smiling, brushing a strand of black hair from her forehead. "Oh, my, look at you, the wounded warrior."

"Just a shell-scratched scribe," Martin said. He looked her up and down, forgetting the pain in his hip at the sight of her. "Gosh, but you're a tonic, Ivy. Do you remember Jacob?"

"Oh, yes," she said, holding out her hand. "How are you, Mr. Golden?"

"Jacob," he corrected. "Only my enemies call me Mr. Golden. Let me take your bag while you help this Boswell of the Somme back to his sofa."

Ivy wandered about the house while the cook prepared lunch. She looked at everything in silent wonder and then sat in a chair next to the couch where Martin half reclined, his legs propped up on a pillow.

"It's a beautiful house, Martin."

411

"I've never seen the upstairs. Not worth the pain of climbing up there."

"Don't tell me you sleep on the couch?"

"There's a small room off the hall with a bed in it and a kind of trapeze bar above it so I can lift myself in and out without any trouble."

"You didn't leave the hospital too soon, did you?"

"No. And anyway, they needed the bed. They had cases in the hallways on cots."

She stood up and held out her hands to him. "Come on, up you get. I want you on the bed with your trousers down."

"What?"

"You heard me. I want to take a look at your wound."

"It's okay," he protested. "Coming along just fine. A surgeon from Harvard – American volunteer group – did the operation. Good man."

"Well, he's not here to examine it, is he? Do as you're told, please."

He led the way into the bedroom, lay on the bed and glowered at the ceiling as Ivy took down his trousers. The red weal traversed the right hip and dipped down across the upper thigh so there was no question of trying to cover anything. He closed his eyes and clenched his jaw as her gentle fingers traced the scar.

"No inflammation," she said. "You're a lucky man, Martin. You missed emasculation by an inch."

"I know," he said thickly.

"Do you have any unguent? It looks puckered and must itch badly."

"I itch all over."

"You do?" She ran her hand with professional sureness across his belly. "Odd. Your skin doesn't feel dry."

"It's not my skin, Ivy. I sort of itch inside. A visceral burning. It's called 'yearning for Ivy Thaxton disease' and it's curable."

"Where's the unguent?" she asked crisply. He told her where to find it, and she rubbed the yellow ointment into the edges of the scar and then stepped back. "You can pull up your trousers now."

He did so gratefully, letting his breath out through his mouth.

"This is a hell of a time to propose, Ivy, but I wish you'd reconsider the whole thing. Look at it from my point of view. I wouldn't expect you to quit the nurse corps any more than you'd expect me to give up reporting the war, but, I mean, you do have two weeks of leave, and two weeks of happiness isn't a bad deal in these times. Anyway, I only ask you to give it some thought, weigh it up, examine all the angles."

"I made up my mind when I wrote to you last week. It wasn't an easy decision to reach."

"Oh," he said, his tone hollow, "I guess not."

"But if you really *want* to take on the obligation of having a wife – "

The trapeze bar clanged as his hands gripped it. "Oh, boy, do I!" He pulled himself upwards, shouting for Jacob.

"What's the commotion?" Jacob asked, peering around the edge of the door. "The girl assaulting you?"

"Call for a taxi! Alert the mayor that he's got a wedding to perform!"

"Congratulations. And now you know what 'ah' means. I'll walk down to the inn and see if there's a car there. The telephone's on the fritz."

"We'll all go," Martin said, easing his legs off the bed. "There's a wheelchair in the hall closet and it's downhill all the way. Come on, Jacob, don't just stand there!"

"Impetuous rascal, aren't you?"

"Will it be legal?" Ivy asked, looking worried.

"Of course it's legal! What kind of a guy do you take me for? *Monsieur le Maire* can marry anyone, like a ship's captain. We can always have a church ceremony one day, Ivy, if you'd like that."

She leaned forward and kissed him on the cheek. "I don't care, Martin, just so long as I can write to Mum and Da with a clear conscience."

There was no car at the inn, but there was also no lack of strong backs willing to push *le bon Americain* into St. Germain, especially for such a purpose. Bride and best man walked beside the chair as two stablehands pushed Martin at a brisk pace down the centre of the road and into town. After a brief ceremony in the lobby of the town hall, the mayor drove them back to the house in his wheezing Renault.

"I am happy," Martin sighed. "Drunk with joy."

"And champagne."

"'Fill every glass, for wine inspires us, and fires us with courage, love and joy . . .' *The Beggar's Opera*. There's more to it – something about women being the most desirous things on earth. But only one woman, Ivy."

She sat beside him on the bed in her army-issue nightgown, plaiting her hair into braids. He reached out, brushed her hands away, and began to loosen the neat coils.

"I like your hair long and loose. You're very beautiful, Mrs. Rilke."

"And a bit drab looking. I never imagined I'd spend my wedding night in a flannel shift with the initials of Queen Alexandra's Imperial Military Nursing Service embroidered on the hem."

"I'll buy you a dozen silk gowns tomorrow. They say there are some fine shops in St. Germain. Or we'll go into Paris – shop, then spend the night in the best suite at the Crillon."

"Hush now. We're in our own house. What could be better than that?"

She stood up and blew out the lamps.

"Sorry about the electricity," he said, "but we get none after eight at night. Power shortage."

"There was a permanent power shortage in my home. I like lamps."

She moved around the bed in the darkness and after a moment slipped in beside him. The flannel gown was gone and her body was cool and fragrant beside him. He attempted to turn towards her, but let out a groan and lay back.

"Damn the Boche," he muttered.

"Shush," she whispered. "No bad thoughts. If you hadn't been hit by a shell, you might be in China now, or Mesopotamia, or some other far-off place, and not lying beside me." She undid his pyjamas and rested her head against his chest. "Your heart's a trifle fast."

"A trifle? It's trying to hammer its way through my ribs."

"And your breath is shallow."

"It's a wonder I can breathe at all. If you only knew what I'm going through right now. I was a fool to marry you until I was capable of doing handstands, and jumping fences, and . . . Well, lots of other things."

She burrowed closer to him.

"You can hold me, Martin. Hold me very tightly."

"Sure," he said thickly. "Sure I can." He folded his arms about her, his hands gliding up and down. "Velvet, pure velvet; the most wonderful body on earth."

"All Norwich girls have good bodies."

"Gosh," he whispered, "what a place that must be if they're half as wonderful as yours."

"Oh," she said, "I didn't measure up, that's why they chucked me out. I shall never take you to Norwich to see the women they kept."

"God, but I love you, Ivy."

She sat up, her body slender and as pale as ivory in the moonlight.

"Will you mind terribly if I discard maidenly modesty, but there's no point in our pining away if we don't have to. I mean to say, I *am* a nurse, so if you will just move your good leg – your left leg – as far to the side as you can . . ."

"Is this going to hurt?"

"I'm supposed to ask that, Martin, not you. No, it won't hurt a bit if you keep your right leg very, very still. And I shall just shift my left leg, like this, and raise up a bit, and . . . and . . ."

"Oh, Ivy! God! You're a wonder. You're . . ."

"No! Please, Martin, don't say anything. Don't say a word."

Jacob cut a small pine tree and dragged it through the snow, the first real snowfall of the winter; soft, wet flakes drifting from the grey sky. Ivy helped him to get it into the house and set the sap-dripping trunk into a wooden keg filled with sandy soil. They decorated the branches with whatever bright ornaments they could find: strips of red and yellow cloth, tiny silver teaspoons tied on with thread, holly berries from a bush in the garden, tin foil from cigarettes.

"A quite acceptable tree," Jacob said.

"I think it's beautiful. If we had some tiny candles to place on the branches . . ."

"We could burn the house down."

"Yes," she sighed. "I suppose you're right." She glanced at the mantel clock. "I'll wake Martin from his nap. He'll be ever so surprised."

"Let him sleep a bit longer. He's a lucky man having you to wake up to."

"Thank you, Jacob. That was a nice thing to say."

"I mean it sincerely. Tell me, Ivy, do you know about me?"

"Your being a pacifist, you mean? Yes, Martin told me."

"I hope you don't despise me for it."

"Despise you?" She smiled bitterly. "I've had two full years of seeing what war does to men. There are no sabre-rattlers in the medical services, Jacob, and no enemies. We treat a German's pain the same as an Englishman's. There hasn't been a night when I haven't prayed that the war would be over when I woke in the morning. I don't know very much about politics, or the balance of power, or any of those things, but I do know the terror a man feels when he comes out of the ether and realises his legs are gone. God in heaven, Jacob, how could I despise you?"

"Thank you." He bent down and kissed her on the forehead. "Merry Christmas, Ivy."

Observations and reflections. The House. January 2nd, 1917. The House, *our* House. My present to Ivy. Gerard Dupont drove out from Paris in his limousine and we signed the papers in the drawing room. M. Dupont casting uneasy glances towards the windows, expecting to see German infantry emerge from the woods before he had my cheque in hand. The price for house and two acres of land is ridiculously low, but Dupont is more than happy with the deal. He views the Allied line from Arras to Rheims as a sheet of glass about to be hit by an iron Teuton fist. Snow is thick on the ground, but M. Dupont remembers that the German hordes struck at Verdun in the dead of winter. "I shall be leaving for Geneva in a day or two," M. Dupont says. "For my health." I feel sure that, win or lose, M. Dupont will survive the war with all his assets intact.

January 6th. I was able today to mount the stairs with no problem – except spasms of intense pain which I stoically ignored. Two fine bedrooms upstairs, one room empty, the other partially furnished. I sat down on the bed to ease my leg and Ivy sat beside me. We made love, she protesting at first that making love in the middle of the day is wicked. Pale sun through large windows. Is there anything more lovely than her body tinged with such a light? If there is, I'll take an option on it, as Uncle Paul would say. Silent, reflective exhaustion afterwards. How fragile we are naked. Distant thunder growled and bumped along the horizon making us both think of the Somme barrage. Had we been lying here between July and November it might well have been the guns we heard, but the Somme battles are bogged down in mud, snow and freezing rain, the armies more exhausted than spent lovers could ever hope to be. Still, the sound was sobering. She goes back to Rouen tomorrow for reassignment, most probably to All Souls in London – which is how my luck runs. Still, I'll be able to wangle a trip to Blighty every month or so and we can use Jacob's flat. I know now what Sherman meant when he said war was hell.

Major Charles Amberley studied the lists placed on his desk by the adjutant. The names of the living and the names of the dead. Few of the names were familiar to him. The battalion had received far too many replacements for that. Names without faces: Jenkins, A. P.; Johns, D. R.; Johns, L.; Johnson, R.

> Roster – 2nd Royal Windsor Fusiliers
> Duty strength, July 18th, 1916
> Officers 36   Other ranks 1005
> Duty strength to date: January 3rd, 1917
> Officers 8   Other ranks 325

He signed his name on the bottom of the typewritten sheet: Maj. The Lord Amberley (Acting Colonel).

"And that's that, I suppose."

"All correct and properly executed," the adjutant said as he retrieved the lists.

"What happens now?"

"I send this to brigade who will send it to corps who will pop it up to Fourth Army who will in turn flip it along to the War Office. Sometime between now and spring we'll be fleshed out. Rather like ordering so many links of sausage from the butcher's shop."

The allusion seemed appropriate. Sausages to be fed into some future sausage-mincer. Charles stood up and looked out of the window. The village of Guyencourt-sur-Noye lay beyond the ice-rimed glass, its narrow, cobblestoned street meandering down to the frozen river and a wooden bridge. What was left of the Second Battalion was billeted in the houses and barns. An exhausted unit licking its wounds and waiting for replacements before being sent back up the line. The barns where most of the men had their billets were far from warm, but they were infinitely cosier than the freezing mud of the Somme trenches. Food was good and plentiful and there was an *estaminet* in the village that served wine and beer at a fair price. For the officers, Amiens with its bars, restaurants and brothels was only ten miles up the road. Yes, life was sweet in Guyencourt-sur-Noye, not that it mattered to Charles. His leave papers were in his pocket. The signing of the roster was his last official act. The new battalion commander, a lieutenant-colonel, would be arriving from St. Omer in a day or two.

"Well, Charles," the adjutant said, holding out his hand. "You did a bloody fine job."

And that was that. Lorry to Amiens, train to Rouen, leave boat to Southampton, train to London. Twenty-four hours after shaking the adjutant's hand he was walking through Waterloo Station with a thousand other men back in Blighty on leave, carrying his own kit bag, just one with the khaki mob.

"Charles! Charles!"

Her voice was thin against the clatter of hobnail boots. He

had almost forgotten that he had written to her, certainly hadn't expected her to meet him at the station, but there she was, beautiful in dark furs, waving to him from the far end of the platform.

"Hallo, Lydia."

"Charles." She bent slightly towards him and kissed him on the cheek. He put down his kit bag, took her firmly in his arms and kissed her on the mouth – a hard, lingering kiss.

"That's the way, ol' sport," a passing sergeant called out.

"Yes," Lydia murmured when he released her. "It is." She touched his face with a gloved hand. "It's good to have you back, Charles."

"And it's good to be here."

"I didn't tell Hanna and your father. Felt you wished to surprise them or you would have written to them."

"One letter was all I could manage. But, yes, it might be nice to just walk in."

She was looking at him oddly. "Are you all right?"

"I'm fine. Not a scratch."

He couldn't tell her how he felt because he couldn't explain how he felt; disembodied, as though he were two people walking side by side. Flesh and shadow and difficult to know which of the two was *him*.

"Do you want to go to Park Lane now and see them?"

"No," he said. "I'm horribly dirty. I'd like to go home, take a hot bath and get to bed."

She gave his hand a squeeze. "Whatever you want, Charles."

Odd. The house seemed alien to him. A stranger's house. He was afraid to touch anything. It was all too clean, too fragile. Tables gleamed with polish. Silver sparkled in the late afternoon sunshine. His bath was drawn by a maid he could not remember ever having met, although she seemed to know him and was obviously pleased to see him again.

"So nice to have you back, m'lord."

Back where?

The bath was warm and pleasantly scented with crystals. He sat tautly in its steamy murk and ran his hands lightly across the surface of the water. He felt disembodied and sat in the tub until the water turned chill and he could hear Lydia tapping at the bathroom door and calling his name.

"Charles? Are you all right, Charles?"

"Perfectly," he said in a flat, tired voice.

The palest of light filtered through heavy silk curtains and glowed against the cream-coloured walls of the bedroom. He was not there. He was floating off in some vast distance of time and space. Silent shell bursts crawled through a wasteland of pollarded trees. A man writhed against ripped sandbags, mouthing screams. The naked woman on the bed writhed as well, head twisting on the pillow. He was above it all. Serene. An impassive watcher. He felt nothing, neither pleasure nor pain. Beyond feelings of any sort. No room for frenzy. One must remain calm at all costs. The woman clutched at his back as the shadows of the second platoon slipped through curtains of rain. They became lost to view, then re-emerged beyond the wire. Half a dozen bent figures.

Christ! Where's the rest of them?

Whose voice was that, he wondered? It hardly mattered. They were dead, of course. Foolish of the chap to have even asked.

"Lovely," Lydia whispered against his cheek. "Not the old Charles."

"No," he said stonily. "Not quite the same."

Watching his father made him think of the parable of the prodigal son, a roast sirloin of beef being a fitting substitute for a fatted calf. The earl carved the meat to perfection and Coatsworth served. Not his job in the old days, but the servant problem was acute, a condition that seemed to dominate the conversation.

"I really don't know what we'll do, Charles," Hanna said. "We're one of the last houses on the street which is still a private residence. The Prescotts donated their house to a branch of the War Ministry, and Lord Doncannon gave up his place to the Red Cross. It's becoming quite impossible to maintain and I expect we'll have to move into a flat."

"Nonsense!" Lord Stanmore growled.

"I quite agree," Lydia said. "That is nonsense, Hanna. I

know I can find you a perfect little house near Regent's Park that would suit you."

"Alex not home?" Charles asked, just to change the subject.

His father paused in his carving to swipe the knife against the steel.

"No. Decided to spend her leave in Paris. Can't for the life of me understand why."

"And William? Still at Eton?"

Hanna laughed nervously. "Good heavens no, Charles."

"The lad's eighteen," the earl said. "Training with the Public Schools' Battalion. He gets passed out as a second lieutenant next week."

"Difficult to believe," Charles said as Coatsworth bent forward to serve him. The slices of beef sent rivulets of scarlet juice across the white plate.

His mother seemed to be sending signals to him, and so when she excused herself right after dinner, complaining of a sudden headache, he dutifully escorted her up to her room.

"Headache better?" he asked as he closed her door behind him.

"Much." She faced him, her face pale and drawn. "May I be blunt, Charles?"

"By all means."

"William has become a terrible concern to me."

"Being in the army, you mean?"

"I can understand his anxiety to join up. He's big, strong, fiercely patriotic. He was in the Eton Boys' Brigade last term, and the term before that, I believe. All of his friends joined up as well, all with the same excessive impetuosity to serve their country. I can't fault that, can I?"

"No." He thought of young Baker waving his pistol. Second Lieutenant Owen Ralston Baker. In hospital now. Both eyes blown out by the same shell that had ripped poor Martin's hip. "It's becoming a boy's war now, Mother."

Her hand darted to her throat, fingers worrying a string of jet beads.

"William is such a superb horseman, as you know. It would please your father and me if he took a commission in the Queen's Bays, the Second Dragoon Guards. One was offered."

"Oh."

"That's all you can say?" she asked sharply. "*Oh?*"

"Oh is simply an interjection, Mother. It gives me time to think. Naturally he turned the offer down."

"Why *naturally?* It's one of the most prestigious regiments in the army."

"If this were the Boer War he'd jump at it, but the cavalry is something of a joke in France. All dressed up and nowhere to go. His refusal to join the Bays is understandable. He's a true Stanmore."

"If . . . if he were *ordered* into the regiment . . ."

"As I was *ordered* into N.S. 5?" He smiled and shook his head. "It won't work, Mother. You and Lydia should know better."

"What has Lydia got to do with it?" she asked cautiously.

"You know perfectly well what Lydia has to do with it, mother. Lydia has *entrée*. Now more than ever with Lloyd George in Downing Street, Archie Minister of War Production and David Langham as . . . what? The grey eminence? I'm sure Lydia could get Willie posted to the Dragoons – ordered, if you will – but he'd only slip out of it."

"How could he slip out of a direct order?"

"By resigning his commission and then re-enlisting as a private in an infantry regiment. He'd be commissioned by that regiment the same day. The infantry is starved of young subalterns after the Somme. Officers with fighting spirit are ducking out of the cavalry every day using that dodge."

Hanna's laugh was like a wail. "Fighting spirit! I think William is too young to have *fighting spirit*. He thinks the war is some sort of game, like a rugby match!"

"Football," Charles said blandly. "Quite a few chaps kicked footballs towards the German lines when they went across. They were shot down, of course. Germans are such poor sports."

"Don't be so glib!" she hissed.

"Am I being glib, Mother? I'm sorry. But we must all take our chances. There's no room for cowardice in the British army."

The fervidity of his tone surprised him.

*

The cocktail party had become firmly entrenched as a London social custom, replacing afternoon tea. There were those who claimed that the cocktail party had been invented by Lydia Amberley. Not true, London's leading light comedy actor remarked. It was simply that Lydia had raised the rather barbaric custom to a fine art. The house in Bristol Mews sparkled from sunset to early evening with bright and brittle conversation, or huddled, serious talk among huddled, serious men – the conversational gamut depending on which circle of Lydia's friends one happened to drift in upon. Charles found all of the talk boring. He stood apart from the crowd, barely touching the contents of his cocktail glass and let the verbiage wash over him the way waves wash over a rock in the sea.

A woman with an ample bosom, only partially concealed by the latest style in gowns, came up to him and said, "I understand from Ivor Novello that you've seen a good deal of the fighting in Picardy."

And he said matter-of-factly, "You know, the first thing that strikes one about the front is the almost overpowering stench of human faeces. It's the shells, you see. Men tend to become terribly constipated – for a variety of reasons – and then when they're hit by a shell all of that *accumulation* simply bursts forth and is scattered everywhere. It's more pronounced in summer, but that stands to reason. Does it not?"

"What on earth did you say to Lady Beaumont?" Lydia asked with a frown.

"Who? I haven't said a word to anyone all night."

"She feels insulted."

"Does she? How curious."

And there was David Langham speaking to two admirals and the First Lord of the Admiralty.

"Haig is certainly aware of this U-boat problem. He would like to break out of the Ypres salient and smash for the Channel ports, past Langemarck and Passchendaele to Bruges, cutting off Ostende and Zeebrugge. He smells victory in that direction sometime this summer."

"Only if the wind is in the proper direction," Charles said.

He felt the sensation very strongly while walking down Regent

Street. It was morning, shopkeepers opening their shutters, the day bright and clear. Brisk, cold wind. Patches of snow in the street, dirty grey piles in the gutters. He walked slowly until he came to Conduit Street before daring to stop and look back. No one was behind him, and yet he could have sworn that had not been the case since turning into Regent Street from Hanover Square. Someone had been following him step for step, practically at his elbow. And yet that was clearly impossible. Odd. Shadow and substance. Which was which? He lit a cigarette and blew a stream of smoke into the wind, standing on the corner of Conduit Street until he had finished it, then crushing the butt under his foot. He continued walking, more quickly than before and he was quite alone this time. Just Charles Amberley in uniform, his Burberry trench coat well buttoned up against the wind. He turned sharply, a drill turn, pivoting on the heel of the right foot, into Burlington Street and then into Savile Row. In the window of one shop he spotted a small, neatly printed sign which read: OFFICERS' TRENCH ACCESSORIES ALSO SOLD. He went in, the door ringing a copper bell as he opened it. It was a uniform shop primarily and several young men were standing about in various stages of their fittings. One sat astride an elevated barrel which had been painted red and had a saddle fastened to it.

"Make sure the jacket doesn't blouse out."

"No fear of that, sir," the tailor said. "I can assure you."

He selected what he wanted from a display case and the clerk nodded his approval.

"A fine choice, if I may say so, sir. Would you also be interested in a truly first-rate trench compass?"

"I don't think so," Charles said.

"Or a guaranteed water- and moisture-proof matchbox."

"No. This will suffice. Thank you for your patience."

"No trouble at all, major. We are here to serve."

"Quite so. As is everyone in these times."

He swung on to a bus leaving Piccadilly Circus for Southwark – Battersea – Clapham Junction – Wimbledon. He got out at the end of the line and walked to Wimbledon Common, towards neat rows of canvas-roofed wooden and tarpaper huts. A wooden gate barred the path, a sentry from the Public

Schools' Battalion standing beside it with rifle and fixed bayonet. The man presented arms and Charles walked around the gate, which was no more than a symbolic barrier to traffic, and on into the camp.

"Dashed nice of you to drop in, major," the second in command said, leaning back against his desk. "I believe we met at Albert last August."

"Perhaps. There was a Public Schools' Battalion at High Wood."

"Yes, but we're primarily a training unit now. Our lads are being posted to any number of regiments."

Charles looked out of the window of the hut. He could see the drilling ground, squads of men marching in lines, a group of men far away at the old cricket grounds spearing straw dummies with bayonets.

"The training looks efficient."

"We turn out first-rate infantry subalterns, a credit to any regiment they join."

"Where will my brother be sent?"

The second in command, also a major, rubbed the side of his ear with his thumb.

"Well, a sticky situation, don't you know. Been ordered to the Dragoons, but refuses to go. Wants to join the Fifth Bedfords in trenches near Arras." The man chuckled. "And he'll do it, too. Young William has a mind of his own."

"Yes, he does. I bought him something useful to have in the trenches."

"Dashed good of you. He'll be along shortly. By the way, perhaps you'd like to give the lads a bit of a talk after mess. They've all heard my tales of the Somme any number of times. Another view of the show might be refreshing."

There was a crisp knock on the door and then William stepped into the hut, his boots and puttees covered with mud. He saluted his own major smartly and then grinned at Charles.

"Major Lord Amberley, sir!"

"Hallo, Willie," Charles said. "There's something I want you to have."

The duty clerks and the O.O.D. heard the quick splatter of shots and burst into the room from the outer office. Acrid blue

425

smoke hung in spirals, drifting down towards the figure writhing on the floor, clutching a bullet-splintered knee. They hurled themselves on the trenchcoated man holding a pocket pistol and bore him down across the top of a desk. He did not offer any resistance as he let the gun fall from his hand.

"What in God's name did you do?" the second in command shouted, coming out of his momentary paralysis.

"I gave him a Blighty," Charles said calmly. "He didn't shoot himself . . . he didn't shoot himself."

6

THE RAIN HAD CEASED, BUT OMINOUS BANKS OF CLOUD OBSCURED the peaks of the Welsh mountains and slipped like dark smoke into the valleys. The crenellated façade of Llandinam War Hospital was shrouded in mist.

"Ugly-looking place," Fenton muttered as the driver of the car pulled up in front of the iron gates and called out to the gatekeeper.

Martin, seated beside Fenton in the back, leaned forward to peer through the windscreen.

"An old castle?"

"No, just some Victorian coal baron's idea of a fitting house for himself. Wales is littered with such monstrosities. All of them," he added bitterly, "eminently suitable as lunatic asylums."

The sprawling house became less forbidding when they drove up to it. The dark brickwork was mellowed by a sheen of ivy that covered many of the walls and the windowframes had been freshly painted white. The grounds were neatly pruned and mowed and the gravel drive freshly raked. It could have been the clubhouse of some ancient and noble golf club if it hadn't been for the ambulances and drab-coloured army cars parked in front of it.

"I shall wait for you, shall I?" the driver asked in a sing-song voice.

"Yes," Fenton said. "We want to catch the London train at Llangollen at six thirty."

"Oh, yes, sir, can be done, I think. If you have a mind to it."

"We do. I'm sure you can get a cup of tea if you can find the kitchens."

"Oh, yes, sir, I know my way about it, sir. I have been here before and that is the truth, sir."

"Nice little man," Martin said as he walked beside Fenton to

427

the front door, slowly, leaning on his cane – only one cane now, a major advance in his recovery.

"All the Welsh are pleasant, but independent as hell. I hope he remembers to wait for us."

The once-spacious foyer had been partitioned into cubicles for the use of the clerks and medical orderlies. A corporal in the R.A.M.C. took their names, asked them who they had come to visit and then led them out of the foyer, opened a thick, locked, security door and told them to go along the passage to the office of the resident doctor on duty. Once they stepped into the corridor the oak and steel door closed with a thud behind them.

"I don't like one damned thing about this," Fenton muttered.

Neither did Martin, but he refrained from saying so.

The doctor was a jovial, heavy-set man of fifty who introduced himself as Major Wainbearing. "Trained as a general surgeon, became a specialist in brain disease and then in psycho-analytic science, a field of medical endeavour barely scratched. Learning a great deal from this war, quite a gold mine of neurasthenic ailments . . ."

"It must be very interesting," Martin said.

"Yes, it is." Major Wainbearing leaned back in his comfortable chair in his spacious and pleasant office and smiled affably at the two men seated across from his desk. "Now, then, you are Mr. Rilke, I take it, Lord Amberley's cousin."

"Yes, that's right."

"And you, of course, are Colonel Wood-Lacy."

No reply seemed necessary. Fenton fingered one of his shoulder tabs, tried to smile pleasantly, but found it impossible to do so. The doctor folded his hands across his stomach and pursed his lips, a sudden frown appearing on his elderly cherub's face.

"Lord Amberley was brought here as a clearly diagnosed neurasthenic. He was passive, no restraint was needed, but he was hallucinating; deep in conversation with a certain Second Lieutenant Baker, a rambling monologue on Blighty wounds and firing squads. Are either of you familiar with a Lieutenant Baker?" They shook their heads. "No matter. He was soon out of that form of shock and quite normal within a week. He has remained so. We walked out of the grounds last Monday and played a round of golf at the links in Glyn-Ceiriog."

"How nice," Fenton murmured.

"He did damned well, considering the appalling state of the greens. On the way back we stopped at a place and had tea. I told him how pleased I was at his progress and that I was prepared to release him from here and to recommend a medical discharge from the army. Cured, you understand, but obviously too . . . *carefully* balanced to risk further military duties. I told him to go to some quiet spot and avoid stress of all sorts."

"Sound advice," Fenton said with thinly-veiled sarcasm.

"He told me, in his gentle way, that if I did such a thing he would contrive, in some unspecified manner, to kill himself."

A wall clock chimed three dulcet tones.

"Do you think he was being serious?" Martin asked.

"Oh, no doubt in my mind at all. Quite a number of patients talk of suicide, but they are mostly impassioned threats, verging on the hysterical. It is the quiet, lucid statement of intent that we become concerned about."

"Perhaps if we talk to him . . ." Fenton said.

"Yes, by all means do. He's been looking forward to your visit, the only two people he wishes to see. You know, his mother and his wife came here last month but he stayed in his room and refused to come down and talk to them." He reached out and pushed a button on his desk. "One of the orderlies will take you to him. He'll be in the rec room, more than likely. And do stay for tea. We have a wizard pastry chef here."

Men in grey dressing-gowns and pyjamas stood staring out of windows or walking aimlessly in the corridors. A few of the patients were in uniform, but the badges of their rank and emblems of their regiment had been removed.

"All officers here, I presume," Martin said.

"Quite correct, sir," the orderly replied. "The men have their own shell-shock hospitals."

Martin noticed a tall, grey-haired man who could easily have been a colonel or brigadier. He sat huddled in a corner with his hands firmly locked on top of his head. A younger man lay near him in a foetal position. Rank could mean nothing to those two, Martin thought, but class divisions had to be maintained no matter what the circumstances.

The rec room was large and airy with banks of windows on three sides. It might have been a ballroom or music conservatory at one time, but now it was an untidy collection of sofas, chairs, card tables and benches. A dozen men were in the room, the majority of them in uniform, reading or playing cards. One player's hands shook so violently that he could barely hold on to his cards.

"Lord Amberley is over there," the orderly said. "At the corner table."

He was in uniform, bent studiously over a writing tablet and did not look up until they walked up to the table and stood in front of him.

"Hallo, chaps," he said quietly. "Good of you both to come."

"The least we could do, old boy," Fenton said with forced affability.

"You look good, Charles," Martin said.

"I feel very well," he said gravely. "They say that I'm cured."

"Yes," Martin said. "The doctor was telling us."

"Of course, they don't say exactly what one has been cured *of*, but I suppose they know what they're talking about. They do some quite remarkable things here in their quiet way. All through the gentle art of conversation. One simply talks. It supposedly clears the mind."

Fenton pulled two chairs up to the table. "And now you may talk to us, if you'll permit me to get right to the point."

Charles capped his pen and set it down beside the writing pad.

"I'm sure you feel uncomfortable being here, Fenton."

"Not in the least," he said a little too quickly. "If I can help you in any way . . ."

"You can both help me, if you will." He sorted through some neatly-inscribed papers, folded two of the sheets and placed them in envelopes. "I wrote a long letter to my father, and one to William at Charing Cross Hospital. Both were sent back to me unopened. There's not much point in writing to William

430

again. I doubt if he will understand, or forgive, what I did. Perhaps he will one day, but not now. I've written a shorter, more concise, explanation to Father which I would appreciate your handing to him, Martin. He might feel obliged to at least open it if he receives it from you. The other letter is for Lydia, which you can post. It's an apology – of sorts – for all manner of things. But I shan't bore you with that. As for you, Fenton, I ask a favour."

"Anything at all, old chap."

Charles picked up the pen and toyed with it, rolling it across the table from hand to hand.

"I was committed without a hearing. The medical officer of Willie's battalion judged me unsound of mind and I was sent here. Now, six weeks later, I am to be released as cured, handed a medical discharge from His Majesty's Forces and put quietly out to pasture. I'm sure that will please the War Office. They're no more anxious to know why I shot Willie than my father is. The act of a temporary maniac. So be it."

Fenton leaned forward and folded his arms on the table. "I don't believe it was the act of a maniac and neither does anyone else, at least, no one who has been in trenches. You snapped with the strain, Charles. Too many bloody weeks of having to stay calm in that hell. It took its toll. You didn't know what you were doing and the very best course of action at the moment would be for you to accept a medical discharge and regain your full strength of mind."

"I have that now, Fenton. What I don't have is any *peace* of mind. I may not have been very lucid after I shot Willie, but I knew why I shot him. It was a deliberate, premeditated act, and I want the reasons for it to be made a matter of record, if not public, at least official."

"What sort of record are you talking about?"

"I've given this a lot of thought, Fenton, gone over it in my mind time and time again. I've been tracing my steps as it were, but backwards. The shooting of Willie in the knee, the buying of the pistol, the feeling that someone was walking just behind me, those weeks in trenches, in and out with the battalion, the men who shot themselves, or killed themselves or prayed they'd get shot so they could get out of that trap." He

431

paused and shook his head groggily. "So damned many thoughts whirling through my head that it's difficult to sort them all out in proper order, but I shall."

"Maybe you'd like to take a rest," Fenton suggested. "Lie down for a bit."

"No, not yet. I must settle this first. I'm sure that Martin understands the need to put experiences down on paper so others can read them and share them. That's the creed of a journalist, isn't it, Martin? Seeing to it that events are kept alive."

Martin exchanged a puzzled glance with Fenton and then said, "Are you asking me to write an article about it?"

"No, not exactly. That wouldn't suffice, would it? I mean to say, I doubt if many newspapers would want to print it. Too defeatist. And even if it were printed in some anti-war paper, what would happen after it was read? Yesterday's news, just an old scrap of newspaper blowing about in the gutters. What I want is a record, a transcript, the kind of transcript that you could provide, Fenton."

"Oh?" Fenton said. "And what sort of transcript is that?"

"Why, the official transcript of my court martial, of course, for maiming, quite literally, a brother officer."

Fenton could merely stare at him. Martin gripped his cane and tapped it gently against the floor. A tall, ruddy-faced man with a Kitchener moustache, who had been pacing restlessly from one end of the room to the other, suddenly strode up to the table, hands jammed into the pockets of his dressing-gown.

"Now look here, Randall," he shouted, staring hard at Charles. "Get brigade artillery on the blower right away. Tell the bastards that they're fifty yards short and are hitting D Company. Quite wasting the attack, quite wasting it, sir!"

"I'll do it right away, colonel," Charles said in a flat, tired voice.

"See that you do!" the man said. "Bloody skrimshankers!"

"We get a lot of that here," Charles said after the man had strolled away, apparently satisfied and at peace. "There's a young chap in my room, a second lieutenant, I imagine, judging by his age. Spends most of his time seated on his bed with the cover thrown over his head. Still in his dug-out at Delville

Wood and won't come out until the shelling stops. Not much older than William. Only thing is, Fenton, Willie would never have broken down. Too strong and brave for that. The best sort of man England can produce. Willie would have gone over the top like a shot, whistle in mouth and revolver in hand. He might have cleared our wire, gone ten, perhaps fifteen yards and then died, for absolutely no purpose at all, just like Roger."

Fenton licked dry lips, reached out and gripped Charles by the wrist.

"Tell all that to Martin. Tell him everything that went through your mind before you pulled the trigger. Tell him everything that happened on the Somme, every damned horror that drove you to scuppering your own brother. He'll send it to America and a newspaper will print it. That's the only record you need. Don't ask for a court martial because you'll never get it."

Charles shook his head stubbornly. "I'd get a hearing, at least, wouldn't I? A hearing to see if a court martial was justified. They would keep a transcript of it: War Office document number whatever, enquiry into the shooting of Second Lieutenant William Greville by Major Lord Amberley. One day, after the war, Willie could take it out of the archives and read it."

Fenton withdrew his hand and sat back stiffly in his chair.

"I think you're bonkers, Charles. A man can't ask for his own court martial."

"No," Charles said, "of course not, but you could demand that one should be held. I told you I'd thought this out. It may be stretching a legal point, but you were technically my superior officer at the time. I was on leave and my new orders hadn't reached me yet. The Windsors were attached to your brigade."

A bell rang for tea and someone in the room cried out in terror, "Gas! Gas!" Someone else said soothingly, "It's all right, Smithy, all right, lad."

"It happens every time they ring that bloody bell," Charles sighed. "I do wish they'd install something less strident."

"Now look here, Charles," Fenton said firmly. "The brass

aren't fools. They'd know something was fishy if I put in such a request."

"Not request, Fenton, *demand*. You have that right and the Judge Advocate General's office would be forced to hold a hearing. I hate to sound like a barrack-room lawyer, but there it is. King's Regulations."

He looked pleased with himself and Fenton's scowl deepened.

"You want a forum. That's it, isn't it, Charles? You just want to stand up before a panel and a shorthand clerk and voice your outrage at what went on over there."

"At what's still going on," Charles said, so quietly they could barely hear him. "And will continue to go on, and on, and on. Yes. That is precisely what I want." He folded his hands, the fingers as white as the writing paper they rested on.

"Christ," Fenton said, pushing back his chair and standing up. "You're asking a lot of me."

"Yes."

"As a soldier I should turn you down flat, but I'm more than that, aren't I? I'm your friend. This won't change a damned thing. It's just a gesture that no one is going to appreciate, but if it will give you some kind of peace then I'll do it."

"Thank you," Charles said, staring at his hands. "I knew you wouldn't let me down."

Fenton sat in brooding silence during the ride to the railway station at Llangollen. It had started raining again and the dark hills and crags of North Wales looked sinister in the gloom. They barely caught the London-bound train as it stopped briefly on its run from Holyhead. The carriages were filled with Irish troops from County Down and Antrim, most of them sporting bits of orange cloth in their hatbands to show their contempt for the "wearin' o' the green". They were all in boisterous spirits. Out of training camp at last, heading for the war, "Look out Kay-zer Bill!"

"Bloody idiots," Fenton muttered as he slumped into a seat in a virtually empty first-class compartment. An Irish colonel and his adjutant were the only other occupants and the colonel glanced up curiously from a newspaper.

434

"Did you address me, sir?"

"No, sir, I did not. I was discussing the weather with my friend."

"Yes. A man can drown in Wales when it rains. And the Taffies have the gall to say Belfast is wet!"

"I suppose you had no choice," Martin said quietly after the Irish colonel had turned back to his paper. "He obviously has a fixation about this court martial thing and if you had turned him down . . ."

"He might have killed himself. That thought had some slight effect on my decision!"

"What happens now?"

Fenton drummed his fingers on the window ledge and stared at his own reflection in the rain-streaked glass.

"I send in my *demand* through the proper channels and a hearing date will be set. Before that happens there will be a few gentlemanly calls from various staff brigadiers in Whitehall, asking me to reconsider my actions. I shall decline to do so on the grounds that I consider the shooting of one officer by another bad form. There will be a hearing and Charles will be permitted to talk for as long as he wishes in order to explain, justify or defend his act. The panel will then deliberate for a second or two and rule that no court martial is warranted because of the mental condition of the accused. Charles will then be sent back to the hospital and quietly discharged from the service. Rather a waste of everyone's time, isn't it?"

"Reading about this frog general in the *Standard*," the Irish colonel said, looking up. "Nivelle, hero of Verdun, they call him. Claims to have a plan that'll crush Fritz in twenty-four hours. Twenty-four years is more like it. The poor sod." He turned pages and immersed himself in the sporting news.

"And the war goes on," Fenton said wearily. "I'm glad Charles is out of it."

"But he isn't out of it, is he? It's all spinning around in his brain. You were right in saying that he's seeking some kind of peace, and if this hearing will give it to him it won't be a waste of *everyone's* time."

"No, I suppose you're right."

435

"Would they allow me to be there? Not as a member of the press, but as Charles's cousin?"

"No. They wouldn't allow God himself to attend. There'll be a panel of two or three officers, a shorthand clerk, Charles and myself. Charles could request council, what's known as a prisoner's friend, but that would have to be a fellow officer and he doesn't need one."

"Please write to me how it turns out, care of A.P., rue Chambord. Will you do that?"

"Of course. When are you going back to Paris?"

"Sometime tomorrow. As you said, the war goes on."

Wales had been corrosive to the spirit. So had writing up the request for a court martial. Both were behind Fenton now as he arrived at his mother's house in Suffolk where Winifred was staying. He found solace lying on the bed with her, his hands moving gently over the great bulge of her womb.

"We're going to have a forty-pound baby. I swear it."

"Twins," she said. "At least I think so. I'm sure I can feel two distinct pairs of kicks."

"Clever girl," he murmured, kissing the tautness of her skin. He could sense the life beating beneath the surface.

"Happy?"

"Yes."

"Do you want sons very badly?"

"I want children very badly, sons or daughters. I'll leave that up to you. Surprise me."

"Another few weeks."

"Must be pure hell for you."

"Not really. Just boring sitting around, and uncomfortable trying to walk. Your mother and Jinny wait on me hand and foot. I feel horribly pampered, like some grossly fecund queen bee. Do you think my body will ever get back into shape or will I always be nothing but breasts and belly?"

"I like breasts and bellies," he said, kissing both. "And I love you."

They clung tightly to each other as the March winds moaned across the river and hammered at the casement window.

"You haven't said a word about Charles," she said softly.

436

"There isn't a great deal to say. A sad man in a sad place. Just one more casualty of the Somme. Charles and four hundred thousand other men."

He didn't tell her about the request for the court martial, nor the fact that Charles had contemplated suicide. Winifred had enough to think about being with child and worrying about her brothers, John and Bramwell, who had gone through the Thiepval attacks and were now back in trenches near Arras.

"Does Lydia see him often?"

"I gather he doesn't want to see her or his mother. There's really nothing he wants to talk about except the war."

Nothing that he wanted to talk about less, but there was no escaping it. On the third morning home the telephone rang, a Brigadier Tydman ringing up from London.

"About this court martial request of yours for Lord Amberley. Sticky business, don't you know. Be much better all round if you reconsidered it."

"I can't do that, sir."

"Can't, eh? Rather delicate, to tell you the truth. Peer's son and all that. Chap went round the bend and plunked his own brother. Medical wallah of the Public Schools' Battalion did the proper thing, certified him mentally unsound and sent him right up to Llandinam Hospital. That kept the whole sad affair quiet, don't you know. No point in kicking sleeping dogs now, to use a figure of speech."

"I'm sorry, but I insist on a hearing."

"I see. Well, won't interfere with your rights as the lad's superior officer, although I strongly disapprove of your insistence. Rather harsh, I must say. Very well then. Hearing set for Thursday next at Llandinam, North Wales. Better than bringing the chap down to London for it."

"Make certain a shorthand clerk is along."

"We're quite capable of conducting a proper hearing," the brigadier said stiffly. "Good day, sir."

Paris. March 12th, 1917. Observations and reflections. Trying to catch up on this. Too damned busy writing personality pieces on General Nivelle, Petain and all the other new luminaries of the Fench army to pay much attention to

437

this journal. Papa Joffre of the big belly is out. Nivelle with his good looks, good English, good manners and boundless optimism is very firmly in. Every shoeshine boy in Paris knows what Nivelle has in mind, as, I imagine, does every shoeshine boy in Berlin. Keeping secrets is not an Allied military virtue. A million *poilus* along the Aisne preparing to lunge for the Chemin des Dames and burst through the Hindenburg defences like water through a dyke of sand. British to aid the offensive by striking around Arras. God help all of them.

Difficult even after ten days to write about Charles without experiencing a sinking feeling in the pit of the stomach. Shell shock. No two doctors seem to agree on the cause. French medical officer I met at Maxim's one night says that shell shock is caused by a partial vacuum created by a passing shell affecting the brain cells. I believe that it means being shocked, period. Shocked by too many corpses, too much pain, too many hopeless attacks. Too many days and nights of never-ending fear. Shock after shock until the mind can no longer take any more punishment and begins to turn in upon itself. Charles is a shell shock case. Too much sang froid for his own good. I know now what he was thinking when he stood on the parapet at High Wood and watched his men get slaughtered in the wire and among those nightmare trees. He was thinking the thoughts of the damned and keeping them bottled up inside. Something had to give in that noble head of his.

The Earl of Stanmore. More sang froid in action. I went to the house directly from the train, still damp from Wales.

"So, you saw Charles, did you?" he said when I handed him the letter. He opened the envelope and read the contents without blinking an eye.

"Thank you," he said, putting the letter in his pocket as though it were a bill from his tailor. I was invited to stay for a drink, but sensed it was merely a gesture of politeness and so I declined. Aunt Hanna is up in Derbyshire, where they have a small estate, looking after William who is recuperating there. And how is William, I ask. "He will never ride a horse properly for the rest of his life." Odd answer. Charles is in such a delicate mental balance he could end up not knowing a horse from a steamroller. Does Stanmore's attitude come with the blood? Cold and blue? Hard to say. May be no more than a pose. Bad form to reveal one's deepest emotions. The earl stands in his magnificent study overlooking Park Lane very much the way Charles stood on the top of his trench.

About fifteen minutes with Ivy in the main reception room of All Souls. Is it possible she's my wife? Hard to believe. We held hands in a room about the size of Victoria Station, filled with the relatives of wounded men. Simple-looking people. Londoners mostly. The "lower orders", as the earl would say. The Somme offensive has been over for four months, but the residue pack the wards. Eighteen-hour work shifts for the nurses, more for some of the surgeons. Over in Whitehall the lights burn as new offensives are planned. "Mum" and "Dad" wait patiently in the vaulted room to see their sons, bearing small gifts wrapped in newspaper . . .

"Assiduous diarist, aren't you, Martin?"

"Well," Martin said, glancing up at the bureau chief. "I like to scribble away. I find it relaxing."

"Care for a drink at the Café Bombe?"

"No. My hip's giving me hell. Must be the weather. I'll be able to predict rain till the day I die."

"Take a week off. Go up to that house of yours in St. Germaine and forget your troubles. I just got a cable from Atkinson. That piece you did on Petain, the Warrior Monk thing. First-rate reception. The *Atlantic* gobbled up the magazine rights. Congratulations. Your telephone work out there?"

"Sometimes."

"Well, if anything comes up I'll send the kid out to fetch you."

And so that was a break, Martin thought as he took the metro at Parc Monceau. He had had it up to the neck with interviewing generals and listening to all the theories on how the war could be won *rapidement*. At Louveciennes, troop trains rumbled north across the Seine, bearded *poilus* standing in the open doorways smoking their pipes. Impassive looking men. Veterans. The troops no longer waved and cheered from the trains as they had done during the first year of the war. But then no one was doing much cheering these days.

The house looked good to him, a place of his own, the deed signed, sealed and delivered. Rilke Manor. Seven rooms and a kitchen. The trees in the garden were barren and stalky, but they'd burst into greenery in the spring. The windows were tightly shuttered and a pale wisp of smoke rose from one of the chimneys.

"What the . . .?" He stood transfixed on the path and wondered if he should hurry down to the inn for help. But that seemed stupid. A housebreaker wouldn't light a fire. "Jacob," he muttered to himself. And when he unlocked the door there he was, standing in the hall looking sheepish.

"Now how in hell did you get in?"

"Penknife. Slipped it under a shutter."

"That's nice to know," Martin said irritably. "Why didn't you come by the office. I would have given you a key."

"Didn't have the time, old sport. Two beefy *flics* were right on my heels?"

"Detectives?"

Jacob nodded. His face was haggard and there were dark rings under his eyes.

"Sûreté Nationale. I came a cropper, Martin. Only two issues of the paper and every gendarme in Paris came pouring into the print shop busting heads with truncheons. I dived through a window without a sou in my pockets and legged it out."

"It was bound to happen sooner or later."

"One of the writers betrayed us." He ran his hands through his hair and smiled bitterly. "God almighty, never get mixed up with strident anti-war types. Not one damned thing you do pleases even one quarter of them. My particular Judas was an elderly anarchist who was furious with me for not devoting the first issue to a primer on how to assassinate politicians and generals. Not that I'm particularly against that sort of thing, you understand, but I thought it a bit thick for the first issue. Anyway, cutting a long story short, I'm on the run from a charge of sedition and this seemed the best place to hide."

"Stay as long as you like."

"I'll borrow some cash from you and try to get into Spain, or even go back to Blighty. At least they don't shoot you there for having different opinions."

Jacob moped around the house for two days, debating with himself whether to go to Madrid and put out another paper which might be smuggled into France, or to return to England and take his chances as a conscientious objector. His depression was palpable, a dark cloud following him from room to room. It was on the morning of the third day that Danny, the breezy New Yorker who was both the copy boy and general errand runner, arrived from Paris on his battered motorcycle. Along with a few letters and some articles for proofing, he carried a bulky package in his canvas knapsack.

"A Limey officer dropped this off at the office, Mr. Rilke. Said he was doing a favour for a Colonel Wood-Lacy and that it was to be given to you personal."

"Thanks, Danny. Anything new on the wires?"

"U-boats sank another American ship; Congress looks ripe for voting for war in a few weeks; and McGraw predicts the Giants will take the pennant this year."

"Good for McGraw. At least there's some sanity left in the world."

There was a letter attached to the brown paper parcel.

Dear Martin,

Enclosed is a copy of the transcript which I managed to get hold of. After reading it I think you will understand why I sent it to you. Charles's agonised reflections on the war deserve something more meaningful than a filing cabinet in Whitehall. Just what you can do with it in the light of the times I do not know, but I want you to have the ms. nonetheless.

The proceedings went just the way I said they would go. Charles spoke for two hours or more in front of three impassive Whitehall Warriors. Their findings were foregone – no court martial justified and Charles to remain at the hospital until the doctors see fit to discharge him. I have sent this over with a friend so as to avoid censors or other curious types pawing over the contents.

Best, Fenton.

"What is it?" Jacob asked, glancing over Martin's shoulder as he sat reading the typed document. "Copy of a lawsuit?"

"More of an indictment, Jacob. But of course, you wouldn't have heard about it. Charles Amberley shot his brother in the leg in January while home on leave."

"Good God! Why?"

Martin touched the loose pages he had already read. "You can discover that reason for yourself."

Jacob drew a chair up to the desk beside Martin. He barely glanced at the first two pages, the stilted language of the panel judge explaining the purpose of the hearing, but the first paragraph of Charles's statement held his attention as nothing had ever held it before.

"I entered this war with the highest of ideals and the firmest of faith in the rightness and justness of my patriotism . . ."

They read through the document several times, Martin lying on the sofa, Jacob slowly pacing the room.

"It took guts for old Fenton to get this hearing for Charles," Jacob said. "I can see why the War Office was content to just let things lie. A pretty damning statement."

"Only if people read it," Martin said quietly.

"I gather that's what Fenton would like to see happen."

"I couldn't get this published, you know that. It's too critical of the high command's handling of the Somme attacks. Too outraged at the battle being turned into nothing more than bloody attrition, huge losses being justified because the Germans were suffering on the same scale. A British Verdun. The censors would turn it down flat. And even if I took it back to the States in my pocket, I doubt if I could find a paper that would touch it. They've got war fever over there now. No editor wants to print a cold shower."

Jacob began to stalk the room in agitation, puffing on a cigarette and letting the ash scatter across the rug.

"Christ, it isn't propaganda. It isn't even that critical of the war. It just damns the conduct of it, the senselessness of push-

442

ing men against machine guns and barbed wire over and over again. The whole thing is one long cry of despair for men caught in a trap. Every Tommy knows what the Somme was like, but the civilians turn a deaf ear to their stories. Hell, they just like to read the papers and see 'Great Gains' printed on the banner, and study the war maps, the enlarged portions that make every advance look impressive unless you realise the scale is in yards, not miles."

"That's all well and good, Jacob, but the hard fact remains – "

"That the wire services or the newspapers wouldn't touch it? Fine. Sod the bastards! Let's print it ourselves – a thousand copies or more, well printed and bound – send copies to every member of Parliament, every churchman, every intelligent human being we can think of."

"Have you been at the brandy?"

"No. I'm drunk with purpose all of a sudden. I feel like flashing a bright light into dark corners. I'd like to see some M.P. with guts stand up in the House with this statement in his hand and cry out, 'What in the name of God is going on over there? Let's find some generals who aren't dead from the neck up!'" He slumped into a chair, a smouldering cigarette butt pasted to his lower lip. "All right. I'm sober now. That was just Jacob Golden being carried away by his own rhetoric, as usual. You're quite right, Martin, no one wants to read something that might make them question their faith in the war leaders or the holy purity of their cause. To die in battle is such a noble death, isn't it? The wisest thing you can do with Charles's cry to the heavens is put it neatly away in a drawer."

Martin chewed an unlit cigar and stared at the ceiling.

"*Could* we print it?"

"Are you serious?"

"Yes."

Jacob leaned forward and flipped his cigarette butt into the fireplace.

"Not here, unless you care to see the inside of a French prison. Could be done in Switzerland, but getting copies over the border would be very difficult. The French are horribly sus-

443

picious of printed matter. Could be done easily enough in London, of course."

"Why *of course*?"

"My mother's brother, my Uncle Ben, prints foreign books – Russian, Ukrainian, Yiddish – has a fine letterpress business in Whitechapel. Used to go there sometimes as a kid before I got hauled away to prep school and Eton. I can still smell the ink he used."

Martin scowled at his cigar and bit off the tip. "Wouldn't be much point in printing this in Ukrainian."

"Ben? He has fonts of half the world's languages, even English. The man collects typefaces the way some men collect old wines. Type and socialism, Ben's twin passions."

"You'd be running a risk going back to England, wouldn't you, Jacob?"

"Well, I'm running a risk staying here, aren't I? All that can happen to me in England is that they give me a choice, go back into the army or get tucked away in a C.O. camp and spend the rest of the war tilling the soil. Not the worst fate I can think of. It's a risk I'm willing to run. You face a bigger one, Martin. This transcript is definitely critical of the war and would be an embarrassment to the War Office and the general staff. They could label you an unfriendly journalist and take away your press passes. The French war ministry works hand-in-glove with ours, so you might just be twice damned. I can't see how much use you'd be to the Associated Press if you weren't allowed within a hundred miles of the war zone."

"I wouldn't be the first A.P. correspondent ever kicked out of a war zone because he rubbed brass the wrong way."

"And then there's Colonel Wood-Lacy. I wonder how much will come down on his head? If he hadn't pushed for a hearing . . ."

Martin swung his legs off the sofa with a groan and then bent towards the table where the transcript lay scattered. He sorted the pages together with firm purpose.

"He would never have sent this to me if he were afraid of repercussions. This was his cast of the die. Come on, Jacob, if we hurry we can catch the night train to Le Havre."

*

London. March 25th, 1917. Observations and reflections. There is a great sense of satisfaction in setting type. For me, it is a return to print shop – 10 point Baskerville – cranking out the Lincoln High School yearbook on the platen press. A copy of the slim, paper-bound book that we have worked so hard on lies before me. Far better printed than the old Lincoln High thing, although the method of producing it was essentially the same. Jacob's Uncle Ben designed it, chose the typeface, helped Jacob and me compose the type and picked out the paper. A master printer's job. Title page reads:

AFTER THE SOMME

An enquiry into the advisability of court martial of Major the Viscount Amberley, 2nd Royal Windsor Fusiliers, conducted at Llandinam War Hospital.

WITH AN INTRODUCTION BY

Martin Rilke, Associated Press

God willing, I will have grandchildren one day and they may wish to know why the old man stuck his neck out a country mile and put his name on the document. The fact is, I had not thought of doing it, but Uncle Ben, who looks more like one of the prophets than anyone's uncle, argued that the book needed a touch of authenticating, England being the land of the literary hoax and Charles himself not being available for interview. And so I sat in a corner of Uncle Ben's shop and wrote an introduction, explaining who I was and what I had seen of this war to date and who Charles Amberley was to me. My cousin's story, perhaps your son's story, or your brother's or father's story. "Be cool but passionate," Uncle Ben advised. Uncle Ben is a man who speaks in contradictions. Above his desk there are two framed and signed photographs. One is of the anarchist Kropotkin, the other of King Edward VII. The two men appear to be winking at each other and smiling down on Uncle Ben at the same time. "Confusion is not always disorder," Uncle Ben murmurs from time to time. "A poor tool will often blame the workman."

*

445

March 28th. Hyde Park. Managed to spend one night with Ivy, Jacob discreetly leaving the flat to us and taking a hotel room. She has been curious about my stay in London and I told her the truth. She read the little book, sitting up in bed with my robe around her shoulders, not saying anything until she had turned the final page. It is nothing new to her, the self-inflicted wounds, the intense gratitude that once-strong men feel when they are carried out of the line with a crushed leg or a shattered hand or arm. Blighty wound. "Better to be a cripple than a corpse, mate." She knows I may get into trouble when this thing is sent around. May even lose my English visa and my French *permis de séjour*. Everyone very touchy at the moment. British battle casualties well over the seven hundred thousand mark, the French a great deal more, a major battle about to begin as Nivelle completes his final plans for ending the war before summer. Rumours everywhere among the press corps in London that Nivelle is in for a terrible surprise if he tries to take the Chemin des Dames by frontal assault. America trembling on the brink of jumping into this war with both feet and closed eyes. Lousy timing for an indictment of Western Front generalship and the callousness of slaughter. But my Ivy does not try to dissuade me. She is blunt about it, "I have my job and you have yours. Do what you feel is right." Solid Norfolk speech. She may go back to the hospital trains soon – Calais to Poperinghe – so I give her the key to Rilke Manor just in case A.P. ships me to Timbuktu until the dust, if any, settles. She can use the house when she gets short leaves, give it the woman's touch. Go over the finances with her, like an old married couple working out the budget. She is stunned by the balance in the Banque de Rothmann. "You should put it to work for you, Martin." Sounds just like Uncle Paul . . .

"Hope I'm not breaking your chain of thought."

Martin closed his notebook as Jacob sat with a grunt of weariness on the bench beside him.

"No, I was just bringing things up to date."

"Must read that voluminous journal of yours one day, Martin. Give me something to do in my old age."

"All sent out?"

"Well, enough to start things going. Frightening the number of copies Ben ran off. He got quite carried away."

They sat in silence and watched ducks glide across the ruffled waters of the Serpentine. Anti-aircraft guns and search-lights could be seen near the Dell, the slender cannon tubes pointed at the sky, waiting for clear nights and the Gothas or Zeps. There were more guns across the park. Guns all across Europe – Hyde Park to the Swiss border. A thick dark blanket of guns and wire and men.

"It's a very *small* book, isn't it, Jacob?" Martin said softly.

Arthur Felchurch, M.P., member for Twickenhurst, began the book at breakfast and finished it at the Commons before the debate began on the railway expansion bill. He found it quite curious.

"Odd," he remarked to a fellow Conservative. "This fellow appears to feel quite justified in shooting his own brother in the kneecap."

"What on earth did he do that for, Arthur?"

"Damned if I know."

Harold Davidson, Liberal member for Coventry, read his copy as he was driven to Parliament from his flat in Russell Square. He skimmed through most of it because he was a very busy man, but he read enough to stoke more fuel on his already burning distrust of General Sir Douglas Haig. He knew that the House disliked its members to openly discuss war policies, but after the first debate on the Railway Bill had been concluded to no one's satisfaction, he asked for the floor and launched into a tirade about Haig's mismanagement of the Somme offen-sives.

"I 'ave in my 'and a book . . ." he shouted as he began his thirty-five minute speech, but hardly anyone had remained in their seats to listen to him, not even members of his own party.

David Langham left his usual afternoon meeting with the prime minister at Number Ten, Downing Street, and told his driver to take him to Bristol Mews. Only two guests were there, the young Countess of Ashford – without her husband, as usual – and a tall, robust Australian captain who had been a professional rugby player before the war. The captain and the countess were surreptitiously touching hands as they sat on one of the divans. Lydia gave Langham a gin and French vermouth cocktail and then followed him into an adjoining study and closed the door.

"I suppose you've come to bring me a copy of poor Charles's book."

"Yes," he said. "I have one in my briefcase. Care to read it?"

"Not if I can avoid it, but people have been ringing me up all day to tell me about it. The Stanmore family solicitor telephoned this morning, too. Charles is seeking a divorce. Of course, I shall be happy to give him one. I feel just awful, but Charles did bring all this trouble on himself, didn't he?"

"I suppose you could say that." He reached out his hand and touched her lightly on the face. "You look very drawn and beautiful and tired. I am leaving for Paris on Monday to have some things out with Ribot and Painlevé; also to have a private chat with Georges Clemenceau. Why don't we meet at the Crillon – say, Thursday next?"

"That might be nice," she said. "London is so tiresome."

Lieutenant-General Sir Julian Wood-Lacy stalked the tiny office in Whitehall, slapping his booted leg with a leather swagger stick. Through the narrow window he could see Big Ben etched against the sky.

"I can't tell you how painful this is, Fenton."

"I'm sure it must be, sir."

"For the life of me, I can't fathom your obstinacy in requesting a court martial." He looked away from the window and slap-slapped at his leg with the stick. "*A court martial*! Damnedest thing I ever heard of! Well, what's done is done, as the chap said. Sir Wully was fit to be tied. He's thin skinned as it is where Haig is concerned and he found that little pamphlet, or whatever the hell it is, downright libellous, sir. How did that newspaper wallah get hold of the transcript?"

"I gave it to him."

The old general nodded, almost sadly. "Always said I'd thrash you if you ever lied to your uncle. Well, dash it, sir, the truth hurts."

"What happens now? A court of enquiry, I suppose."

"Great Scot, no! The less done about this matter from now on the better. But it means a decided setback in your career, Fenton. You hold only a brevet rank as brigadier. No possibility of that being retained. They could drop you as low as major, and you'll be fortunate to find yourself sanitation officer in a Liverpool training barracks!"

"One other thing you used to say, sir. 'One takes what comes in the army'."

The general turned his back, clearing his throat loudly.

"Quite so, my boy, quite so."

The telephone call was expected. Martin had already been on the phone for half an hour with the London bureau chief. His bag was packed and he sat by the telephone, waiting. When it rang he picked it up immediately.

"Martin Rilke?"

"Speaking."

"Ah, yes, Davengarth here, Ministry of Information. You caused a bit of a flap here. Do wish you'd taken the trouble to clear the document with the press censor's office. Ah, well, the impetuosity of the fourth estate, what? Well, look here, Rilke, no point in your coming in here now. Your Mr. Bradshaw phoned us and said you were being re-assigned. Going back to America, I take it."

"That's right. New York."

"Well, *bon voyage* and we hope to have you back here again one day. Perhaps after the war."

"Yes," Martin said, hanging up. "After the war."

Lord Trewe turned the book over carefully, then thumbed slowly through it, feeling the paper, tracing the clean imprint of type, sniffing the ink. A Benjamin De Haan printing job if ever he saw one. He laid it carefully, almost reverently, on his table while Ranscome, feature editor, watched him expectantly.

"Damned fine little book," the editor said. "Wish we could give it a play. No chance of it, of course."

"That's correct," Lord Trewe replied. "No chance of it. A bad wind for that type of sail." He folded his large hands across

449

his middle and leaned back in his chair. "Did we get that piece from Logan yet?"

"Just came over the wire. Having it typed up now. He says the spirit of the troops at Arras is first rate – buoyantly optimistic, as he puts it."

"Good. That's what people want to read, Ranscome, the buoyant spirit of their lads."

Jacob Golden carried the paper box through the streets of Whitechapel until he spotted a bus heading for Charing Cross. He sat on the open top deck, savouring the sunshine and the wind, the heavy box resting on the seat beside him. Traffic was heavy along the Strand, the huge War Savings rally in Trafalgar Square spilling over into the adjacent streets. He got off the bus and pushed his way slowly through the crowd, moving towards the throbbing drums and shrilling fifes of the London Rifle Brigade band. A man clutched at his arm and tapped the side of the carton.

"Sellin' ices, chum?"

Jacob balanced the box on his hip, opened the top flaps, pulled out a book and pressed it into the man's hands.

The man stared at it in surprise. "What's your game? London Bible Mission?"

"Something like that," Jacob said, moving on into the crowd.

The Rifle Brigade band marched slowly around the broad stone platform at the base of Nelson's Column, round and round with firm step, the sun glinting off fifes and the drum major's baton, the strains of "The British Grenadiers" stirring the crowd to cheers. Tiny Union Jacks held in a thousand hands were being waved in time to the music. Ranged wheel to wheel in a square below the platform, were artillery pieces of pristine newness, polished like gems by the proud gunners who stood before them: six-inch howitzers, eight-inch howitzers, a battery of field guns and two monster fifteen-inch crushers which nearly dwarfed the lions that sat hunched far below the admiral's distant figure. And attached to each gun was a small, neat sign giving its price to the taxpayer in pounds, shillings and pence.

"INVEST IN WAR SAVINGS!" a voice appealed over a loudspeaker, the words contrapuntal to the martial music. "HELP THE BOYS DO THE JOB! YOUR KING AND YOUR COUNTRY NEED . . . YOU!"

Jacob stood by one giant, olive-painted iron wheel, the barrel of the howitzer looming above him, angled towards the upper storey of Admiralty House seen beyond Cockspur Street. Raising the box above his head, he placed it on an iron-flanged tread at the top of the wheel and then quickly climbed up the spokes and straddled the breech.

" 'Ere, now!" a sergeant gunner called out. "Get off there."

He reached down for the box, picked it up and held it in front of him. The gunner made a grab at him but he propelled himself forward, thighs gripping the sun-warmed barrel, up and up and out over the crowd, hearing laughter now and shouts of encouragement from below.

"Pop down the spout, mate!"

He smiled at them, an ocean of white faces below, fluttering squares of red, white and blue:

"KAISER BILL SAYS KEEP YOUR HANDS IN YOUR POCKETS . . . BRITANNIA SAYS . . . BUY THESE GUNS."

On the lip of the barrel now, the box before him. Reaching in, he picked up book after book and sent them flying off into the crowd, whirling flutters of paper, grabbed for by eager hands. Half a dozen constables shouldered their way through the crowd, hard faced and implacable. When the final book was gone, he lay contentedly back along the great steel barrel and waited for the Bobbies to climb up and get him.

Martin asked the taxi driver to wait for him and then hurried into All Souls. The hospital had never seemed so huge, or so crowded, and he felt a momentary panic that he wouldn't be able to find her, but the clerks at the reception desk located her without any trouble and he was soon walking quickly down a long corridor towards the multiple amputee ward where she was on duty. She was his wife and he wanted her with him, but he knew the impossibility of that, couldn't even ask her as he held her hands tightly in an aisle between rows of beds, the mutilated men watching them with drugged eyes. He held her hands and kissed her on the cheek and then the matron called for her impatiently from the far end of the ward.

He could still feel the softness of her skin against his lips as he sat in the back of the taxi, the driver speeding down Gower Street and through a maze of streets towards Charing Cross Station. Crowds streaming away from Trafalgar Square suddenly blocked their progress like a wall.

"Sorry, guv'nor," the driver said. "Can't be 'elped, but you won't miss your train."

He didn't really care if he missed it or not. "Going home," the A.P. man had told him. A wry joke. He felt that he was home now and on his way to a strange and alien place. He sat stiffly on the seat, not seeing the crowds or the line of big guns being hauled slowly out of the square and into Whitehall, the great iron wheels churning up paper, the wind taking the scraps and blowing them like pale leaves across the pavement and into the street.

Book Four

Shall they return to beatings of great bells
In wild trainloads?
A few, a few, too few for drums and yells,
May creep back, silent, to still village wells
Up half-known roads.

—WILFRED OWEN, 1893–1918

I

November 2nd, 1920

HôTEL GAILLARD, HAZEBROUCK. OBSERVATIONS AND REFLECTIONS. Heaven knows there has been enough soul-searching about it, but now it has been done and the rightness of it must wait for the verdict of history. Benteen of the *Journal-American* felt it would do more harm than good, would reopen the wounds now so delicately healed, but I argued against that as did Fletcher and Wilde and the other A.P. men, as well as Warrington of U.P. It seems, somehow, right to have waited for the second anniversary. Last year was too soon, the armies barely demoblised, the shock of the war still too numbing for any quiet reflection on it to be possible. But we have turned a corner now, stepped into not merely a new decade but what would appear to be another age. The promised return to "normalcy" made Warren Gamaliel Harding president-elect last week. Perhaps it is now a "normalcy" to express grief in one final public outpouring and then permit the dead to rest for ever in peace, forgotten except in our own memories. Anyway, the deed has been done. Two days ago, just up the road from here in Flanders, plain wood coffins containing the remains of six nameless Tommies, chosen at random from the forest of graves marked "Unknown" that stretch from Ypres to the Marne, were placed in a hut. A British officer was blindfolded and led inside. The coffin that he touched at random was carried out and taken to Boulogne. There it was plced in a giant casket of oak, the lid bound with iron straps and, where the straps crossed, there was attached a great seal which is inscribed:

A British Warrior
Who fell in the Great War
1914-1918
For King and Country

454

A soldier unknown, a warrior familiar only to God. Today that poor flesh will be taken through the streets of London for burial in Westminster Abbey on Armistice Day, the gun carriage trailed by admirals and field-marshals and the dead man's King.

Fletcher had suggested that I go to London, but half the world's press will be covering the story and I preferred to stay on this side of the Channel with Ivy and gather notes for my own elegy, starting in Paris and driving to Hazebrouck and Ypres in the Citroën.

Brief impressions. Convoys of trucks on the road to Albert, filled with bricks, bags of sand and lime. No more *camions* packed with troops inching towards the front. The monstrosity of a basilica at Albert, so badly shelled in 1916 and again during the German breakthrough in 1918, is being rebuilt, complete with new golden virgin high atop the tower. Beyond Albert there is nothing but a wasteland of dead ground, a moonscape of craters and tumbled-in trenches. Salvage crews still work cutting and baling the miles of wire and demolition men find and explode or defuse shells. Mametz and Trones and Delville and High Wood have been cleared of splintered trees and new ones planted. In time there will be glades and leafy paths on those scarred hills and in time there will be cottages on the patches of brick dust where the villages had been. The view from Bazentin towards High Wood and Flers is something of a heart breaker. How short the distances seem now, how vast they were then – paths of eternity. Such a small wedge of ground to have changed so many lives . . .

Colonel Sir Terrence L. De Gough and his second in command, Major Fenton Wood-Lacy, rode in the back of the Vauxhall, the driver keeping as close as possible to the armoured car racing ahead of them on the twisting road between Ballingarry and Limerick.

"Dash it, Fenton," the Colonel said. "The whole idea of having a ceremony here is most foolish. There are bound to be demonstrations. The garrison stands for two bloody minutes in silence and the blasted Sinn Feiners will take advantage of it. You mark my words."

"We won't all be standing silent," Fenton said. "The cars will be out, and the constabulary."

"They'll still manage to blow up something. When Paddy has a will he'll bloody well find a way. You're fortunate to be leaving. When do you take off?"

"Tonight."

"I hope to God Hackway can do the job. I shall miss you, Fenton."

"Hackway's quite competent, sir."

"Perhaps, but he's not *you*." The elderly colonel toyed absently with the revolver resting on the seat between them, his eyes on the armoured car, its turret revolving, the Vickers gun menacing the hedgerows on both sides of the road. "They expect you to chuck it in, Fenton, I suppose you know that."

"Yes, I know it."

"Sending you to Mespot – "

"Iraq now."

"Same bloody difference. If the Arabs or Kurds don't get you the climate will."

"It's not all one-sided."

"Because they kick you up to lieutenant-colonel again and give you a battalion? Don't be foolish, my boy. They have a mark by your name. Every job you get will be a damned tough bullet to chew. The promotion is just a sop to keep your esteemed father-in-law from writing angry letters to the War Office. They'll be most happy to accept your resignation and put you in civvy street with your honour and colonelcy intact. You should jump at the opportunity, Fenton."

He should, by all that was logic, do just that. God knows it would make Winnie happy. Become a country gentleman and manage one of the marquess's estates. Or learn some sort of trade. A bit late for the law. Business perhaps. Import and export. Twelve years a soldier. It was the only trade he knew. The regiment was drawn up on the square of Limerick barracks, the band turning into it now, "The Bonnie English Rose" played on drums and fifes. Corporal Harris, the best trumpeter in the band, stood to attention by the flagpole facing the chaplain. Fifteen minutes before eleven on the morning of the eleventh day of the eleventh month. A mild day. Great fleecy clouds blowing in from the Shannon. He glanced

456

upwards and there was the flag whipping in the wind, the colours bright and crisp against the sky. Oh, damn, he thought. Right or wrong it was what he did and it was too late to leave it now . . .

> Take 'old o' the wings o' the mornin',
> An' flop round the earth till you're dead;
> But you won't get away from the tune that they play
> To the bloomin' old rag over'ead.

"You're not packing, surely," Lady Margaret asked as she came into the room, the twins hanging on to her hands, dragging their feet and shrieking with the fun of trying to pull their grandmother's arms out of the sockets. "He hasn't written you yet. He may give up his commission, you know."

"He's your son," Winifred said as she sorted through a pile of the twins' dresses. "You should know better than that."

"Baghdad," Lady Margaret whispered. "I can't bear the thought of it."

"It wouldn't be Baghdad, Mother, he wouldn't allow us to live there. No, we shall go to Egypt and rent a beautiful cool house in Gezireh. Jennifer and Victoria will adore it and so will you."

"*Me?* You'll never drag me out of Suffolk, my girl."

Winifred smiled, watching the twins tug and pull. "You're being dragged already. Anyway, it would only be for a year or two at the most and Fenton will get ample leave. We could hire a houseboat and go up the Nile. It will be very pleasant."

Lady Margaret detached herself from the girls, who raced off like puppies, and sat on the edge of the bed.

"Oh, dear. You're not suited to be an army wife. Why in heaven's name don't you tell him so?"

Winifred sighed and touched her mother-in-law lightly on the shoulder.

"Because if I told him that he'd give it up and it has to be his decision, not mine. I'm Fenton's wife and that's all I really care about. That he happens to be in the army is just something I've learned to live with and will go on living with, I suppose."

"Well, they say Egypt is delightful in the winter and we can purchase two tiny donkeys for the children to ride."

Winifred bent and kissed her on the cheek. "*We*, is it? Good, but the twins are a bit young for donkeys."

"Oh, are they?" she said ruefully. "A couple of Amazons! I always imagined girls would be gentle lambs, but they're almost Fenton's equal at that age, although I must say that Roger was – " She stopped abruptly and looked down at her hands folded in her lap. "*That* day again. Two minutes to remember in silence. I don't need one day a year to think of him."

Winifred turned back to the piles of clothes and continued her sorting.

"I feel the same way about Andrew and Timothy. And if the bullet that hit Bramwell had been a tenth of an inch further to the left I would have another brother to remember as well."

"Armistice Day is for the sort of person who only goes to church one Sunday out of fifty-two."

"I suppose it is," Winifred said quietly. "And yet when they ring the bells . . ."

They looked at each other and then held hands, very tightly, waiting for the first doleful peal of eleven.

It had been an exhilarating drive back from Biarritz with Prince Michael.

The prince had escaped the bullets which had felled many of his kinsmen, not to mention his cousin the tsar, by having been an aide to the Russian military attaché in Paris from 1915 until events in Holy Russia had made such a post less than super-fluous. He had also been fortunate in having had the foresight to transfer a million rubles in gold from his bank in Petrograd to the Banque de France. This money had not only allowed the thirty-five-year-old prince to indulge himself in his primary passion – the quest for speed – but had given him something that few of his émigré countrymen of noble blood could boast of – independence. He had not been reduced, as had so many dukes, grand dukes and princes of the Romanov swarm, to selling his name to one of the daughters of the new "war rich", who were beginning to flock to Paris from such places as Birmingham, Bradford, Liverpool and even Gary, Indiana, U.S.A., in search of titles on the cheap. No. He was Prince Michael and he was beyond being bought. The Isotta-

Fraschini that he drove, the Breguet biplane that he flew, had been paid for out of his own pocket. It was for this reason, if for no other, that Lydia sat beside him. She did not like men with price tags on their family crests.

Yes. Exhilarating. The trees flashing past, the dust whipped back from the tyres in long, flat streamers of the palest yellow. The wind in her face as it whirled over the glass screen in front of her. Paris rising in the dawn, spires and towers glinting above the haze. Montparnasse. The Faubourg. The squeal of rubber as the prince braked in front of the Deux Magots. The sleepy kitchen staff opening up the place to serve them coffee and brioches. When at last he parked in front of her house on the edge of the Bois she felt totally satisfied. It was fifteen minutes before eleven.

"Shall I come in?"

"Shall?" she laughed. "Or *may* I come in?"

He shrugged. "How can I tell your mood, Lydia?"

"My mood is vaguely reflective at the moment. And besides, we have had quite enough of each other in the past week to last us some time. Drive to the aerodrome and fly your little machine somewhere exotic."

He held her hands and kissed them. "*Au revoir*. I will go to Tangier. Do not entangle yourself *too* deeply with someone else before I return or I shall crash land my machine on your roof."

Galant. But then he was a prince and the right phrases and gestures came naturally. If she married him she would become a princess with a five-hundred-year-old name. The idea did not intrigue her. They were equals now. "Money," David Langham had once said, "is the only important aristocracy." And then had added with a wink, "But power is the votes of the poor."

Langham crossed her mind as she walked slowly up the staircase, a maid scurrying ahead of her to open her bedroom door. She thought of him because he was so opposite in every way to the tall, athletic prince. It was Langham who had induced her to buy this house so that he could have a place of quiet retreat during the interminable months of stormy conferences at Versailles. He had solved the complex problem of dividing Hungary after a particularly satyric weekend in this

459

very room, on the very bed that she now stretched out upon as her maid hurried to draw the bath. Her closeness to Langham had not gone unnoticed. It had given her an *entrée* into the new society that money alone could never have bought. Money was desirable in this post-war world, but influence was everything.

The bells of St. Jean Baptiste in Neuilly began to ring. Not Sunday, surely? Thursday morning, Thursday the Eleventh of November. The bells had the same soft, melodic sound as the churchbells of Abington and memory came in a rush, a flood of images that stunned her with their clarity. She felt that she had but to reach out her hands and grasp Fenton's and they would be up, up, up, the scaffolding to the tall brick chimneys with Charles far, far below calling out, *"Lydia, Lydia, don't fall . . . don't fall!"*

The Earl and Countess of Stanmore and their son, the Hon. William Greville, were warmly greeted by the Reverend Mr. Toomey, Vicar of Llandinam, as they stepped from their Daimler, the earl remaining behind the wheel for a few moments to double-check his parking procedure, gears in reverse, hand brake pulled up, wheels turned at a sharp angle. A meticulous driver of motor cars. The Reverend Mr. Toomey then ushered them into the vicarage for a cup of strong tea to offset the morning's chill. The tea was served, appropriately enough, in a Georgian silver service donated by the Stanmores. Their generosity over the past three years had been extreme and their company, as always, genuinely welcomed by the young clergyman and his wife.

"So tell me, William," the vicar said, "how is Cambridge treating you this term?"

"A bit better than I'm treating Cambridge," William said with a laugh. "I don't think I'm quite suited for classics."

"He's thinking of leaving King's and studying for the bar," Hanna said.

"I couldn't be happier," the earl remarked, drinking his tea with relish. "We could do with a lawyer in the family, what with all these new laws and taxes the government, in their arrogance, see fit to impose upon us."

William laughed again. "Now, Father, let's not get embroiled in politics on Armistice Day."

"Quite so," the earl muttered. He finished his tea and held out his cup for more. "Well, John, what sort of service can we expect this morning?"

"Simple, as usual," the vicar said as his wife poured the tea. "When I was a padre with the South Wales Borderers, the men would become restive if my sermon was too high flown. Simplicity of language and directness of thought, that's my firm belief. And the choosing of the more popular hymns, the ones the chaps can sing without looking in their hymnals."

"I have always been most fond of 'Oh, for a Thousand Tongues to Sing'," Hanna said.

"Ah, yes," the vicar agreed. "Very lovely indeed. But 'Onward Christian Soldiers' is still the one the chaps like best. They always give full lung power to that one."

William stepped over to one of the windows and looked up at the hill behind the house.

"Is he up there, Vicar?"

"Oh, yes. Every morning, rain or shine."

"I'll go and fetch him."

"Shall I come with you?" his father asked.

"I'd rather go alone this morning, if you don't mind, sir." Hanna watched him leave, could see him through the window as he went up the path. Walking so much better, she reflected, after the surgery in New York in August. A stiffness, but no marked limp even going up a hill. The stiffness made it very difficult for him to drive a car, but that was a minor enough restriction on his activities. How tall and strong he was. Powerful shoulders and arms. A young, handsome man and so very much alive.

William walked slowly up the steep, sandy path to the top of the hill. A number of wooden benches were placed among oak and chestnut trees and Charles was seated on one of them, leaning forward, hands on his knees, gazing out across a valley at the distant slopes and crags of Moel Sych. William sat beside his brother and took a silver cigarette case from the inside pocket of his jacket.

"Care for a smoke?"

"I don't think so," Charles said, leaning back and folding his

461

arms. "Odd how the shadows race in and out of the ravines and gullys."

"Cloud shadows. A very peaceful sight."

"Quite lulling, as a matter of fact. I often find myself falling asleep watching them."

"It's peaceful, all right."

"Quite. I walk up there sometimes, but one can only appreciate the chiaroscuro effect from a distance."

"I imagine so."

"The shadows race over you, terribly quickly, sweep on by, you see. One hasn't time to notice the clean definition of light and shade."

"I understand."

"But seated here, or even further along, near the old wall it's quite a different matter. Do you come here often?"

William lit his cigarette with a windproof lighter he had bought in New York.

"As often as I can."

"I rather had the feeling that we had talked before. Perhaps not here exactly . . . but . . . somewhere."

"Oh, we've talked together many times. Last time I was here we talked about Derbyshire."

"Did we?"

"Buxton in the Peak district. It's a very lovely spot. Masses of hills and crags. We've owned a house there for years. A smallish place, but comfortable. There's a hill beyond the house and from the terrace one can watch the patterns of light. A great many clouds sweep over and the shadow patches change constantly all during the day. Quite an interesting sight."

"Ah, yes, I'm sure it must be."

"Would you care to see it one day? Perhaps even stay there?"

Charles frowned and looked back at the hill, at the shadows of the wind-driven clouds as they dipped in and out of the hollows and raced across the slopes.

"I'm not sure I could. I really don't know about that. I must watch this hill, you see, watch it in case the men come back."

Observations and reflections. There were touring buses

parked beside the road near Beaumont Hamel, the occupants – almost all of them with cameras slung over their shoulders – being led by a guide to see the old trenches. Quite a new industry. More touring buses north of the Somme at Arras. Middle-aged people for the most part, tramping gingerly over new duckboards laid down by the tour companies to keep their clients from being too discomfited. Near Cambrai a few rusted tanks remain partially entombed in mud. Along Vimy Ridge the wire has turned orange with rust. At Messines, great flocks of ravens along the skyline wheeling above the stumps of bombarded trees.

Odd how peaceful it is. No major stories to be gathered here. The storms have shifted. The Riffs cutting up French and Spanish legionnaires in Morocco; Turks and Greeks fighting to the death at Adrianople; the British pouring troops into Iraq, into Ireland, into Northern India. And Russia at war with the Poles, at war with herself. White Russians, Red Russians, Denikin, Semenov, Trotsky, the Czech legion. No lack of work for me among those whirlwinds. Jacob, too, in those winds, somewhere between here and Siberia. A special observer for an agency of the League of Nations, keeping an eye on political developments in the new nations carved from the old empires. "Watching the new hatreds grow," as Jacob put it so sardonically when we sat in the Hotel Adlon in Berlin last year. New hatreds breeding to replace the old on this second anniversary of the end of the war-to-end-all-wars. I wonder if Wilson sees the joke in that, lying half paralysed in the White House, listening to the cheers for Harding and his "normalcy"?

All of us scattered. The beginning of the rootless age? Or is it just a new restlessness, the old horizons no longer as safe and comforting as they once were? Back and forth we go like so many migrating birds – Petrograd, Berlin, Paris, London, New York. Back and forth. Trains to Milan, Belgrade, Warsaw. Back and forth across the oceans without giving travel a thought any more.

Strange to think of Alexandra living in Canada and working in a clinic for war wounded with a doctor who may or may not be her husband. She seemed so much a part of the ambience of Abington Pryory and Park Lane. The lovely belle of all the balls. An English society girl to her fingertips. All is changed. She wrote to Hanna that even Toronto is not far enough away. She and her doctor plan to keep moving west once the reservoir of the maimed is lowered, to get as far away as possible from where I now sit, Hazebrouck, the edge of the great salient.

It's a good, new road from Hazebrouck over the Messines Ridge to Kemmel and Ypres, but the earth is sour on both sides of it. Mustard gas and lyddite permeating the soil. Still, grass is beginning to grow, inching over the lips of the shell holes, sprouting rawly along old parapets and amid sand-bagged bunkers. Sandbags to Sandburg. Yes, Carl, the grass does cover all.

There is no one Golgotha for the British army, but Ypres will do and it is the closest battleground to the coast. It is here, near the waste of stones that had once been a lace-making town, that the six unknown Tommies had lain side by side in a hut, waiting for one of them to be chosen for immortality, to symbolise the apotheosis of all the million dead. Those who remain here are not forgotten. The Commonwealth War Graves Commission has spared no expense to lay out ceme-teries. Low walls surround them and trees and shrubbery soften the lines of stone. At Poperinghe the cemeteries are like English gardens and the caretakers dedicated and efficient men. It takes only minutes for them to locate any grave for visitors – the neat rows of white crosses, the names on each. On one of them, Ivy Thaxton Rilke. Beneath the name are the initials of the military nursing service and a date, October 9th, 1917.

There are at least a hundred thousand other graves from Passchendaele; not that that's any comfort. She lies in a special plot beside twenty of her patients who died with her when the shell hit. Alexandra saw to that. An earl's daughter getting her way.

A grave in Flanders. Far from the places she had hoped to see. Chicago, Illinois, on Lake Michigan; railways and cattle-markets.

No. I couldn't face going to London and witnessing the pomp at the Abbey, not with her on this side of the Channel. A quiet spot. Just the wind and a blackbird swaying on a cypress tree and then, at eleven, the distant tolling of a bell.